G000168109

Whale Rock

Diana Plater

This is an IndieMosh book

brought to you by MoshPit Publishing
an imprint of Mosher's Business Support Pty Ltd

PO Box 147
Hazelbrook NSW 2779

indiemosh.com.au

Copyright © Diana Plater 2019

The moral right of the author has been asserted in accordance with the Copyright Amendment (Moral Rights) Act 2000.

All rights reserved. Except as permitted under the Australian Copyright Act 1968 (for example, fair dealing for the purposes of study, research, criticism or review) no part of this publication may be reproduced, stored in a retrieval system, or transmitted in any form or by any means, electronic, mechanical, photocopying, recording or otherwise, without the written permission of the publisher.

Cataloguing-in-Publication entry is available from the National Library of Australia: http://catalogue.nla.gov.au/

Title:	Whale Rock
Author:	Plater, Diana (1956–)
ISBNs:	978-1-922261-41-0 (paperback)
	978-1-922261-42-7 (ebook – epub)
	978-1-922261-43-4 (ebook – mobi)
Subjects:	Fiction: literary; women; thrillers/general

This story is entirely a work of fiction. No character in this story is taken from real life. Any resemblance to any person or persons living or dead is accidental and unintentional. The author, their agents and publishers cannot be held responsible for any claim otherwise and take no responsibility for any such coincidence.

Cover design by Diana Plater and Ally Mosher

Cover layout by Ally Mosher at allymosher.com

Coming Back to Life:
Words and music by David Gilmour
© Copyright Pink Floyd Music Publishers Ltd
All rights administered in Australia & New Zealand by Native Tongue Music Publishing Ltd on behalf of Imagem Music BV
Print rights administered in Australia and New Zealand by Hal Leonard Australia Pty Ltd ABN 13 085 333 713
www.halleonard.com.au
Used by permission. All rights reserved. Unauthorised reproduction is illegal.

I knew the moment had arrived
For killing the past and coming back to life

Coming Back to Life
David Gilmour
Pink Floyd

Chapter One

"If Tom had died they would have brought me casseroles," Shannon said to herself, knowing full well her lips were moving. "But when you split up with your husband the neighbours don't give a damn."

She was standing at the coffee machine, which sat on a huge wooden bar, a slab of polished timber that felt connected to the earth. But she didn't feel connected anymore. Not to the ground. Not to most people. And certainly not to her customers. None of them cared about her personal situation – they were more interested in their next social gathering or whether the surf was up. Her life wasn't going to affect their choice of a latte over a flat white on an April autumn's day at Shannon's Café perched on top of a hill between the beaches of Tamarama and Bondi.

Well, she didn't care what people thought. It was her café, and she'd talk to herself if she wanted to. The yummy mummies and their designer-dressed babies, scary real estate agents and bronzed surfies could all go about their exciting lives partying, working and swimming in Sydney's eastern suburbs. So long as they paid for their cappuccinos and carrot cakes, they could do what they liked.

"You still have the café," that's all Tom had said as she'd agreed to move to their upstairs flat after the tenants left. He'd stay on at their Paddington terrace. Shannon's was not a particularly imaginative name but that's what she'd christened the café when she started running it two years before. Her five minutes of fame. It was tiny; there was just enough room for four tables inside and two long benches and a table out on the street but it was big enough for her. It used to be a groovy little place, wedged next to a post office, where wannabe Hollywood stars photocopied their latest scripts and sent their resumes to agents. But sadness had descended on it. And the customers seemed to feel it.

She brushed her long dark-brown hair out of her eyes as she packed the coffee. Her style hadn't changed in the two decades since she was a teenager. She cut her fringe herself in the hope she could put off the inevitable trip to the hairdresser. She didn't want to be talked into dyes and foils and perms and curls, but the other day she'd found her first grey hair. The clock was ticking. Whatever happened, she'd never change her uniform of jeans, sloppy jumper, a scarf on cool days and walking boots.

Tom had suggested she tame those waves. "Do something with your hair, Shannon. Other women look after themselves, why can't you? And wear something feminine for a change."

She'd wake up next to him, her eyes red from night-time crying. He was way over the other side of the bed, deathly quiet.

Stop nightmare dreaming. Better to check out the latest less-than-enthusiastic assistant, Nick. How did he wear his apron so casually chic, overlapped and tied at the front? But that's where the sexiness ended. His white T-shirt revealed more rib than muscle and his skin was pale. His longish black hair curved into his tattooed neck, and a wispy beard didn't quite cover his chin. He came to her in need of a dollar, saying he was an experienced barista but his froth came out like runny yoghurt. And when he tried to do designs with the chocolate on top it turned into a mushy mess. But she told him he could keep the tips if he learnt quickly.

"Here you take over, *Señor* Barista," she said. At least the young female customers liked him, with mutual flirting and winking at times brightening up the sombre atmosphere.

She pulled her powder-blue woollen scarf up around her neck; the café felt the ocean winds. The colour of the sea that she could smell in the air. Fringed by 1930s red-brick flats and yellow bungalows, the road the café was on led down to parks and a coastal walk past ancient Aboriginal engravings, which overlooked the ocean. The parks were filled by six am with skinny women who were addicted to exercise. They ran up and down the volley ball field, did weights and boxed with each other or their personal trainers, who barked orders at them. She used to like men like them. Look at Tom. He was heavily into exercise.

Many of these trainers were her customers; they ordered fresh juices in front of their clients but she'd spotted them chilling out after hours drinking beer at the nearby pub with their tradie mates.

She now preferred her arty clients – filmmakers and actors, who had given her signed photos of themselves, which lined the wall above the counter. On the other walls were black and white framed photos of old Paris and Frida Kahlo prints that Tom had ribbed her about when she bought them at the Art Gallery shop. So what if they weren't avant-garde?

Today a bunch of exercising mothers were sitting outside the café, their strollers and prams taking up every bit of footpath space. When her five-year-old son, Maxie, was born Shannon had inherited her sister's old-fashioned pram, which converted into a stroller with one flick of the wrist. Tom had turned his nose up at it; he wanted her to use a super-duper child-mover. She resisted; that old one was so much easier. But these mums had the latest inventions, worth more than her second-hand Toyota.

They ordered babycinos, talking to their toddlers in sweet, high baby voices as they screeched like seagulls at Shannon for their caffeine and chocolate hits. Their voices rose even higher as their spoke to each other and into their mobile phones, so the whole world could hear every word. They were like paddle pop sticks, tanned even in winter with gorgeous hair in every different colour. She couldn't imagine having to look that perfect all the time.

One of them grabbed Shannon's arm as she collected their cups. "Shannon, isn't that girl inside with the blonde pony-tail famous?" she asked.

"A legend in her own lunchtime?" her particularly thin friend commented as they laughed in unison.

"She's an award-winning actor actually, Jane," Shannon answered. She knew Jane from Maxie's school, the local public one. Her older daughter, Clarissa, was in his class. Jane was always the centre of a scrum of mums at the gate at drop-off and pick-up time. They would spend an hour making sure their little darlings were settled in at school, or at least using that as their excuse to have a good old gossip. And then they'd go off to exercise.

At school assemblies Jane's set would clap like mad for their own children but ignore others like Maxie, whose mothers weren't one of the clan. And when Shannon picked him up from school she felt as if she needed to be wearing riot gear to run the gauntlet.

She was forever late, and the ones at the gate tut-tutted as she raced past them, finding Maxie alone in the playground. Or she'd be the last one to collect him from after-care. She did have a business after all and what the hell did they do?

"So, Shannon, how is your handsome husband?" Jane asked. "When are we going to see him at canteen duty again?"

"Don't you see him when he picks up Maxie from after-care?" She didn't want to explain her separation although she guessed Jane knew all about it. She didn't want to explain anything to her.

"Oh no, we don't send our girls to after-care," her friend, who wore her hair pulled back in a hairband, said. Shannon hadn't come across her before. Her daughter must be in another class.

"I did see Tom's mother at school the other day," Jane went on. "Aren't you lucky that she's helping out with babysitting while you run the café?"

Irina? Shannon hadn't heard that her mother-in-law was now on pick-up duty. Tom had insisted lately that he have Max stay over more often and the two days a week had stretched to six and even seven sometimes.

"Better for you to concentrate on one thing at a time," he'd said to her.

But didn't he know women were geniuses at multi-tasking? Shannon turned up the iPod music – a Radiohead album that Nick had chosen – to blot out the mums' conversations. Now they were discussing what high school their daughters would go to but even the loud music didn't work.

"Saint Joan's, I've already got Clarissa enrolled," Jane, who had pulled up her skin-tight top in order to breastfeed her baby, said. "But I'll get her to do the selective schools' test just in case."

"Oh you wouldn't want her to go to a selective school would you?" her friend asked. "Do you really want her to do all that coaching?"

"She'll be fine without coaching. I'm so blessed to have an intelligent child. The others wouldn't get in without it though."

Didn't seem too bright to me, Shannon thought. Maxie, in his innocent way, had told her about the dumb questions Clarissa asked in class so she doubted she would get into a selective school with or without coaching. Of course, her Maxie would sail in! Well, she hoped he would.

"Taking places from local children, it's just not fair," Jane continued. "Stop it Clementine." She pushed her toddler away, who had jammed her whole hand in her babycino and was now trying to feed the baby.

Shannon thought the really unfair part was being stuck with a mother like Jane, especially somebody who would call her poor child Clementine. Why did people with nice, simple names come up with such pretentious ones for their children? It wasn't as if they'd grown up playing banjos in Louisiana. It was time a one-name policy was brought in here; if the Chinese could introduce a one-child policy why couldn't the Aussies insist on only one name for children – Janet or John perhaps? Or Max, now that was a nice, simple name. But not one Tom had liked that much.

Oh no, she was thinking about Tom again. It had been eight months since, standing at the Paddington front gate, he'd announced he couldn't live with her anymore. It wasn't a surprise. He'd hide away in his office when he came home from work and go to bed after she finally fell asleep. She guessed he couldn't cope with her melancholy.

"Can't you see how much you're hurting me?" she'd said to him.

But he didn't even say sorry.

I am floating above my bed, my mind has left my body. But my soul lingers on. Am I dead?

I can see midwives and the doctor hovering around. Tom is standing next to my body, holding my hand, his usually tanned face now pale.

"We've still got Maxie," he keeps saying, over and over and over again. We still have our beautiful little boy.

The mothers were leaving but Jane wasn't in a hurry. "I feel like another coffee," she said to her friend, who reluctantly waited for her, muttering something about being late for book club.

Jane put the baby back in the pram and went inside to order another soy latte and babycino for Clementine.

Shannon was standing next to Nick. "Maybe her breast milk's soy too," she whispered after Jane sashayed back to her table.

He rolled his eyes.

She thought of how Maxie loved his treat when he came to the café, referring to it as "my cupofcino". Was he alone in the playground now munching on his apple, she wondered as she went to the iPod and turned off the music.

"I was enjoying that," Nick complained, working the coffee machine.

"There's a reason why this café's called Shannon's," she said, putting her hands on her hips. "I just want silence."

"Wish you'd make up your mind."

"Wish I was down at the valley," she responded, shaking her head and pursing her lips. At the family farm a couple of hours' drive south of Sydney, away from all this clutter and chaos, walking up hills or jumping from rock to rock in the creek. She loved the peace of the bush, punctuated only by the mooing of cows and bird calls – the Eastern Whip-bird, with its drawn-out whistles and whip crack, and the female's "chew chew". They were a pair, those whip-birds, staying together for nearly a lifetime.

Shannon took the drinks out and noticed Clementine kneeling on the bench, playing with the sugar she had spread all over the table. She tried to edge past the double pram to place the cups away from her. But the toddler turned around at that precise moment and leant back to rock the pram, pushing it into Shannon and forcing her to trip and spill the coffee. Soy froth went everywhere. Maybe it was because of her years of dance classes but Shannon was able to plonk the cups on the table without dropping them. Her face was red. "Get those bloody prams out of the way," she yelled.

"Don't swear in front of Clementine." Jane swung round, her hair moving in sync with her head.

"Mummy, my babycinoooooooo," Clementine yowled, putting her hands in the mix of milk and sugar and licking her fingers. The baby was howling now too.

Shannon passed the half-empty babycino to Clementine, trying to soothe her by touching her arm but Jane snatched her away.

"Keep your hands off my daughter," she said.

Shannon couldn't contain herself any longer. "Oh go fuck yourself," she burst out.

The toddler poked her tongue out at Shannon while Jane bundled her into her pram. "We're never coming back," she said.

Pain sears through my body. It comes again in a rush of blood. The midwife puts a mask over my face. Gas. I'm starting to go. Is this what it feels like to die in a hospital ward? Ugly grey walls, chrome bed, all so clinical. Is this where I want to die? No, not here surrounded by nurses and doctors who don't know me.

I want to leave this wretched place, this Earth, when I'm alone far away from other people, deep in the valley, way up my creek, where all you can hear are lyrebirds and water tumbling over the steep rocks.

Shannon felt a reassuring hand on her shoulder. "The Mums and Bubs Club giving you grief?" a stocky man in khaki overalls asked.

She looked up and he gestured at Jane and Hairband retreating with their jangle of prams, toddlers and babies.

Shannon was relieved it was her regular, Colin. "Did you see it all?"

"Sure did," Colin nodded. "And heard the swearing too."

"I wish I had some smokes."

"Now, now. I thought you were giving up."

"One day."

Gliding between the double-parked cars and the phone boxes was another labourer, who grinned at her and she felt herself blushing. She tossed her scarf over her shoulder so it wouldn't trail in the milky mess as she attempted to clean up.

Colin turned to introduce him. "This is my mate, Rafael. He's working with me on the building site. This is Shannon, the proud owner of this establishment. I convinced him you had the best coffee in town."

Shannon wiped her hands on her apron, then shook Rafael's hand. "Sorry about my swearing. We're really all just one big, happy family here."

Rafael smiled. "They need a licence to operate those prams."

"Yes, a truck licence." She observed something she couldn't quite make out in his dark eyes. She turned to Colin. "Cap, sir?"

He nodded. "Of course, my dear."

She loved Colin and his crinkly face, even if it was looking a bit the worse for wear. He must have been handsome once. He reminded her of the Koori boys she went to school with. They were witty, knowledgeable about nature and never wasted time talking about nothing.

"And for you, Rafael?" She guessed he would have to be at least ten years younger than Colin, who was possibly in his mid-sixties. He had a face that had seen a lot of life but he was still good-looking, dark-skinned with long black hair. She liked the look and smell of men who did physical work for a living. Muscular men with strong arms that it must feel good to be wrapped in. She bet Rafael knew how to chop wood, like those Koori boys.

"Short black please."

"At least I don't need cocaine to be manically depressed," Shannon looked up as Jane's massive Range Rover passed. She was honking her horn as she tried to steer it around a car parked in front of the café.

"She must have got her truck licence," Rafael joked.

"Truckies and their uppers!" Colin joined in.

Nick looked amused as he made the coffees and passed them to Shannon. "You're always friendlier to the male customers, you know," he said.

"I am not." But she was glad she'd put on her blue scarf that morning. Shannon knew that colour suited her.

She took the men's order over to their inside table, where they'd divided their newspaper in half. Colin was checking out the dogs at Wentworth Park and Rafael had the foreign news.

"So, Salsa Queen, you've recovered?" Colin put down his paper.

She nodded. "But I've lost my rhythm, man."

"It'll come back, Shannon." Colin looked fatherly.

"You can dance the salsa?" Rafael asked.

"Yes, I guess."

"But not like in my country." He went serious. "Here they are artificial, here they try too many moves but they just look stupid."

"That's not very polite, Rafael," Colin said.

Rafael looked embarrassed. "Excuse me," he said.

"He's right," Shannon nodded. "They count the steps and most have two left feet. Where do you come from, Rafael?"

"Latin America. You wouldn't know my country. It's tiny."

"Maybe not," Shannon wondered why he didn't want to mention its name but she let it pass. "Anyway, I believe the world's divided into those with rhythm and those without. It doesn't matter what country you come from. I've even met black men who can't dance," she paused. "Colin."

"You obviously haven't seen me on the disco floor, Shannon," Colin replied, also pausing before her name.

"I'm looking forward to that. Provecho! Enjoy." She went back to the counter.

"And that, my dear man, is my friend, Shannon," Colin said to Rafael, taking a sip of his coffee.

"I agree with her theory about rhythm," Rafael said.

Colin wiped his chocolate moustache and went back to his newspaper.

Shannon had given Nick a break and was working the coffee machine when the men went to pay. Colin pushed back the sleeves of his work shirt as he took his wallet out of his pocket.

"Your ink's sick, man," Nick at the cash register said, glimpsing the anchor tattooed on Colin's arm.

"Got it when I was young and foolish," Colin said. "And I wasn't even in the navy."

Nick came round the counter to show them his latest tat – a cactus – on his skinny, white ankle.

"Cool," Colin admired it.

"Don't encourage him, Colin," Shannon said.

"What about you?" Nick looked at Rafael.

"None for me," he shook his head. "Tattoos are only for gangs in my country."

"I'm with you on that one," Shannon said, ignoring Nick's expression.

"Let's go, clean skin," Colin led Rafael out, waving as they left the café.

"Can you take over again, Nick?" Shannon went out the back door to grab some soft drinks from a crate. Most of her customers wouldn't be seen dead drinking such sugary drinks but she needed to be prepared. But then she forgot why she'd come out there; she felt confused and annoyed with herself.

The midwives in their drab blue cotton tops and baggy pants pull my legs wide open. Something is half out of me. It's a baby's bottom, then her tiny legs and arms and her head.

"It's a girl," one midwife says.

The other takes a photo of her. "Perfect, she's perfect," she says.

Perfect? How can she be? She's struggling. To breathe. She was only in my womb for twenty-one weeks.

I whisper: "Don't go, don't leave us yet." I stretch my arms out for her but the midwife turns away and places her in a tiny crib. The doctor shakes her head. Tom walks to the window, stares out.

"Shannon, I need some help," Nick's voice broke through the fog.

"Soft drinks, that's right." She found the crate of Coca Cola and lemonade and came inside to stack the fridge. Then she turned the iPod on again. She found a Rubén Blades number, filling her space with the sound of salsa. And she moved in time to the music.

Chapter Two

As Vesna awoke and turned over in the crisp, white sheets, she could hear whistling coming from the bathroom and it dawned on her she wasn't in her own grotty bed. She was alone as usual but this time in somebody else's place. Tom, wasn't it? She thought she remembered his name.

She'd been woken by a dog's incessant barking. Why do people have dogs if they don't look after them? Her mind was still half left behind in a dream about a pack of animals roaming the streets of a Kosovo village as crows flew overhead. And why own a dog when you're living in a city? What was it about Sydney people that they had to have everything?

She surveyed the bare room, dominated by a fireplace with a marble mantelpiece. Once coal was used to heat the house, now a gas heater was inside the fireplace. She gathered it was a terrace house that had undergone a major renovation. A few Aboriginal prints hung on the wall. Desert art by the look of them. That'd be right. Bloody dot paintings. What a trendy! And a clean one too. The place was spotless. He must have a cleaner, who wouldn't have much to do – there was no clutter at all. Quite a contrast to her own slovenly digs; she was never home so why bother with housework?

It was almost claustrophobically warm; that gas heater really worked. French doors led to a balcony and she guessed rows of courtyards, each with their own pacing dogs probably.

She heard the toilet flush and the memory of the night before returned. She saw the glass of water next to the bed and downed it. How much had she drunk? At least eight wines? Her head was throbbing and she felt dizzy. The evening had started at Sweeney's just around the corner from her city office and ended in some trashy joint at the Cross. It was all coming back to her. The waiter had insisted: "You have to eat if you want to have a drink here." So she ordered garlic bread. So demanding for such a dive.

The door swung open and a tall, slim, swarthy man, wearing only a towel around his hips appeared. Vesna was reminded again how much she'd admired his body when she first saw him in the bar and now she was admiring it even more. She didn't like to think of her own flabby tummy or her bats' wings. Or as one unkind personal trainer had called them, her tuckshop arms. No wonder she only lasted two sessions. She pulled the sheets and the Laura Ashley doona up to hide them. She really hated her chubby body but she couldn't be bothered doing anything about it. She made sure the bed linen covered the tattoo of a rose on her chest. Her early forties was perhaps too old for a tattoo but she'd got it when she was young and wild.

"Oh you're awake," the man said, not in the friendliest manner.

"Yep. I'm Vesna, how are you?" She let one pudgy hand emerge from under the sheet.

"Tom," his fingers were long and thin. He shook her hand but didn't smile.

"Yeah, I know." Their encounter in a bar with her slipping off the stool came back to her.

"Look I don't do this …"

"What? Get pissed in a bar and end up with a stranger?"

"No, well." He looked uncomfortable as he searched his wardrobe for a shirt. Hanging in a perfect line, they were all as clean and crisp as the sheets.

"Why not? Too many knock backs?" she asked from the cosy bed.

He didn't laugh.

"Look, it's fine." Vesna thought she might have gone too far but still stared at him as he dropped his towel and put his clothes on. "Takes two to tango, as they say. My turn in the bathroom?"

He nodded and she swung out of bed, grabbing her clothes along the way, hoping he wouldn't notice her wobbly bum. She closed the bathroom door. Kids' toys were on the edge of the gleaming bath and a Thomas the Tank Engine towel was hanging on the rail. Oh no, not an ankle biter, Vesna thought. Ah well, beggars can't be choosers, even if the man has baggage.

There didn't seem to be any sign of women's products though, no fancy shampoos, or moisturisers. No makeup or tweezers even. Or maybe they were hidden away. For a moment she almost stopped herself opening the bathroom cabinet door, but a recent comment by one of her fellow sub-editors came back. He accused her of not digging enough. "What kind of journalist are you anyway?" he asked her. So she looked but found nothing much inside, just some razors and blades and men's deodorant. Not even tampons. Aha, a packet of condoms – phew, he was separated or divorced. He hadn't offered to use them last night though. Thanks a lot!

She picked out a clean, fluffy towel from a pile on the shelf, the sort that good hotels provided and that she never owned. The only woman's touch was a sachet of lavender on the top of the pile. She climbed under the shower carefully avoiding any glimpse of herself in the mirror; the boiling hot water helped drown some of the hangover. Spotting a razor on the shampoo shelf she dragged it through her hairy legs, hoping Tom hadn't noticed how bad they were.

Outside, Tom was pacing the room, continuously looking at his watch. He had to go to work, and Vesna was using enough water to flood the bathroom.

But Vesna was blissfully unaware of his impatience; she felt slightly better as she emerged, dressed again in her work clothes. "Where's your kid?" she asked.

"My kid? Well if you have to know, he's at my mother's for a couple of days."

"Oh your mother? So that's why your place is so clean. And your wife?"

"Wife?"

"You're wearing a wedding ring," she took his hand, noticing how perfectly manicured his nails were compared to her ragged ones. "And don't tell me your mother gave it to you."

"My finger's swollen, can't get the damn thing off." He pulled away from her. "We're separated, if you have to know."

Oh great, a bitter divorce coming up. "What happened?"

"Hey, you're not a journo are you?"

"Good guess. My interviewing techniques must be showing." She looked inside her handbag for her brush, dragging it through her thick, dark mane, then depositing the brush back into her bag, complete with her strands of hair.

"What do you do?"

"Lawyer. Where do you work? SBS?"

"Oh God, just because I have a wog name. No, aust.com.au. What do you specialise in?"

"Immigration mainly."

Tom didn't offer her coffee or breakfast or mention a future rendezvous. But Vesna wasn't going to let him get off that easily. "Immigration! You're kidding. You're just what I need at the moment."

"Why, what are you working on?" Tom looked again at his watch.

"I'm doing some Muslim stories, you know how they're being harassed all the time."

"Doesn't sound very digital."

"I had to convince the features' editor."

"You can be convincing."

"Oh ha ha." Vesna liked his tone hoping it meant he could be convinced again. "Have you any contacts that could help?"

"I know an interesting Lebanese woman," he finally answered. "Her name's Amany. She's a social worker at the hospital. I'll email you her number. What's yours?"

"Oh great," she tore a piece of paper from her notebook and scribbled down her email address and phone number. "And yours?"

He slowly took his business card out of his wallet. "And by the way I'm a wog too."

"Yeah, I can see," she glanced at the card. His last name was Markovik. "Well Kraljevic Marko, your faithful horse, Sarac, awaits you."

"And you must fly away, Vila Ravijojla, my fellow Saturday Serbian School victim," he replied.

But Vesna knew only too well the power of ancient Serbian poems and folklore. She well might have been a Vila, a nymph that haunted the woods and springs. She too was not unfriendly to earthly beings but she also could be jealous and capricious. And hungry.

As she opened the door to leave she turned to Tom: "Is there a Macca's around here? I'm starving."

Chapter Three

Shannon wiped down the benches and started the coffee machine, the gorgeous smell of roasted beans filling the café. She felt good, for a change. Maybe it was the weather – a warm autumn day with no clouds. Maybe that dark stranger – Colin's friend – would come in for a coffee, she laughed to herself. That would give her the necessary eye candy to keep going.

A motorbike roared past, its driver in a world of his own. Didn't matter if there were kids walking to school or mothers pushing prams. If he ran over somebody it would just be collateral. He was on his way somewhere and nothing was going to stop him.

A couple of surfers in wetsuits and tousled, dripping hair stopped just outside the café. They looked bemused as he tore past. "What funeral is he rushing to?" one asked, his skin glistening with drops of salt water.

"Not mine, I hope," the other, a girl, said and laughed.

Their surfboards still had sand on them. The morning waves were rough and the lifesavers had closed the beach. But that never stopped surfers. A "do not swim, danger" sign was like a red rag to a bull to them. All the more reason to jump in. And it also meant there were no kids playing in the water or yuppies training for their next marathon to stop them catching the wave of the day.

Shannon signalled as she opened her door. "How's the water?" she asked. "Freezing?"

"About fourteen degrees," the girl said. "Bloody beautiful."

Inside, Shannon took out some pastries and bread and turned on the sandwich maker to make a toasted sandwich for her breakfast. As she was popping it into her mouth a familiar car – a black BMW – pulled up. "Oh God," she groaned. "Knew it." Just when life was looking good, there had to be somebody to come along and spoil it.

Tom. She peered out to see if Maxie was in the back seat, her heart beating. She hadn't seen him for a couple of days and she was dying to hold his warm, little body. But the seat was empty.

"Where's Maxie?" she asked Tom as he came through the door.

"Good morning to you too."

She gave him a questioning look.

"He's at mum's. She's taking him to school. How about a coffee?"

"So now your mother is doing my job?" She threw the sandwich in the bin, filled the jug with milk and steamed it for his usual flat white, wishing she could add some hallucinogenic drug to it. God, he was so straight, in his lawyer suit, boring tie and white shirt. He dressed badly when she wasn't around to help him choose something just that little bit different from all the other corporates. His mother had probably bought him the shirt.

Such a city boy. Not a wimp. He was fit. He looked good in Lycra, heading off from home on his bike to Centennial Park at the crack of most dawns. But he was a lawyer, an office man in a glassed-in space high up in the city. Not the valley for him, but work lunches, meetings, consultations, cocky tails. An art lover, of course. Member of the Art Gallery. Drinkies amongst the Archibalds.

"Hideous, ugly paintings of hideous, ugly people," Shannon told him once, but he wasn't amused. "Come on, let me see your perfect teeth. Have a laugh." She'd taunted him when he didn't laugh at her comments. She'd showed off in front of his friends in their suits and ties and cocktail dresses. She knew the names of the painters, their style, their history – she had friends who went to art school when she was a dance student.

The café was filling with people, and a young woman came up to the counter to order, asking what sort of muffins they had that morning.

"The bloody usual," Shannon snapped.

Tom grimaced. "I think that looks like apple and cinnamon," he tried to help. "Would you like one?"

"Thank you so much," the customer said.

"You're welcome so much," Shannon said, glaring at Tom as he sat down at a table, staring out the window. She bet he was probably thinking that she was a bad investment. She'd lose the café if she kept putting her customers off like this. Tom's frown was normal but

Shannon noticed something different about him. Was it his smell? He always wore cologne, but not today. He was a bit sweatier than usual too. Or shiftier. That's it. He looked shifty. As if he had something to hide. And it wasn't just about keeping Maxie. Must be screwing around. That'd be right, couldn't keep his prick in his pants. Ah well, the marriage was over. She knew Tom thought she was mad and just too much hard work. Maybe his mother was right, she was a bit crazy.

Her phone rang and she took the call. One of the greenies she knew from the valley; they were organising another sit-in to protest against the cutting down of trees for the new highway.

Maxie kept begging to go down to the valley. The old farm house was close to the rainforest, the nesting ground of lyrebirds whose sounds mimicked those of the calls of all the birds in the forest, weaving a tapestry of song through the trees. She'd taught him the names of the birds. Already he could pick them out from an ancient book she'd kept for him. He loved the satin bower-birds the best, with their crazy bowers next to moss-covered rocks or fallen logs. He'd put out blue bottle tops and pegs just to see if the bower bird found them and ferreted them away to his bower.

"Sorry I can't make it down this weekend," she told the greenie. "Next time, OK?" She felt slightly guilty as she served the woman customer her coffee and muffin and brought the flat white over to Tom, pulling up a seat and sitting down for a minute. Well, she couldn't be everywhere.

"Don't forget to bring Maxie on Friday," she said to Tom. "It's my weekend."

"Ah, that's why I'm here. Shannon, I think he's better off at mum's. He's having a good time there. And it's dad's birthday on Saturday."

Shannon's face dropped. She knew the day was looking far too benign. Something just had to happen. She turned away; she didn't want Tom to see how easily he could affect her. And why wasn't she invited to the old man's birthday? They got on well; she liked him and he liked her. "What do you mean? My lawyer said ..."

"Your lawyer?"

"Yes Tom, my fucking divorce lawyer."

"Don't swear Shannon, calm down."

A couple of women with blue-rinsed hair sat at the table next to Tom. Where was Nick when she needed him? Late as usual. She noticed the women look up at the raised voices, but she didn't care. "Tom, it's my weekend."

"Next weekend, OK?"

"Tom!"

"Your customers, Shannon, keep your voice down," he whispered.

"Don't tell me about my customers."

"Look, I think it's better for him to stay there most of the time," he stirred his coffee. "I've had to work late a lot."

"Well, bring him back here. For Christ's sake, I'm his mother."

"You're still not coping."

"I am. I'm much better. I can manage."

"Just give it a little bit longer, Shannon."

"How much longer? Come on, Tom."

"A few more weeks."

"No! I want him back. You're in breach of the arrangements. You're a lawyer, you should know."

"Yes, Shannon, don't forget, I am a lawyer."

"Yeah, a fucking Immigration lawyer."

Rafael was smiling as he came in the door of the café but he stopped at the sound of the argument. He turned around quickly and went back outside.

Shannon saw him. "Tom, I do have to look after my customers. Do you mind?"

"OK, but please be reasonable." Tom gulped down the dregs and scuttled out the door.

What a way to start the day. And where was that bloody Nick? She went outside, where Rafael was standing awkwardly, his hands in the pockets of his overalls. The morning had suddenly improved and she thought he looked particularly handsome. "Come inside, I'll make you a coffee."

As he waited at the counter he asked for a ham and cheese croissant.

She shook her head. "Sorry, Rafael, I forgot to order them. There aren't any."

"There aren't any. *No hay.*" He repeated.

"What did you say?"

"Nothing. What you said it just reminded me of something a long time ago."

"In your country?"

"Yes, back home. Can I have a tuna sandwich then?" Rafael was miles away, his brown eyes seeing something she could never see.

"I forgot to buy tuna too. How about a chicken wrap?" Shannon asked.

He nodded.

"How's the job going?" she toasted the wrap, moving slowly. She didn't want him to leave.

"It's OK. Not long to go. I'll have to start looking around again soon. Were you arguing about your child?"

So he had heard the argument. Oh well, what did it matter? The whole café must have heard. Great for business. "Yes, he just started school this year. He's staying with Tom. His father, who just left. Have a seat, I'll bring it over."

"Oh, right."

Just then a tall woman wearing a purple hijab, which matched her skin-tight pants, edged past two paddle-pop customers and their children sitting at a table near the door.

"I thought all the Lebanese restaurants were in Cleveland Street," one of the customers said to her friend.

"It's OK, I'm just here to recruit for Hezbollah," the newcomer, who had heard her, responded.

Shannon looked at Rafael and they both laughed as the woman came up to the counter. He sat down to wait for his order while he read the paper. Nick arrived puffing from running from the bus stop. Today he was sporting a man-bun and Shannon shook her head at him as he took over at the coffee machine. "Hello, Amany. What are you doing here?" she said.

"I was in the area. For an inter-faith meeting at the Jewish school," Amany said, loud enough for the mums to hear. "How are you? And Tom?"

"We're fine I guess."

"He must still be grieving?" Amany looked concerned.

"He never tells me anything."

"Not very communicative? That's normal for men in this situation."

"Well he wouldn't win the Nobel Peace Prize."

"Can I have a coffee please?" Amany said. "I've had a busy morning and a long drive from home."

"We don't do Turkish here." It was Shannon's turn for a bad joke.

"Lebanese, actually but I'd prefer a flat white, thanks. Can you take a short break?"

"I'm kind of busy. Do they pay you extra to do home visits?"

Amany laughed. "Not likely. You cancelled your counselling sessions?"

Shannon looked under the counter for her cigarettes and took one out of the packet, admiring the way the barista's black pants clung to his bum. "Nick, can you make Amany one of your special coffees, you know with a design in the froth and all," she asked.

Amany followed Shannon out the front. She gestured towards the mums and their babies. "Must be hard for you."

"I'm not like them, even if they are mothers," Shannon replied, enjoying the blast of nicotine as she took her first drag.

"You're smoking?" Amany looked disapproving as Shannon flicked the ash.

"Oh no, not you too."

"But if you're wanting to get pregnant?" Amany tried to put her arm around Shannon but she brushed her off. "What did Dr Taylor say?"

"Nothing. Just that it would be an immaculate conception."

"Oh, well you need time to grieve."

"Look, I've got work to do." She turned to go inside but Amany grabbed her arm.

"So have I, Shannon. I don't normally come to a client's place of work."

"I didn't ask you to come." She pushed Amany's hand away, she'd had enough of this.

"How's Maxie handling it all?" Amany was like a dog with a bone.

"How would I know?" Shannon was going from annoyance to anger now.

"What?"

"I only have him every second weekend and one night a week now," she shrugged.

"Really? Have you and Tom broken up?"

"Yep and he's got Maxie. I was meant to have him this weekend and Tom's even made that difficult."

"But why? Max should be with his mother."

Their conversation was interrupted by Nick appearing with a takeaway coffee for Amany, who nodded thanks.

"I know that. But I'm a bad mother. I lost my baby, didn't I? I smoke too much." She put out the cigarette, grinding it into the pavement with her shoe. "I drink. I don't look after myself. Maybe you should have come with somebody from welfare."

"It wasn't your fault. You can try again. Well, once you and Tom get back together."

"That won't happen."

"Don't torture yourself, Shannon." Amany's eyes looked into hers.

Shannon put her head down. "The café's not a good place for this conversation, Amany." She hoped the social worker wouldn't visit her at home but she had to get rid of her.

Amany followed her inside to pay for the coffee but Shannon waved her hands to say she didn't need to. Amany was adamant, she took the money out of her purse and pushed it across the counter at her. She tried to give Shannon a kiss on the cheek but Shannon swerved to avoid it.

"I'm only trying to help," Amany said as she took her car keys out of her bag. "I feel for you."

Far out! Why does Amany upset me so much? Shannon thought as she opened the fridge, taking out a bottle of water. It slipped out of her hand and smashed to the ground. There was water everywhere, seeping across the floor and under the fridge.

"Oh shit," she cried out, her arms in the air.

Rafael jumped up from his table, dropping the newspaper on the floor and ran behind the counter. "What happened? What happened?"

"It's OK, only water." Shannon assured him. She didn't like people invading her private place – the kitchen was her escape from the café crowd.

"Do you have a broom?" Rafael asked.

She pointed to the corner and he picked up a dustpan and broom to sweep up the broken fragments. He cleaned up the mess, going back to collect his newspaper to wrap the broken pieces of glass, not saying a word. He put the broom away and found a mop, soaking up the water from the floor.

"Thanks, Rafael." Shannon was bemused but also grateful. "Want a job?"

"I've got one, thanks," he smiled.

She went to the fridge again and this time took out a bottle of wine, found a glass and poured a big one. As she leant against the cupboard she went to take a sip but stopped. For the first time she noticed Rafael had a pony tail. Normally she hated them, especially on somebody who must have been the wrong side of fifty, but on him it looked just fine.

"Would you like one?" she asked.

He shook his head as he pulled a tiny shard of glass from his thumb and sucked the drop of blood.

"Too early for a drink?" Shannon asked, gesturing to the wine bottle.

Rafael stared at her. "I must go, we must finish the job as soon as possible."

Shannon felt stupid. What was she thinking? It was early morning, for God's sake. And why was Rafael eye-balling her as if she was a ghost? She put the bottle back in the fridge.

"Who was that woman?" he asked.

"Oh the social worker from the hospital."

He turned to leave. "How much do I owe you?"

She went to the cash register at the counter. "Fifteen dollars, thanks."

"A little boy should be with his mother." Rafael reached inside his pocket for his wallet and handed over a twenty dollar note. "I am happy to help you get him back."

Shannon was surprised at his words; she smiled and thanked him as she gave him his change. She imagined a picnic in the park with the three of them, Maxie playing on the swings as Rafael fed her camembert and prosciutto. She took some blue straws out of a container and threw them in her bag; Maxie could take them to the valley to leave out for the bower birds.

Stop dreaming. Back to work as another contingent of mums and bubs landed on the café. There was no more time to think about how Maxie was feeling or guess what diabolical move Tom was going to make next. There were men and women who needed coffee and perhaps even a muffin.

Chapter Four

Vesna's neck and back were killing her. She'd been sitting at her desk in front of a computer for hours. She was sub-editing, trying to fix one abysmal story after another. They'd land in the subbing basket on the computer; it was never-ending. And they'd all be equally bad. Hadn't anybody ever taught these people to write? How did they ever get a job in journalism? She couldn't fathom it. They couldn't even get the lead right. There was nothing interesting or gripping that would entice you to read further.

"Look at the bottom of the story, you'll usually find the lead there," one elderly sub, Grahame, had once told her and they'd both chuckled. His fingers were yellow from nicotine, he had horrendous bad breath and he wheezed as if he was going to die any minute. But she loved him. He had that famous sub-editors' wit. Scathing and cynical but not cruel. She used to often hear him on the phone, gently asking young reporters questions about their copy. Not screaming at them, not putting them down, just wheedling the information out of them.

"Your story needs to be cut. We're not *The New York Times*," he would joke. "Do you want me to send it back to you or do you trust this old fella to do it?" He would put this question time and time again. There was nobody around who in any way could replace him. He was humble but funny. He'd keep his head down whenever the boss was around, shuffle off to the kitchen to get a cuppa about ten times during his shift, always work overtime when the others around him clocked off as soon as the big hand hit knock-off time. Then one day he told Vesna he wasn't feeling that well. "I'm going out for a bit of fresh air," he said, surprising her, as he never went out to the atmosphere-less shopping centre next door. He would always eat his lunch at his desk as he worked – normally sandwiches made by his wife and a cup of tea from the kitchen.

"Can you get me a coffee," Vesna asked and then explained where the best coffee shop was in the dreary centre.

Ten minutes passed, then twenty and then thirty and he still hadn't returned.

"Where's Grahame?" the chief sub asked. "That queue is getting very long."

It was just then that she heard an ambulance's siren. Another ten minutes and the phone rang on the chief sub's desk. It was the police. Grahame had been found in the shopping centre, lying on the floor. He'd had a heart attack.

Vesna rubbed her eyes. She could imagine her takeaway cup of coffee spilt next to him on the dirty shopping centre lino. She didn't want to think about Grahame now and what this unforgiving place had done to him, or whether having to line up behind a bunch of suburban mums and over-dressed office workers in the coffee shop had been the final straw. The following day the editor had sent out a nauseating email to all staff, talking about "our beloved Grahame".

"You never called him beloved when he was alive," she thought. "Just good, ol' Grahame or bloody ol' Grahame." And just as she predicted the editor-in-chief sent out another email a week or so later announcing a new prize for journalism at the office would be named after "our beloved Grahame". The cynicism was breathtaking to her and she was the queen of cynics.

An email pinged. She had butterflies in her stomach, hoping it would be from Tom. But no, just another long email from the management about staff changes. All the wrong people for the right jobs, as usual. She felt disappointed. Would he ever contact her again?

God, this office was grotty. Her keyboard was covered in crumbs; she attempted to tweeze some indescribable bit of food out from between the letter 'r' and the letter 't'. The cleaner wandered past, muttering to himself in Greek as he emptied the rubbish bins – cardboard boxes with plastic bags in them. Was this part of the cost-cutting – first the rubbish bins went, then the jobs? Somebody had strategically placed bottles of Spray'n'Wipe around the room to drop the hint that the journos could now and again clean their desks. She decided to ignore the hint. It was hard with shift work though. Nobody knew whose desk was whose and who had responsibility over the dirty coffee cups and glasses. Vesna sighed, got up and went into the kitchen to make herself a cup of tea.

She had little choice but to stick at this job. The years as a foreign correspondent in hellholes like Kosovo hadn't won her any Brownie points. She was bitter but how else was she going to pay the bills? Still, she couldn't help herself working on other stories, in between her subbing shifts. The sort of stories she wanted to do, in the vain hope that they'd get a run. No extra money, she just gave them to the Features desk and begged them to use them, but at least it made her feel alive. That's what she was planning to do with the Muslim story.

The fridge was full of other people's food, all neatly labelled. She never brought any food in. That was because she never had any at her house. She was known as "empty fridge Vesna". She wondered if somebody would notice if she pinched some of their food; one of the salads looked nice. Nah, not a good idea, she thought. I'm already unpopular enough here. Well, will just have to be a bickie this time. But of course there were no biscuits left. There never were. There was one shrivelled apple in the bowl and she grabbed that. She wondered what Tom had in his fridge – cabbage rolls and stuffed peppers made by his mother, fetta cheese, olives?

She looked up, feeling somebody eyeing her. It was Steve, the grinning editor-in chief, a squat man who had attempted to get fit by running at five am every day, but had more recently given up on the idea. She wasn't sure if she liked the fit editor or the slobby one.

"Fruit Vesna? You're changing," his grin seemed to smear his face like toothpaste.

"I'm starving, there's a queue of crap stories a mile long to sub and I can't go out to get lunch because the casual never turned up," she retorted. "What choice have I got?"

"Well it's good to see the fruit I'm supplying all of you is being eaten," he said.

Yeah, fruit instead of "upgrades" or being promoted and more money, that'd be right.

Behind her the new reporter who'd just got the travel writing gig had crept in. She was tossing her long fair hair around taking all her bits of vegetables out of the fridge and moving over to the same side as the editor, placing them on a chopping board ready to make a salad.

"That looks healthy," he said.

"Oh yes, a breast-feeding mother needs to eat healthy food," she said in a school ma'am tone. "I've just pumped some milk for my little one."

He laughed. "How is your baby?"

"Oh beautiful. Do you want to see a photo?"

Vesna groaned to herself and stopped in the nick of time from commenting on the wet patches on the travel writer's jumper. Typical that they'd give the travel writing job to somebody who would find it difficult to travel, she thought, heading back to her desk. Her mobile rang just as she got there. She didn't know the number but answered it. She didn't believe in blocking calls. Who knows? She might miss the scoop of the year.

"Hello, is that Vesna? I'm Amany Abdoul," a crisp, efficient voice with just a twang of western suburbs, announced.

"Oh yes, thanks for calling back. Tom Markovik gave me your number. He said you'd been attacked for wearing a hijab, for being Muslim? Could I interview you about that?"

They arranged to meet the following morning at the hospital where Amany worked, Prince George.

"Vesna!" Gary, an older overweight check sub, who was past his journalism prime by at least ten years, yelled. "Oh God, she's on the phone again. Vesna, are you going to do any work for us today or just your own stuff?"

She hung up. "Yeah, yeah OK."

"Well, can you pick up 'Prime Minister'. We've gotta get that out fast. Just a sub not a rewrite. Don't do a Grahame on us."

Vesna clicked on the story, trying not to let her fury erupt at Gary's comment. He would never, ever be capable of "doing a Grahame". And with a horrible, sinking feeling she wondered if she could even be half the journalist poor, old Grahame was. But at least she was trying. Her Muslim story was going to be a beauty.

Chapter Five

Rafael sat on the edge of the concrete slab at the building site eating his sandwich. He had ten more minutes of lunchtime to go and he was enjoying the sun. He didn't want to go to the pub with the other workers, and today he'd rather sit alone than join Colin at the café.

He knew Colin from other jobs he'd been on; they'd worked together a few times and he liked him, he was a good bloke. He also liked his fellow workers – a crew of guys from the western suburbs and Wollongong, the Maori boys from Bondi, Iranians and Chinese – but he didn't want to have to spend every lunch time with them either. They only had half an hour and he didn't want to waste time listening to them making crude remarks about the barmaids there and boasting how they were going to score. Sex, sex, sex, that's all Aussies talked about. OK so at home the men loved to "catcall" women, yelling out sleazy comments as they drove past them waiting at intersections or bus stops. He didn't like that either. That wasn't the right way to treat your *compañeras*.

And it wasn't because the others knocked them about going to a trendy café instead of the pub. In fact, he'd noticed they'd discovered Shannon's too. Her falafel rolls were great, one of the Maori boys told him the other day, making him laugh as he said: "Yeah, bro and she makes the best aioli sauce." It was just that he needed some time alone, and anyway he'd rather see Shannon when Colin or the others weren't around. He was a private person; he didn't want everybody knowing what he was up to.

While he was grateful for the job, he was sick of this sort of work. It was boring, menial and damned hard. His overalls were filthy by the end of the day. He had breathed in enough dust to make his lungs completely snow white. His nostrils were full of the powdery stuff and it didn't even give him a hit. Prefer some cocaine, he smiled to himself, thinking of Shannon's comment. But that was counter-revolutionary too. He remembered photos from forty years before of Contras loading boxes of cocaine onto planes parked on jungle airstrips. One side would say they were photos of his revolutionaries, the Sandinistas, the other the counter-revolutionaries, the Contras. He knew it was the Contras.

He thought of Nicaragua, his poverty-stricken country – so poor it didn't have enough wheelchairs to give the amputees. Legs blown off from land mines, the injured sat on the footpath outside the co-operative for returned soldiers in the once-rich suburbs of Managua. They waited, oh-so-patiently, bored and expressionless, for their own set of wheels. Then their families wouldn't have to leave them there each day – like old sacks of beans and rice.

He would walk past the co-operative on his way to buy food in a shop where every day he was told by the storekeeper: *"No hay, señor."* There isn't any. It was only a few blocks from the Intercontinental Hotel, where the journalists he worked with as a cameraman hung out. There also the *internationalistas*, known as *Sandalistas*, found relief from the intense humidity by dipping their toes in the silvery-blue waters of the kidney-shaped pool. As they sipped their rum and cokes, they claimed they had discovered the truth of the revolution and all his country's problems.

He would nod and say *"holá"* to his limbless *compañeros*. They'd look up from their card games and nod back. *"Hola, Rafa."* They'd ask for cigarettes that he couldn't supply as he no longer smoked. It had become a joke, because each day they would ask and each day he would say: *"Lo siento, no hay."*

But one day he realised there was one thing that would never run out in his country: rum. Almost one hundred per cent alcohol. Turned Dr Jekyll into Mr Hyde. Marx said religion was the opiate of the masses. But in Nicaragua *Flor de Caña* did that trick. He went back into the store, returning with a bottle for each of them. It was cheap, he could afford it. He would be in deep trouble from the authorities, from their families. He didn't care. From the footpath they reached their arms, nodding in gratitude. *"Gracias, hombre."*

"Viva la revolución." He mouthed the lingo as he handed each a bottle they would most certainly drink until they passed out in the boiling, tropical sun. *"Patria libre o morir,"* he said to them knowing full well they'd never have a free fatherland.

"I still have my legs, my arms, my body," Rafael spoke to himself. "I'm not dead. I've survived. But what use is that? Am I the last revolutionary?"

What choice did he have but labouring in a country that didn't welcome him? Things were supposed to be different – there'd be lots of good jobs, great sight-seeing, nice houses to live in. But that was years ago anyway. He'd learnt to live with the solitude and the boredom of his life. Australia was somewhere safe but he felt no loyalty towards the country. Maybe he was *apátrida*, a stateless person.

He'd tried once to get work in his old job as a cameraman here but his English just wasn't good enough then. And now he had no desire to go outside his circle into something more challenging. He had his routine and it suited him. He didn't mind his time alone in his little flat at the weekend. As the late afternoon sun shone on his bed, he'd read his tattered books of poetry. All the revolutionary ones he once believed in. That was his religion. Forget Catholicism and all that mumbo jumbo. Ah those poets could write, of revolution and patriotism and love for their country, of revenge by educating the country's children instead of keeping them poor and barefoot.

Occasionally he would summon up the courage to visit his past and go and hear a salsa band just for the music that went straight to his heart. He'd buy a drink and sit on his own watching the dancers. Some were good, they had the rhythm. Others resembled a bunch of escaped convicts as they attempted the moves. *It's not the hips, it's your solar plexus*, he wanted to tell them. *Don't jump around so much. Listen to the music, listen to the beat. Feel the rhythm, let it flow from inside you.* But he kept quiet, just laughing into his Coke.

Tomorrow he would go to Shannon's café for breakfast or lunch, but not today. He liked her too – she seemed tough outside but she was suffering. Poor thing, having to beg to see her son. Maybe she really could dance the salsa. How he missed the music of home and the camaraderie of the dance floor. Perhaps he could invite her to go with him sometime.

Today he didn't even want to drink coffee or move anywhere. He just wanted to enjoy the feeling of warmth on his skin as he ate the toasted ham sandwich he'd picked up earlier on the way in. If only they made *pinolillo* here life would be so much better.

The others returned and two of them sat down next to him, talking loudly. "Jeeze, I got blind last night," one of them, Wayne, said.

"Me too. Were you with the missus?"

"Nah just having a bit of *me* time."

"Sweet."

Rafael wondered what language these two were speaking. It didn't sound like the English he'd picked up on the streets of Managua. Bloody Aussies they were so uneducated. Imagine if any of them knew he read poetry, his wonderful Gioconda Belli or Carlos and Luis Mejia Godoy or the assassinated Salvadoran Roque Dalton.

"Es bello ser comunista,

aunque cause muchos dolores de cabeza."

Yes it was good to be a Communist even if it gave you a headache!

It was an unusually warm day for April – humid even, like home in the dry season. An Indian summer day even though autumn had arrived, with still the scent of jasmine in the air; too nice a day to be working here. Labouring and general dog's body – there must be something better to do. A couple of new guys had turned up that morning for a day or two's work. No training. Didn't have a clue. He wasn't sure where they came from, but they certainly weren't speaking Spanish or English or even Australian. They sat together for their lunch over in the shade of the only remaining tree on the block – a messy hibiscus bush – yammering away in their language. Probably Iranian cherry pickers. He grimaced. Iranians were always trouble. Never had any papers and they attracted unwelcome Immigration visits.

The Maori boys weren't that much better. They'd been in Australia so long they called themselves Mozzies. But some of them didn't have papers either. Didn't matter where they came from, they were all so negligent when it came to safety. He'd told Tony the other day to do up his safety harness but he'd ignored him. A big tough guy, a Rugby player, covered in tattoos. A good bloke on the whole. But he would never have been accepted by the Movement; he wouldn't take orders.

"It'll be cool," he'd said when he called out to him. "No worries."

"But you need to secure it."

"Mate, I told you, it's cool, I've been doing this for 30 years. They just cause problems." He stuck his tongue out as if he were doing the Haka.

Rafael had just shrugged. These Mozzie boys, they knew better than anybody and he didn't feel like arguing with him. Tony's safety wasn't his responsibility anyway. The company wanted the job over and done with as soon as possible and the workers wanted to be paid. Just get on with it.

Back home, at least the revolution tried to educate the masses, not like here where they seemed proud of being as anti-intellectual as they could be. Aussies: they'd gambled the country away to professional punters, who built phallic symbols for the generations-to-come to remember them by. But now it was bad back home too. Oh his poor, poor country. What a mess it was. Sexual deviates running the place, just like the Gringos. Doing favours for their mates, building unsafe monstrosities, planning a huge canal which would destroy peoples' homes. What had they fought for? What was the point of it all? No money, no food, and then once the Sandinistas lost the election, no revolution either.

He thought of his favourite band, from the Atlantic coast, Dimensión Costeña, and the words of one of their songs:

Everybody love money.

He wished he still had something to believe in and fight for. But those days were long gone.

Colin tapped Rafael on the shoulder. "Are you OK, mate?"

Rafael swung round. "Aye, you gave me a fright."

"Have a good solo lunch?" Colin asked. "You were missed."

"Who missed me?" Rafael knew exactly who Colin was talking about.

"You know!" It was in his nature to stir his mate.

"Mañana, hombre, mañana."

Colin laughed. "Better get back to it. Can you help Tony put the safety netting up on the scaffolding this arvo?"

Much as he liked Colin, Rafael didn't need to be told it was time to get back to work. Even if he hated the job he still had initiative. His time fighting in the streets and in the army and later working for television crews and filmmakers had at least taught him that. He strapped his leather tool-belt on and climbed the scaffolding ladder up onto the platform, where Tony had left his buckets of cement-render all over the place. What a mess! He started to attach the netting left there but Tony stopped him.

"No need for that, mate."

"Colin told me to do it. He's the foreman."

"Listen, Raf, that's not your job. Leave it to the scaffolding guys. They'll be back tomorrow."

Rafael shrugged. "But …"

"I'm telling you, she'll be right, mate."

What was he to do now? He climbed back down the ladder and closed the hatch, which seemed a bit tight. He wanted to fix it but with Tony's attitude he decided to leave it. There must be another job he could find in this God-forsaken place.

Chapter Six

What was it about hospital coffee shops? They were just so depressing, Vesna thought. Maybe it was the smell of death or of fear, or just plain disinfectant. Doctors deliberating over people's lives, patients shuffling around in their dressing gowns and slippers. They didn't seem to care what others made of their get-up as they stood in line ordering their pineapple donuts and caramel slices. Didn't they know it was that sort of food that had got them there in the first place?

"A takeaway cappuccino and a blueberry muffin please," Vesna ordered.

"Sugar?"

"Two, thanks."

She made her way to the lift and up to the social workers' area and its waiting room, and took a seat as far away from the daytime television as she could, even though it meant being next to a woman with a small child playing on the ground in front of her. Why couldn't they make up their minds whether to turn the TV up full blast or completely off, not that annoying continuous murmur? It was hard to ignore the presenter cooking some awful concoction or dancing with a politician or pretending she was interested in somebody's sob story.

A pregnant woman on the other side of Vesna was talking on her phone as if she wanted the whole world to hear what she was going through and this was the only way to do it. There were signs on the wall alerting people to not use their mobiles but that made no difference. The little girl on the floor even had a plastic one she was playing with.

"I'm calling because my partner has a crook back and he's been trying to get into the pain clinic for months," the woman said loudly on perhaps her fourth phone call. "He's an alcoholic and he's in a lot of pain. I need some advice."

Vesna tried to ignore her by observing a tall, well-built woman cleaner who reminded her of the silent Indian from *One Flew Over the Cuckoo's Nest* pushing a mop around. Even with her lack of housekeeping skills, to Vesna it looked as if the mop and the dirty water in the bucket were making the floor even filthier.

"That's what I call a Clayton's clean," she said to herself and laughed out loud at her own joke, which raised a curious stare from the mother.

The woman on the mobile made another call explaining again that her husband was an alcoholic with a sore back. "My husband is in a lot of pain. Can I book him in here? What, a nine to ten-month wait? You've got to be joking."

The room sighed as one when she was finally called in for her appointment but Vesna wondered whether it was such a good thing for her and her alcoholic husband to bring another being into the world.

The relief was broken when the little girl spoke loudly into her toy phone in a high-pitched mimic of the disappearing woman: "You've GOT to be joking," and the waiting room erupted in laughter, including Vesna.

"Smart kid," she commented to the child's mother, who tried to hide her embarrassment by engulfing herself in a magazine graced with a cover of a TV personality from the 1960s announcing: "Cancer won't get the better of me."

Well I guess this is all good colour for the story about a Muslim social worker in a hospital full of Bogans, Vesna thought. Ten minutes later she looked at her watch and impatiently wondered if she'd got the right place when a woman, possibly in her late-thirties, wearing a bright purple hijab, tight jeans and a fashionable cardigan that matched her scarf called her name. They all look alike, she smiled to herself, getting up to meet her.

Amany introduced herself, shaking Vesna's hand and apologising for being late, explaining she'd had to meet the parents of a baby taken to the neo-natal unit.

"Mm, that must be tough," Vesna tried to sound concerned. "Will it survive?

"Oh yes it's amazing how babies of only 22 weeks gestation live and prosper these days," Amany answered, showing her into her office and sitting down at her neat desk, while Vesna took out her notebook, pen and tape recorder.

The room was bare, with no pictures on the walls, but on the desk was a photo of a young girl of about ten, her long black hair framing her shy smile.

"You were attacked by some boys in a train. Is that right?" Vesna turned on the tape recorder, declining an offer of coffee or water.

"Yes," Amany didn't seem to enjoy repeating the story. "I was travelling home from here."

"Right? Do you always get the same train?" Vesna scribbled in her notebook.

"Most nights, yes, around six. Some boys started calling me names."

"What sort of names?" Vesna's questions came thick and fast.

"Well, rude names."

"Like what?"

"Muslim bitch, that sort of thing," she spoke with reluctance. "Then they pulled at my hijab and one of them spat at me and told me to go back to where I came from. I was born here, for heaven's sake."

"Were you scared?" her tone still remained the same.

"I was but I felt protected by God. I tried to ignore them."

"Did you call the police?"

"Yes, when I got away from them."

"Oh so how did you do that?"

"I jumped off at the next stop and they were too cowardly to follow me. It's important people know what is happening to the Muslim community here." She paused. "What exactly are you planning to do with this? How do you know Tom, by the way?"

"I'm writing a feature about attitudes towards Muslims here. I'd asked Tom for contacts, he's a ..." She paused. "A colleague. We've worked together."

"Oh that's good," she smiled. "So sad about Tom and his wife losing their baby."

Vesna didn't have a clue what she was talking about, but tried not to show it. So maybe that's why they split up?

"People need to know about the prejudices we face," Amany continued.

"Can I ask you, why do you wear the veil when you know it's going to cause trouble?" Vesna could feel herself becoming bored getting ready to hear the same old gripes about racism in Australia. There's racism every bloody where in the world, some places worse than others. Been to Kosovo lately? Or Syria? But she needed case studies and wanted to hear Amany's answer to a question that all non-Muslim Aussies asked.

Amany grimaced. "As a Muslim woman we have the opportunity to respect our femininity and the veil is a religious ritual that offers us this respect." She spoke quietly but with authority.

"Right." Vesna tried to sound sympathetic. "When did you start wearing one?"

"I put the scarf on when I was twenty. I was pregnant with my first child. It was after a dream, I felt it was time to do it. We have rules and regulations. The aim is that you have the right intention in your heart, not to hurt anybody. You need to have self-control, discipline, respect for other people. Our religion is based on five points: prayer, fasting, charity, going to the pilgrimage and the belief there is only one God."

Vesna was worried she was getting a religious lecture, but she let her continue.

"Wearing the veil is not a constraint for us, we are not restricted from fulfilling our aspirations nor keeping up to date with the latest fashions."

"Yeah, I can see that. But what about the sexual aspect? The idea that men are telling you what to wear?"

"It's nothing to do with men. I'm not wearing it because of my husband. Actually, he does most of the cooking at home; all those ideas about women being subjugated are so stereotypical. But I think you should be able to understand that I don't like to be treated like a piece of meat by anybody."

Vesna was getting annoyed. "Do you think I'm seen as a piece of meat?"

"No, not at all. I hate it when people think I am oppressed because I wear the scarf." Her eyes widened but her voice was still calm. "What is really misunderstood in western society is that our religion does not oppose women's personal fulfilment, but it is the diverse extremist cults and cultural habits, not religion in itself, that is gaining bad publicity."

"So would you call yourself a feminist?"

"Yes, I suppose so. There are many Muslim feminists – have you heard of Nawal El Saadawi, the Egyptian feminist and writer? I love her books."

Vesna nodded. She had read of her.

"Look, I can do anything non-Muslim women can do, I know that. But maybe western-style feminism has failed anyway. And the sort of moral freedoms you've won for yourselves only bring unhappiness."

"But isn't freedom important? Freedom of speech, of expression?" Vesna was getting fired up but still taking notes.

"Not when morals are lost along the way," Amany was emphatic. "Sometimes upholding ethics is more important than freedom."

"But not all Muslim women think that way. What about the stories of women wearing forbidden lipstick under the Taliban or having their fingers cut off just because they wore nail polish?"

"We don't agree with what the Taliban or ISIS or any of those fanatical groups do to women." Amany continued to speak softly but firmly. "That's not real Islam, that's taking it back to some kind of mediaeval cult. We're not against makeup, of course. In the Koran it says to tell the believing women to lower their gaze and be modest. Islam doesn't say women are inferior to men; it says they are different."

"But this is Australia," Vesna could feel herself burning.

"Exactly, this is Australia. That means multiculturalism and diversity, and respect for other cultures. But we get attacked for being different and still maintaining our religion and cultural habits." Amany sighed and shifted in her chair. "Do you realise how tired we are of having to answer these same, old questions. Why don't you ask something new? Something a little deeper that may really educate your readers. Aren't you at all interested in our religion? And please don't ask me about female circumcision, either. That is a practice that came about way before Islam."

"Yeah, our guys took hundreds of years to find the clitoris and don't know what to do with it. Yours find it and get rid of it." Vesna gave up on the argument.

Amany finally laughed although her cheeks were red. "I can assure you that hasn't happened to me."

She moved the papers on her desk. "Vesna, have you ever been attacked just for the clothes you wear?"

Vesna shook her head. "Not me, personally but I know about hate between religious groups. I covered Kosovo. You can't tell me anything. The world is dominated by mad people who believe in witchcraft. We haven't come further than the primitives denouncing women as witches."

"I don't agree. We have sophisticated rules to live by that many are now seeing the benefit of. Even some Aboriginal people here have turned to our religion. And wasn't it the Serbs who started the war in Kosovo? Your name? Are you Serbian?"

"Some blame CNN for Kosovo. And anyway my parents were Yugoslav. Our lounge room had a photo of Tito on the wall, right above the tray of Turkish coffee cups," she said. "You know all us Yugos, well Serbs or whatever, we were brought up with those stories of mothers cutting off a finger of their first born son to stop them being taken away by the Turkish army. Without all their fingers they couldn't use a gun. You have to understand hatred goes back a long way."

"My family's Lebanese; of course we understand that," Amany started picking up the papers on her desk, putting them into manila folders.

Vesna was feeling jaded and could see she was irritating her subject and it was time to lighten up. "Well everybody thought it was a little Lebanon here when we had those so-called race riots at Cronulla. But I reckon it was just a drug gang war, with the Lakemba mob trying to take up the Bra Boys' territory. Spoilt Lebanese boys maybe?"

Amany smiled. "Thank heavens I have a daughter."

Vesna turned off her tape recorder and put her notebook in her bag. Her thick, black hair lay in a mass around her olive skin. She was feeling hungry and thought about hummus and tabouli.

"Is there a good place around here for falafel rolls?" she asked.

"I prefer your stuffed cabbages so long as they're filled with beef." Amany smiled again. "You're Orthodox Christian right?"

"Me?" Vesna snorted. "Sorry Amany but all religions are fucked if you ask me. Anyway it doesn't matter what I believe. Can I get a pic of you in your veil?"

Amany nodded as she pushed a stray hair beneath her veil and Vesna pulled her phone out of her bag. "But please, no more swearing." She posed for the shot but then her phone rang and she excused herself to take the call.

"He's been picked up, but why? Really? I thought he had a work visa. When they came here he had a Medicare card. Oh OK, I'll make some calls." She hung up. "Sorry, Vesna."

"Some legal problems?"

"No, well, you know some people try and beat the system."

"Illegals?"

"I can't really say." Amany put her head down. "I hope you write a good story, thanks Vesna. We need journalists who have some understanding of history."

On the way home on the train Vesna started thinking of a totally new story. Illegals and how they managed to get Medicare and every other type of card and stay under the radar. Much more interesting than harassed Muslims. Tom would come in a lot more useful than she'd realised. Mmm, and he was useful in other ways too. Maybe she could kill two birds with one stone.

Chapter Seven

Shannon decided to leave the café a bit early. Ever since the visit by Tom the previous day she had felt bad and hadn't been able to concentrate on work. It was the last place she felt like being. And Rafael hadn't come in that day, which would have brightened her up.

Like most days, Nick had finally turned up around ten; his man-bun looked ridiculous, and so did his two-day growth, and he was possibly sporting a new tattoo. But she didn't want to know about it and just asked him to finish off and lock up. He'd been goading her lately about making the café more hipster, bringing in a groovier clientele. She could see his point even if she still felt plates rather than bread boards were fine to serve food on, but if he really wanted to make changes he needed to get to work a bit earlier.

He nodded. "Don't worry, trust me. Just go."

She looked at him as if she really didn't trust him but went anyway.

She liked doing this walk in the late afternoon, passing the renovations along the way in trendy Glamarama. Colin and Rafael and the other labourers had gone home by then. They'd spent the day pulling down old houses and blocks of flats and putting up new concrete ones to replace them. Charmless, but that's what people seemed to want. Every day there was a new real estate sign out the front with a gleaming portrait of a real estate man or woman, teeth white, suit formal and black, like an undertaker.

"As if a picture of somebody slimey like you would make me want to buy this place," she'd speak to them as she walked past, even though some were her customers. But now the ocean walk was choked with joggers and loud walkers, who she tried to ignore as they took over the whole path. "Doesn't anybody know how to stick to the left anymore?" she muttered.

The wind was picking up and a woman walked past, dragged by

her dog on its lead. It was unclear who was taking whom for a walk. Both also didn't seem inclined to move out of the way.

She climbed over the metal fence the silly council had erected to stop even sillier walkers or joggers falling off the cliff. As if they would, although an occasional fisherman did get swept into the water by huge waves and sometimes she saw tourists taking photos a bit too close to the edge.

Shannon looked out ahead, the sea seemed to stretch for ever. That's New Zealand over there, she'd tell Maxie, where they do the Haka. A tanker was sitting on the horizon, waiting for the call to come into port. Further down the coast was the cliff-top cemetery. People come and go, come and go but this rock had been here for thousands of years. The Aboriginal people might have had a special name for it but to Shannon this was "her" whale rock. Flat with ripples that ran through it like waves, it had a huge engraving of a whale with a calf inside her. She only noticed it one day by chance. It faced directly east to the wide expanse of ocean and Shannon wondered if this had been a Koori spectators' site for whale-watching. She must ask Colin about that one day.

The whales had their own special routes all over the world. But here their cycle was to leave the freezing waters and feeding areas of Antarctica in the winter for warmer Queensland seas. And then they would turn around and steam south in spring, around October. An unending cycle of migration which, depending how you looked at it, also began with the birth of calves in the lagoons of the Great Barrier Reef or near Fraser Island.

"They head north in winter and home again for Christmas," Shannon would tell Maxie when he walked to the rock with her.

"I like whales," he'd said. "They like swimming, just like me."

But when Shannon was young she had never spotted whales; they were much further out at sea. Two hundred years of whaling had almost wiped them out. Now the Eastern Australian humpbacks and other breeds were recovering from years of slaughter. Some cheeky ones even crept into Sydney Harbour and frolicked under the bridge and near the Opera House. Or knocked Bondi surfers off their surfboards with their tails.

"Catching a show," Shannon would joke to Maxie.

"Naughty whales," he'd giggle. "I have a joke. Where do whales come from?"

"I don't know," Shannon would shake her head.

"New South Wales of course, silly."

A few years ago spotting a whale was an exciting event that drew crowds but now it was almost passé. Still Shannon always hoped she'd see the giant mammals from her rock, on her daily pilgrimage. Well at least at the right time of year when she was there. She'd read somewhere that the whales had their own songs that they sang.

"A new top of the pops whale song every year," she'd say to Maxie. "Can you hear their songs coming across the ocean to us?" Or was it just the crash of the waves on the rocks below?

Spray hit Shannon directly on the face and her feet squelched the mossy grass that had grown next to the rock. A seagull flew so close she felt as if its wings were brushing her cheeks. She sat down on the edge of the rock, trying not to harm the engraving in any way and spoke to the whale as if it was alive and could hear everything she said. "How's your pregnancy going? Is the baby whale doing OK?" she asked. "Hope yours survives. I hope you'll be fine."

She remembered the counselling session she was forced to go to. Actually, she didn't really have to go but Amany had persuaded her that it would do her good. Talk with other people who had gone through the same thing as her. Communally feel the pain. God, she hated it. She arrived late and there was already about eight couples sitting on chairs placed in a circle. It was in a hospital meeting room, cold and khaki green with no atmosphere.

Amany, wearing her usual brightly-coloured headscarf, jumped up and found her a chair. The others moved their chairs a tiny bit to make space but not enough and Shannon had to edge into the circle. One of the women was speaking. She looked brown; everything about her was brown, her skirt, her stockings, her sensible shoes, her cardigan. "I was 41 weeks and finally they decide to induce. But it was too late. They couldn't find a heartbeat." She was sniffing and her husband, an equally drab man, handed her a hanky.

"How sweet, so supportive," Shannon was thinking, looking at the landscape paintings on the wall that she hoped, like a scene from *Mary Poppins*, would open up and allow her in.

But then Amany turned the attention on her. She smiled at her, without actually introducing her to the group: "And Shannon, what is your story?"

"I didn't want to come," Shannon mumbled. "I'm missing *Housewives of New Jersey*."

Nobody laughed, they just looked at her oddly. They probably wondered what planet she was on. But Amany was used to her sense of humour. "I think it will help you to talk. Shannon, you lost your baby at twenty-two weeks, right?"

"Yes. And?"

The sniffing woman turned to Shannon: "You need time to grieve, to cry."

"I've cried enough," she was indignant, scraping her chair back. "I need to move on. I want to have another baby. I want medical answers, not grief counselling."

"The doctors say you should wait at least six months after losing a baby," one of the men said, another less-than-handsome type, who had lost most of his hair and succumbed to shaving the rest of it off. He seemed one of those know-all husbands who she guessed had read every pregnancy manual available. Shannon imagined him talking about "our" pregnancy before whatever dastardly thing that happened to them happened.

"It's been more than that already. My husband's not interested."

"Oh and he couldn't come tonight?" the annoying husband asked.

"No way."

"Mm, what a pity," he looked directly at her. "Partners need to support each other. Men feel grief too, they just don't know how to express it.'

"He's not my partner, he's my husband." She was so sick of this talk. "And he's quite capable of expressing himself."

Amany interrupted, asking another woman for her story. When they stopped for a break to have a cup of teabag tea or instant coffee and tasteless biscuits Shannon pretended she was going to the bathroom and escaped. She poured herself a huge glass of wine when she got home. Never again.

She didn't want to think of these depressing stories. She needed a bit of fun. She thought of the mysterious Rafael. Boy, he certainly was sexy. She wondered how long he'd been in Australia. What was his story? Was he married? Children? The man of so few words. She wished he hadn't heard the argument between her and Tom. She didn't want him to know that side of her. Well, not yet. But to say he would help her get Maxie back – that was unexpected – and even though it was a bit weird when he hardly knew her, she was grateful. Nobody else was helping her. Well, except for dear, old Colin.

Her other friends seemed to have disappeared since the stillbirth, and her sister was living in Western Australia so she really couldn't do much. Mum and dad were gone. Oh no, she was beginning to cry again. She breathed in strongly and let the air gush out towards the ocean. Think of something good, think of something hopeful. Think of a man with a pony tail that actually suited him. She laughed quietly to herself. It had been ages since she'd had sex, but she wouldn't knock Rafael back. He could put his workman's boots under her bed. She wondered how well Colin knew him, she must ask him about his workmate. Just as her thoughts went to Colin she felt somebody watching her and turned to see him coming around the bend from Bondi.

Colin tried to do the Bondi-Tamarama walk most days when the weather wasn't too fierce. Feeling the wind and the salt on his skin made him come alive. As he rounded the path he was pleased to spot Shannon, her hair caught under a red cap. "A lovely woman," he thought. "Good-looking. Come on, Colin, you're miles too old for her. Anyway she's got problems with a capital P."

He sniffed under his arm, wishing he'd used deodorant that morning, not just talcum powder. At least he was relatively fit, these walks helped him keep his creaky bones moving. He didn't want to end up in an old people's home, being fed soup through a straw. And there was no way in the world he ever wanted to spend time in an institution again. He thought of that time inside. Lined up for the bathroom, his towel over his shoulder, his soap in his hand. Hard, yellow soap, rough white towel. The daily morning trek to the wash-house. No fear never again. Nobody was interested in him and there was no standovers or violence. Nobody ever asked what you were in for, that was against prison etiquette, but they knew about him. They knew it was better not to wrestle with his Sunshine soap.

He smiled when he realised Shannon was sitting next to his whale rock. "That's my rock."

"Oh really," she spun round to see him. "I thought it was mine."

He raised his eyes at her.

"I was hoping you could explain its story."

"I'm trying to find out more," he said. "It's part of a songline, I can tell you that much. Are you open tomorrow?"

"Anzac Day, no I'm thinking of just opening in the afternoon," she said. "Are you going to the dawn service or Redfern for a march?"

"Huh, Redfern! I only go there for funerals."

She motioned him to come and sit beside her and he pulled his body over the fence and sat down next to her. "Too early in the year for whale spotting isn't it?"

"Hope this whale managed to keep her baby."

"You'll have another one, Shannon." He felt so sorry for her and what she had gone through. Losing the baby seemed so unnatural, but as he'd told her before not that unusual. Modern medicine couldn't account for everything. It was hard to convince her though.

"You're not another one of those bloody grief counsellors are you?" she said.

"No, more like a Koori Buddhist."

Colin had been at the café the day she started having stomach cramps. He'd popped in for his usual coffee and noticed how pale she'd looked. She'd been so healthy through this pregnancy and really looking forward to the baby. He remembered trying to get her to sit down as she doubled up in pain but then she'd gone to the bathroom for a very long time. She'd emerged, looking even paler.

"I think I better get to the hospital, Colin," she'd said. "Something's not right. Can you call Tom for me."

Colin had copied the number from Shannon's phone but Tom hadn't answered. Must have been in court or something that day. He'd left a message telling him he'd called an ambulance for Shannon. While they'd waited Shannon sat bent over, groaning. Colin had been really worried about her. He'd put his arm around her, trying to comfort her. "It'll be fine, you'll be OK," he'd whispered, brushing her long hair out of her eyes. Her forehead was sticky with perspiration; she was burning up with a fever. He'd been relieved when the ambulance turned up and the male and female paramedics put her on a stretcher. The woman shook her head at him, as if to say, "Not this time, mate."

"Where are you taking her?" he asked.

"Prince George," he said. "Are you her husband?"

"No, no. I've let him know. He's at work."

He'd hung around for a while at the café after closing it, leaving more messages for Tom, who never called him back, but he assumed had gone straight to the hospital. It was a sorry business, it really was.

Shannon looked out to sea again, as if she was hoping to see a pregnant whale on the horizon. "Yeah a bit early for whales." She took off her scarf as the sun came out.

Colin wanted to put his arms around Shannon but he stopped himself. She was so vulnerable, he didn't want to make it worse. He hoped she'd eventually get over it, she'd have another baby. He tried, in his own way, to cheer her up. "I guess it's like when your favourite footy team loses the grand final by one point."

"Yeah, I guess so."

"I remember my mum saying she lost her first baby, but I'm not sure of the whole story. Anyway, she had us, then Johnny was taken and my sisters and me. And then she must have suffered so much after what happened to Johnny."

"Who?" Shannon looked sympathetic.

"My older brother." Making himself more comfortable on the rock, he dragged out his wallet and from it a crumpled black and white photo, which he handed to Shannon. It was of a much younger Colin, maybe five years old. He was holding hands with a taller boy; he looked about ten years older. Their skinny legs poked out of oversized khaki shorts and shirts, some kind of school uniform. "Me when I was a kid. That's Johnny."

"He looks sad."

"Missing his mum. He died from a burst appendix, not long after this photo was taken. Bastards at Kinchela, that's the boys' home where we were, they wouldn't take him to hospital in time." He thought of the day of the funeral, forced to scrub up with soap and wear their best, patched clothes. The Kinchela boys lined up to go to the cemetery – shadows being pulled along a hill. The white kids in their ironed school uniforms calling out from across the road, jeering at the 'boongs'. The home boys putting their heads down, they didn't know where to look. They didn't even know what the words meant but they felt the cruelty, the derision. They knew what it was to be orphanage kids. And they weren't even orphans. Poor Johnny. He just wanted his mum. And she wanted her kids.

Colin thought again of his prison cell, his iron bed, his filthy single mattress – black and white striped and stained yellow. He deserved to be in there. He did something he shouldn't have done. But God damn it, his victim deserved it too. No woman should have to put up with that. But Johnny, he didn't deserve to die in a hospital bed with the sides up and the blankets down. In a room stinking of stale urine and bleach. He didn't deserve to die calling out for his mother, calling to be taken home. Disinfectant and dashed dreams. Nope. He didn't deserve that, no, not at all.

He'd lie on that mattress and think about digging a tunnel like that bloke in *Shawshank Redemption*, cover it with a poster of Madonna or Cher and wiggle his way out to freedom. Drive down the highway with the wind in what's left of his hair to Mexico – or even Tassie.

But no, it wasn't Hollywood. No tinsel town aery-fairy happy endings here. Just did his time. Graduation Day: Long Bay Jail. Head down, nose clean. Read, read, read. Hang out with his Koori brothers. Play cards, win tokens. One day, he had wondered, will I be able to collect my dues?

"Don't forget, I'm the ace when it comes to poker," he spoke out loud.

"What did you say?" Shannon asked.

"Nothing." He mumbled.

"But why didn't they take Johnny to hospital?"

"Because they didn't care. They wouldn't even let mum visit. He screamed in agony but they still wouldn't take him to the hospital. By the time they got him there it was pretty well too late. And you know he was about due to leave the home and go into the big, wide world. How could you treat a boy like that?"

She shook her head then looked closely at the photo. "Where was Kinchela?"

"Up the coast, about six hours' drive from here. Horrible place." He brought out another photo from his wallet, folded in half with a crease down its middle. It was one of those photos that you often find in albums of the 1940s – a snapshot of a man and woman, sometimes with children, walking down the main street. They're wearing their best clothes, gloves and hat and possibly carrying a parcel or two. They've been in town shopping and some anonymous photographer has snapped them and then flogged them the photo.

This one was of a soldier, complete with slouch hat and a cigarette in his mouth holding the hand of a little boy, wearing shorts, long-sleeved white shirt and a tie and a cap and next to him a slim, pretty Aboriginal woman clutching a purse and wearing a cotton dress and straw hat with a flower.

Colin turned it over, being careful to not let the wind blow it away. On the back in black fountain pen somebody had written: "Father and mother and son Jim Barnett, 1945."

"This is our little family, before I was born. My dad was in the army. That's Johnny. Must have been around three. He got taken when he was like seven I think. You know I found out later that dad came to the home, wearing his soldier's uniform mind you, to take him home, but they wouldn't let him, even him being a returned serviceman and all. That is what Anzac Day means to me.

"Mum must have given me both these photos when they took me away, poor thing. I just know I always had them. Mum wrote so many letters, well that's what Johnny told me. She begged the Board to send us and my sisters back home. They were in Cootamundra, the girls' home. She used to tell them that it was time we came home now. But she'd get letters back saying we had to stay at least until we were fourteen. They said she neglected us. I don't believe that – look how well and clean Johnny is in this photo."

Shannon reached for the photo and looked at it carefully. "Yeah, you're right. She's lovely. She looks very young."

"Yeah she had Johnny pretty early I think."

Shannon frowned as she stared at the photo. "She looks familiar. What was her name?"

"Lily. And hey we all look alike don't we?"

Shannon hit Colin on the arm. "You know I'm not like that, Colin."

Colin pulled his collar up. The temperature had dropped and the wind was blowing but he didn't want to leave this spot. "I don't know that much about her, except I think she met dad when she was working on a farm down south. But you know I think she was from round these parts. Maybe she was Cadigalleon of the Cadigal people. She'd been taken from her mum too. I think she might have first been sent to Bomaderry Children's Home and then to the girls' home at Cootamundra."

"Bomaderry? That's near our farm down the coast, well my parents' farm. You know the valley, where I often go? I didn't know there was a children's home there. How could they be so cruel to small children? And I can't even keep a baby inside myself."

"Sorry I was trying to take your mind off that. Bloody hopeless, I am."

She smiled. "It's OK, it's not your fault."

"Be kind to yourself, Shannon. You don't get over that sort of thing that quickly."

"But I'm sick of thinking about it. I keep adding up the dates and the weeks. A pregnancy is nine months, mine was five. Life's not worth living. It's only for Maxie."

"It is worth living. Your biological clock isn't ticking that fast. You have time to have another baby. You're still young and gorgeous."

"I named her Emma," Shannon seemed to ignore the compliment.

"You know it's taboo in some tribes to mention the names of the dead. They're known as Kumanjayi."

"My little Kumanjayi."

Colin looked at Shannon, wishing he could make her happy. She handed him back the photos and he felt the brush of her hand. He wanted to grab it and hold it tight, even kiss it, but he stopped himself. He tried again to change the topic from dead mothers and dead babies.

"This whole area south of the harbour was Cadi and that beach over there is Cramaramma," he said.

"Cramaramma I always call it Glamorama with the people that go to the beach here!" Shannon smiled and looked out at the sea, where silver gulls were sitting on the waves, as if they were laying eggs.

"Yes, true. And did you know Sydney was once known as the golden city because so many buildings were constructed from its sandstone, what we are now sitting on?"

"No, I didn't. You know so much, Colin."

"And I love talking to you, my dear," Colin said. "It's like being plugged back into my charger."

They both laughed when Shannon's mobile phone rang. She hesitantly picked it up, her voice getting louder and more agitated. "OK, OK, I'm coming now."

Colin guessed it was Nick. Hopeless lout. More beard than brains, that one.

"Nick says Tom came in looking for me – probably just checking up on me – and started yelling at him. And now he can't get the milk to froth and customers are complaining. I better go."

"What's that got to do with Tom?"

"He gave me the money to start the café and so he thinks he can order me around. He's got Maxie, can't he just leave me alone?"

They stood up together.

"I'd kill for a coffee." Colin didn't want to end his time with Shannon.

"OK, I'll make you one but you have to tell me more about that cute Latino friend of yours."

"Ah, Rafael," he shrugged, as they climbed over the fence and headed back up the hill towards the café. "I don't know him that well really. Bit old for you, don't you think?"

Chapter Eight

The thought of Colin's mother nagged at Shannon. The photo rang a bell, that's for sure. He'd done so much for her, she'd really like to help him find his mum.

Anzac Day was sure to be quiet. She'd rather spend the time researching Lily than working at the café and she wasn't going to let Tom decide her work hours, especially with him not allowing her to have Maxie. On Saturday afternoon, she rang him right around the time they'd be singing happy birthday to his father – just to annoy him. It was unfair that she wasn't even invited to his party.

She'd always liked Aleksandar; he made her laugh. She felt sorry for him, stuck with Irina. At family events they would conspire together over their shots of *rakia*, the warmth of the brandy burning her throat and making her feel mellow. But now she was banned from seeing him too. "Stay away from the café, it's my business," Shannon told Tom over the phone.

"It won't be for much longer if I stop paying the loan. Get your act together, Shannon." He hung up on her.

She had to get away. She'd go to the valley for a couple of days. Hopefully she'd missed the trees protest. Why did she have to give all of herself to everybody all the time? She knew she just had to try and trust Nick to look after things so she could escape. He'd finally sorted out his milk frothing, at least. She just hoped she didn't return to a totally different deconstructed décor or menu.

The traffic had died down by the time she left and it was easy to get out of town. The Buena Vista Social Club made the journey easier. Ah salsa. She always felt a sense of freedom when she made it to the freeway south – nearly halfway to her little piece of paradise. But she couldn't stop thinking about Rafael, wondering about him. Who was he? What was his background? Where had he sprung from? She would love to salsa with him, he must be a good dancer. She could see him on the dance floor, sexy women with flowers in their hair lining up to take their turn with him.

As she turned off the highway, then drove down the hill and across the causeway an owl stared straight at her, before it took off from its branch and flew across the road in front of the car. It didn't startle her, she liked putting a face to the sounds of the hooting in the night. Sometimes she'd be woken from her dreams by the sound of flapping wings outside her window – must be flying foxes. Owls fly on silent wing beats, you can never hear them, and neither can their prey.

She swung the car in through the gate and across to the garage next to her parents' old timber farm house, turning the engine off and just sitting in the dark for a while. It was a relief to get here, away from all the drama of Sydney's eastern suburbs, and the never-ending coffee making.

Before she could go inside though she needed to walk, to see the sky and the moon and any animals out in the night – wombats perhaps or other creatures. She needed the cold night air to make her feel alive again, to move her thoughts away from her lonely body, to forget her troubles. The full moon shone a light across her path and she could hear rustling in the bushes and trees.

She spoke to the moon, that moment's manifestation of Mother Nature. Please, please bring Rafael even more into my life. Slightly mad, but aren't we all? Definitely has issues, but that made him more interesting. She loved the way he ordered his short black and made banter with her. At last, a man with a sense of humour.

"Thank you goddesses of the valley, Mother Nature, whale rock and all that is," she mouthed the words, staring at the moon, then moving slowly to the music in her mind, her feet beating out the rhythm of the Latin music she loved. "It's about time something good happened in my life. And I promise I'll give back what I take."

Returning to the car, she brought her bags inside the creaking house. She took a bottle of wine and her iPad to her favourite spot on the verandah and wrapped her cardigan around her; her addiction to genealogy and her curiosity about Colin's family was calling her. What happened to your mum, Colin? Where did she go?

She fired up her iPad and logged into an ancestry site where she had an account; she had been piecing together her own family history.

One day she would visit her long-lost relatives in Ireland. There were emails there from people who could be these rellies, some correcting her version of the family tree. Genealogy is an exact science, one told her. You must have an unbroken line of descent and unless you have an authentic, unbroken line, you can trace your ancestry to anyone you like. One missing link is all it takes. Just because they have the same name, that means nothing. It's amazing how many people on Facebook have the same name as you, even when you don't have a common ancestor. OK, she thought, but I have to start somewhere.

Shannon was envious of Tom's certainty about who he was and where he came in a long line of Serbian peasants. His grandfather had lived through five different regimes; they changed so much the only way he could remember which one was now in power was by the hats people were wearing. The family yarn went that he was running from the Turkish soldiers but stopped to pick up his fez. It wasn't until later that he realised he was risking his life to fetch the headwear of his oppressors.

Tom had worked his way up and his parents were so proud of him, their first child to gain a university degree. They couldn't understand why he'd married an Anglo girl, with no culture and very little knowledge about her background. Irina even had to show her how to make Turkish coffee, the stupid girl. "Don't let it bubble over, Shan-non. Don't let it burn. Don't make a mess on the stove. Keep an eye on it. Stir the sugar in early. Tom likes one spoonful. Be careful, Shan-non."

Well, she'd show them she too had culture. With a name like Shannon Foran, she couldn't deny her Irish heritage. She thought of her dad, with sadness. When she was little he used to say to her: "You could ride a surfboard on that nose with its Irish freckles." She'd giggle and climb up onto his knee, pulling his nose and ears. "You look like Santa Claus," she'd say to him. "You've got white hair like people in the North Pole."

She wanted Maxie to know about his Irish heritage too, not just his Serbian. She wanted to take him on a trip to Ireland, to see the green rolling hills, the quaint villages, the leprechauns. She'd tell him stories about the little people, not having a clue what she was talking about.

"Tell me the little people story, mummy. More, more, don't stop." She'd weave stories with all sorts of crazy children's TV references into them. It wasn't unusual for Bart Simpson to pop up in a story about leprechauns. Anything to get Maxie to go to sleep at night. He was a terrible sleeper and it was exhausting night after night coaxing him into Dreamland. She'd try to sneak out of the room but he'd catch her. "One more story, please mummy." He'd also call to her if she left out a verse from *Where Have All the Flowers Gone?* It was a song she'd often sing to him.

Ah, she didn't want to think about Maxie. It was killing her. This time she was more interested in somebody else's family history. She shifted in her chair and stretched her arms. Then a big gulp of wine. Maybe she could find a way to help Colin. He was a smart cookie but perhaps there were avenues he hadn't thought of such as ancestry sites. But first she needed to educate herself a bit. She typed in 'Cadigal'.

She read of the Cadigal people the British first encountered when they arrived in Sydney Harbour. But what happened to those people? She read of the smallpox epidemic in 1790 and how whole tribes were decimated, how bodies were floating in the water or found in caves along the harbour foreshore. She'd grown up with Kooris but she'd never really thought that much about the history, or the brutality they had faced. They were just country kids like she was.

How could she find out where Colin's mum had come from? He had said he was a member of the Stolen Generations – he had been taken from his mum when he was a kid. She knew a little about that but she Googled Stolen Generations to find out more. There were hundreds of entries. She tried to narrow it down to NSW, and opened one link, which talked about the homes the kids were taken to including Kinchela, Cootamundra and Bomaderry.

She started to think about the boys she went to school with. What had happened to those Koori boys? She'd heard that a gang recently ransacked a house in the valley. They were looking for guns. The police called them the Teflon Gang because they were so slippery. Were they in that gang or their kids? Or did they have responsible jobs in town now?

A face suddenly came into her mind – Ainslie, the woman her mother had once employed as a housekeeper. Short, cropped dark hair, smooth, swarthy skin. Pretty, slim. Was that the same face from Colin's photo? It was too late to ask her parents anything now – her dad died when he was in his sixties – a heart attack. He was quite a bit older than her mum. He told her once he got married late, it took him a long time to find the perfect woman. Shannon was only in her teens, and then her mum got cancer a few years later. She and her sister were left with the farm. Now she just let the neighbour agist cattle on it and kept it as her retreat.

Her parents were of the generations who didn't explain too much to their children. Where maids came from or farm help or what happened when the money ran out. They just got on with it, milking cows every morning and evening, feeding the chooks, growing a few veggies. Maintaining the mismatched house with all the rooms tacked on, verandahs closed off, fireplaces sealed with asbestos and electric heaters installed. But warm and cosy even when the wind blew up through the white ant-eaten floors. She loved this old house.

She tried to think back to when she was five years old – her bed covered with a floral eiderdown, her arms nursing her teddy and her feet touching the pale pink hot water bottle, Ainslie perched on the end, telling her those spooky ghost stories. Scary stories about the bogeymen who might get her if she didn't go to sleep. About the ghosts that lived in the gums.

Why would an adult tell such stories to a small child? Was it because she never wanted to go to sleep? She'd run all day across the paddocks, exploring along the creek and climbing up the weeping willows that hung over the muddy water. Barefoot and wild. Ainslie's stories were to warn her to be more careful, maybe. But Shannon didn't know that. She didn't know anything about Ainslie.

As she studied the internet, wisps of conversation came back to her – stories of being locked all night in the morgue at the home. Listening to the whoosh of ghosts outside the door.

"When I was your age I was punished for being naughty," Ainslie would tell her. "Just silly things like talking to the girls after lights out. Or poking my tongue out at the matron. They'd put me in the place where they kept dead people before when the home was a hospital. Leave me there all night. Shivering in a corner. Let me out in the morning."

"Weren't you scared?" Shannon asked.

"Baby, I was terrified."

Ainslie, Ainslie. What was your last name? Why did you leave us?

She tried combinations of Ainslie Barnett and Bomaderry but nothing turned up. Colin really just wanted to know more of his mum's background, who her parents were, what tribe she was from, what happened to her after her kids were taken away and her husband died. Somebody must know that down here. She'd try and ask old Joe, the former manager, who still lived in the valley. He might know something.

And then to bed. She finished her wine and turned off her iPad.

It was a clear, blue day when Shannon woke up. The old house creaked its smells of generations who had lived here, who'd added rooms and pulled down walls countless times to allow for more and less children. The babies who had been born here, the people who had died. They were all part of her in some way or other.

She put the kettle on and made herself a cup of tea, checking her phone for messages and emails. There was one she didn't want to read. From Tom: "You forgot to pack Max's project in his school bag. He needs to do it today. Typical."

So few words but enough to ruin her morning. "Fuck," she said out loud, then wondered if she had in fact forgotten it. "I'm sure I put it in," she thought, trying to go back to the week before when she'd taken Maxie back to his father. She and Maxie had sat at the kitchen table doing the project together, finding pictures of dinosaurs and sticking them on coloured pieces of cardboard. He'd tried to write the names of the different ones, misspelling them but at least getting the phonetics right. She was so proud of her intelligent son.

They'd rolled the cardboard up and stuck it in his backpack. Or had she? Had she left it on the table? She just couldn't remember. She was forgetting a lot of things lately, clothes that Maxie needed, food she was meant to buy for the café. She'd go into a room to get something and forget what she was looking for. Time and time again. What was wrong with her?

She wrote a text back to Tom: "Sorry but I'm sure I put it in the backpack." As she sent it, she was annoyed with herself. Always saying 'sorry' – when she wasn't even sure it was her fault. When did Tom ever say sorry? Never.

She took her tea out to the verandah sitting with her long, slim legs up on the rails. The smell of grass and manure swept over from the paddock on the other side of the fence. She sipped her sugary tea as a familiar feeling swept over her. Guilt. Always in the wrong. "Oh fuck you, Tom," she said so loudly one of the cows turned round and stared at her, a mournful look on her face as her calf tugged at her udders. "Fuck you!"

Why couldn't she do anything right? Why was she always stuffing up? This thing with Rafael wasn't going to go anywhere, she just knew it. It would just be more disappointment. Life was just one big bloody failure.

Oh to hell with it. Yes, mother cow, sunshine, blue sky and green escarpment, I do want to have sex with Rafael. I want to be held by him, to be wrapped in his arms, to be kissed and touched and loved and brought a cup of tea in the morning, like the one in my hand.

She wandered across the garden, past the neglected hydrangeas to the oak tree in the corner by the fence. She knelt down to pull out the long grass, trying to avoid the stinging nettles around a small plaque. To: Emma, the baby who would never become a woman. To her darling little girl. "Hello, Kumanjayi," she spoke to the ground where the ashes were buried, remembering Colin's words about not speaking the name of the dead. "I'm always thinking of you, you know. I'm so sorry for what happened. I wish you were here. It's all my fault. I should have looked after myself better. I should have looked after you, so much better. I'm so, so sorry."

Then she remembered who had taught her the flowers song. This time she sang the verse asking where all the graveyards had gone. She always missed out this one when she sang to Maxie – the words for her dead baby and Ainslie, her long ago housekeeper, who as a girl, used to be locked in the place of the dead.

Chapter Nine

The warmth in the air was unseasonal but clouds were building and Rafael thought there could be rain later. That was the last thing they needed. The pressure had been on to get the job finished, especially with the short week they were having for Anzac Day. Bloody public holidays – what was the point of them, especially ones that celebrated defeats at war?

The developers had under-quoted and were having cash-flow problems. The tradies and contractors were clamouring to get paid. This meant corners were getting cut, and Rafael had no desire to be affected by their shoddiness. He was a man of morals, he always tried to do the right thing. Well, that's what he was taught by the Frente. Not like the Mozzies and the Chinese and all the other slackos on the site. He was sick to death of them all. He was sick of labouring. He was sick of everything. Strange elements of nature were making him edgy. Ants everywhere, mosquitoes, and he'd noticed a wasp earlier and had tried to kill it until Wayne had warned him he'd get stung.

"You wouldn't want to be attacked by one of them buggers, mate. Hurts like hell. And they don't just stop once they sting you. They keep coming back."

"Maybe with any luck it would kill me."

"Ah come on mate, you're depressing me."

The wind started to pick up and a dark cloud passed across the sun. The sky went black. Dust blew everywhere.

"Storm coming," one of the workers said. "Might finish up early today."

"Sweet," the other retorted.

Must be his favourite word, Rafael thought as they laughed. *Dulce*. They loved any possibility of getting off work. They were all bored and lazy too.

"Penny for your thoughts," Colin seemed worried about his mate.

"Not in the mood today, Colin. Just not in the mood."

"Come on, only a couple more hours." Colin, always the efficient one, brought Rafael back to the present.

Rafael grabbed his shovel, pushed his large, filthy boot down on it and lifted a pile of dirt. He felt dirty all over, his face, his ears, his overalls, his boots, even his underwear. Another wasp flew near his face and in a pure moment of unadulterated cruelty he lunged at it.

"You're right, you are in a violent mood today, Raf," Colin said.

"Yeah, full moon," Rafael responded.

"What's that got to do with it? Have you got your period?"

Rafael normally would have laughed but not today, still waving the wasp away.

"They're European wasps, bloody nuisance," Colin said. "Only been here since the seventies. Been a plague of them this year apparently. Maybe cause it's been a mild summer. They'll be gone by winter."

"How do you know all this stuff, old man?"

"I just take an interest in feral animals that compete with us natives, I guess. Suppose I better get a pest exterminator in to spray but the company will say they can't pay. Anyway, Tony could do with a hand; company wants all the cement rendering done by next week." Colin pointed to Tony up on the scaffolding, which was swaying slightly in the wind. "And why wasn't that netting ever put up?"

"He reckons it's the scaffolding boys' responsibility, I don't know." Rafael dropped his shovel.

"Just make sure nobody goes within three metres of the live edge."

"Col, you know I've done my working-at-heights training."

"I know, Raf, that's why I'm asking you to help Tony."

Rafael climbed up inside to where Tony was leaning over the rail, applying cement. The wind was stronger now and grit was blowing into his eyes. He nodded at Tony; he could see he wasn't wearing a harness but he wasn't going to say anything to the bloody daredevil this time. He knew the rules. Realising his trowel was on the level below he climbed down, closing the hatch above him.

As he was bending down, he heard a yowl and looked up to see Tony madly flailing as a swarm of wasps seethed around his face.

Bloody hell, he must have disturbed the nest. He was leaning so far over he was losing his grip on the rail.

"Hold on, I'm coming," Rafael yelled as Tony waved frantically – the wasps were everywhere. Must have been an army of them. Rafael tried to get the hatch open but it was stuck; he was calling hysterically: "Wait, wait." Then he saw the body fall. Could have been four metres down. He wasn't sure if the crash he heard was the body's impact or thunder but almost immediately lightning scraped across the sky.

Nicaragua
March, 1978

Inside the helicopter is dark and khaki. Everything green and khaki. I'm terrified. It's almost my turn. The people before me are screaming: "No, no, no." Catholic revolutionaries, crossing themselves.

The helicopter is flying low over the top of a volcano. You can see straight down into the gases and fumes, the bubbling mud. Clouds of grey gas. I think I can see the bodies of other people, hurled out into that poisonous air, their arms outstretched, for forgiveness, for hope of life after death. Will any of those thousands of Hail Marys whispered over a lifetime in church or in confessionals help now?

"Fuck! Oh fuck, Tony!" Rafael screamed madly, scrambling back down to the ground where his workmate's body lay, stretched out in a weird, contorted shape.

Colin arrived at the twisted body at the same time. "Jesus!"

"Get some help," Rafael yelled, frantic, scared, going down on his knees, taking Tony's hand in his own.

Colin pulled out his phone and called triple zero. The rain was coming down in big droplets and the dust was turning to mud. "One of our men. Looks like he's broken every bone in his body," Colin was speaking to the operator. "Hurry, please hurry."

"Hang in there, mate." Rafael kept talking, as if in a dream. Now it was just him and Tony. The rest of the world had been locked out. The words were garbled, nonsensical but anything to keep Tony alive. "Fight it, mate. You'll be right. My country – my poor, poor country," he mumbled.

Tony's hand was going cold. Where was the ambulance? Where were the other workers? The Iranians had probably taken off, they didn't want to be around if anybody official turned up. But Wayne and the others, where were they? Rafael felt fear knifing his body. Why wasn't anybody here to help? Tony might die and there was nobody around to hear his last confession.

"Tony, mate, are you with me? Wheelchair, we'll find a wheelchair."

A groan emerged, "Help me."

"*Tranquilo, hombre.*"

Tony's eyelids fluttered and he opened his eyes and stared into Rafael's with no recognition.

"The land mine, it blew your skinny legs off. They're bringing a wheelchair, the only one left."

Tony groaned again: "My wife."

As the rain came sheeting down, Rafael squeezed Tony's hand and broke the labourer's taboo. He kissed it and held it close to his cheek – the rough hand of a labourer, dirty, split nails, a thick, gold wedding ring.

The other workers had run to get the ambulance men. They pointed to where Tony lay, with the strange Latino holding his hand and muttering at him like a priest. The two burly paramedics dragged Rafael away so they could get to Tony, put him on a stretcher and lift him into the ambulance.

Colin called the union and then went to the side of Rafael, who wept into his chest, like a woman whose husband has left her.

Shannon saw the ambulance arrive across the road from the café. Her first panicky thought was Rafael. Had he been in an accident? Or Colin? She was too scared to go herself but commanded Nick go across to find out what had happened. Customers rushed outside then Nick returned with the news that a labourer had been taken away on a stretcher.

"Did you see who it was?"

"They reckon one of the Maori boys," he answered. "Could be a heart attack."

Shannon felt guilty to be relieved it wasn't Rafael or Colin. But she also felt an unnameable haunting – a premonition that everything was going to turn topsy-turvy from now on.

Chapter Ten

Things were looking bad. There'd been more retrenchments at all the news organisations and the numbers still weren't adding up. Nobody knew what to do. They understood newspapers were dying but had no idea how to get the readership back. Meanwhile, Vesna and her colleagues still had to cope with much less staff, the extra work piled on them, being told to cut everything back to as few words as possible so the masses could cope when reading stories on the internet. Nothing too serious and hundreds of breakouts and boxes to make it easier to read. Short and sharp. That's what people wanted, they were told daily. Nothing over three hundred words. No depth. No colour. No humour.

God, what else can I do? Vesna thought. What other options are there for a burnt-out former foreign correspondent? Washing dishes, minding children, prostitution? She laughed to herself as she clicked on a story to sub. When she read the lead she groaned loudly. "Kourtney Kardashian's agony: posts sad tweet about lover." What are we now, Hollywood Life? Prostitution as a work option was looking pretty good.

Now what I need is a good pimp. She grinned. With his job, Tom would have to know a few.

"What's the joke?" A bright young thing – a new sub – sitting at the desk next to her smiled widely. She wore a garish hair band and lots of cheap jewellery and Vesna had taken an instant dislike to her, nicknaming her Pollyanna. Anybody that cheerful all the time must have something wrong with her.

"Oh, just laughing at the awfulness of this story, never mind."

"I'll do that one if you want," Pollyanna offered. "I've done all my work on Digital already. It's such an easy job."

"Don't worry I can cope."

"Do you want to have a look at my blog? I'll email you the link."

Pollyanna looked eager.

Vesna tried not to groan out loud. She'd better put her head down or somebody might swap her with Pollyanna and she'd be stuck on Digital, fixing up misspelt headlines and literals. At least she knew what she was doing on the news subbing desk. And she could be creative with the abstracts which led readers into the story, if not with headlines which weren't witty anymore, and didn't use puns. They just wanted click bait.

Her Muslim story involving the interview with Amany was finished and she'd given it to her friend, Sarah, on the features' desk, who had put it out that morning. But she knew in order for it to get a better run it needed to go out on the news wire. How was she going to do that without anybody noticing? Features were meant to go on Features, as those clients paid a different premium price compared to the news' clients. But all they ever wanted was entertainment fluff and celebrity crap. Most of it was unsourced gossip or if they did use sources they were incredibly dodgy. She knew her story would have more of a future if it went out to newspapers and online sites.

Sarah had said she'd drop it into the news basket when nobody was looking and hopefully they'd put it out. In a place like this you needed friends and Sarah was a good friend. She'd sent Vesna an email, saying she was putting it there now and to cross her fingers nobody said anything. There'd been a habit of late of editors spiking or deleting stories without asking anybody about them, anything that looked the slightest bit highbrow. Only the other day Sarah's book reviews had disappeared after she'd put hours of work into them.

Vesna was nervous when she saw a red dot on her story, and realised Gary, who was acting as production editor today, was reading 'Muslim', having noticed it in the queue and wondering what it was doing there. Oh bugger, she thought.

Without asking Vesna, despite her byline being on it, he turned to the deputy editor, Liz, yelling across the desk, "That feature, Muslim, what's that doing here?"

Liz shook her head. She was more interested in keeping an eye on the Prime Minister's Twitter account than worrying about a lone feature. "I don't know, Gary. I don't know about every story that goes through here."

"Well I see no news value in it whatsoever. It's a busy afternoon and I think it should be spiked."

Vesna wanted to throttle him, but she kept her head down while Liz had a read of it. "Oh it's OK, Gary, just put it out."

Thank God for her, she was an old toughie but a no-bullshit person and Vesna liked her.

"More crap," Gary said as he hit the transmit key. "What are you up to now, Vesna? Going to do any real work or are you writing another towel-head story?"

"Immigration is one of the major political issues of the day, shouldn't we cover it?" She felt braver now that the story had gone out.

"Yeah, but you're not in Canberra, Vesna. You're on the subs' desk. So sub OK?"

"You'll be sorry when I win a Walkley Award for my in-depth piece on illegal immigration." She felt like sticking her tongue out at him.

"Huh! Didn't your union membership run out years ago?"

"Yeah well they're a corrupt mob too. But I'll re-join just to be able to compete."

They both chuckled. Gary wasn't so bad really, old school and old fashioned, but most of the time he had good news sense. He pretended to be a racist, but he wasn't really. He just didn't like his file being cluttered with features and do-gooder stories, as he called them. He was a list person. He kept immaculate ones containing every story that ever went out, so that if there was a blue they could check. He also kept a computer basket containing the names of all the people that had ever gone through the place, including people he thought were a total waste of time, and others he had five minutes for. Keeping lists is meant to be anti-depressive behaviour but Vesna wasn't really sure what the psychology was behind Gary doing it so thoroughly. Maybe giving him a reason to be there.

Why he kept working, nobody knew. Surely he had enough money. Couldn't he just go and play tennis? He must enjoy the company, Vesna thought, shaking her head. She could think of better things to do with her time than hang out here.

Liz's voice woke her from her daydreaming. "There's an update here on the death on that building site at Tama, Vesna. Can you turn that around?"

Vesna knew that for all the bullshit Liz knew she could sub a story, put a decent headline on it and an abstract that people would click on in the time inexperienced subs would have only read the lead. She'd also make sure the facts were as correct as she could and turn clunky prose into something readable.

The story stated that the 35-year-old labourer had died of a suspected heart attack.

"I don't think so," she thought, calling the reporter and asking her to check. "Who mentioned the heart attack?" She waited for an answer. "Well, you need to quote the company spokesman saying that then, not just report it like gospel truth." She wasn't as nice to the reporters as Grahame had been.

Gary left her alone while she worked on the story. "Better put bells on that one too, there's been so many deaths lately, what with the royal commission into the building union and all," he said when she finished her edit.

Vesna did what she was told then hit transmit. She really wanted to concentrate now on the wider immigration story. She was hoping if this Muslim story went well Amany might help her with some more contacts; she must know illegals by the sound of the phone call she heard in her office. And even if Tom only ended up being a one-night stand he might at least be able to give her some more names and details. She reckoned it was a beauty, how people managed to stay underground with everything you would ever need, and no visas, residencies or anything else. Drivers' licences, Medicare cards, tax file numbers, ABNs, but no legit working visas.

She had Tom's number – she just needed to get up the courage to call him. A drink after work was definitely the way to go. But she didn't want to piss him off by coming on too strong.

She subbed a few more stories then checked to see if her Muslim story was live yet. Yes! It was up on Yahoo Nine already with Sarah's apt headline: "Lifting the veil off an unknown world."

Great. Now she had an excuse to call Tom, to say thanks for giving her Amany's number. Pretending to go to the bathroom, she took her mobile into a stall and rang his phone but his voice mail came on. "Ah Tom, this is Vesna, you know the journo you met the other night in the bar," she started to leave a message. "Well, I just wanted to say thanks for your help. Amany was great. The story's gone out. I was thinking, maybe we could have a ..." But the phone beeped; she'd used up all the space.

Chapter Eleven

You'd never seen so many suits on a building site, Shannon thought, recalling the lawyers, their take-away coffees in their hands. They'd swarmed all over the site like wasps, come to see what evidence they could dig up in order to blame the other party. The police had arrived soon after the ambulance and had taped off the site where the body landed. WorkCover had been called in to investigate but they had no desire to see the body or have anything to do with that. The company had marched all the workers off the job and tried to stop any information being leaked to the press. It was they who had put out a press release saying the worker had died of a suspected heart attack, Colin told her.

He'd also said the lawyers tried to tell the union rep he had no right to be there, but he argued, as foreman, he had every right in the world. The president of the construction arm of the union had gone to see Tony's wife to give his condolences and arrangements were being made for his Cbus to be paid out to his family, who were organising the funeral. All this in twenty-four hours.

The weather had taken a cold turn, and a gale was blowing rain straight across the sea, and up the headland, soaking the outdoor benches at the café. Rafael and Colin were sitting at a table inside. They were wearing their overalls, despite not going to the site. They looked despondent, staring into space and Shannon was worried about them.

"There's a community response throughout our industry that when we lose someone, we stop work the next day, we acknowledge their loss, we raise funds if the family circumstances require it," Colin spoke as if in a dream. "We do safety inspections of our jobs to focus the awareness on preventing any further death and then we go back to work."

"Is that right?" Shannon didn't look impressed. "So that's why you're not at work today?"

"Well, that's what the boss told us."

The heavy rain had kept the customers away; better to stay inside on a day like this. Since Saturday morning rush there had only been one bedraggled mum, obviously desperate for her caffeine hit, with an equally bedraggled baby hiding in its pram beneath a plastic cover. Shannon had told Nick he could have an early mark for a change.

Now the café was empty except for an older woman sitting at a table on her own, devouring a novel and a piece of banana bread lathered in butter. She might have been reading a bestseller – the latest female erotica – but she showed no interest in her two fellow customers, despite them being single men.

"I've been in accidents like this before, *hombre*," Rafael, too, was dream-like. "During the war. High up in the mountains, where there was nobody. Just land mines that caught little children out if they played too far from their village or farmhouse. Would blow their tiny legs off. They'd have to do some kind of rough surgery with no anaesthetic."

"What are you talking about, Rafael? What's Tony's death got to do with land mines for God's sake?" Shannon tried to bring him back to earth. "Why did the company say it was a heart attack?"

Colin shook his head. "They just said that to cover themselves. They know he died from the fall."

"Falling ... yeah, kids had to crawl along the ground on little platforms with wheels underneath," Rafael ignored them. "Like the skateboards you see boys riding here. But they weren't toys. They were the only means of transport. What kind of life was that for children? *Patria libre o morir*. Problem was many got *la muerte*, usually not their first choice."

"It's OK, my boy." Like Shannon, Colin seemed to have no idea what his friend was talking about.

"I did nothing, if only I could have helped him more. The wasps, I should have told him about the wasps. I shouldn't have shut the hatch."

"You did what you could," Colin said. "You didn't leave him. You held his hand the whole time. If anybody's to blame it's me. I should have got the pest exterminators in. And that netting should have been up. I just don't understand that. The scaffolding had been certified. There weren't any parts missing. Everything else was right."

Rafael looked at his own hands. "He'd lost a finger. Right at the knuckle. But he had a ring, a gold one. Where's his wife, his kids? Did he have kids?"

"Two. Girls," Colin nodded.

"Girls? Those poor *niñas*." Rafael stared out the door across to the building site to a bridge in another place.

Northern mountains
Nicaragua
March, 1986

Two little girls are holding hands and looking down towards a ravine near their village. Their faces show no emotion, no sadness, no nothing. *Nada.*

I ask them, "What are you doing here?"

They have just come to look at the river, they say. It's moving faster after the storm.

And then again, "Do your parents know where you are?"

"The Contras dragged mama and papa out of our house. They did bad things to them," the younger sister answers.

"We found their bodies out on the rubbish tip, outside the village," the older sister fills in the details.

The reason? Because they were teachers and they were showing the *campesinos* how to read and write. Some of them were even starting to write poetry.

Those girls have nothing to live for. *Nada.* Only sorrow.

Colin jolted Rafael. "I guess there'll be an inquest into Tony's death."

Rafael's eyes lit up with fear. "You're not getting me in court."

"I told you it's not your fault. I should have checked that scaffolding. Pressure, too much pressure. Those bastards and their mad rush."

"But it was my fault. I should have got up there to save him." Rafael jumped up from the table and ran to the bathroom as Shannon was coming out with the coffees.

"Hey slow down." She tried not to spill the coffee. "Your usual, Colin. And the crazy one's short black."

Rafael came back and sat down as if nothing had happened, still talking. "Where I come from, after they had the earthquake, the only buildings that still stood were the ones built five hundred years ago." He put a spoonful of sugar in his coffee as he took up the conversation where it had been left off. "All the modern buildings, they just fell down. Bricks and concrete. The murderers who run the construction companies, they bribed the city officials."

"We're getting more and more Third World here, brother," Colin nodded. "Shoddy apartment buildings, freeways, cruelty to greyhounds. The almighty dollar while people live in slums."

"Then after the earthquake there were still people stuck under the rubble," Rafael continued. "At one factory the women dressmakers had always to be locked in when they went to the bathroom. So many could not get out. You know what the owner of the factory did? *Hijo de puta.* He crawled in, took his sewing machines and equipment and crawled out again, straight past the women moaning and begging for help."

"They'd do it here too," Colin stirred his coffee and sucked on the spoon.

"It should have been me," Rafael said. "I don't have a wife or kids."

Shannon broke in. "C'mon, cut the guilt trip. He was my customer too. We all feel sad."

"Well, it's a nice change for a Blackfella to feel guilty," Colin attempted to joke.

"Accidents happen on building sites. What could you have done?"

"Yes certainly, my dear, accidents do happen. But there was no risk assessment done by the company. They were in too much of a rush."

"Well then it's the company's fault."

"I was the foreman though, I had responsibilities. I should have seen that nest. And I should have made him wear a harness. Should have checked the live edges. It's not sufficient to say we have a policy that says there's a need to secure yourself at a height. Tony thought there was no risk whereas a more experienced worker would have seen it."

Rafael shivered. "I think he broke every bone in his body."

"What did the company say?" Shannon asked.

"They said it was a foolhardy escapade by the employee."

"That sounds like one of those lawyers talking."

The lone woman customer looked as if she'd had enough of the maudlin conversation, deciding to take her mummy porn elsewhere. As she paid she suggested that perhaps Shannon should, "shut up shop".

Shannon thought that was a good idea; she wanted to show her respect to Tony, although her only contact with him had been to make him an occasional takeaway. She put the "closed" sign up; she'd lose half a day's takings but who cared? It had been a slow week for business with her escape to the country anyway; she didn't make as much money when Nick was in charge. She needed to count her takings too; she knew Tom would be on her back.

The men didn't notice and continued to be sucked down into their melancholia as Shannon tidied up, putting cups in the dishwasher.

"Have you ever felt like you were dying? Or wanted to die?" Rafael asked Colin.

"I've felt like I didn't want to keep being alive," Colin played with the froth on his coffee.

"So many times I've seen my life flash before my eyes," Rafael stared out the window as his coffee too went cold.

"Your whole life – like from when you were a baby? In nappies and a bottle?"

"My mother's breast. Aye, Colin, do you think Tony saw his whole life when he was dying?"

"Maybe God waiting at the Pearly Gates."

"I got the feeling he was an atheist," Rafael frowned.

"They all turn to God in the end."

"Do you believe?"

"The home beat religion out of me."

"I thought your people believed in the rainbow serpent and the Dreamtime stories."

"Yeah sure, Mother Earth, the giant wombat, how the kangaroo got his tail. What about you? Liberation theology?"

"The revolution embraced Catholicism but it's all bullshit in the end."

"So you won't be visiting them pearly gates, brother?"

"Only if they need a handyman to stop them squeaking." Rafael finally smiled.

"Ha. I think they've already got a carpenter there," Colin laughed. "I can't understand why a good looking man like you is such a loner. You need a woman's touch."

"I know you love me, Colin, you just don't want to admit it."

"You might be right there, mate."

Shannon was relieved to hear quiet laughter coming from the two and reappeared with cans of beer.

"You guys look like you need a drink," she offered them.

But they both shook their heads.

"Oh come on, isn't anybody going to join me?"

"Not today, sweetheart," Colin repeated. "I gave up a few years ago."

"Alcohol, it sends me crazy," Rafael agreed with his friend.

"That's what it's meant to do," Shannon chuckled as she pulled the ring top from a can.

"You should try life without it, you can see colours again," Colin smiled.

"I thought it was good to be colour blind," Shannon replied.

"I mean real colours, not black and white. The sky might be grey today but usually it's blue, not like the old days."

"Was it really that bad?"

"It's bad when you can't remember what you did the night before and how you ended up in some stranger's bed."

"Well, I hope they were good looking, at least." Shannon found it hard to imagine Colin in bed with anybody.

"Not usually."

Rafael spoke thoughtfully. "I could always see colours," he said. He turned to Shannon, who had opened her can of beer and was sipping it. "Maybe I will have one, Shannon."

She was surprised but happy to have a fellow drinker, especially Raf. "I think you might need one." She handed him the freezing can.

"*Salud*," he raised it and she followed.

She'd been nervous about asking Colin about his mother but her memories of Ainslie had been disturbing her since the weekend. "Colin, you know how I said I'd help you with some research about your family?"

He nodded.

"Could your mum have worked on farms as a housekeeper after she left the home?"

"That's a possibility, my dear."

"Was her real name Ainslie?"

"No, just Lily. Why?"

"We had an Aboriginal housekeeper called Ainslie."

"You did? Maybe she knew mum." Colin squeezed her hand.

Rafael stared at Colin. He swigged his beer and crumpled the empty can, putting it on the table as he pulled his chair out. "I'll leave you two to it," he said.

Shannon called for him to wait but he'd already headed up the street towards the bus stop. Damn, she was hoping he'd stay.

Chapter Twelve

Shannon's apartment above her café had a small balcony – a Juliet balcony as they called them in real estate ads. If Romeo had climbed onto such a balcony, the two of them would never have fitted. But she could sit on a chair inside the kitchen and her legs could reach the railing – a perfect spot for the first wine of the evening after a rather depressing day. If she cricked her neck and peered out sideways she had "ocean views" as the ads would again say. But tonight the view was of rain and more rain.

She found solace in the flat, away from the two-storey Paddington house which she, Tom and Maxie once called home. That modern terrace was definitely his, she hadn't even chosen the art for the walls. The flat and her parents' farm house were hers.

She'd never felt that comfortable in the Paddington house, perhaps because Irina assumed she could drop in at any time, and look contemptuously at the messy kitchen and unmade beds. She'd even sneak into Maxie's room and tidy up his toys and books, perhaps to make herself feel better – she didn't want her grandson growing up in a chaotic household.

Shannon had gone as far as succumbing to the custom of leaving shoes at the front door, and padding around on bare feet, but she couldn't do the slippers routine – putting on special slippers to use in the bathroom and so on. That was just too un-Australian for her. Even Tom didn't really go for that. But if Irina was in the house and saw Shannon barefoot, she would hand her a pair of slippers from the hall stand, as if it was her house. Or she'd fill the sink and start washing up, even when Shannon explained they had a dishwasher.

"I don't like those. They don't make the glasses clean enough," Irina would say, polishing the sink so hard she could see her reflection in it.

"We do have mirrors if you want to put your makeup on," Shannon would make a joke that Irina did not find funny.

Why was she thinking about Irina on such a cold, wet evening? Cars drove past and a dog barked as her mind turned to its owner, her neighbour, an old, lonely woman who never seemed to take him out. That poor dog, Shannon felt sorry for it. Her old dog, a bitser who had died a couple of years earlier, loved to go on walks through the bush, sniffing at wombat holes and growling at every kangaroo it saw. This dog probably wouldn't recognise a roo if it ran into one.

It was going to be a freezing winter this year, that's for sure. She hummed to the Dixie Chicks playing on her iPod as she gulped her wine. Café closed, customers gone home to their own little abodes. All's right with the world, well, except that Maxie wasn't here. That bastard Tom hanging onto him. She'd have to wait another few days before she saw him. It was killing her. At least she'd spoken to him on the phone and he sounded happy. He'd had a bath, he told her, and was watching TV. She used to love giving him baths, his slithery little body covered in soap diving under the cloudy water. Playing with his bath toys, telling them stories. "Are you having a bath, mummy?" he'd ask and she'd climb in with him. Irina didn't approve, she thought it was unhygienic.

A bath, now that's a grand idea. She poured herself another glass on the way into the bathroom, and turned the taps on, pouring bubble bath under the water until it frothed and smothered the tub. She found some lavender oil in the cabinet. To calm my nerves, she thought as she poured the oil into the burner. The candle alight, the smell filled the room with its pungent reminder of massage rooms and relaxation tapes. She sunk down into the bubbles, emerging to sip on her wine.

Back in her bedroom she got up the courage to stand in front of the full-length mirror but she was faced with a sight she didn't find at all pleasant. She hadn't been eating despite the great food she was surrounded with in the café, and had lost weight. At least eight kilos since the separation. She was scrawny. And now even her face was beginning to sink in. But there was one advantage. Her wedding dress might fit again. She was very slim when she got married. She'd give it a try.

She pulled out her underwear drawer in the old dresser and found her white silk undies and a bra-corset, which was covered in lace and still so pretty. She slid open the cupboard door. Covered in a plastic bag and hanging on a clothes hanger was her wedding dress. Carefully, she took it out of the cupboard and laid it on the bed. First the white pantyhose. She took a pair from the drawer and pulled them up her legs. She climbed into the wedding dress, a designer one Tom had forked out for. Cost fifteen hundred dollars. A bargain at the time, she'd told him. Ivory silk with thin straps and a lace bodice, it hung loosely on her frame.

"Ah I'm forgetting something. The piece-de-resistance," she spoke to herself. She climbed onto a chair and lifted down a white, cardboard box from the top of the cupboard. There it was in all its glory. She gingerly took out a gauze veil with a tiny tiara studded in fake pearls and put it on. "Where are my wedding shoes? Oh these will do." She found her fluffy, pink slippers. Irina would approve.

In the mirror her reflection stared back at her. What a lovely bride. What a gorgeous dress. What a pretty church. What beautiful flowers. What a nice service. What a handsome groom. What an enormous waste of money. What a stupid decision. What a short time it took for Tom and her to separate.

Well, she drove him away, didn't she? Her and her depression. You'd think she'd get over the stillbirth. It's just part of life anyway. Babies die. But why did it have to happen to her? What did she do to deserve it? Women who are terrible mothers have children. They bash their kids. They even kill them or let their moronic boyfriends do the deed. Burn them with cigarettes, make marks all over their sweet, little tummies. Lock them in dark cupboards and leave them for days. A telephone book on his head and then a bang with a hammer. What about that woman who killed her daughter and buried her body in the bush?

How come these women didn't lose their babies at twenty-two weeks? Oh no, they smoked right through the pregnancy and still had their un-wanted, snotty-nosed brats. But she, she who'd only ever wanted to have kids lost her beautiful little girl.

She went to another drawer and took out an envelope. Inside was a Polaroid photo of a baby with her almost see-through skin covered in blue and red veins, her huge eyes staring up at her. What kind of reminder was that to keep? How could she show it to anybody? How could they believe how perfectly formed she was? So much more real than the ultrasound X-ray images that every happy couple was given these days.

Her thoughts were disturbed by a knock at the door. She was startled and dropped the photo on her bedside table. She wasn't used to visitors, especially at night. She found a cardigan on her chair near the bed and, draping it around her shoulders, went to the door in her wedding dress and veil and slippers.

It was Rafael, in his civvies – black leather jacket, black polo-necked jumper, jeans and checked scarf – looking a bit wet but more handsome than in the dirty overalls he had been wearing earlier, although he looked good whatever he wore.

"All dressed up and nowhere to go," Shannon laughed, trying to cover up her embarrassment. "You're wearing different clothes?"

"Yes I went home and got changed." He put his fingers to the lace of her bodice, touching the scratchy material.

Shannon pulled back, this guy was acting a bit odd. Then he slid his hand down her side to her hips, and she shivered.

"Beautiful. Is it silk?" He kept his hand on her hip.

"Yes. Too big for me now." She knew her ribs were showing, there was no cleavage to fill it out; her breasts were almost flat.

She took off the veil and he put his hand out to touch it. "Let me smell it."

"It's dusty."

"I don't mind," he took it in both hands and put his face into the tulle.

He was taking too long and she wasn't sure what to do. She reached for the veil and put it on the hall table, catching a glimpse of her un-brushed, still-wet hair in the mirror. She looked a mess.

"What happened at the wedding?" His expression changed to one of horror as he stood behind her staring at her reflection.

Northern mountains
March, 1986

I stop the car as a soldier waves me down. It's a Contra. I'm shitting myself. He wants to know where we're going. I tell him the next village. All over the road are strewn dead bodies. It's a wedding party. All massacred. Thirty-three of them right there. The bride is wearing a white blouse and skirt embroidered with red flowers, but it's not the red of the flowers I see but blood all over her. And mud. The groom lies a few feet away. Till death do us part.

The Contras must have ambushed the party returning to the village, believing they were Sandinista supporters. I am sure we too are going to die but Lana speaks to them. In her usual charming American journalist kind of way, she just goes and charms those Contras out of killing us.

"Hey, where were your rifles made?" she says. "FAL. In Belgium right? My government helped with that, right? You going to let us go, you know we're CNN and we don't take sides? Give us your message to the people, we'll let the world know what you're fighting for."

Lana, she just charms those Contras out of killing us.

Rafael's expression changed to a smile as Shannon moved sideways away from the mirror. Then his eyes narrowed as his smile turned cynical. Shannon was getting the creeps. What was she going to do with him? "What wedding? Mine you mean?" she asked him.

He turned to her. "Yeah, yeah. Sorry."

"The wedding was OK, the marriage was horrible. Glass of wine?"

"I'd prefer a tea." He followed her to the kitchen where he sat on a stool at the bench. There was only the sound of waves in the distance; the dog must have finally gone to sleep. Shannon lit a cigarette but Rafael snatched it from her, stubbing it out among the other butts in the ashtray.

"What the hell?" She was almost amused at his actions.

"I hate smoking."

"It's my place, Rafael," she shrugged. She pulled her cardigan around her as the night closed in, sensing it was going to be a long one. He still seemed to be disturbed. Seeing his friend Tony die in that manner, it was no wonder and Shannon was sorry she hadn't appeared as understanding when they'd talked about it at the café earlier. She didn't mean it in that way. "I'm sorry if I said something in the café that offended you," she apologised as she handed him a cup of black tea. "You left so quickly."

"Those bastards, somebody has to pay for Tony's death." Rafael ignored her comment as he stared into the cup.

"Why didn't he have a safety harness on?" Noticing her bottle was finished, she opened the fridge door to find another, filling her glass.

Rafael shook his head. "The unions, they're paid off too."

"What do you mean?"

"The company was in a rush. They were losing money. They didn't care about safety. I think they told Tony not to worry about the netting. I'm not sure. But something was wrong. They cut corners and then somebody dies."

"We should go to the media."

"I can't," Rafael looked down again.

"Why not?"

"I just can't."

"Well, I can," she pleaded with him. "I've had experience using local journos for the conservationist actions I've been involved in down at the valley. If we find somebody we can trust, I think they could talk to you off the record."

"A journalist you can trust? Huh!" He banged the cup down on the bench. "They're just trouble. Especially the women."

Women! Look at me, my baby dies and then my husband splits up with me, she thought. It's men who send women mad, who take their children from them. Crazy women are due to crazy men, she'd heard that in a song. But there was a way to do something right, to help people. "They're not all like that, I've dealt with good local ones," Shannon said. "It's so unjust. We've got to stand up for these guys. The doctors never really helped me. Imagine Tony's kids, they've got no father now."

"Leave it, please Shannon."

She looked at her watch. It was midnight.

Rafael apologised. "You have to work tomorrow. I'll go."

"I'm not working until the afternoon."

The one-bar heater had made no difference in the icy kitchen and they were both shivering. Shannon's slippers had been brushing his ankles and she pulled her wedding dress up and put her stockinged legs between his calves. "You don't have to go, Rafael, there's absolutely no reason for you to go." She took him by the hand and led him into the bedroom.

"What's that smell?" he looked around to see where it was coming from.

"Lavender oil. It's soothing."

Fumbling, he undid her wedding dress, remembering another time with another woman.

Managua, Nicaragua
November, 1985

It's Lana's bedroom in the run-down house she's rented with a group of other journalists. We're so hot we can't even bear to have the sheets over us. They're in a crumpled heap at the end of her single bed. But she still insists on burning that damn lavender oil. What is it about hippy *Gringas*?

She has her hair up again but bits are falling out all over her face from her ponytail. We're kissing and carrying on. I'm about to mount her but she stops me.

"Why? Come on," I plead.

She's leaning over to the drawers next to her bed, and pulling something out. "If you want to do it honey, you're going to have to use an ... *anticonceptivo*."

I groan. "*Plastico*! No way, that's like washing your feet with your socks still on."

"I don't care, here," and she thrusts the packet at me.

Shannon turned over in her bed to look at Rafael. He was snoring now and grumbling to himself in his sleep. His grinding teeth made a sound like chalk scraping a blackboard. She couldn't sleep, her head was spinning with what had just gone on and all the talk and all the memories coming back, of being touched again, of feeling somebody's hands on her body in a tender way. It had been so long, so long. Tom had given up on sex with her. He'd lost interest or perhaps he was just worried about hurting her. All that blood, it would put anybody off. He had told her when she was pregnant with Max that he probably wouldn't come to the birth. She had threatened to kill him if he didn't support her. She didn't want some "support person" there, she wanted him. But Irina had warned him not to go. "It will put you off sex," she had said. "What about me?" Shannon had asked. "I'm the one giving birth and going through all the pain. You're just watching." So he came and he was good, very supportive in a quiet sort of way. But later after the stillbirth he had tended to roll over and go to sleep when they were in bed together.

Now she just couldn't get up the strength to go looking for another man. Well, nobody had turned her on. But Rafael, he was different. Exotic, handsome and mysterious. But also neurotic, she thought. He'd turned the lights off as soon as they came into the bedroom and the darkness was only broken by the moon's reflection on the skylight. She thought she'd be the one worried about her body but it appeared Rafael was more concerned about his. He got into the bed and pulled the covers up over both of them, slowly moving on top of her, kissing her on her neck. Pretty rudimentary but she gave him the grace of forgiving him. It was their first time together.

Shannon turned the bedside light on and gently moved the sheet and doona down off his body, she wanted to admire his arms. But as he turned onto his back she was shocked to see scars all over his stomach and chest. They looked like cigarette burns, like somebody had ground them into his skin. She could imagine Tony Soprano's underling lighting a cigarette. Taking a long draw. Putting it out on him. Using his body for an ashtray. She was startled when she heard Rafael's voice. He was talking in his sleep: "Be careful, *cuidado*, mud on your wedding dress."

"Shhh it's OK," she comforted him as he stretched his arm out and stroked her face, still dreaming.

"*Mi bonita Lana, Lana. Que pasa?*" But then he became more restless, shouting. "No, no, not me. *Es mi trabajo.* No. No, not the kids' fingers. No, don't do it."

Shannon pushed Rafael to wake him, to bring him out of his nightmare. "It's OK, it's OK, Rafael. It's a dream, only a dream."

Chapter Thirteen

It was the barking dog that woke them both the next morning but Rafael's reaction was more violent than Shannon's. He jumped up with a start and fell out of the bed, rolling onto the floor. "Work, I have to go," he yelled.

"It's Sunday," Shannon consoled him, trying not to laugh as she realised what had happened. She moved over to the edge and gave him her arm to pull him up.

"I thought we'd been attacked."

"It's just the bloody dog." Shannon felt sorry for the poor thing but this morning she really wanted to throw him a bait.

"I'll make you some breakfast," she offered, putting on her dressing gown and fluffy slippers.

"Just coffee please. I don't eat breakfast. I must go soon."

"No, don't go. We don't have to rush anywhere."

Rafael leant over to pull her back into bed this time. But as he looked down he saw the photo on the bedside table and picked it up. "What's this?"

"My little girl." Shannon hadn't meant for him to see this.

"She's like a doll," Rafael's fingers traced the outline of the dead baby.

Northern mountains
March, 1986

Inside the church a woman is bent over a child's coffin. Bent over the tiny, white coffin. Made by the father, the poor, poor father. She is willing the corpse to rise from the dead.

"I couldn't keep her in," Shannon took the photo from him. "She was born too young. Her tiny lungs weren't strong enough to help her breathe."

Rafael touched her hand. "I'm so, so sorry, *querida.*"

Shannon put the photo back on the table and pointed the way to the bathroom, asking if he'd like a shower. She was dying to question him about the burns on his body but didn't want to scare him off or let him know she'd been staring at him while he was sleeping.

Rafael went into the bathroom, climbing into the bath and turning the shower taps on as Shannon hummed to herself, making plunger coffee. Short black, of course. Then realising she hadn't given Rafael a towel and hearing him in the shower she went into the bathroom without knocking. Behind the curtain she could make out his strong back and perfect bum. He was singing something that she couldn't quite make out because it was in Spanish but she picked up Nicaragua, his country. He had finally told her last night where he was from.

"I'm just putting a towel out here for you," she called out through the sound of the water and his sweet singing as she pulled the curtain open.

"What?" he covered his lower body with his hands, the cigarette burns still stood out on his chest.

"Oh sorry. Didn't mean to startle you."

"Can you leave please?" he pleaded.

"Hey, don't be shy. I saw everything last night."

Rafael turned his back. "Please can I have some privacy?"

"Be like that." She slammed the door and went back to the kitchen.

The sun was streaming in while she rummaged in her bag for her smokes, taking one out and lighting it. As she sat at the bench nursing her coffee, she wondered what the hell she had got herself into. Tom was difficult with a capital D as Colin would say but he wasn't mad. Maybe he just hadn't loved her enough. She wasn't the perfect wife that he wanted, the good housekeeper, the one waiting at home for him in an apron with his dinner in the oven. She wasn't that and she never could be. But she had loved him, she hadn't wanted him to leave. They just clashed too much, all that fighting all the time. It wasn't good for him either. But Rafael, what was his problem? What were those burns on his body? What kind of an accident would cause them? Shannon knew nothing about Nicaragua except for its coffee. She felt so ignorant, but wanted to know more.

She heard Rafael coming down the hallway and jumped up and opened the balcony door. She put her cigarette out and hid the ashtray under the chair, then closed the door. He came into the kitchen, clean and dressed with his thick black hair slicked back. Whoa, it took her breath away. Like wine, some men just get better with age. But most just let themselves go. Perhaps he even had some Indian blood in him, she wasn't sure.

"I have to go now," he said.

She wanted him to stay, she was in no rush. "Can't I make you some eggs and bacon?" she asked, giving him his coffee.

"No really," he said.

"What did you have for breakfast in Nicaragua?"

He laughed. "*Gallo pinto.*"

"What's that?"

"Beans and rice mixed together. It looks like a painted rooster, that's why we call it that. That's all there was. And bean soup for dinner with tortillas."

"Oh why?"

"It's a long story, Shannon. Sometimes we'd have fried plantains. And mangoes grew everywhere."

Shannon smiled, she liked the sound of that. So tropical. So different to Sydney in winter. "I'd like to go there one day."

Rafael laughed again, but this time with derision, as he put on his leather jacket. "No you wouldn't. It's a dump."

Shannon couldn't be swayed. "So how was she trouble?"

"Who?"

"The journalist? The one you were talking about last night? Lana, I think. You were saying her name in your sleep."

"Lana? *La Gringa.* You don't need to know about her."

"Of course I do."

"Forget it."

"Come on. Sit down, don't go yet."

He sat at the table and picked up the cup. "She thought she was doing us a favour. But she was only doing herself a favour. But in the end that wasn't enough to save her."

Shannon felt as if he was talking in riddles. She wanted to lighten things up; she was sick of heaviness. She moved to the CD player and put on a salsa CD. She danced in time to it, her rhythm just where it should be. "Could *La Gringa* dance the salsa?" She moved closer to Rafael.

"She wasn't bad but she always wanted to lead," Rafael recalled.

Managua
January, 1986

The bottle of *Flor de Caña* is almost finished. There is only a bit of rum left at the bottom. So opaque you would hardly know it was there. Under the black sky, people dance the salsa, their movements in sync with the rhythms of the band, their sweat pouring hot and sticky like the rum. Husbands, wives, grandmothers, grandfathers: in my country they have the rhythm from birth.

But Lana doesn't want to dance. She just wants to drink – and talk. "El Salvador was the place for torture." She continues her monologue. "They'd tie electric wires to their vital parts and shock the Christ out of them. People would find their bodies strewn like garbage in the rubbish dumps in San Salvador – not pleasant."

I have been trying to get her to slow down on the alcohol but she takes no notice. "You could put some Coke in it," I say.

"That Imperialist drink. And I can see your non-smoking is going really well, Rafael." She nods at the pile of butts on the floor. "There might be an economic embargo but thank God there's always rum and cigarettes." She sweeps her arm across the table. The bottle smashes to the hard concrete floor. Broken glass glitters at my feet. The sickly sweet aroma of rum rises from below, and as she leans towards me I can smell it on her breath. She dives down onto her knees, picking up bits of glass, laughing wildly, not caring what anybody has to say. Or what they think.

Luckily for me, the crowd freezes just at that moment. We can hear loud voices and then the band changes mid-song. In struts *Comandante* Manuel, our vice president and Sandinista leader, followed by a tall, beautiful woman. She could be Russian or even Canadian, I don't know.

"What's the matter?" Lana looks up from under the table. "Why are they playing the national anthem?"

"It's *Comandante* Manuel," I hiss. "Get up, for God's sake."

People stand up for the *comandante* as a waiter shows him and his lady friend to a table, right at the front near the band. Of course there will always be anti-revolutionaries amongst us and supporters of those ratbag Contras, and some stay sitting, staring into their drinks or making muttered comments behind their hands. I have no time for these insects; they only add fuel to Lana's fire, who is always trying to find so-called talent who will speak against the *Frente*.

Lana pulls herself out from under the table, peeking over the edge, her knuckles gripping the plastic table cloth. "Who's that?" she asks.

I tell her I have no idea.

"I bet she's a visiting revolutionary poet from the Eastern Bloc or something." She's laughing hysterically again, as she drags herself onto her chair.

"So what's so funny?"

"I doubt it if it's the sonnets the *comandante's* interested in."

"Oh give the poor man a chance. Remember Somoza's National Guard tortured him and murdered his wife. But after the revolution he still forgave his torturers." I immediately regret bringing up her favourite subject.

Lana picks up her glass and turns to look at the *comandante*, across on the other side of the dance floor. "*Viva la revolución*," she shouts, raising her empty glass to toast him. Her cotton skirt has risen and I notice a cigarette butt has stuck with blood to her lacerated knee.

This is my place, where I have been coming for years to dance like there's no tomorrow. How dare she embarrass me here? This stupid *Gringa*, who doesn't know how to behave. They may say they're here to support the "leftist" revolution, or in Lana's case to report on it, but really they just want to run their banana republic. But it's my country!

But then *Com* Manuel sees her, and picks up his glass and raises it, toasting her. "*Viva los Estados Unidos, mi periodista bonita, Señorita* Lopez," he shouts so the whole place can hear it.

"Ah what a gentleman," Lana giggles as she gestures to the waiter to bring more rum. "Why aren't you like him, *amorcito*?"

"Don't call me that." I am seething.

"You liked it before. The moon, the stars, the heat," she pauses as she slaps a mosquito. "Maybe not *los anticonceptivos*." She shrieks with laughter. But then she keeps going on about a story she wants us to do, using me as her cameraman as usual. "I have heard that deep in the mountains to the north the Sandinista Army has set up a psychiatric hospital where poor demented soldiers are being kept hidden away, even from the *campesinos*. They have gone mad from what they have seen or had done to them by the Contras – *El Enemigo*. They are known as *Los Locos*. The official line, of course, is that no such trauma exists. The soldiers are happy, pleased, honoured to fight – and die – for The Fatherland, Nicaragua. *La Patria*!" She does a Heil Hitler salute.

"Shh, don't speak so loudly," I whisper, worried that people will hear who could convey this information to one side or the other.

"But it's a good story, *sí?*"

"Not one your Yankee TV-land audience would be interested in," I say. "What a load of *mierda*." I'm so sick of her conspiracy theories but I do wonder where she got her information from.

"Or *miedo*, perhaps?"

I am not afraid until she looks at her watch and asks whether we're going to her place or my smoke-filled hovel, behind my mother's house. I drag her away by her arm, out to the waiting queue of taxis from the Carlos Fonseca co-operative as she continues to argue with me.

"I once was a dancer, you know," Shannon said, trying to get Rafael's attention.

"Were you the star?" Rafael asked, allowing himself to be pulled up from the table.

"There were no stars. It was a co-operative. Only decisions by the group, which meant not much was decided on. It fell apart in the end."

"Sounds familiar," he smiled as he moved, but then stopped and went to put his scarf around his neck. "I have to go."

"Come on, it's Sunday. Let's go out."

The music stopped and she found her bag and took out her lipstick, walking to the mirror on the wall and applying it in front of her reflection. Rafael moved up behind her and swung her round to kiss her but she pulled away from him. No dance, no kiss. "Careful, you'll smudge my Lana Turner lips." She emphasised Lana.

Northern mountains
March, 1986

I can hear the eerie sound of wailing drifting over from the church. It's raining and the drops are turning to mush on the windscreen. Lana pulls herself up to the rear-vision mirror and starts applying her lipstick. It's a deep, dark red like blood.

"Do you really need makeup to film a funeral?" I ask as I park the car.

"*Amor*, I have to look good for my stand up, no matter what I'm filming, or they will switch to another channel."

I'm trying to contain my anger as I climb out and go to the boot for my equipment. All this *Gringa* cares about is her job and her appearance as my people are dying. The people I fought for. The people our revolution is finally giving dignity to. I hate that she cares nothing for everything I believe in. I hate myself that I have to work for her, just for the *Gringo* dollars.

Lana finishes her cosmetic routine, as the wailing becomes louder and louder, almost piercing. And we go into the church together. It's the *abuelas* who are wailing. All in black, their faces covered by cheap, synthetic veils, they cry for all the grandchildren who have been killed in this filthy war. The sight even stops Lana. But it's only a minute's pause before she goes over to them. "Film us while I shoot a few questions at the grannies," she commands.

Shannon lifted her jacket down from the hooks near the mirror and put it on, taking Rafael by the hand. "Stop dreaming, Romeo."

"What?"

"I'll take you down to my rock, to my whale rock."

"Oh alright then, I will come with you. I need a decent coffee anyway." He tickled her and she laughed.

"Oh thanks, *Señor* Smooth. Well, when are you going to take me dancing?"

"Not here, it's too depressing."

"Oh come on. I've heard about a new salsa club in Marrickville. How about you take me out next Saturday night? I want to see if you really can dance, or if it's all talk."

"OK if you don't believe me then *bueno* it's a date."

Rafael and Shannon made their way down the hill to the beach, where families held barbecues and the smell of burnt sausages rose in the air. One group had strung up a volley ball net as they pitched to each other, while small kids played on appropriately safe slippery dips.

Shannon held Rafael's hand, guiding him past the children. "I used to always take Maxie to this playground. He should be with me."

"Do you want me to speak to Tom?" he asked.

Shannon shook her head. She knew this might make Tom angrier. "Just leave it for now but thank you so much." She wanted to know more about this man – how he came to Australia, and the reasons why. Did he have a wife? What happened to Lana? Where was his family and how many were there? Did he have brothers and sisters? Where were his mother and father? And did he have any children of his own? She was trying hard not to let the questions tumble out of her mind and onto her tongue. She didn't want to make him angry as well, but she wanted answers. "Have you ever been married, Rafael?" she asked.

"Wouldn't you like to know?" he said.

"Oh, you're so annoying." She laughed.

He followed her around the cliff walk as they stretched their eyes for whales and any signs of life out on the horizon. But they couldn't see anything except miles and miles of sea. The wind was blowing in from the coast as they zipped up their jackets and pulled their hoods over their heads. When they came to the whale rock Shannon explained what Colin had told her about its significance and age.

"So old? We have indigenous culture in my country too," he said. "But I know very little about it. Colin probably knows more than me."

She grabbed his arm and kissed him on the cheek and he put his arm around her waist. "You're so small, two of my arms could go round you," he said.

"I stopped eating … after the baby, you know. Now come on, tell me about Lana. How did you first meet her?"

"I told you, I used to work with her. She was a correspondent for CNN."

Managua
January, 1985

It's my little bar in my barrio and the radio is playing Atlantic Coast

music. The timber walls are shaking as people dance barefoot on the dirt floor of the shack. I have been coming here since I was barely a teenager. I'd just hang around and talk to the girls as I sipped on a beer. They knew I didn't have a girlfriend or even a friend who was a girl. I was not into all that romantic stuff. And even when I came back from the war I was still so young, so inexperienced that sometimes they would take pity on me and give me what I needed. Lead me to the room out the back and the narrow bed with its dirty sheets, used by one after the other. The door was another dirty sheet nailed up over the entrance.

It's a still and steamy night. Up in the mountains the Contras are doing whatever they can to wreck the revolution. But in the city people only care that they don't have what they used to have before the war.

The door of the bar is fringed by hibiscus trees, their bright crimson flowers falling on the ground forming a red carpet of mushy petals. Inside, the bar is crammed with patrons sitting at rough, wooden tables, mostly covered with beer, rum and Coke bottles, plastic bowls of ice and small containers of salt.

It's noisy. When the Atlantic coast music stops Latin love songs take over. So sentimental but everybody loves them. I'm sitting in the corner with two of the girls, Rosita and Maria. They're like aunties to me really. Aunties with conjugal rights.

There's a woman at the bar, trying to ignore Silvio, that old *borracho*, coming on to her, his breath sickly sweet from the rum. I don't know who she is but she is beautiful. Rosita and Maria catch me staring at her and goad me on. "What are you waiting for, *chico*? Go for it."

I can see she isn't from my barrio or even my country. Too white and her teeth are too even and she has a *Gringa* look about her. Her clothes are modern-looking and clean too, not the worn-out cotton shifts that the other women wear. She has a tight skirt that shows her bum, and long strawberry blonde hair. And when I hear her speak, her accent is different. *Sí*, it sounds Mexican. Or maybe Chicano.

"If you're going to annoy me then give me a drink at least," she says to Silvio.

The grubby crocodile's words in reply are slurred and incoherent, his leering eyes look down her blouse.

"*Hola, señorita*," I say. "Is this man bothering you?"

"Don't worry, I can look after myself."

Silvio has by now managed to actually find a glass and pour her a drink, which he hands to her, reaching across and trying to touch her breasts in a rather awkward manoeuvre. She pushes his arm away and turns towards me. She has a look in her eyes as if she knows me from somewhere. "Are you Rafael?"

"*Sí*," I wonder how she knows my name.

"Did Carlos tell you I was looking for a cameraman? I'm Lana, from CNN."

"Oh Carlos," and then I put two and two together. He rents out cars to foreign journalists.

"*Sí*, I'm available. Why don't you join us? Can I get you a drink and not Silvio's rum?"

"Yes a beer, but I hope they give you glasses here. I don't like drinking beer out of a plastic bag."

This is what they have to do in our country – pour the beer from bottles into bags, as there's not enough bottles. I order the drinks and she follows me over to my corner and I introduce her to my "aunties".

Rosita asks her if she's American and Lana nods.

"So, are you with this government or not?"

Lana only laughs.

Maria butts in. "Don't worry, love, it's just a joke between us and him" and she points with her lips at me.

"Oh really?"

"He's for the government, you know. And we're not too happy with them."

"Why not?"

You could almost see Lana taking notes in her head. Aha a group of pro Contra prostitutes who hate the revolution, useful for a coming story.

"Well, if this government had its way we wouldn't be able to feed our kids," Maria says.

"*Es la verdad*," Rosita agrees. "And these police, *hijos de putas*, they never leave us alone."

I attempt a joke. "Hey, if they're sons of whores they must be family."

"Ah, Rafael."

I give my views: "You ought to explain that the revolution wanted to eliminate prostitution. It's a social evil that exploits women and hurts their dignity."

"But we have to eat, *amor*," Maria pleads.

"Even if there's no food to buy," says Rosita.

"And when there is food you have to stand in line half the day for it." Maria gives me a friendly cuddle and helps herself to one of my cigarettes. "Ay *compañero*, you make me laugh. Now the government says that apart from the war the big problem is *machismo*. But without *machismo* we wouldn't have no work at all."

"Maria, Maria. Politics, politics," Rosita begs her to stop. "Ay Lana you must be crazy leaving your beautiful country to come to this mad place. *Mucho gusto*. Hope to see you again." And the two aunties shake Lana's hand and walk to the bar, joining in an intense discussion with two ugly and coarse men of the barrio.

"So *machismo* and prostitution are top of the government's hit list, huh?" Lana asks me. I answer yes. I am trying to be The New Man, and wonder why she has the right to be cynical. Where was she in the revolution or during the time of Somoza, when we suffered so much? I don't care what she thinks, I'm keeping to the government line. "*Sí*. The revolution announced the new women's policy recently. And it admitted there had been some problems – eliminating prostitution is still a long way off. *Machismo* in Latin America is the first thing we have to tackle. We consider it a retrograde ideological position unacceptable by true revolutionaries."

Lana rolls her eyes. It's as if she's heard it all before.

The cafés facing the beach were crowded, packed with couples and friends and families.

"What would Aussies do on their days off if they didn't have cafés?" Rafael asked. "And don't any of you know how to cook breakfast yourself?"

"I offered to cook before." Shannon was indignant.

They found an outside table and Shannon opened the menu. "I'm starving," she said. "I feel like the big breakfast. Must be all that exercise last night."

Rafael rolled his eyes. Another Aussie custom he didn't understand – talking about sex all the time. "About the burns – it was my older brother," he finally said after he reluctantly ordered some toast. "He got hold of papa's cigarettes and tried to smoke them. He couldn't inhale. The smoke went everywhere and he was coughing like mad. I started laughing, you know and he got angry with me. He started to burn me with them, one by one. Twisting them into my belly. He was holding my wrists so tight I couldn't run away."

"Wow, even my bossy male cousins wouldn't have gone that far. Unbelievable," she shook her head, gulping her coffee.

"Crazy Nica kids. We grew up on the street, not in cafés, like the children here." He gestured at some little devils monstering their parents for more fancy food. They were yelling at the waitress to bring them Coca Colas, as if they needed more sugar to add to their hype.

A couple pushing a pram and dragging a small white dog stood staring at the table next to them, discussing whether they should choose this spot.

"Make up your minds," Rafael whispered to Shannon.

They sat down after tying their pooch to a pole near the table, where the café had thoughtfully left a bowl of water.

"Do they have a doggie menu too?" Rafael asked Shannon. She smothered her laugh as she turned to the couple and asked them what sort of dog it was.

"A caboodle," they answered, their faces serious.

"You know what the name of this dog would be in my country?" Rafael whispered to her again.

She shook her head.

"A bloody mutt," he said.

Shannon almost choked on her coffee.

One of the naughty toddlers stumbled out onto the footpath, pulling himself along people's chairs, a mangled muesli bar in one hand, and found the dog. The couple with the baby smiled at him, but Rafael saw that the toddler was not attempting to play with the animal. He was hitting the dog in the face with what was left of his treat, and splashing water from the doggy bowl at it. Rafael wondered why the dog didn't bite the kid and was about to pull him away when an older woman wearing sensible sandals and calf-length cotton pants passed the café, dragging a black Labrador. Her dog looked as if it couldn't believe its luck when it saw there was both a mutt and a child to bark at.

The toddler threw water at the Labrador, who backed away and in the excitement, both dogs' leads became entangled, tripping the woman over. She landed on her backside on the footpath, knocking a table. Coffee cups smashed to the ground. The toddler yelled in confusion and his father ran out to grab him.

"I'll sue, you stupid bloody cow," he screamed at the poor Labrador-owner.

Rafael pulled the woman up off the ground while Shannon scurried to pick up the cups and place them back on the table, in between shouting parents, red-faced dog owners and noisy babies.

"I have to get out of here," Shannon grabbed her bag and crossed the road to the park.

Rafael stared after her. And they say my country is under-developed, he thought.

Managua
March, 1986

All the dogs are boney in my country. You never see a fat dog. You see every other variety though – bitsers of every breed, mongrels all. They hang around in packs, roaming the streets, barking at everybody who walks past. They have no fear, they own the streets. They're the Mafia of Managua.

But one of the side products of poverty is these dogs are starving. You can't go to a restaurant without half-starved dogs moving around your feet, as you sit at the table. You push them away, they growl and come right back.

We're at an outdoor restaurant eating fried chicken. It's a treat. I haven't eaten chicken in weeks. It's scrawny chicken but it still tastes good. Covered in batter from corn flour, oil and salt. The restaurant owner has killed a couple of chooks so our timing is perfect.

I'm down to chewing the last bit of meat off the drumstick when I notice the similarities between the chicken leg and the bony, white dog sitting on my feet gnawing on its paws, waiting, hoping I will throw it my last bit of bone. Am I eating dog? I want to throw up.

Lana is looking at me strangely. "Are you OK, Raf?"

I jump up, knocking my chair over and run for the bathroom – no door, just a scrappy curtain – and mud on the floor and it all comes out. It's like *The Exorcist* – out in a giant spray like a waterfall. I flush the filthy toilet and wash my face with water from what passes for a basin. Sweat runs down my chest.

Back at the table, Lana is chewing on those bones as if it's The Last Supper. I grab my plate and tip its contents on the floor. The dog can't believe its luck, pouncing on the meat still left on the bones, before one of the pack bounds over to join it. He snaps at his mate and next thing they're fighting over my meal, almost toppling the table over.

Lana pulls her seat back and yells at me. "Rafael. What are you doing?"

I shrug my shoulders. What can I say? My country has gone to the dogs!

Rafael found Shannon sitting at a picnic table in the park opposite, holding a cigarette in her yellow-tipped fingers, sucking the nicotine in and blowing great clouds of grey smoke out her nostrils. Her hands were shaking in time to her chattering teeth.

"Don't worry, Raf, no more questions about Lana or anybody else." Her eyes pierced his.

"That woman should have brought her dog in a doggy pram," he tried to break the mood by joking, just as her mobile beeped a text message.

"It's Nick, he needs help. There isn't any food made." She jumped up and ran up the hill.

Rafael sat for a minute and then followed her.

Northern mountains
March, 1986

Lana and I are up in the mountains, driving north, to her crazy idea of a story. A hospital for insane soldiers? What next? We've hired this little white Datsun from Carlos-rent-a-car – he's called that because that's what he does, rents cars to foreign journalists and film crews, one of the few guys in Managua who's making money out of the war.

We stop for a cigarette break – Lana won't let me smoke in the car. I pull up right next to an army truck. The soldiers are having a break. A smoke in the shade. Loyal soldiers hiding beneath their big green truck. Some are still sitting up in the cabin where there's two rough wooden benches with piles of sacks in between. The soldiers' guns are lying by their sides. There are boxes spread around with Chinese characters on them.

I ask them, "What's in these boxes? They're from the People's Republic of China, *sí*?"

"*Sí*," one of the kid soldiers answers. "They're polio vaccines. There's a big health program on now all through this country."

Lana pricks her ears. "So there's not so much fighting going on now?"

"No, all quiet."

The second baby soldier, who looks even younger than his *compañero*, must like the look of the *Gringa* journalist and pipes up: "But you heard about the Contras blowing up the power plant at Ocotal? No water or lights now. Your president doesn't like us much."

"Hey, I didn't vote for him," Lana's indignant.

"Ah, no offence, lady. We've got nothing against *Gringos*, just your government."

"So how much longer you got to go, *muchacho*?" I ask.

"Three months, man, then I'm going home."

"Did you volunteer?"

"No, *hombre*. I was dancing with my girlfriend at a disco in Esteli when they came in and took us. Hope she's still waiting for me."

Lana, ever the journalist, wants to stick to the topic and asks if the Contras blew up the bridge ahead.

"Yeah, man," the younger soldier answers.

The other soldier gives him a look. "We can't say really. We don't know."

"But it must have been the Contras eh?" I ask.

He shrugs his shoulders. "It's dangerous all around here, man. Be careful where you drive. Even *Gringas* aren't safe around here these days."

We turn to go into the tiny village store and Lana hisses at me, saying I should stick to filming and let her ask the questions. I'm hungry and thirsty, hoping to find some breakfast. And I'm not in doubt that if the Contras knew I fought for the revolution I wouldn't be safe either. Those drug-dealing bastards. We all know they're funded by that crazy movie star, Ronald Reagan. Lana follows me in.

Behind the counter is a middle-aged woman wearing a scarf. I say good morning and she answers: "*Buenas dias.*"

"Can I have a mango *fresca, señora*?" It's the fruit drink that I love.

"There aren't any." She shrugs her shoulders.

"No frescas?"

"*Sí*, there aren't any."

"And sodas?"

"*No hay.* There aren't any." She doesn't even look sorry.

"Can I have a sandwich?"

"*Sí*, there's ham or cheese."

"Can I have ham and cheese together, please?"

"No, we can't do that. One or the other."

I'm going mad with frustration and Lana is almost red from trying not to laugh. The shopkeeper goes to make the sandwich but returns a minute later.

"Sorry, *señor*, but there's no bread, or ham or cheese."

"*Señora*, what do you have?" I'm going crazy asking these same old questions.

"There's nothing. No water, no lights. I can't make ice for *frescas*. The truck hasn't come with the supplies from Ocotal. I can't help you."

I look up at the shelf and point to some cans of sardines. Puffing and heaving, the shopkeeper climbs up on a stool and gets the cans down, handing them to me. I pay, and Lana and I walk out of the shop together.

But Lana, the practical one, asks how the hell we're going to open the cans with no can openers. She imitates the shop owner. "*No hay, chico.*"

We walk back to the soldiers and I hand them the dusty cans. They probably need them more than we do.

"Sardines? We live on these for weeks in the mountains. But it's food, eh? *Gracias, hombre.*" The baby soldier takes them.

"And did you know in Sandino's time they filled sardine cans with stones and used them as grenades?" I say.

He shakes his head. Lana can see he's on side so she goes for it, asking if they've heard of a hospital that treats soldiers for mental problems. The older one says he hasn't heard anything like that. But the younger, not so cautious one, thinks a bit and answers: "*Sí*, I know. Could be Esteli, maybe. Hey ask the fellows at Esteli. They should be able to help you."

The other one gives him a look to say shut up. But Lana is happy.

"*Gracias, muchacho*," she gives him one of her big, sexy smiles.

I don't feel so happy. Lana has no idea what the Contras can do to Sandinista sympathisers. She's never fought in a war. Her only enemy is her annoying boss.

Chapter Fourteen

Colin had been living in his flat for twenty years now. He'd got a loan for it and had very slowly been paying it off. The whole building reeked of leaking gas but it was home. Red brick, two up, two down. His apartment was on the ground floor, on the right through the glass-paned front door. Other people had pets here, cats and small dogs, but he preferred to live on his own.

He had his routine. Up every morning at six. A good brekky of eggs and bacon and white sliced toast. Plenty of butter. Had to keep those cholesterol levels up. Bit of vegemite on one piece. Not too thick. You don't want to die!

He liked a good pot of tea. Not those ranky tea bags they give you in cafés – well not at Shannon's, she had class and served tea leaf in pots. He liked it real hot and real strong, with two spoonfuls of sugar. That's why he needed to walk every day, to give the calories somewhere to go.

Before breakfast he did his weights and his push-ups. He'd learnt this routine a long time ago in the Big House where an iron bed made a good base for your legs, while you did your sit-ups, even with short pins like his.

He'd catch his reflection in the mildewed full-length bedroom mirror and look away. He wasn't the handsome devil he used to be in his youth. But for a 65-year-old who'd seen a fair bit of death and doom in his life, he didn't brush up too badly.

In front of the cracked bathroom mirror, he lathered up and shaved. Didn't miss a day. He hated that unshaven look that youngsters like Nick seemed to think was so attractive these days. The permanent three-day growth. They even went to the church and the reception without a shave. Make up your mind: a beard or clean-shaven. Not this in-between business. Well, not that he was too keen on the Ned Kelly look either. He wiped the last bit of soap off with a towel. "Watch out, Casanova," he joked to his reflection. "Ugly mongrel, actually."

He flushed the toilet again. Always getting blocked, probably those Spaniards in the flat upstairs putting in wet wipes and things that should never go in a toilet. He climbed into the bathtub to have a shower. Grimy marks around the edges. Better get the Ajax out next weekend, he thought. But not today. After his walk he was going to head to the State Library to do some more research.

Colin passed the bookshelf in the sitting room, full of history books about first contact between the colonialists and his mob. He had them all, but he especially loved the First Fleet Diarists like Captain Watkin Tench, and his masterpiece, *A Complete Account of the Settlement at Port Jackson*. Pity Tench became a bastard later and fought against the great warrior, Pemulwuy.

He was looking forward to looking up documents, turning over dusty books and tracing whatever information he could find. There wasn't any white professor who could lecture him on Australian history.

He wanted to know more about his mother's people and he'd gleaned most of it, from the white historians' perspective at least. But Shannon's belief that Lily might have worked for her family down the South Coast made him want to find out more about what had happened to the girls at Bomaderry and Cootamundra after they left the homes.

What a weird coincidence. She could have come to work at their farm after the children's home. But the dates didn't quite make sense because if Shannon was a child, Lily would have been a lot older and why call herself Ainslie. It must have been a fair while after she met his dad and had the kids. He still didn't know where she was born or where she came from, or what happened to her later. But if he could get hold of her records that showed her time in the home that would make a big difference.

A pile of unopened letters sat on the telephone table near the door. He didn't feel like opening them. He knew what was inside. Just more bills. He had opened one though which arrived a long time ago. A birthday card from Lowanna. "Happy birthday, grandpa," it said in her lopsided handwriting. Gee he missed her, lovely little thing she was. He wondered when he'd ever see her again. He'd put the card up on the bookshelf, next to a photo of his mum, keeping the envelope with her address just in case he ever had the courage to visit her and her mother.

Grabbing his corduroy jacket from the chair next to the table, he smiled and nodded at them both. As he opened the door to go out the neighbour's black and white cat skittled past him. He swore to himself, but hoped that meant good luck.

Colin was well known to the librarians. His bandy legs, his well-worn colourful shirts and mismatched pants, his whiff of Old Spice. A bit bent over as if he had something to hide. But they seemed to like his cheerfulness, and his silly jokes.

"You want more on Barangaroo?" a middle-aged librarian with pale blue eyes asked him when he arrived on this cold, windy Sunday.

He nodded and she gestured to a desk and told him to wait there while she found the documents. He'd get to his family's files and research on the Coota and Bomaderry girls after he first read the accounts of the first settlers of Barangaroo, the second wife of Bennelong, the well-known colonial figure, who was famous for journeying to England.

The librarian returned with a pile of documents and plonked them in front of him, as he took his glasses out of the top pocket of his jacket. He was always excited when he received new material to read, and colonial history was his favourite subject.

Although Bennelong was captured by the first governor, Arthur Phillip, the odd couple became friends but Barangaroo never liked the idea of this friendship. She loved to fish; she was good at it and could often be seen with her line bobbing over the side of her canoe. She was a member of the Cameraigal people, from the north shore of the harbour. She'd already had two children, from another man, but they'd died, apparently of smallpox. She was a toughie, she didn't want the British here and she didn't want Bennelong having anything to do with them. She was especially angry when Bennelong sailed for England. She was a fiery one. Colin was amused to see her described as a "scold and a vixen".

Barangaroo was upset about how the newcomers treated the land, the sea and also each other. She hated their greed – the way they fished out the harbour, leaving little for her people. She also hated their cruelty. When a convict was being flogged for stealing fishing tackle from one of her women friends, Barangaroo grabbed a stick to whack the soldier who was flogging the convict.

She wore a bone in her nose and got around with no clothes on. Tench though described her as feminine, soft and modest, even if the saucy woman did take off the petticoat they gave her to cover her nakedness. Bennelong asked the British soldiers to help and they combed and cut her hair. And she seemed to like it, Colin gleaned from what he read.

But in 1791 she was pregnant. By this time hundreds of her people had been decimated by smallpox. There were bodies floating all over the harbour, washing up onto the beaches. She may have been thinking of a way to protect the rest of her mob. She asked Phillip if she could have her baby at Government House, down by Circular Quay. She used to go there often for meals. This was partly because Bennelong had brought Phillip into their kinship group by calling him 'father, uncle'. He was known as Be-anga. So if born there, her child would have responsibility for that area, and power.

Another account says that Bennelong came to Phillip explaining that when Barangaroo's time came he would bring her to his house, so that she could deliver there. The symbolism was if the child was born under Be-anga's roof it would be under his protection as he was regarded as a king or godparent.

Phillip refused, believing she just wanted somewhere safe to have the baby and so suggested she go to the hospital. There's no way Barangaroo would go to a hospital, Colin thought. She must have seen it as a place of death. His heart sank further thinking what a terrible dilemma she must have faced.

Colin read on. She had her little girl, Dilboong, which means bellbird, nearby in the bush. Phillip saw her only a few hours after the baby was born, pottering about picking up sticks for her fire, while the new-born child lay snugly in a soft bark cradle nearby. The baby only lived for a few months. Barangaroo also died later that year. They were both buried in Government House's gardens.

Nobody knew why she had died. One of her family, Gooroobarooboolo, thought it was all a part of the evil influence of the white men. Barangaroo had felt great uneasiness as her husband became more familiar with them and took to the magic drink.

Colin felt choked up as he read, taking his glasses off and wiping his eyes with a hanky. He didn't want the librarian to see. Barangaroo was everything that had ever happened to Aboriginal women, all the sadness, all the fear, all the hopes dashed one after another. But there was more he wanted to know about: more recent history. His own. Years before he'd been in touch with Link-Up – the organisation that helped Stolen Generations people find their families – and they had helped him track down his files with the Welfare Department. It was here he learnt how his parents had tried to get him and his siblings out of the homes. But he didn't know the full story of his mum and dad; he wanted the gaps filled.

He packed up the files to take them back to the librarian. He wanted to ask for his parents' Welfare files but wasn't sure if they would keep them here. Walking up to the desk, he noticed the librarian who normally helped him had left. There was a younger girl there, all pale and pretty, and totally lacking in the sort of understanding he needed, he thought. What if his time in jail popped up or other personal information? His hands grew sweaty as he tried to get up the courage to ask her.

"You're interested in Watkin Tench right? He was a captain on the First Fleet; his diary has been published in paperback, they should have it upstairs," she said to Colin, who found her tone patronising.

You're stating the obvious and by the way shouldn't you still be in school, he thought but instead just smiled as he put the files back on the desk, said a brusque thank you and left. He'd get those files another day.

Coming out into the cool air he turned right and headed for Circular Quay. As gusts of wind blew he wandered past the Museum of Sydney, where Government House had once stood, and past the AMP building, thinking about Barangaroo resting under those tall buildings there. No mark, no grave, not even an ugly cross covered in plastic flowers, like people erect for those who have died in road accidents. Nothing. A forgotten victim of colonial history. Just like his mum.

He remembered the car accident he'd had many years before. He'd been driving late at night on the highway not that far from the boys' home, and he'd felt a rush of wind pass across him. The car went into a spin and hit the guard rails. He was taken by ambulance to the local hospital. He'd always wondered if Lily had died around there.

On his way home he decided to stop in at Shannon's for a cuppa and a chat. She might have found out more about Lily, although he wasn't sure how to respond to her information. He couldn't quite put two and two together. Shannon's family had Aboriginal maids? Well, lots of the Coota and Bomaderry girls did go off and work as housekeepers on farms. Treated abominably too. He'd never had the chance to ask his mother about any of this. Welfare stopped all that, didn't they?

He got out of the bus near the café but it was closed. "Strange," he thought, looking at his watch. "It's usually open until five on Sundays."

The sound of salsa music drifted down from the window above, Shannon's flat. He was about to climb the stairs and knock on her door but he heard voices, ones he recognised. Was that Rafael? That sneaky Latino. Why did he always get the feeling Raf wasn't totally honest with him, about many things? And now he'd wheedled his way into Shannon's bed, he guessed. What did she see in him? Well, of course he was exotic and not bad looking.

He tried to do his belt up a further notch but it was too tight and he returned it to its original setting, then turned around and headed home, pulling his jacket around him, and pushing his fists down into his pockets. Never mind, there was still time to get up to the pub for one last bet, he told himself although his heart was full of jealousy.

Chapter Fifteen

Pink feathers, writhing bodies and brown, sensuous skin. Drummers' arm muscles throbbing as they beat the rhythm harder and harder. Pushing through the party crowd of young, over-dressed and under-dressed people. Men in T-shirts and baseball caps – the under-dressed ones. Women – or over-aged girls – in their gold lamé frocks and giant white shoes, the heels so high that they tower over the bar as they order their frothy pink cocktails.

To get in the door of the newest bar on the block, Vesna had to pass a security guard marking his territory. He stood in front of what seemed to her to be the shortest red carpet in history. Was it short because of the size of the celebrities or the actual lack of them? There seemed to be more photographers than celebs anyway.

The guard reluctantly unpinned the Velcro barrier, and Vesna took a cigarette out of her bag and put it in her mouth, standing on tip toes to reach up to the towering figure as she gestured for him to light it. She thought she might be able to get some information out of him.

"Here, keep it," the beefy guard handed down a lighter with the name of the bar on it.

"So who owns this bar?" she asked him, trying to look nonchalant.

"Fucked if I know," he answered, looking disdainfully down at her.

"Somebody with money to throw around," she threw back at him. Knowing she had little chance of getting more than that from him, she moved inside.

"No smoking inside the club," a gaunt hostess holding an iPad piped in her high-pitched voice.

"I'm outside the club," Vesna retorted, throwing the butt on the ground.

The hostess took a few minutes to find her name on the guest list then checked it off, waving her inside.

"Hostess with the mostess – not," Vesna thought as the girl frowned at her. A couple in front of her hovered and she pushed past them to grab a champagne from the tray a waitress was carrying. She'd be waiting until Christmas if she didn't help herself. And what was the point of being here if she didn't get a free drink? Was that the notorious stand-over man, leaning on the bar? Great, there might be a shooting tonight, she thought. Even the Bada Bling had more class than this place.

Her friend, Sarah, the Features Editor, had given her the invite and asked her to write a few pars but what could she possibly write? "Another sleazy bar opened in Kings Cross tonight." Actually, that was all they really wanted these days, an acknowledgement of an opening in a town where there seemed to be a lot more bars closing, with all the toughened liquor laws and rules and regulations. A sign of the times. "A bar opened in Kings Cross tonight, despite the nanny state."

The drummers started up their relentless pounding, and she made her way to the bar, having finished the champagne in two gulps. At least the barman was good looking, she thought as she attempted to flirt with him. She asked for something stronger. "And put a bit of alcohol in it please," she yelled over the loud techno music. It must have been the same track they'd been playing for twenty years.

Good old Kings Cross. It kept trying to be trendy and reinventing itself but nothing really changed that much. They might think Brazilians in feathers and bikinis added class but even male pole dancers would be better than that.

Vesna squeezed past the stiletto-clad PR girls with their musty perfume smell towards the dance floor. She needed to get the lay of the land. And then she saw him, looking uncomfortable in a suit and tie. What the hell was Tom doing here?

Tom swayed from side to side trying to move in time to the music but missing the beat by half a second. Why had he let his work colleague talk him into coming here? He'd only wanted a quick drink on the way home – the last thing he needed was another night of heavy boozing and drunken driving. He only had two points left on his licence, so he couldn't afford to be pulled over by the cops. Especially being a lawyer. Not a good look.

"Oh come on, just one drink," his mate had said, displaying a very fleshy-looking invite to this bar opening in the Cross.

"What, do you think I'll pick up a few new clients there?" Tom asked.

"Yeah sure to be full of queue jumpers," his mate made his idea of a joke and Tom winced.

Just one drink. It'd been a long day. Immigration court and pleading clients. An older woman dragging a Balinese gigolo here for some kind of doomed marriage. Lying Lebanese. Sleazy Cambodians. Sneaky Chinese. So he'd agreed, left his car in the office car park and found himself at a bar full of celebrity illegal immigrants, or that was the way he saw it. He felt a bit guilty about his mum looking after Maxie. She loved the little boy but she was getting older and it was tiring for her. And he'd been a bit naughty lately; Irina had told him Maxie had yelled "no" at her the other night when she told him it was time for bed. Pity his dad didn't have the energy to do much to help. He spent most of his time sitting in his arm chair watching SBS or listening to the radio. He adored Maxie but he was too much to handle sometimes, especially when he tried to climb up on his lap. Tom suspected the old man had dementia but his mother wouldn't let him take him for check-ups. Something had to be done soon, he'd make an appointment next week. Bugger mum.

He saw Vesna mincing across the dance floor towards him. Oh my God, the one night stand, who just happened to turn out to be a journo. He'd hoped that when he hadn't returned her calls she'd got the hint. Her grin was plastered all over her face and red lipstick marks smothered the rim of her champagne glass. Her black shoulder-length hair definitely needed some styling and the gold loopy earrings betrayed her ethnic background.

"Bloody Serbs," he thought as his eyes went lower towards her black T-shirt and tight jeans. Not a bad set. Stop it, Tom. He tried to look away, wishing he could hide; he felt like a frightened rabbit but it was too late.

"Hey Tom, back at your old stamping ground? Whatcha doing here?"

"Oh hi. Vesna, isn't it?" Tom pretended not to remember their night together. "I'm with a friend," he looked towards the bar, hoping he'd be rescued. He felt as if the nymph, Vila, from Slavic mythology was coming down from the sky to trap him. "And you? Are you covering this for a story?"

She shook her head. "Nah, just got an invite and felt like a drink." She didn't want to admit she wrote such lightweight dross. "Hey, my Muslim story went out. Got a good run too."

"Oh right," he nodded.

"Didn't you get my messages?" She didn't wait for an answer. "I wanted to say thanks for the contact. I'm still wanting to do a wider story, about how illegal immigrants manage to work the system and stay underground here. Do you think you could line up an interview with one of your clients for me? Off the record of course."

Tom looked doubtful. "That's a bit tricky, Vesna. What would they get out of it?"

"Publicity for their cause." Her yellow teeth showed when she grinned.

Tom grimaced, turning to his friend who handed him a huge flowery cocktail. He gave him a look as if to say, "Get me out of here," his eyes moving in Vesna's direction.

"Who's she?" his friend asked.

Tom just shook his head, keeping his back to Vesna, as he toasted his friend, then allowing himself to be led to some teeny boppers in short, tight skirts and wide smiles.

"Fuck you, Kraljevic Marko," Vesna muttered under her breath, as she was left stranded on the dance floor.

Tom gulped down his cocktail, grabbing another one from a passing waitress.

Vesna had to get out of the nightclub, her humiliation was beginning to show on her face. She again squeezed past the bottom-of-the list celebs, the ones she unfortunately knew she would have to remember later for her story and almost threw her glass down on a table. At the door she pushed past the gaunt hostess still holding her iPad over her size twenty-eight chest. As she scurried past the security guard, he called out: "Did you get your story?"

Vesna didn't normally cry. She'd seen too much tragedy in her life to let small things bother her. Maybe it was the alcohol but for some reason the tears were flooding down her face. Tears of embarrassment, of anger, of just damn sadness. At being alone, at being a fool, at not knowing what the hell she was going to do with herself.

She staggered down the road, already filling with drunks and kids on ecstasy, losers on ice, yelling and screaming, in their own little worlds. Their voices were so loud they blocked out the music screeching from open doors of even more gangster bars. It had been raining and water flooded the gutters, sweeping along cigarette butts, plastic cups, odd bits of newspaper. She stopped and stared at the deluge, wondering how she was going to get to the train station in this foul weather. She moved back to a damp, brick wall, huddled under the canopy and pulled out her ciggies, finding the lighter among the lint, used tissues and escaped tablets at the bottom of her bag. As she smoked, she tapped out a three-par story on her phone on the bar opening and sent it through to the subs' desk. Even in the midst of depression, she was still a professional, she thought. Well, at least for Sarah's sake.

"Smoking's bad for you, you know," the voice made her swing around. Tom must have followed her.

"What do you want?" she wiped her snotty nose with her sleeve.

"I'm not normally so rude; they're people I work with." His words were slurred.

"Other lawyers? That'd be right."

"Yeah," he took the lighter from her and turned it around, inspecting the writing on it. "Jon's Bar, well at least you gained something from tonight."

Vesna laughed her deep, guttural laugh, right from the back of her throat. "I didn't steal it. The security guy gave it to me." The lines around her eyes creased her swarthy skin, still wet from her tears.

Tom took the hand that wasn't holding the cigarette, trying to avoid the smoke, wrapping his long fingers in it. "C'mon, let's go for a coffee."

It was a night of surprises, that's all Vesna could think. Of co-incidences, and strange meetings. But maybe it wasn't lost yet. Maybe she could get the information she wanted – and even more. Whoa, she wasn't expecting that. Serbs. They were so bloody unpredictable. He'd obviously been enjoying the free cocktails and was horny; she didn't mind that one little bit.

They found a small café, with oily red and white plastic checked tablecloths covering the tables. It had missed the Hipster phase. Vesna asked for a hot chocolate before finding a table, surveying the scene of toothless types that looked like they'd lived at the Cross since the days of the witch, Rosaleen Norton. It was a bit like a dentists' convention, only they were the problem patients waiting to go on stage to display their worn-out dentures to the fraternity. Why did she always end up in seedy places late at night? At least this time she wasn't alone.

Tom came back from the counter with two hot chocolates, soggy marshmallows floating on the top.

"Can't drink coffee at night," she said almost burning her tongue on the drink as she took a sip. "Insomniac from way back."

"Ah but we Serbs don't need to sleep. We have too much honour for that." He laughed as he leant over and wiped a smear of chocolate from her forehead. She pulled a grotty tissue from her bag and tried to wipe it off. He lent forward again and kissed her as she wrapped her knuckles around the tissue.

He was a good kisser. Her memories of Serb boys were of the ones she grew up with at Bankstown – jeans up around their middles, neatly ironed by their mothers, mullet hair-cuts, driving purple Valiants with plastic skeletons dangling from the rear-vision mirrors. Their idea of foreplay was to bend you over the front bucket seat; at least in those days there was no console to get stuck in. But Tom had a bit of style – maybe his wife had taught him. And she didn't want to stop. She kissed him back as softly and sensually as she could, hoping her nose wouldn't run again.

"'ey you two look like something out of a toothpaste ad," a bag lady sitting opposite them croaked, forcing them to emerge from their romantic haze.

Tom laughed. "I'm Colgate, she's Palmolive."

"Me Olive Oil, You Popeye." Vesna took a large sip of her hot chocolate.

"Come on, let's go to my place," he said, putting his arm around her to shield her from the rain as they walked out onto the road to hail a cab.

"Only if you promise to help me with my story," she shot back.

He laughed again, opening the door for her and helping her inside. "Here is Sarac, ready to take us home."

"Ah your trusty steed, Kraljevic Marko. I think I prefer Uber," Vesna pulled Tom in beside her.

Chapter Sixteen

There wasn't any choice but to go back to work after the accident. Neither Colin nor Rafael wanted to but they had no desire to front up at Centrelink neither. Life had to go on and the building had to be completed, even if it meant pushing past a raggedy band of demonstrators out the front, holding placards with: "The boss needs you, you don't need him" and "An injury to one is an injury to all."

It was still cold and windy and Colin dragged his orange fluoro jacket's collar up to protect his wrinkled neck. He pulled his backpack strap up onto his shoulder, as he pressed his hand into that of a striking Maori brother.

"You still working here, Colin?"

"Yeah mate, but there's an inquiry. They'll find the answers."

"Don't count on it, mate."

"How's Tony's wife?" Colin was genuine in wanting to know.

"How would you be if the capitalist pigs killed your husband? I would've thought you'd be on our side, bro."

"I'm with you, brother, but we're not officially on strike." Colin walked on, hoping his guilty feelings wouldn't show on his face.

Rafael saw the picket line from a distance and thought about turning round and going home. But he needed the money. It was OK for these people with big families and hard-working wives to not work, but he had nobody, and nothing he could fall back on. He was also in a tricky situation in more ways than one. For the time being it was better to zip his lips and not get involved. He walked past the Mozzies, his head down, but he couldn't escape them.

"Raf, I thought you were a good Commie. What you doing back at work?"

He ignored the comment, and the next that was yelled at his

back: "We never thought you'd be a scab, Raf."

"Or a murderer," another whispered to his mate.

The words stung but he had to keep going, masking his emotions, trying to keep a straight face as he made a beeline for Colin.

"Did you have a good weekend?" his mate asked and Rafael nodded, his head still down, trying to keep the grit out of his eyes.

"Yes, I went to see Shannon on Saturday night." Rafael knew he couldn't pretend to Colin about his affair. He'd see right through him.

"Ahh, so that's where you were? So how was it?"

"Don't be disgusting," he grimaced at the thought of discussing sex. "She's a beautiful woman."

"I know that. You're a lucky man."

"We went to the beach for breakfast too."

"Ah, came for the wedding, stayed for the honeymoon?"

"Strange you should say that," he looked puzzled at the joke. "She was wearing her wedding dress when I arrived."

"Really? Be careful, Raf. She's been through a lot." Colin's protectiveness was impossible to hide, as he rummaged in his backpack for his milk and sugar.

"She lost her baby," Rafael nodded

"That was careless of her." Colin took his thermos out of his backpack and poured himself a coffee to keep him going until morning tea time at Shannon's.

"Don't joke."

"Hey Raf, don't teach me how to suck eggs. I was there when it happened. I called the ambulance."

"She showed me the photo of the baby," Rafael covered up that Shannon hadn't mentioned Colin's role in helping her. "And her ex-husband taking her son now too."

"Yeah, I know. What a bastard. People are still taking children from their mothers. I thought they only did that to Blackfellas."

"I don't know about that. But I don't like that she wants to get a journalist to write about the accident, about the building company here. I don't want people sniffing around. Bad enough these bloody Mozzies hanging around with cardboard signs. Even I write English better than them."

"What are you so worried about? You don't still feel it was your fault do you? Tony was a great bloke but he was careless and you know it, Raf."

Rafael shook his head, he didn't want to talk about it. He wanted the memories to go away.

"You know I feel guilty about a lot of things too, Raf. But come on, there's a question I've been meaning to ask you for ages."

"Yeah, what's that?" Raf took out his tool belt.

"Do you play pool?"

"I used to." He nodded as he did up his belt, shifting it onto his hips, but looking way past the Mozzie brothers.

Esteli, Nicaragua
March, 1986

It's a dark room full of old pool tables, the material ripped and balls missing. You improvised if there was no black ball. Red meant black. The Sandinista colours.

Boys are hanging around leaning on the tables, trying to look tough as we wander in. Lana is the only woman there but that doesn't stop her picking up a pool cue and handing it to me. "Do you play Raf?"

I stare at her as if she's an idiot. Of course I play. What else was there to do in the days before the revolution but to play pool? No jobs that's for sure.

Lana is surprisingly good and the teenagers ogle her backside as she leans over the table, carefully sizing up the ball and then giving it a gentle but effective hit. But she's no match for me. I've been playing this game since I was a dirty little kid, let into my barrio bar by my prostitute aunties. I pocket the ball. She laughs but you can see she's annoyed. Lana is used to winning.

When she doesn't get her way she goes back to her journalistic mission – to find out where the damned mystery hospital is. "Hey *chico*, have you heard about a hospital for soldiers up this way?" She asks one of the boys, a particularly skinny one who has been watching her ever since we walked in.

"*Yo, no. No sé.* Maybe he knows," he points with his lips to an older boy with wild hair.

They all snigger as Lana goes up to the kid and grabs him by the arm. "I'll buy you a beer if you tell me where the hospital is," she says.

The boy is not afraid of her. He's one of those cheeky types who thinks all women love him. "*Señorita,* I need more than a beer for that information," he responds as he hitches up his perfectly ironed, waisted jeans.

Lana laughs. "Don't ask for more than you can cope with." She turns to walk away.

"Aye *señorita*, or is it *señora*? I might be able to help you," he gives in.

Lana swings around. "Yeah?"

"I've heard of ambulance trucks heading up into the mountains, up near the border with Honduras, near Ocotal I think. They are full of soldiers but empty when they come back."

Lana's eyes light up. This is what she's looking for. I'm silently groaning but I'm not going to get involved. This kid could end up in a lot of trouble but Lana doesn't care. The story is number one.

"Do you know what village they are going to?" she asks.

"I'm not sure but I know it's near Ocotal, Santa Maria maybe. My friend told me he sees them often. Go to Ocotal and somebody will know. Now how about a kiss?"

Lana laughs, then grabs him round the waist, pushes him back and plants a smacker on his lips. That kid will never get over it.

The pool table at the pub round the corner from the building site had seen better days. You still put your coins on the table, to show it was your turn next but the green felt was faded to almost white. Rafael and Colin sat on stools at the bar, both feeling slightly uncomfortable nursing their Cokes. They hadn't gone home to get changed and their overalls were covered in dust. But nobody seemed to care. It was a tradies' pub anyway.

The pair playing before them nodded and gave them the cues and they wandered over to the table. Colin carefully placed the balls in the triangle and made the first shot. Big balls for him. They played silently, both equally good and finished the game, Rafael just ahead.

Back at their table Colin tried to coax some information out of his mate. He knew there'd been a revolution in Nicaragua in the late 1970s; he'd heard of the Sandinistas. But he didn't know much more than that. He'd get a book next time he went to the library, read up on it. "Where'd you learn to play pool?" he asked Rafael, who just shrugged.

"In the *barrio*, just a bar near my home. And you?"

"I'm a late starter. I didn't get to play until I left the home."

"How old were you then?"

"About fifteen. They got me a job on the railways. Stayed there for a few years. There was a pub opposite the depot, full of pool tables. We'd end up there after work."

"Staggered home after I'm sure?"

Colin smiled, yeah he remembered those nights full of booze and bravado, thinking he was King of the World. He was out of that bloody home, he was freeeeee at last. But his temper kept him pinned down to the earth. A few drinks and anybody who muttered anything to him under their breath deserved a wild swing. He didn't even register what they said to him. He only heard words like boong, and black bastard. Yeah, he would stagger home to the little boarding house down near Central and sleep it off. Up at five am for the next day's toil. Hardly felt a thing, he was young and what was a bit of a headache to a skinny, energetic kid? They knew he was underage at the pub but they didn't care back in those days if you paid for your beer. They'd only kick you out if you got into a fight.

"The girls were good sorts too, back then," Colin sipped his drink.

"Yeah working girls like I knew back in my bar too, I guess?"

"Probably. I never asked them. They were nice to me. They knew I was lonely but they never took advantage of me. I was a virgin till I got married, I was that damned innocent."

Rafael almost choked on his soft drink. "Aye Colin, I didn't need to know that! But hey I never knew you'd been married. What happened to your wife?"

"She went stir crazy and left."

Rafael laughed. "Any children?"

Colin nodded. Yeah he'd had a daughter, a daughter who never spoke to him. And Lowanna, his granddaughter. One day he'd get to see her again. "What about you, Raf? You ever been married?"

Rafael snorted. "Huh. Nobody would have me. Girls don't like me."

"Well except for Shannon. What does she see in an ugly mutt like you?"

"I have no idea, Colin. No idea at all."

They chuckled as Colin went over to put more coins on the table for another game. As he executed the first break, they talked about the building site, and Rafael wondered whether the Mozzies would force it to be shut down.

"Nah," Colin hit a ball, narrowly missing the pocket. "They'll be back at work by the end of the week, I'm sure of that. It's just their way of grieving."

"That's good," Rafael lifted his cue. "Don't need government people. They might ask me if I've paid my tax."

They both laughed.

"Anyway, I've done enough fighting for causes and pushing through the red tape." Rafael studied the balls on the table.

Jinotega, Nicaragua
March, 1986

We're in a government office in Jinotega applying for a permit to get into the war zones further north, up near Ocotal.

The room is dotted with photos or illustrations of our heroes of the revolution – Carlos Fonseca, Sandino in his hat of course and others. White asbestos walls covered in grainy black and white photos.

Lana is looking through a booklet on the table. It's one of many in small neat piles, all revolutionary material and information on *campesinos'* rights. "Look Raf, it's Carlitos," she says, pointing to a photo of Carlos Fonseca's son. "Oh my God, he's the spitting image of his father. He's even wearing little kid fatigues." She starts laughing so loudly everybody in the room turns round to stare at her.

"Shoosh," I nudge her, embarrassed.

But then I look at the photo and it IS funny. This little Carlitos is even wearing the same horn-rimmed glasses as his serious father. And I start giggling too. We're both laughing so much the tears are streaming down our faces. And we're gulping, almost sick.

People are looking angry now and uncomfortable and wondering what all the fuss is about. Are we making fun of their revolution? No, of course not.

My name is called out and I have to sober up. I wipe my eyes and put on my best Carlos Fonseca expression and walk up to the counter. I need that all-important piece of paper or we ain't going nowhere, as they say in the *Gringo* movies.

It had been a long day but when they left the pub Rafael decided not to go straight home. There was somebody he couldn't wait until the weekend to see. And not just for the conversation; he'd been feeling in the mood ever since Sunday.

When Colin turned the corner to walk to his place, Rafael waited for a while before heading back towards the café. He hoped Shannon would be home; he just wished she wouldn't ask him questions he couldn't answer.

Chapter Seventeen

It was Rafael's talk of taking her dancing that had finally got Shannon going again. She did want to dance. But not salsa this time. The music on the CD player in her lounge room stopped and she went to change it. She had some Irish music she never played, somewhere in her collection. She thought of those Irish dance classes her mum sent her to as a kid. She never really wanted to be an Irish dancer. It all seemed a bit ridiculous. She really had wanted to do jazz ballet, bugger her Irish roots. But tonight, Irish music was what she wanted to hear. She put on a Chieftains CD of Celtic folk songs and rocked to its rhythm, moving one foot after another from side to side. That fiddle-playing and plaintive ballads had always moved her, and the sound of Gaelic was so romantic even if you didn't understand a word of it. She swayed, moving around in a circle, closing her eyes and letting the music take over.

She hadn't danced like this for so long. Free and on her own. If Tom had been home he would have laughed at her. Everybody knew Australians had no culture. Not like the Serbs, who were the most cultured and literate people in the world. OK, he might admit the Brits had Shakespeare but that was about all. There was no better literature than the great Russian novelists, closely followed by the Serb poets. Didn't matter that nobody outside Belgrade had ever heard of them.

Who cared anymore? She just wanted to move with the music, and be herself again. It was so loud that she didn't hear the knock on the door. And then a much louder knock. She went to answer it. God, is it Rafael again? Her spirits rose for a moment but sunk when through the peep hole she could see Amany, her kohl-circled eyes peering at the door.

"Oh damn," Shannon thought she should just ignore her, but

knew she couldn't – the music was a bit of a giveaway. "Just getting back to my roots you know," she said as she opened the door.

Amany sat down at the table, making herself at home, much to Shannon's displeasure.

"You don't have something to drink do you?" she asked.

"Wine?" Shannon opened the fridge door but Amany shook her head and Shannon felt slightly guilty for offering, knowing full well Amany didn't drink.

Shannon poured herself a glass and some orange juice for Amany, hoping the glass was clean enough. "So to what do I owe this pleasure?"

"I was in the area for the Inter-Faith program, you know at the Jewish school near here. We take turns to cook."

"Oh, right. Again? It's rather late."

"Yes, it's every month. We cook the night before. And you did say it's better to visit you here than the café. How is it going anyway? Good business, I guess with all these people in the eastern suburbs and their love for coffee?"

"It's all right, I guess." She sipped her chardonnay.

"Too much hard work?" Amany picked up the glass of juice.

Shannon wondered why Amany was here. She'd always appeared a bit too good to be true. "It's long hours, yes."

"Good customers?"

"I could do with a few more. Why all the questions?"

Amany's hands shook as she put her glass on the table. Her thin frame shifted in the seat. "I need somebody to talk to sometimes too."

Shannon's eyes widened. "Oh God Amany. What's wrong?"

"We've been through similar experiences. We are women, we know how it is to suffer." She took a tissue out of her handbag and blew her nose.

Shannon felt she should touch her hand, or give her a hug but she just couldn't. She was curious but she didn't want to get involved. She didn't feel they had enough in common – religion was not Shannon's strong point.

"God tests us in different ways," Amany spoke to break the silence.

"It's been a hard couple of weeks," Shannon was apologetic. "There was a death on the building site opposite my café."

"Oh yes, I heard that on the radio. I didn't know it was that close to you."

Shannon nodded. "Yes it was terrible. A Maori guy. Tony. One of my customers. Because of the bad safety standards."

"Do you know that for sure?" Amany put the tissue away.

"Well two of my customers think so. There's so much cutting of corners. It's because of the company's greed that Tony died. They don't care about safety."

"Shouldn't the union be doing something about that?"

"I don't think the union cares. They're in with the bosses. It's all so unfair. The poorer people are always at the bottom."

"I see the same exploitation here of our people," she shrugged. "So many don't speak English well. They have to get whatever work they can."

"I've been thinking we should go to the media with it," Shannon stood up to get a glass of water. She was tired and there was another long day of work ahead of her. She offered another orange juice to Amany but she shook her head.

"Do you know any journalists?"

"Only ones down south where our farm is."

"I know a Sydney journalist. She interviewed me the other day."

"What about?"

"The stupid men harassing me and our women for wearing the veil."

"Did that happen to you? That's terrible."

"Yes, my daughter was very upset when I told her. But since then on the train some people have come and sat next to me – you know the ride-with-me movement or something like that."

Shannon laughed. "Pity if you just want to be on your own."

Amany smiled. "I know, I have thought that, when they talk too much. But it's very kind of them." She rummaged in her bag for a pen and paper, and copied Vesna's number, writing "journalist for safety story" next to it.

"Here, this is the journalist. Her name is Vesna. She works for a news agency. I have the feeling she's ultimately interested in justice even if she prefers to show her hard exterior, if you know what I mean. I'm sure she'll be interested if there's corruption involved, she seems to go for the difficult stories."

She handed Shannon the piece of paper.

"Fantastic, I will call her." She stuck it on the fridge with a magnet.

Another knock on the door interrupted them and Amany stood up. "That might be Tom. We'll speak next time, Shannon."

Shannon opened the door as Rafael bounded in, still in his work clothes. Amany's surprise showed on her face. She grasped Shannon's hand with both of hers but Shannon pulled back. She didn't want to be kissed by this woman, no matter how nice she was.

But she did want to be kissed by Rafael and he was already taking off her clothes as soon as the door closed.

Shannon's pink bedroom was as pretty as a picture except that the bed wasn't made. But at least she'd changed the white sheets a few days before – cosy doona, lots of pillows and cushions and her teddy bear lying in the middle of it all. She'd had that teddy bear since she was a kid – once she'd lost it when she went to visit her mother's friends in the city and it had to be posted all the way home to her. She cried and cried until it was returned safely to her bed.

She hoped that the sex with Rafael this time would be better. She'd had a few drinks, which always helped loosen her up. And his hand on her arm had sent shivers through her. He was pretty gorgeous, she thought. Handsome. That olive skin. She really would have to ask him if he had Indian heritage.

He touched her face and whispered: "*Querida* Shannon, let's go to the bed."

She didn't need to be asked twice. She'd thought about him all day, and was very happy when he'd turned up unannounced. But he seemed a bit out of it, she thought. He didn't ask her why Amany had been there; he didn't want to talk, except to say he'd been playing pool with Colin. For once, she, too, just wanted to enjoy the moment.

She pulled down the covers and moved Bear over to her bedside table. He pulled her jumper off and threw it on the floor – she was wearing mismatched undies and bra – why hadn't she taken more notice when she got dressed? Why such raggedy old underwear?

But he didn't seem to care. "You have beautiful breasts," he said as he kissed one and then the other. "You are so beautiful."

Shannon's hair fell all over her face as she rose up to kiss him. "You are too." I guess it's like riding a bicycle, she thought and smiled, as he sucked her nipple.

"What are you laughing about?" he asked her. "Does it tingle?"

"No, nothing. You mean tickle. Don't stop. Please don't stop."

The moon light from outside the bedroom window crossed his face – the shadow of the shutters left lines along it, he looked so serious and determined in what he was doing. He seemed to want to do it right, as if he wanted to satisfy her right down to the last drop of sweat.

He kissed every part of her body until she could take no more. They lay back on the pillows and Shannon traced her fingers along the scars on his chest but he pushed her hand away. "Why was the social worker here?" he asked, turning towards her.

"I'm not sure," Shannon answered. "I think she wanted some help herself but I didn't know what to do. I guess everybody has problems."

"You can't help everybody, Shannon."

Ocotal, Nicaragua
March, 1986

We're in a pensión up in the mountains near Ocotal and sitting on single beds opposite each other. Lana's crossing and uncrossing her legs. She's restless I think because she's onto a story but it hasn't quite jelled.

"They used to call it Shell Shock during World War One. But nobody wanted to admit that their soldiers were going mad from war. That would be weakness, cowardice. Isn't that what happened to you, Rafael?"

She just has to bring me into it. "Me? I'm fine." The ash tray is full of butts as I add another one to it, and light up a new smoke. So much for giving up.

"I don't think you're fine. You act like you don't care when you film horrific things. The wedding party."

"You know I can't take sides. That would be the end. I've had to film children's fingers being cut off. Am I meant to stop filming and stop them doing it?"

"Yes, yes, I think you are. There has to be a line drawn somewhere."

This surprises me, from Lana who is always after the story. "When you're dead nobody cares," I say.

"I thought I was the cynic. We'll get into that hospital somehow.

We need that footage. Nobody else has got this story."

"Yes, but I'm sure the Sandinistas are only trying to help our soldiers."

She ignores my comment and scratches herself, something has bitten her. "God, this place is a dump. They could change the sheets now and again. And couldn't you have asked for separate bedrooms or even an *en suite*?"

She is the one who used to want to sleep with me. And an *en suite*? The only bathroom here is a bit of dirty plastic curtain strung up in front of a shower.

Rafael sat on the edge of the bed and pulled his jeans on, but Shannon pushed him back down to stop him getting dressed. "More, more."

"You're so spoilt."

"Oh yeah, really. And you're not?" It was cold and she pulled the doona up over them.

"No, I'm not." Rafael laughed.

"Didn't your parents spoil you?"

"With what? They couldn't even pay for my education. I wanted to be a doctor, like Che."

"Who is Che?"

He looked at her like she was mad. "What did you learn at school?"

"Not much. I went to a country school. And you?"

"A terrible Catholic one, but we did know about Che Guevara, the great hero of the Cuban revolution. Anyway, it's a bit hard to study when your windows are being pelted with rocks."

"Rocks?"

"And gun shots can be distressing in the middle of a class."

"Whose side were your parents on?"

"Let's just say we didn't have a family Christmas during the revolution." As Rafael spoke he pushed Shannon back onto the pillows. "My mother went one way, my father the other. He left the country to find work or more women or alcohol, I don't know what. My mother stayed. She had five children, what else could she do? Every Friday night she made bean soup with poached eggs. A little bit of chilli. Ah bean soups and cigarettes, I lived on that." Rafael kissed her neck and chest, slowly moving down her body.

"Did Lana teach you to dance? I can't wait for Saturday night."

Shannon sat up and put her arms around his waist. "I love your washboard stomach. And yet you can still eat anything. Men who worry about their diet are very unsexy."

"What about women? They are always worrying about their diet. But you are very sexy, *amor*." As he talked his hands found every little crevice and crease, even where her skin sagged and her hip bones jutted out.

"Oh yeah sure." She worried now about her hairy legs, and wished she'd shaved them.

But nothing stopped him putting his lips to the downy hair on her legs, her feet, her toes. "There is nothing wrong with your body, Shannon, and don't let anybody ever say there is."

"It's OK, you can stop talking now." She lay back again on the pillows while Rafael gave her what she had been missing for a very long time.

Managua
Late February, 1986

I'm in my room at the back of our shack. I have an iron bed and a small table and chair. I lie on the bed and take a long draw of my cigarette, flicking ash on the floor. I'll clean up the carpet of cigarette butts and ash later. One of my nephews, Luis, wanders into the room.

"*Hola*," I smile at him. His big, brown eyes widen as he sucks on a mango seed. He must have eaten every mango in that damn tree. His face is covered in messy orange goo and he reaches out his arms, wanting me to pull him up onto the bed.

I know I will be covered in mango juice too and my mama will berate me for messing up my sheets but I feel sorry for this little one. He's three but still hardly says a word. My sister just leaves him with my mother and goes out to find men, every day. She doesn't give a damn about him. As if my mum doesn't have enough kids to look after. I drag him up onto the bed and he sits between my legs, chewing away on that mango seed. I stroke his thick, black hair. "Ah, *hombresito*, what is going to happen to you? Will you join the army when you grow up? Will our country still be at war? What future is there for you?"

He just silently sucks away until there's not a drop of juice left. He turns round, hands me the seed and climbs down from the bed.

Out the door he goes looking for yet another mango.

I light another cigarette and lean back on my pillows, thinking about Lana. She insisted, even though I told her about the risk. She wasn't going to keep my baby. I throw the mango seed across the room.

If he still smoked, this would have been the moment Rafael lit up a post-coitus cigarette. But much as Shannon would have loved him to do that, there was no way he could. He would never smoke again, not after what he did. Shannon will never understand, he thought. She is charmingly naïve. And better that she doesn't know my history, my life too closely.

But much as he tried to reason with himself, and answer her silly questions about his family with the most basic of information, he could feel himself being drawn more and more in. Even when she asked if he was Indian, it didn't bother him. Of course, he was. Everybody in Nicaragua was a mix of Spanish and what Australians so annoyingly call Indigenous. Indian or whatever. It's just some didn't admit it. And the whiter ones, like everywhere in the world, pretended they were pure.

He had to laugh when she asked him about macho Latin men. "You don't seem that way at all," she said.

"You know, my first commander was a woman, so I overcame that matter."

"You really were a revolutionary then?"

Rafael knew he had said too much, he was tired of answering her questions about him. He needed to change the topic. He held Shannon tightly around her tiny waist and kissed the back of her neck, as lying on her side, she curved her body into his. "Tell me what's happening with Maxie," he said.

"Tom won't let me keep him overnight or hardly see him, it's killing me," she stared at the wall.

"I said I could talk to him."

Shannon shrugged. "You're so gorgeous," she turned to kiss him. "But I don't think Tom will listen to you."

"I can try." He returned her kiss. "Why don't we take him on a picnic one day?"

"OK, that would be lovely," she said. "There's one more thing you haven't done yet for me."

"What's that?"

"Make me a cup of tea."

In the kitchen Rafael sang a song from home as he filled the pot and boiled the water.

He opened the fridge, looking for the milk. But then he noticed something on the fridge door. "Shannon! Come here," he yelled.

When she came, he pointed to the piece of paper with Vesna's details on it. "What the hell is this?"

"She's a journalist Amany recommended, you know the social worker from the hospital. To write something about Tony's death."

"No, Shannon," Rafael said. "Just leave it alone."

"It's not just about you, Rafael," Shannon's anger rose. "Tony was one of my customers too. Somebody should take responsibility."

Outside the window a helicopter hovered. The sound was deafening. A fisherman must have slipped off the rocks. Rafael dropped the milk, which splashed all over the linoleum floor.

"What are you doing?" Shannon jumped away from the puddle.

"They're coming for me." He grabbed his jacket, ignoring Shannon's calls to stop, as he banged the front door shut and ran down the stairs.

Nicaragua
May, 1978

Gold and silver. When the Spanish conquistadors first saw the Tago Volcano they thought the lava was molten gold. No riches, not there. Only a pact with the devil. Even those greedy Spaniards would have turned back at this sight.

And for a reason I don't understand the helicopter is turning around. I'm the only prisoner left but fate has saved me. I think the pilot has been called back but I can't hear over the din of the engines.

The *guardia* smiles roughly at me. "*Suerte!* Not your turn today. Back to the prison for more fun, *hombre.*"

It's not my turn today to be thrown into the volcano, into the roaring lava. I can't believe I'm still alive. We fly low over the earthquake-ruined city. I'm taken in a jeep through the sleepy, siesta neighbourhoods, my arms shackled, my eyes covered, but of course I know the way. I'm dragged back to my cell, the stinking, sticky, graffiti-covered one I never thought I'd see again. Covered in black and red etchings – somehow sympathetic guards had found those paints for us. Who knew where you could find an insider? Even at a filthy prison, full of political prisoners. We'd left our mark on the damp, thick walls – Sandino in his trademark hat, the initials of our movement, the words: a free fatherland or death. *Patria libre o morir.* For my *compañeros* it's *muerte.* For me, for some unspoken reason, it's *libre.* Or at least *la vida.*

Why me? I never even said my Hail Marys. Maybe, I wonder to myself as the cell door closes hard in its metal frame, it's because I never confessed.

Chapter Eighteen

Vesna's mobile rang as she sat at her desk in the newsroom. It said "Blocked" but what kind of journalist wouldn't answer a call just because they didn't know who was calling, unless it was the Tax Department?

It was a young woman's voice – Aussie accent, but not from around where she grew up. She could pick that up immediately. "Who's this?"

"My name's Shannon Foran, I own Shannon's Café at Tamarama."

"Right. And …"

"Well, I was given your name by Amany Abdoul, a social worker at Prince George Hospital. She recommended you because I have a story. But it needs somebody who's prepared to dig a bit."

Amany recommended her? She was surprised but pleased.

"OK, sure. When can we meet?"

"Tomorrow after I close around five. Would that work?"

Vesna agreed and hung up. She noticed there were now about twelve stories in the queue, and could feel her fellow sub-editors' infuriation with her, as she jumped into one. Oh no, another one from the entertainment desk about somebody from *Married at First Sight* being seen at an event with somebody from a soapie. You call this news? She was about to drop the story back into the computer basket but Gary had already noticed.

"Oh Princess Vesna has finally decided to do some work, but she's still picky," he said. "I thought that story was right up your alley – aren't you going for the job as the new entertainment writer?"

Vesna ignored him. He was referring to her longer story about the opening of the Kings Cross bar in which she'd attempted to weave in as much colour as possible. Filed the following morning after a very memorable night of about three hours' sleep. Always a professional.

Tom and Vesna. She was beginning to like the ring of that. They made a good team, even if he was more posh than her. Once he let his guard down he turned out to have a great sense of humour. They cackled in bed about the weirdos and try-hards at the bar, the hostess with the mostess, and even the security guard.

"He called out after me asking if I got my story," Vesna told him, the sheets wrapped round her.

"Investigative journalist of the month," Tom grinned.

"I was really hoping there'd be a shooting there, then at least I'd have had a decent story."

"Oh police reporter too. Kings Cross's Seedy Underbelly! By Vesna Bojic."

"Well, it's better than Kim Kardashian's Bum."

"I prefer yours," he grabbed her backside and slapped it as she howled.

She turned him over and climbed on top of him. He was totally ready for her, as they continued their marathon session well into the early hours of the morning.

Shannon had turned the coffee machine off and was finishing cleaning up as Vesna arrived. "Sorry I can't offer you a coffee," she said.

"No worries. Is there a pub around here?"

"Yeah there's the grotty one down the road or the trendy bars. Which do you prefer?"

The grotty one used to be a workers' pub, one of the few left. Its patrons had been men in blue singlets and stubby shorts, even in the middle of winter. But overnight it appeared to have gone trendy, with low lighting and young, bearded barmen. Nick's crowd, Shannon thought.

They ordered two glasses of white wine, but were quizzed about whether they wanted sauvignon blanc, chardonnay or some other variety, pointing to the new wine list. Shannon was beginning to think the barman would ask her if they wanted cat's piss next. He rolled his eyes when they asked for the house sav blanc, then knelt down to the fridge below to find the bottle. He unscrewed it and taking the largest wine glass perhaps she'd ever seen poured it out for Vesna, asking for twelve dollars. There wasn't much wine in it. It seemed to only be a quarter full, leaving the rest of the glass looking very lonely.

"Hey fill it up," Vesna said, giving him the evil eye.

"I can't," he argued, pointing to a line on the glass. "Legally we're only allowed to go to here."

"What?" Vesna put her hand over the line to hide it. "For twelve dollars? I'm thirsty, I'm an alcoholic and I want my money's worth."

Shannon laughed. This Vesna was a hoot.

The bar had a normal week-night Bondi crowd of tradies, surfies and older single women hoping to pick up. Not packed but a few people there for the fifteen-dollar steak special. Or just a quick drink after work. Shannon had liked coming here for a drink because it was one of the less pretentious places around. But now she agreed with Vesna; the glass was so big you'd be hard pressed to find the wine in the bottom of it.

"Sorry," she said to Vesna, as they found a seat away from some of the noisier patrons.

"Yeah I'm used to places where it's twelve dollars for a bottle of wine, not a glass," Vesna said, putting her drink on the table as she took off her coat and scarf.

"That's what happens when the trendies move in."

The room was a cacophony of sound – TV screens competing with each other across the space. They were on sports channels, mostly footy but others blared out music videos, hits from the 1980s.

Shannon noticed there were a few guitars out on stands and a drum set, ready for a gig for that night, she guessed. That'd be nice, some live music for a change. An older man with a scraggly white pony tail going yellow at the ends and a matching beard was carrying speakers and gear, setting it up next to the guitars.

"Looks like a band playing here tonight," she said to Vesna.

"Hope it's not country and western. He looks like Willie Nelson risen from the dead," Vesna took a sip of her Sav Blanc as she indicated the ancient roadie. "So what's the story?"

"There's a block of units going up just opposite my café."

Vesna nodded.

"Well there was a bad accident there a couple of weeks ago. One of the men died. He was a customer. My friends who work with him were really shaken up by it. One of them is the foreman."

"Yeah, I heard about that one. They made out it was a heart attack. But accidents on building sites, that's not that unusual."

"I know, but there was something they said. About the company being dodgy and cutting corners, safety and all that. And as you say, it's par for the course. But I'm worried about these guys. They're my customers. It's not fair that Tony died. I thought there might be a story in how often it's happening, and how dangerous building sites have become."

"Could be." Vesna started writing in her notebook. "Any Albanians working there?"

"Albanians?"

"Sorry, just a bad joke. Look, give me the name of the company and the people involved and I'll start looking into it."

You weren't allowed to smoke in bars any more, and, as usual, Shannon had run out anyway. She was dying for a cigarette. Vesna opened her bag for her notebook and Shannon noticed a packet of fags on the top. You couldn't miss them – they were covered with the faces of people who looked like they were just about to die in a cancer ward or cough themselves to death, limbs missing, teeth decaying.

"Mind if I have one of your cancer sticks," she asked Vesna, who laughed as she handed it over.

They went outside onto the footpath to have a smoke and Vesna pointed to the half-built block of apartments. "So that's the one?"

Shannon nodded as she took a long draw. "I don't get your joke about the Albanians."

Vesna laughed. "I can't seem to get away from Albanians. If it's not Albanians, it's Croatians. Or Bosnians. Or Bosnian Muslims. Or Macedonians. Or Greeks. All fighting with each other.

"I think it's worse here than it is over there. They still think the war's going on. Haven't they heard the UN sorted it all out years ago? Pity a few thousand people had to die in the process, just because the West always has to take sides."

Shannon had no idea what Vesna was talking about but she liked her, she hoped she could trust her to do a decent story on the building site. Somebody needed to find out what was going on there.

As they butted their cigarettes and went inside, Shannon saw the familiar figure of Colin standing at the bar. That's funny, she thought he didn't drink. He was filling in some papers and handing them back to the bartender with a fifty-dollar note. The bartender put a midi under the Coke tap then passed it over to Colin. Placing a bet, she gathered.

Shannon turned her back. She had a feeling Colin wouldn't have wanted to be seen there and she didn't want him to know she was talking to a journalist either although she would have to give Vesna his name once she did the initial research. But she was dying to ask him about Rafael and his strange reaction to the sound of the helicopter. Rafael had come into the café the next day and he'd just said sorry he had to leave so suddenly. No mention of Vesna. She knew she was taking a risk talking to her but it was important something was done about the safety issues.

She suggested to Vesna that they go and look at the site, maybe pick up a few clues from there. Together they wandered down the road to where dirty red and white barricade tape was lying in the gutter, the only sign there'd been an accident there.

"Don't suppose you know if there's any illegals working at this site?" Vesna asked. Shannon looked hard at her – what had that to do with a story about slack safety standards? "I really don't know. And I don't think anybody would be telling you."

Vesna smiled. "I can't imagine a building site where there aren't workers with dodgy visas, ABNs and everything else they need."

"Don't ask me. But I don't think that's the issue for this story." Tom was the one who'd know all about immigration issues, she thought. But she wasn't going to give Vesna his number.

Chapter Nineteen

"Didn't you just hate Saturday school?" Vesna asked Tom.

"With a passion."

"All those dead poets. And patriotic songs."

"Well, at least I learnt the language."

"Kako si?"

"Dobro sam, hvala. A ti?"

Tom and Vesna had spent most of Saturday morning in bed. He'd been out to get the newspapers and coffee and brought them to her on a tray. She was lying on his freshly-laundered five-hundred-count Egyptian sheets, leaning against matching white pillowcases. She hoped she wasn't going to leave copious amounts of her thick hair on them.

The papers were full of stories about the Middle East blowing up, refugees in third world detention centres, terrorist attacks and Americans fighting a 21st century Civil War. Vesna wondered why she was bothering with her illegal migrants' exposé. It was going to be swamped by all this other doom and gloom. But there was something about this story that intrigued her – maybe it was the extent of the underground world, or how easy it was to fly under the radar for years and years. Or how the billionaires running the show got away with murder. Everything had a cost.

Tom had promised to find her some over-stayers to interview, so long as they weren't named or put in danger. He had several clients who would be perfect but he had to persuade them. He had wondered what was in it for him, did the world need to know how they operated? But, he'd said to her, he couldn't see why people who were prepared to work hard couldn't stay here. So long as they paid their tax – and him.

"So many refugee stories," Vesna said, flicking through the World section. She'd divided the paper and Tom preferred Sport anyway.

"Where did your parents come from?" she asked Tom.

"A bit serious for a Saturday morning, Vesna," he turned the pages of the paper.

"I'm interested."

"Belgrade born and bred. Mine."

"Ah well, you can't have everything."

Tom laughed. "They were partisans and supported Tito but came out for economic reasons in the sixties. Yours?"

"They came earlier, after World War Two in the late forties. Dad was only a kid, he'd been in a displaced persons' camp back there. Had to stay in one of those migrants' camps in the country first. Mum came later. She was a lot younger. Mine aren't city people like yours though. Peasants."

Yeah, she thought, they fled a devastated Europe before Tito's walls went up. Not that Yugoslavia was anything like other Eastern Bloc countries – people were much freer to travel. Well, that's what they always told her when she went there.

"Our parents came here legally," Tom said. "They did the right thing. They waited their turn. Why shouldn't other people?"

"Oh come on, I think we should break down the borders. Let people live where they like. Sooner or later they would go home – if they could. There should be one big, giant WU or world union with visa-free travel everywhere. OK you might have to find a new occupation but who cares?"

"Divorce lawyers make more money anyway. But I don't know, there's only so much capacity here for refugees. They're not all legitimate. Some say they're political but they're mostly economic. I get to hear a lot of bullshit, Vesna."

You don't mind taking their money, Vesna thought. But she knew it was time to change the subject or she might get into an argument with him. He pulled his beautiful sheets down and climbed on top of her to tickle her, finding her vulnerable spot. "I'd prefer to discuss something a bit lighter, Vila Ravijojla."

She laughed and pushed him onto his back, then climbed on top of him, spreading the newspapers all over the covers and floor.

When they were finished, Tom got out of bed and put a towel around himself. He picked up the newspapers and put them neatly on the side table.

"Did your mother teach you housework?" Vesna asked, worried she could never live up to his standards.

"Yes, I hate mess. "

"Do you still take your washing to her to do?"

"Sometimes when I'm too busy."

Vesna groaned, remembering what her mother told her when she came home from Europe with a backpack full of dirty laundry. "Vesna, I need hammer to break underpants before I put in washing machine."

"Hey, I'd like you to meet my mother." Tom cut into her memories.

Vesna wasn't so sure. She wasn't a meet-your-mother type of girlfriend. Her relationships usually didn't last that long. She screwed up her face. "Oh really? I might be too uncouth for her."

"After Shannon, she'll love you."

"Shannon? Is that your ex-wife's name?"

"Yes. Hadn't I told you that before?"

Vesna smiled sweetly at Tom, while her body went ice cold. "No, I don't think so. That's not a very Serbian name." It couldn't be the same Shannon, surely?

"Exactly, she's a bloody bogan. And a spoilt one. Everything I've done for her she wrecks. Her café in Tamarama. You'd think she'd be raking it in. But no, I'm sure she's going broke."

How could she have been so dumb? Oh God, it was all too close. Tom. Amany. Shannon. Tom. Should she tell him she knew her? No, not when things were going so well. For once in her life she'd try and keep her mouth shut. But why had he never told her about his baby dying like Amany had mentioned? That might explain why Shannon seemed a bit off the wall. Well, she wasn't bringing that subject up either. Instead Vesna tried to look as if she'd never heard of Shannon or her Tamarama joint. "That's no good."

"Don't worry about it. I'm hungry, let's go for breakfast," he dragged her out of bed and into the shower with him. As the hot water steamed, he bent her body towards the wall so that he could take her from behind. "My mum'll love you," he went for it, slapping her on her bottom. "You're from the old country. Just make sure you pour her the first cup of Turkish coffee so she gets the crema."

But Vesna was not so sure about that. Tom shared a few similarities with the boys she'd grown up with, and their mothers were never great fans of her.

Chapter Twenty

Rafael climbed up a steep set of stairs in a disused warehouse. It was down the road from the new train station, across a loop in the road that he'd had to run across to dodge the trucks. The station was the only bright thing in the area, beaming neon and silver metal. But a few metres away it was dark and gloomy, abandoned shops in between walls covered in non-artistic graffiti. It took him a while to find the club; the music led him there.

At the top of the stairs a girl took his twenty dollars and, without a smile, stamped him on the wrist. He couldn't see the point of this; it was doubtful he'd be going out for a smoke in the street or a gasp of cigarette air. He hated the cold; he could handle the heat and sweat of being amongst a throng of dancers. It made him feel at home.

Inside, camels of every description decorated the walls. Ones next to pyramids. Palm-edged oases. Crowded souks. He couldn't see how this had anything to do with salsa music. When was the last time a camel was spotted in Latin America, apart from on a cigarette packet?

A band swallowed the stage – guitars, piano, brass. An overweight but still sexy woman singer channelled Celia Cruz. There was something not quite right though, the band seemed to be out of time with each other but he tried to ignore that.

Pushing his way through a group of women dressed in swirly skirts and dance shoes, he made it to the bar. He became impatient as the pale-faced patrons in front of him ordered mojitos, which seemed to take forever to make. The barmaid smiled at him when he ordered a simple beer. He winked at her and told her to keep the change. He felt good, acting as if he was made of money, and still sexy despite his years and battered brown skin. He leant against the bar, watching the band and feeling the music pulse through his body but keeping his eye on the door for Shannon.

A couple were dancing in front of him. They'd moved from the actual dance floor and were taking up the space near the bar. "Must have been to salsa class … the one held in the women's prison." He laughed to himself, as the lumpy male displayed his total lack of rhythm.

Rafael no longer thought it was a joke when the man swung the woman around and knocked him. He saved his drink just in time. *"Hijo de puta!"*

"Oh sorry," the woman giggled as her partner pulled her away.

The barmaid smiled. "You've got good reflexes," she said.

Rafael grimaced. He didn't think it was funny, just plain rude.

"The worst part is they're the salsa teachers," she pointed out and his eyes moved to the heavens.

Then he spotted Shannon at the door, wearing black pants and a shimmery top and her hair in a high pony tail. He barged his way through the crowd, not caring now if he too was rude. He wanted to pay for her entry. Just as she was reaching for her wallet he thrust a twenty dollar note at the girl on the table and grabbed Shannon by the arm.

"What! I need a stamp," she protested putting her wrist out for it.

"You don't need a cigarette break. Come and dance," Rafael pulled her onto the dance floor, as she dragged her small shoulder bag over her chest.

Their bodies moved in perfect time to the salsa beat. At first they held each other around the waist and shoulder but then Rafael spun Shannon in a neat semi-circle. She knew the moves and was in complete time with him, neither of them taking up more than the necessary space on the dance floor. They laughed together and he leant down and kissed her on the cheek. "You are the Salsa Queen of Sydney."

"And you're the Mover of Managua!" She'd been studying the map.

He kissed her again as Ms Cruz, covered in sweat right down to her tight white pants and midriff top, announced the band was having a break. Taped music took over, and Rafael felt the easier beat – without all the showing off of the brass musicians – but never mind, he was thirsty.

"What would you like to drink?" he asked, pulling her again by the arm towards the bar.

"Just a beer, thanks."

Rafael pushed his way to the front, eyeing the barmaid who again took his order.

"What'll it be *guapo*?"

"Ah just two beers. Maybe those Mexican ones tonight, *guapa*." He winked again at her.

He could see she thought he was corny but liked it, even blushing a little.

As the band started up again they left their drinks on a table and moved back onto the dance floor. But Rafael was finding it difficult as more and more people swarmed on to dance including a couple of overweight women. At least when our grandmothers dance together they can move, he thought.

He whispered to Shannon that maybe they should sit this one out and he led her back to the edge of the dance floor. A couple left their table and Rafael snapped it up.

"I had a drink with that woman journalist the other night," Shannon said, staring into her glass.

"What? I told you not to bring the press into this."

"But she's good," she raised her eyes to him and pleaded. "She was recommended by Amany. She'll get to the truth."

"Truth?" Rafael snorted. "Please just leave it alone."

"But Rafael … Think of Tony's family."

Rafael turned his back to her; he didn't want to discuss it. His body was stiff, his arm outstretched to pick up his beer from the small table. Shannon had no idea what she was getting herself into or what it meant to him personally. He couldn't go back to Nicaragua, he just couldn't. He'd spent enough time in prison cells. He'd … but just as he was putting his glass to his mouth, the annoying couple who had been throwing themselves around the boundaries of the dance floor swung into the back of his chair, bumping him and this time it was enough to knock the beer out of his hand, smashing to the ground.

"What the fuck!" he exclaimed. There was beer all over him and he felt like an idiot. His carefully-ironed shirt was wet and he felt his whole body on fire. He jumped up and landed a punch right on the man's cheek. The man was stunned for a minute but came back with his own force, punching Rafael in the stomach, who bent over in agony.

Shannon grabbed Rafael before he could keep going, while a

security guy emerged from nowhere and told him to get out. But then he vomited and the floor became a yellow mess of spilt beer and that night's dinner, unfortunately not a gourmet meal in a chef's cap restaurant.

"I didn't mean to knock them, I said sorry," the dancer was saying but nobody was listening to him except the barmaid, who arrived with a mop.

"Shut up," she yelled at the dancer as she cleaned up the mess.

"Come on, Rafael, let's get out of here," Shannon took him by the arm.

Rafael didn't want to know; he pulled himself up and shook her off, bounding to the door without turning around.

"Fuck you and fuck your club, and fuck your fucking camels," were his last words to the astonished girl at the door as he heaved his way with as much dignity as he could down the creaking stairs.

Ocotal
March, 1986

Lana's taking me by the hand and pulling me up and onto the dance floor. Her hips are swaying and she has a come hither look on her face.

The band is from the Atlantic Coast and is playing a *Paolo de Mayo* song, the ones they used to dance to there, making fun of the British and their stupid May Pole.

So Lana is doing her own version of what she thinks is *Paolo de Mayo* dancing.

"It's not meant to be pole dancing, you know," I say.

"I know, it's an erotic version of the May Pole, which actually I'll have you know was an erotic dance in the first place. Well if the Brits could ever be erotic." She thinks she's hilarious and witty but she doesn't realise it's the rum talking.

She bends her back and widens her legs, gyrating on my leg now. I'm so embarrassed I'm dying. *Hijo!* But then what the hell? I love to dance and she's a willing partner. The rum is taking over and I can feel my body giving way to the rhythm. I bend forwards too, and take her by the arms, and lift her onto my waist. Her head almost touches the ground. I pull her back up and her face is right opposite me. Her blonde locks are stuck to her cheeks by perspiration. Her whole body is wet and so is mine. My jeans and T-shirt are drenched.

We don't care. We're laughing and alive with the music. And then it stops and we're left alone on the dance floor, clapping the musicians. But she wants to keep dancing, she doesn't want to stop and although I'm already back at the table ordering more rum she's looking for another partner. She goes to another table and pulls up a soldier. He's embarrassed but intoxicated by her beauty. Nica men, we love blondes; we can't help ourselves. And he starts to dance with her, even more erotically than we were. She is so drunk.

I can't stand to see her making a fool of herself, and making a fool of me in front of my own people. It's too much and I go to her and drag her by the arm. "Come on Lana, come for a drink."

"No. I don't want a drink. I want to dance." She pulls away from me and continues to move with the poor soldier.

As I leave the bar I sweep my hand across the table, smashing everything on it – rum, Coke, ice and glasses. And I leave her the bill.

As Rafael did his jacket up and crossed the road to the train station, he passed a group of Salsa smokers, puffing away and chatting like they were still dancing – off-beat. They didn't feel the cold, the warmth of the nicotine was all they needed, before they headed back up the stairs and inside to the music from Celia Cruz and her band.

Ocotal
March, 1986

I'm back in the *pensión* sitting on my bed having a smoke and trying to calm down when Lana comes back. She's much earlier than I thought. I imagined she would have gone home with the soldier.

"Thanks for leaving me with the bill, *hombre*." Her eyes are wide.

"Well, you were embarrassing me in front of those soldiers," I say.

"You *loco*. I had to do the come-on. How else was I going to get the information out of him?"

"What information?" I find Miss Excuses hard to believe.

"The information, *compañero*, about where the mental hospital is. I even have a map now. Da daa." From her bag, she pulls out a napkin covered in a roughly-scrawled mud map. X marked the spot of the hospital.

Even I am now feeling the adrenalin of a good investigative story, for all my misgivings about the treatment of cowardly soldiers and potential damage to the Sandinistas.

"Can you follow this map?" she asks.

"Follow it? I think I know exactly where that is. It used to be a convent, back in the day when we Nicas were being brainwashed by the Catholic Church."

Lana hugs me and we fall back onto the bed together. But I don't want to do anything, I don't want to hurt her.

Shannon was left on her own, in the scene of destruction in the midst of a sea of dancers. She felt like she was floating above herself, looking down. "Dead, dead," she muttered.

The barmaid, who was cleaning the neighbouring table, swung around. "Are you speaking to me, love?"

Shannon didn't answer. The room swam around her, the salsa music still pulsing.

Chapter Twenty-one

Vesna was day-dreaming as she walked to her car down the road from her office. It is 1999 in Kosovo, just on dusk. The sky is pearly pink, the clouds sitting on the horizon. It would be breathtaking if there isn't a war going on.

When a journalist travels with the army it's known as embedded but she doesn't want to "embed" with these scraggly soldiers. It's the remnants of the Yugoslav Army – what was left after Tito died. All 18-year-olds had to do military service and some stayed on. Baby soldiers trained as killers.

The one whose job it is to keep an angry eye on her keeps his rifle as tight as his buttoned-up flak jacket, his black beret pulled down closely over his curls. He could be Serb or Montenegrin. No longer are there Albanians, Macedonians, Croatians, Bosnians or Slovenians in an army where the ethnic groups once mixed freely together, especially if they were officers. It was their level of education that united them. No more! Now their hatred is unleashed like waves of terror. They starve, maim, rape and do whatever they can to hang on to power. But there is another side to the story. Later the world discovered NATO tested their depleted uranium weapons out here – their dirty war – even bombing Orthodox churches, as black-bearded priests ran weeping.

Now Vesna is with her brothers-in-arms as they roll into a small village. The Albanian flag with the black double-headed eagle silhouetted against a red background is flying from the poles and roofs of the crumbling, mud-brick houses. It's deathly quiet. The soldiers alight from the tank and trucks and stealthily move through the narrow streets. She follows; the only sound the screams of stray cats and the bark of dogs.

The whole population has deserted the village. No sign of KLA either, just piles of stinking garbage and wrecked cars. She pulls her shirt over her face to cover the stench. Inside the broken-paned window of one house she thinks she will see stacks of stolen televisions – Serbs talk about Albanians trudging through waist-deep snow to nab TVs. But there is just an engraved rocking chair and a small table, on top of it a pair of rimmed glasses next to an abandoned book. The Koran maybe?

The sudden ringing of her phone brought Vesna back to reality. "Hello, Vesna here," she answered.

"This is Peter Simpson of WorkCover. You left a message for me." His voice was thin and high pitched.

"Oh yeah, thanks for calling back." Great, this was the guy who her contact at the union suggested she talk to, the bureaucrat who handled work safety complaints. "It's about a death on a building site in Tamarama," she said.

"Oh that one, there's going to be an inquest into that."

"Right." This was news to Vesna but then she should have realised there would be. "Did the post mortem find anything?"

"Just that he died about fifteen minutes after he hit the ground but they need to look into how the accident happened."

"And whether anybody's to blame I guess?"

"Well, maybe. But really I can't comment on that."

Vesna realised she had pushed him too far, he was clamming up now. Damn! But she was going to keep trying. "I'm interested in complaints that were filed and never acted on, about lack of safety procedures on that site," she said. She had been given this information by her contact.

"I don't know anything about those. I'd have to check. And that wouldn't be information we'd be free to release to the media anyway."

"Why weren't the complaints acted on?" Vesna could be like a ferret when she wanted to be, especially when she felt she was being blocked.

"I didn't say there were complaints. Look, any media questions need to be handled by our PR department."

"Oh come on, all I want to know is did you receive any complaints about the company and if so what were they?"

"Really Miss Bojic, it's better if you email your questions to the PR department."

"Now you know that would be a complete waste of time. Somebody has died. It's a matter of public interest now."

"I'm sorry I really can't help you. Goodbye."

Vesna threw the phone into her bag as she pulled herself into the car. Bugger, sounds like a cover-up, she thought. She turned the engine on and the radio blasted a hip hop song. "Fuck!" She tried to change the station, at the same time reversing into the car behind her. "Fuck, fuck, fuck."

Putting the car back into Drive, and hoping nobody had seen her, she tore off past the ugly shopping centre. Well, there was going to be an inquest. It had been years since she'd covered something at the Coroner's Court but she was like an elephant, she never forgot.

Macquarie Street opposite the Botanic Gardens in the city was unnaturally quiet; Shannon hoped she wouldn't run into Tom, whose office was close by. Offices full of workers, heads-down, bums up. God knew what they did all day. She remembered a younger Maxie standing in their Paddington courtyard mumbling "meet, meet" and when she asked him what he was doing he'd said, "I'm at a meeting". That's about all she knew of office meetings herself.

"Breathe in, breathe out. I just need to breathe. I'll get Maxie back, I know I will. The lawyer will help, he'll have the answers. He'll know how to deal with the bastard. Give him a deadline, make him come in for mediation, make him agree to give me back my little boy." Shannon talked to herself as she entered a grey, twenty-storey building.

This divorce lawyer had been recommended to her by a friend; he was smart, sharp, Jewish. He'd sort it all out. Tom wasn't the only clever lawyer around. Sorting out her divorce and the custody arrangements was costing her a fortune but she knew it would be worth it. In his chambers, he was sleazy, that's for sure but he made her laugh. Must have been having an affair with his secretary, she was sure of that. Never mind, that's his business. All she wanted was results.

The thought of dealing with Tom gave her butterflies. Divorce: it felt even worse than losing a baby, just because at least she and Tom had still loved each other then. They'd buried their little girl's ashes together, joined in their grief.

She thought of that day. Maxie's holding her hand as Tom digs a hole and they carefully place the box in the soil. Maxie places the card he made, To Baby, on top of the box. "You be good, baby and go to sleep. Me and mummy and daddy, we love you." When the hole is filled in, he puts a bunch of daisies he's picked from the garden on top of it. Tom, as usual, shows no feelings, just puts the shovel back in the shed after shaking the soil off it, leaving Maxie and her at the graveside, both crying.

But now it had all become so aggressive. And there were also money issues, the lawyer had told her. There needed to be a financial settlement too. She dreaded this.

Shannon was the only one in front of the lifts; she hit the up button. The doors opened a few seconds later and she was surprised to see the lawyer there with his secretary, a squat, dark woman with a thick fringe that almost covered her even thicker black glasses. The lawyer was holding the handle of a small suitcase with wheels. The secretary had a stack of files in her hands, so tall they came up to her chin, and she wasn't very tall.

"I thought I had an appointment with you now," Shannon said, holding the door open.

The lawyer looked at the floor.

"Didn't you get my message?" the secretary asked.

"No."

"David's retired," she spoke for her boss, who said nothing. "Health reasons. Sorry, we've given your file to Deborah Secombe upstairs."

Shannon's mouth dropped open. She had no words.

The lawyer pushed past her wheeling his suitcase behind him. The secretary turned around. "Oh, there was also a letter from your husband's lawyer. Something about your assets. Do you have a family farm or something?"

"Yes, but that's nothing to do with him."

"Speak to Deborah about it. You'll be in good hands. Don't worry," she said, touching Shannon on the arm. "She's on the tenth floor."

The lift doors closed as Shannon slumped backwards on the cold mirror, feeling the walls closing in around her.

Shannon thought the whale engraving would know how she felt. She was caught between a rock and a hard place, herself. A magnificent piece of art etched thousands of years ago just sitting there, with hardly anybody even noticing. Shannon climbed over the barrier, edging carefully around the whale, speaking to it in Koori terms that Colin had told her about – announcing her arrival, explaining why she was there. "What am I going to do, whale? I've had it."

She could almost see the whale's smile – one eye cocked and a wink. "Don't worry, love, I'm here for you."

"Why me?" It wasn't just Tom and the lawyer. She also hadn't heard a word from Rafael since Saturday night. She wasn't going to call him. He was the one who left her at the club. He could be dead for all she knew. She wondered how in God's name she'd got involved with him. It had seemed too good to be true. "What is wrong with me? Why do I attract the bastards and the crazies? What do you think, mother whale?"

But there was no answer from the whale – just the sound of gulls, the feel of the briny air, the salt on her tongue and the endless sea.

Shannon went as close to the edge as she could so she could see the rocks washed with waves below. Fishermen would regularly be swept off those rocks but others would return the next day, their fishing rods over their shoulders. A helicopter hovered out to sea, probably looking for one right now.

It wouldn't be hard to jump here. Nobody would notice. They didn't notice the whale rock so why her? She still had her good clothes on that she had chosen to go into the city. So there would be no need for an undertaker to change them before the burial. Straight from the bus to the rock to the coffin. It was getting late, soon time to collect Maxie from after-school care, but no, Irina would already be doing that.

"What's the point of living?" she called out to the seagulls, her boots slipping on the rock and she nearly fell; she felt dizzy as the sky and the sea seemed to come together as one. She felt a large arm grab her and pull her back, holding her tight around the waist.

"Shannon, what in God's name are you doing?" Colin almost fell over too as he dragged her back towards the engraving.

"Nothing." Everything was blurry as she knelt down on the rock.

"You weren't going to jump were you?"

She shook her head. "I don't know, Colin. I don't know." She hummed as she rocked back and forth, and Colin cradled her like a baby.

Chapter Twenty-two

The protesters were still out the front but not the large crowd of the week before. They'd lost interest and had moved on to another site; some had gone back to work on the apartments.

As he walked through the small throng, Colin was deep in thought, and a bit unsettled. He'd gone to the whale rock to look for Shannon because he wanted to find out more information about his mother, especially since visiting the library. But that had been impossible yesterday. He'd walked her home and tucked her into bed, amused to see a teddy bear there. He made her tomato soup from a can and toast with lots of butter, and she'd eaten a little of it. He quietly closed the door as he left. He was worried about her. He'd drop in to the café later and see how she was.

Rafael was sitting on his own on a small wall next to some scaffolding, drinking from a thermos cup.

"Coffee's better at Shannon's," Colin said, sitting down next to him.

"I don't think I'd be very welcome there." Rafael finished the coffee and screwed the cup back on.

"Oooh," Colin was the last to admit it, but he loved a bit of gossip. Over the soup, Shannon had told him a little of Saturday night's drama. "Did you give the other dancers too much competition?"

"Do I have to tell you, old woman?" He stood up, putting the thermos in his backpack.

"Yes, you do, sonny boy," Colin followed him. "So how was the salsa club?"

"I am never going there again."

"You didn't get into a fight did you, brother?" He pretended he didn't know.

Rafael looked at the ground and his dusty boots. "Yep."

Colin was serious. "My dear man, that is not the way to behave on a first date."

"Well, it was the other guy's fault. The worst part is this Aussie bloke with no rhythm is paid to be a dance teacher. He bashed right into the back of me while we were sitting. He made me drop my beer. I told you Aussies cannot dance."

Colin imagined the scene. "Oh dear. And what about Shannon? Was she hurt or anything?"

"I don't know. I left. She made me so angry. She's found a journalist to write about poor Tony."

"You left her there? Oh that is not good. Not good at all." Colin was trying not to look too pleased at the outcome of their first real date. Maybe the girl would come to her senses now and stop seeing Rafael. "She's been though a lot. Be gentle, Raf."

He looked embarrassed. "I suppose I should apologise."

"She's a beautiful woman but she's fragile. She needs to be treated well. I made her soup yesterday." Colin turned around to find the others to go over the day's jobs, hoping Rafael wouldn't take up his advice.

Rafael nodded: "I'll treat her like *mi madre*."

Managua
May, 1978

I close my eyes as they push my head down into the bucket of water. I'm imagining myself back at home sitting at my mother's table, in her kitchen in her hot little shack, eating her bean soup. How I love that soup – hot and spicy with poached eggs floating on top. Full of goodness and protein and energy. Black beans. And rice. We eat them every single day. But the *sopa* is the highlight of the week.

Why didn't they throw me out? Why was I returned to my cell? I know now. They had this in store for me. They were saving me to give me more horror, to scare me into telling things I can't even tell myself. To lift the veil from the secrets I've stored for so long. The only ventilation in my damp cell is a tiny window so high I can't even climb up to reach it. There's nothing to climb on anyway. I just sleep on the wet stone floor.

As they pull my head up by my hair I see the paintings others have done of Sandino in his black hat and jodhpurs staring down at me as if to say: "You coward, you're going to give in, you're going to tell all about your friends, your comrades, your *compañeros*. You will spill it all – give details of the hiding places, of attack plans, of plots against the government. Just the thought of being thrown out of that helicopter into the volcano is enough for you to tell everything."

Sandino in his red and black colours, laughing at me, laughing at my cowardice.

"Come on, eat up, Rafa." My mama breaks some crusty bread for me. Bread she has lined up for hours to buy.

The nieces and nephews are running around my feet, in and out of the table and chairs, laughing and pulling at each other.

Mi madre in her simple cotton shift: blue and white, her hair pulled back in a bun, weathered brown skin, calling to the kids to go outside and play. "Leave Rafael to eat his soup in peace."

Madre mía. I won't give up the secrets, just for her and her bean soup. Never. They can threaten to throw me out of that helicopter, they can dunk my head in water all night long but they'll never get anything out of me – not a single word. Perhaps only: "*Sopa.*"

Rafael was startled by a white sedan and a van pulling up outside the building site and an official-looking woman climbing out. "Hey, who's that?"

"Could be Centrelink, the car has Feds number plates." Colin never missed a trick. "Or Immigration. Damn. I'm sure I checked those Iranians' four-five-sevens. They seemed hunky dory."

"I'm getting out of here," Rafael was panicking.

"What's wrong?"

"I don't like government people," Rafael said as he grabbed his backpack then walked as quickly as he could without making it too obvious around to the back of the building, climbed over a fence and took off down a laneway. He was puffing but got to the bus stop just as a bus pulled in. Bloody Persians, he knew they'd be trouble, attracting Immigration to the site. The Movement had taught him how to keep his head down. He wasn't sloppy.

The bus driver stared blankly ahead while Rafael found his card and tapped it. Then he took off, braking heavily as a car pulled out in front of him. Rafael almost fell over in the aisle but grabbed the rail as the book a young seated woman had been reading fell to the ground in front of him.

"*Hijo de puta*," he swore out loud, as he picked it up, studying the gaudy cover. It was some kind of thriller, showing a man peering through bars. He pulled himself into the seat across the aisle from the woman and handed her the book.

Managua
May, 1978

The door to the cell next to me clangs shut. I can hear a body being dragged inside and dumped there by two of the guards but I don't want to open my eyes to check. Any movement from me and it will be my turn next. I can't bear it another time, having my face pushed into the water, pulled out by my hair. What is that going to do? No Sandino, that won't make me tell. I don't even know what they want to know.

The body on the ground groans then I hear them kicking it one more time, just for luck. I hear the key turn in my lock. Oh God, it's my turn again. I try to crawl into the corner of my cell, like a cockroach hiding. One guard pulls me by my bare feet while the other drags me by my shirt. This time it's the interrogation room.

"Come on *compañero*," they say in their sarcastic voices. "Time to make love, not war."

Colin watched the official woman, who appeared to be the team leader, walk past the demonstrators, ignoring them and make a beeline for him. About ten officials waited at the entrance to the site.

"You the site foreman?" She was wearing a blue suit, black boots and stockings with a thick, scratchy grey scarf around her neck. She looked sensible but with a bit of hippy flair. She'd teamed her blue suit with azure butterfly earrings, which matched a butterfly pendant on a chain around her neck, visible under the scarf. A pretty face, even if she does work for Immigration, Colin thought as he tried to figure out her age. Early fifties maybe but hard to tell as she obviously dyed her cropped red hair. Good idea, silver fox was for the Grey Nomads and their campervans and two-way radios.

"Yes I am my dear," he said. "And I'm guessing you're from the

Department of Immigration and Incarceration? What can I do for you this beautiful winter's day?"

The official woman showed Colin her badge. "Jenny George, Director of Compliance, the Department of Immigration and Border Protection."

"Oh so that's what it's called these days?" Colin said. "Wish we'd had a Border Protection Department two hundred years ago."

Her eyes creased as her jangly earrings swung in the cold air. "You'll need to shut down the site while my colleagues check your workers' IDs. Have you any Iranians working here?"

"Who, love?" Colin tried to sound nonchalant, hoping Rafael had made it away in time.

"Iranians. Over-stayers. We've been told they're working on this building site."

"We don't employ illegals."

"You know I could print up a list of your four-five-seven visa workers in a flash. Are they all sponsored?"

"Go ahead. You'll find everything's by the book here. And you can't get me, my dear. If my ancestors came by boat, it would have been at least seventy thousand years ago. We're the original boat people."

"We're not after Aboriginal people." She was trying not to laugh but then she gushed: "Leave that to the police."

"Oh the police? Yeah that'd be right." Colin pretended to be offended.

"Ah that was a joke. Anyway, the Department of Immigration is a supporter of Reconciliation and the Recognition campaign."

"And what in heaven's name is that?"

"Supporting native title, the constitution, people all getting along together. We should have a yarn about it."

Colin snorted.

The woman softened her stance. "You're obviously an intelligent man."

"And you're a beautiful woman."

She rolled her eyes. "Right, thanks. Well, maybe you can help me. It's your duty to inform the department about over-stayers."

"And what would you do with that information?"

"Catch them, put them on a plane and send them right back to wherever they've come from. I don't believe in queue jumping."

"Oh right. Forgot about the queues. So where was Captain Cook in the queue? He was the British Boatperson."

"At least he didn't pay an Indonesian people-smuggler to bring him here. We're just trying to stop people dying at sea."

"Huh! Yes we were generous enough to let the old captain in. Lucky, because we were wandering around lost in the bush before he discovered us."

"Look, here's my card. Call me. Anytime. We need eyes and ears on the ground. It'll be worth your while." For the first time she smiled and winked at him.

Colin put the card in his pocket. "Pleased to meet you, Jenny George. I'm Colin Barnett. Perhaps you would like to partake in a liquid refreshment sometime? I'll text you my telephone number."

She laughed. "Charmed I'm sure, Colin Barnett. Now my colleagues will need to have a little chat with some of your employees. It shouldn't take more than an hour." She signalled to the officers to start their investigations.

"I should hope not, Ms George. We're already way behind schedule." Colin hoped to hell those damn Iranians' visas were genuine.

Chapter Twenty-three

Rafael's little flat looked out over the sea. He moved in way before it was fashionable and with a landlord who never did anything to it, he'd managed to stay there without the rent going up every month.

The building had concrete cancer, rust had taken over all the pipes, the window frames needed sanding-back, there were brown stains down the less-than-white walls, the foyer hadn't seen a mop or broom in years but it would do.

He tried not to talk to his neighbours – except to nod hullo to the two gay guys – *los maricones* they called them back home – who lived downstairs. They were OK really, they valued their privacy too and at least attempted to grow a few flowers in pots on their windowsills. For Rafael, a telly and a CD player that had only ever blasted Latin music was enough company. Well, until he met Shannon.

He shut the door, with a last nervous look out onto the landing to make sure nobody had followed him. Phew, that was close – getting away from the building site just in time. He'd caught several different buses just to make it hard for anybody to follow him and then walked cross-country to get home. He was like the Kadaitcha man Colin had told him about, the one who left no foot prints. And now he needed a coffee to calm down.

In the tiny kitchen he filled his ancient coffee pot with water and spooned the coffee in, putting it on the stove and waiting for it to bubble. Outside the window was an ugly car park, with rubbish always blowing around; nobody ever seemed to close the lids properly on the bins. The view from the lounge room towards the sea was much better. Why the cheapskates who built the place had never put balconies on he couldn't understand. At home, houses were built around a courtyard, so you had privacy and pretty gardens. You could lean back in the rocking chair and enjoy nature. Here most hadn't figured out how to bring nature into their homes.

On TV were the usual scenes of war, death and destruction. He quickly changed channels. Ah, *Dancing With the Stars*. Rafael liked that show even though the celebrities had no rhythm. He poured his coffee into a small china cup and sat down on the lounge, trying to forget the government person's visit, but then noticed that his dollar vine in its hanging basket over the window needed watering. He filled a glass with water from the tap, soaking its leaves and admired the view of the sea.

North of Ocotal
March, 1986

We're at the gate to what we think is the hospital – I can't believe it, we've finally made it here. It's a big, iron gate with a giant padlock. Rusted-on iron. It's as if the jungle is encroaching on this mysterious place. Vines are growing over the spikes, twisting in and out of the barbed wire wound around them. If they keep growing like this, they will pull the whole gate down. They remind me of vampire vines or the Devil's Snare as we call them. They grow in swamps and if anybody comes close they wrap themselves around you, trapping you as their dormant mouths feed on your blood. Like Somoza's *guardia*, who would use our revolutionary women as blood banks for their wounded soldiers until they drained them dry.

I can see a dusty track leading from the gate up a hill and in the distance a large brick building. I would never have expected such a sight, looming down on us. It's spooky, like something out of a horror movie.

We've stopped our trusty little Datsun in front of the gate, the windows wound down to get some air in. The grey dust has crept its way through our ancient cassette collection. The salsa is still playing as I turn off the engine.

Lana is ecstatic. "We're here, we've found it," she laughs hysterically. "You didn't believe me, Raf, but look."

I'm worried the guards will jump out at us from the bushes or there'll be a booby trap, or a land mine if we go inside the gate. But it's quiet, so quiet. Only birds in the distance, the humming of cicadas, a slight breeze moving the leaves on the trees.

Native ginger – I can smell that in the air, but not the sweat of soldiers. Where is everybody? This is too strange, too eerie. I'm guarded and I try to warn Lana but she's out of the car and at the gate, checking the huge padlock. "It's not locked, Raf. Oh my God, it's open."

"Shoosh, be quiet." I'm out of the car now too but nervous the soldiers will come hurtling down the track in a truck, scoop us up and take us to the hospital, where they'll perform crazy experiments on us, then leave us there to rot.

But this is my government, my revolution, not the enemy. Why would they do that?

I've seen the way the Contras treat their injured. Makeshift hospitals in between the trees, limbless soldiers on stretchers, drips in their arms, swearing "*Patria o morir*". They look dead. I've been into those Contra camps. I was travelling with a Canadian journalist that time so I had to pretend I was a *Gringo* too. I stayed mute behind my camera. I wanted to kill those bastards but I had to keep quiet.

Now we're here at this secret Sandinista place and I feel sick in the gut. Why were we never told about this?

Rafael's coffee had gone cold, the television was showing some inane reality show as the sky darkened outside. Some surfers in wetsuits were catching the last waves of the evening – that final bit of subdued sunlight before it was all given up to night.

His mobile rang, the jarring sound made his heart jump. Not a catchy little tune that he'd downloaded on iTunes – but one of the more regular rings that came with the phone. The screen said "Blocked" – he had no idea who was calling and didn't want to answer it. What if it was Immigration? Had they finally found his number after he'd changed it so many times? Who'd dobbed him in? But surely they would show a number. He sighed, oh well maybe it was all too late now. He put the phone to his ear. "Hello."

"Hello. Is this Rafael Ramirez?"

"Yes, that's me."

He didn't know the woman's voice; there was nothing familiar about it at all. "Who are you?"

"I'm Vesna Bojic, from aust.com.au. Shannon at the café told me you were there when Tony was killed."

Shannon? He'd told her over and over not to go to the media. "What do you want?" He was blunt; he didn't care if he sounded rude.

"I want to tell your side of the story."

"I don't want to tell my side of the story. Please just forget it."

"But didn't Tony die because the safety rules weren't followed?"

Rafael felt his blood boil. These women were too rude, interfering when they should leave things alone. "I don't know that. It was a wasps' nest."

"Yes, but wasn't there something wrong with the scaffolding? Was the rail too low? Why wasn't there netting? There's going to be an inquest."

"I don't know about any inquest. I'm not going to court. Just forget it."

"Rafael, you can trust me. I just want to tell the truth."

Rafael laughed scornfully. The truth? He knew all about journalists telling the truth. Lana and her fumbling attempts at objectivity. How had that helped anybody? So keen to show the world what really was going on in Nicaragua, but where did that get her in the end? Building her reputation as a brave war correspondent. But who was she doing it for? Not for his countrymen and women, not for the revolution, that's for sure. Yeah he knew all about the media. And they could go and get stuffed. "The only truth is Tony died. And we all have to keep working. Sorry, lady – I have no interest in talking to you."

He turned off his phone and turned the TV up, which was now showing a home renovation show. He'd much rather watch young people making fools of themselves acting like they knew how to renovate a house than talk to anybody.

North of Ocotal
March, 1986

It's the smell of burning rubber that I first notice, coming from way up the track, then the sound of screeching tyres bumping over potholes, slushing through puddles left by the rain. A truck is heading our way and we have nowhere to hide and no time to get there.

"Shit, it's soldiers," Lana calls out.

"*Hijo!* I told you to be quiet." My skin is tingling.

But they aren't the enemy. What am I worried about? This has to be the hospital that Lana has been seeking. There's no way the Contras have a large, brick building under their control even so close to the border.

So why the fear?

A bright red and green king parrot swoops down near us, flying from one branch to another. It gives me a shock and I let out a gasp. "Lana, you really are trouble."

The midday heat is intense. I need some shade or to get back into the Datsun. The air conditioning doesn't work but it's a bit cooler.

But then the sound of salsa music. It isn't coming from our car. The ignition is turned off. It's from the truck, which is getting closer and closer. Then yelling and a soldier jumping up and down in the tray, his AK47 cocked and ready to go.

Lana at the gate has her arms up. "*Periodista*, journalist," she yells. "*Soy una periodista*." But then she hisses at me. "Rafael, quick start filming."

I run to the car and get my camera out but the soldier yells: "Stop, don't move."

They're now at the gate, with the engine still going, the Salsa music blaring, the other already out with his rifle ready to fire, a khaki cap covering his wild, long black hair, his deep eyes intense. "Who are you? What are you doing here?"

"*No hay problema*," Lana repeats in her own flirty way. "*Soy una periodista Americana*."

I turn from the car. I have to speak to them, I don't want Lana to screw this up. She can charm that's for sure, but not all the time. This is my country, my soldiers, my revolution. "We're from CNN, *compañero*. We just found this place. We're not with the enemy. Can we talk to your *comandante*? Can you take us to him?"

Lana looks surprised. She is the one who usually does all the talking. But this time she finally shuts up.

Rafael thought about calling Shannon and abusing her if she'd given his number to the reporter. She didn't understand how risky it was for him to be talking to the media, especially with Immigration sniffing around the building site. He still felt bad about what had happened on Saturday night at the salsa club but that didn't make him less angry with her.

He relied on his job, he couldn't run away – he didn't have access to government payments or anything else. But now work was turning into a danger zone. Still, he'd just have to go back tomorrow and hope for the best. Be careful, like a good soldier should. He'd keep quiet for now. He took his half-empty cup into the kitchen. Coffee might keep him awake, but tonight he needed another one to calm his nerves.

Chapter Twenty-four

Another glorious winter's day at the café meant there were the usual mums and bubs and a few of the regular crowd. Some of the mums had stayed away since the pram incident, which Jane must have told everybody about, but a brave couple of her friends had returned and were chatting at one of the inside tables. They wore their black skin-tight pants tucked into boots, their taut stomachs covered by Kathmandu down vests, their hair perfectly streaked and shoulder-length.

A few customers read the thinner and thinner newspapers that Shannon provided. The choice: a rag that screamed tabloid headlines, with a bonus terrorist beheading thrown in each edition or a bourgeois newspaper that crowed about itself and its staff more than the news it presented.

Like clockwork, Colin turned up at nine am, morning tea time. He sat at a table next to the mums and opened the newspaper. He checked his phone, the tenth time since seven am, just in case Jenny, the Immigration woman, called him. He took out her card from his wallet and wondered if he should call her. He was looking at it when Shannon brought his cappuccino over.

"The usual crap I guess?" she asked.

"Yeah I'm not sure I can read about the Middle East anymore."

"Have you seen Raf?" She had to know.

"No. He's a great guy but I have no idea about his past." He stirred his coffee.

"Well, I have no idea about his future. I was only trying to help when I spoke to that journalist. He didn't need to freak out."

"You should leave it alone, Shannon. The inquest starts later this week. Let the coroner figure it out. Immigration is on the case too." Colin said, taking his wallet out to put the card away.

Shannon saw the writing on it and grabbed it. "What did she want?" she asked.

"Hey, that's mine. Nothing. She was after some illegals but we don't employ them. We're very careful about that."

"Oh she's the one that led the raid?"

He nodded.

"What does she look like?"

"Pretty, red hair. Fiftyish. Why?"

Shannon stared at the card and then put it on the table. "I think she might have put her head in here too. I didn't realise who she was."

"Oh, she's thorough. Anyway she spooked Rafael."

"What happened?"

"He ran off. I hope he turns up soon, we really need him."

"Why? Don't tell me he's illegal?" she joked.

Colin mouthed "Shhh", noticing that the women at the neighbouring table had pricked up their ears. "I really don't know, Shannon. Listen, I've been wanting to talk to you ever since you told me about Ainslie who worked at your farm. What else can you remember about her?" He really wanted to ask her: was she treated like shit, like most farm servants in those days? But he had no desire to discuss these details in front of nosey white women.

"She told me about her time at the home," Shannon said. "I didn't know anything about the Stolen Generations, back then. I thought she was an orphan. But they were cruel to the kids there, I remember that. Beating them and locking them in the morgue if they were naughty."

Colin felt a twinge of jealousy – his mum had never told him any of this when he and his brother and sisters were small. Probably didn't want to scare them. Or maybe talking about it would bring bad luck – she didn't want her kids to be taken. Didn't help in the end, did it?

"I can talk to Joe, he used to be our farm manager; he might remember something about how she got the job and where she'd come from," Shannon said. "Gotta get back to the customers, sorry Colin."

"OK. I just wish I knew more." Colin nodded, taking a big sip of his coffee. The idea of Shannon and some old, white bloke talking about the black hired help made him uncomfortable, but he didn't have much choice. He looked up to see Rafael coming through the door with a furious look on his face. "Hey, speak of the devil."

Shannon swung round as Rafael came straight at her. "Who gave you the right to give some woman reporter my phone number?"

"Did Vesna call you? It's OK, Raf. You can trust her, we need to get to the bottom of what happened."

"Keep out of it, Shannon. You're making it worse, don't you understand?"

Outside a truck's brakes screeched as some teenagers crossed the street chatting, oblivious to their jay walking. The driver beeped his horn and one of the kids turned and gave him the finger.

"Cool it, Raf," Colin said.

But that only made Rafael angrier. "You stay out of it too, Colin."

North of Ocotal
March, 1986

The soldier reaches out to Lana and pulls her up onto the back of the truck. She lands with a thud and moves to the hard bench on the side. There is no help for me; I drag myself up, handing the camera and equipment to Lana as the soldier stares at her as if he has never seen a woman in his life.

"What is this place?" Lana asks the soldier, whose eyes are on her breasts.

But he must know it's not worth his life to give any information away. The other two soldiers are in the front of the truck, the woman is driving. We're bashing over the potholes as the track leads us further up towards the brick building. The salsa music has been turned off and there's only the sounds of the birds in the trees. I'm worried. How will they respond to a Nica cameraman with a *Gringa* journalist?

The truck turns the corner and I see the building is two storeys and imposing. There's soldiers standing out the front, their AK47s by their side. We stop right in front of them. The soldier with us jumps off the truck and puts his arm up again to help Lana down. As before, I get no assistance.

"Wait here," he says to me, and one of the other soldiers guards us.

Guarding me? In my own country? What is this? We are standing in full sun, no shade and no water to even sip. The place smells of petrol and dust and I don't know why I think this, but death.

When I cannot handle the heat much longer, the young soldier comes out and tells us to follow him. His khakis are too big for him, they hang off his skinny behind and his black Russian boots need polishing. Wouldn't have lasted long in my garrison. He must be sixteen, no older.

Inside it is cooler, thank God and the corridor is filled with photos of Sandino and our old friend, Carlos Fonseca. This is most definitely a Sandinista post. Lana and I try to peep into the rooms we are passing – they appear to have iron beds in them and patients but we can hardly see anything. But then we spot a nurse coming towards us, wearing khakis also but carrying a syringe. My hands are sweaty, and I can feel the stubble on my chin. I feel like I haven't washed for days. She doesn't look at us; we probably smell of sweat and fear.

We are taken into a large office with brown chairs and told to sit and wait. I still have my camera with me.

On the crumbling yellow wall there's a crucifix. Jesus is staring down at me. A crucifix? So odd to see that here and then I remember this is a former convent. Just as I'm thinking that, a nun comes out of the office. A nun in full habit.

"I hope she's a Liberation Theologist like Ernesto Cardenal," Lana whispers to me.

Joking even at this time about one of our great Sandinista leaders. Does this woman have any fear or morals at all?

And then the soldier beckons us in to a dark and even cooler room. Sitting at a desk covered in papers and manila folders is *Comandante* Manuel, his uniform ironed down to the last crease.

Lana almost bursts out laughing. She walks straight up to the desk, leans over all the papers and crap on it, throws her hand at him, which he limply takes in his and says: "*Comandante*, we meet again."

"*Hola, Señorita* Lopez," *Com* Manuel says, shaking her hand.

Rafael moved from one foot to another, leaning over and picking up his mate's coffee, taking a swig and finishing it, the chocolate left around his lips.

"Hey, that's mine." Colin was surprised. "Sit down."

He stayed standing but noticed Jenny's card and picked it up. "You friendly with the government people now?"

"She gave it to me. They were just doing a routine check. You made yourself scarce."

"I was worried it was the tax department. Haven't paid for years."

Colin gave Rafael a look as if to say he didn't believe him. "Somebody must have called them. They were looking for Iranians. We don't employ illegals, do we, Rafael?"

Shannon came back from the kitchen, carrying a black coffee. "Here you are. The usual." She put it on the table as he finally sat down. She wondered if he would apologise for the salsa club incident.

"Why should I always have the same coffee?" Rafael didn't change his stance.

"Would you like an orange juice instead?" Shannon tried to be conciliatory, not understanding why. She was the one who should be rude and angry.

"A juice? I'm not a hippie. Why can't I have a hot chocolate?"

"You can have whatever you like, Rafael." She was exasperated. "It's my café."

"Oh is it? I thought it was your husband's."

"Well, technically."

"Did you ever really have to work for anything? Or do you just go to demonstrations? You're so privileged."

"What is wrong with you? Listen, I'll get you a hot chocolate, *amor*. With marshmallows? And since you've drunk most of Colin's coffee, I'll get him one too."

Colin laughed and shook his head. But Rafael was still serious. "No, thank you. And don't try to speak Spanish. It's not cute."

North of Ocotal
March, 1986

Com Manuel somehow knew that we were coming and that we were onto the story. He has travelled here to meet us. He knows in the long run that I'm more loyal to our revolution than to any American journalist and her capitalist television station. You think I would let a *Gringa* tell an anti-Sandinista story, and be involved in that? No way. They can't let the world know that their soldiers are traumatised by what has happened to them and by what they've had to do. This is war, and if you're on the victorious side you have no victims. But I do believe *Com* Manuel is trying to help our brothers, our *hermanos*, even if I still believe they are weaklings.

Lana is tense. "Go get some footage," she whispers to me. But I don't make a move.

Shannon picked up Rafael's untouched cup, made a beeline for Nick and gave the startled barista a kiss on the cheek.

Colin pulled Rafael up by the arm. They were both watching Shannon and the bearded twenty-something-year-old. "Come on, we've got to get to work. You've already missed a couple of hours."

Shannon poured the coffee down the sink, and washed up the cups. God, she needed a cigarette. Tom was enough to cope with. She didn't need another rude bastard. When there was a break between orders, she went outside onto the footpath, lit a smoke and made a phone call to Vesna. She should know that the Immigration Department was looking around the building site. It might connect somehow with her safety story.

Chapter Twenty-five

Amany didn't normally do house calls – Shannon was an exception – and she never did office calls but this time she needed a lawyer. She'd made an appointment to see Tom in his city office and asked for him at the reception desk inside the huge glass doors.

"Level twelve," the bored receptionist said, hardly looking up.

Rude girl, she thought. Young women like her had no idea what she'd gone through to get an education. These Anglos didn't know how lucky they were. Everything on a plate, yet they threw it all away. Even Shannon with a husband, who was rolling in money, only worked as a hobby. He could afford to support her. Even if they had separated. And promiscuous. What was she doing with that Latino? They all had so few morals, or beliefs in anything.

On the twelfth floor there were a couple of chairs and a small table covered in business magazines. Amany picked one up and flicked through it – the dollar had risen one cent against the greenback. That had to be good news. Not really her thing, although she did do one economics unit for her degree. Why had she come here? What was the point? How could Tom help her? She was stuck in her situation, if only for her daughter's sake. Stuck in an arranged marriage – he came from the same village in Lebanon as her parents. She'd gone through Immigration hoops in order for him to stay, but since it was a real marriage his residency was granted. Now she wasn't so sure she wanted to be with him till death-us-do-part.

She didn't know if she was anxious or relieved when Tom came through another glass door and held it open for her but she followed him into a small airless office.

"Amany, how can I help you?" Tom stayed in official mode.

"I'm not here to speak about Shannon or the baby, Tom."

He looked surprised.

"No, this is about me, for a change."

"Sit down," he pulled a chair out for her and sat on his side of the desk. "What seems to be the problem?"

"You know, Tom, my parents came out from Lebanon in the late sixties with almost no English. My father first, he worked on the gas pipes in Western Australia. He really made a go of it. My mum, her English is not so good. She can greet the neighbours, really that's all. She wasn't allowed to go to school back in Lebanon. And here too busy with all of us – I have eight brothers and sisters. "

Tom nodded. "That's a lot to look after."

"I was born here and I still have people asking me how long I've been in Australia, or if I speak English."

"You speak better English than I do."

She laughed. "When we were little in the school holidays my mum used to send us across the road to the Greek church for holiday Bible Club. You know, crafts and all that sort of thing. Anything to get us out of her hair. We spent most of our holidays there. She didn't care if they weren't Muslim. There was none of this segregation back then. I can't see people doing things like that now. They've been brainwashed."

"You're lucky. I had to go to Saturday School every week – to learn Serbian. So boring."

They chuckled together. Amany reached into her bag and pulled out a photo of her daughter, Leila. Ten years old. Cute chubby cheeks and long, black hair pulled back in a plait.

"She goes to a private Methodist girls' college now," she explained. "I know it's Christian but there isn't much choice." They both smiled. "I worry for her future. Somebody spat at me in the street the other day."

Tom sighed. "Ignorant fools."

"I know. Private school is hard but we both want her to have a chance in the world. My husband, well he doesn't earn that much and my salary is pretty basic. Public hospitals, you know."

"Where does your husband work?" Tom asked.

"Just in a factory. His English is not great either. I think he resents the fact I have a university education. Even my father told me no good would come of it. He said, 'You're going to end up at the kitchen sink anyway, so what are you doing?'"

"You're a wonderful social worker, Amany," Tom said. "A lot of good has come of it."

"Thank you. I guess my husband's frustrated. He told me there was no point spending so much money on a girl's education. He's taking his anger out on me. And Leila, she gets scared when we fight."

"You don't have to put up with that." He pushed a tissue box towards her but she shook her head.

"I'm OK."

"What did you want me to do, Amany?"

"I want to see what my rights are. If I wanted, could he be sent back to Lebanon?"

Tom looked serious. "What sort of visa does he have?"

"Permanent Resident. He's not a citizen yet."

Tom shook his head. "There's not that much we can do. If he became a PR quite some time ago he's well and truly on his own now. You're no longer a sponsor as such since this only happens at the first stage of the process."

"Yes but I don't want him here."

"I don't think there's much that can be done there. You can't leave him?"

"It's hard. I don't want any trouble for my daughter, or my family. My parents would be disgraced. They have enough problems with my little brother. I'm trying to keep an eye on him. He's dropped out of school. I'm worried about him with all these evil influences around now."

"What? ISIS and so on?"

"Yes. But I don't think he's that stupid. Our girls are responding much better to education. The boys, well, some of them are in chaos. And he's been hanging around with the wrong crowd lately. Petty thieves, not terrorists of course. But still I am worried."

"Has he had any charges against him?"

"No, but the police keep a very close watch on our youth."

"Let me know if there's any trouble, call me immediately. I have colleagues who are good criminal lawyers."

Amany stood up. She knew that as much as Tom appeared sympathetic he really couldn't do much for her. And maybe her idea about her husband was a bit crazy. She'd just have to put up with it. It was hard to talk to her family about her problems. They saw her as the black sheep. God would find a way for her. She knew she was being tested. She just needed more patience. "Sorry to bother you with all this. Our women are very outspoken, you may have noticed."

Tom came round to her side of the desk. She took his hand and thanked him. "I would have to be the only Muslim here who wants a fellow Muslim kicked out." She smiled sadly.

He saw her out to the lifts. "Have you spoken about any of this with Shannon?"

She shook her head. She'd tried but soon realised Shannon had no idea of what she'd been through. She had hoped that a woman who had experienced pregnancy loss would be more empathetic but she doubted it. "I tried to talk to her about it but she didn't really want to know."

"Typical. She's so selfish."

"Cut her some slack, Tom," Amany still wanted to help Shannon. "I hope you don't mind me saying this but Shannon needs Maxie. She's really feeling it. Can you let her see him more often?"

Tom sighed. "It's Maxie I'm worried about. She's really losing the plot, Amany."

"You think so? Everybody needs to grieve in different ways. I think she's mixed up, sad, depressed I guess. But I don't think she's clinically depressed. She misses him. And he needs his mum too. He's only a little boy."

"OK, I'll think about it."

Before she got in the lift Tom kissed Amany on each cheek. She smiled at him as the lift doors closed.

Chapter Twenty-six

After Rafael and Colin left the café Shannon found it almost impossible to concentrate on work. She tried to hide her red eyes from Nick and her customers by putting on her sunglasses. Slightly obvious, she thought, but ah well. She was still smarting from the night at the salsa club and then Rafael so unpleasant to her here. God, what a temper. That guy sure had issues. She pronounced it to herself like issoooss, trying to make herself laugh. She wished she'd poured the coffee over him. That would have made him realise what a deadshit he'd been. Just when she thought she'd met somebody she could actually be interested in he turns out to be a weirdo as well. Tom, a control freak, and Rafael a traumatised loony. Great, just what she needed. Couldn't she find somebody normal?

Nick must have been able to hear her snuffling because he was on his best behaviour, helping make sandwiches and salads as well as coffee, serving customers with a smile and flirtatious banter, much to the pleasure of the older women. Neither Colin nor Rafael came in at lunchtime and at around three pm when they were due to knock off Nick suggested she go and speak to him.

"I can't, he's so angry with me."

"Well maybe you shouldn't have involved the media. He must have his reasons for not wanting that. An apology perhaps? What have you got to lose?"

Shannon waited outside the building site in her car, thinking she would offer Rafael a lift home. When he wandered out with his backpack strung over his shoulder and a sour look on his face she beeped the horn at him. He swung round and saw her but kept walking. She beeped the horn again and waved but he continued on his way to the bus stop.

"Oh for God's sake," Shannon muttered to herself as she jumped out of the car and ran towards him, the engine still running.

"What are you doing, Shannon?" Rafael was still angry.

"Please, I just want to talk to you. Come for a drive. I'll take you home."

"No, you won't. I don't need your charity."

"I'm sorry, Rafael. I was just trying to help," Shannon touched his arm but he jumped back, then turned again and walked quickly to the bus stop. But she wasn't going to give up that easily; she went back to her car and drove up next to him, almost mounting the footpath.

"*Hijo!* What are you doing?" He shouted at her.

Rolling down the passenger window she called out: "Want a ride, stranger?"

"Stop trying to be funny. You're crazy."

'I'm deadly serious, Raf. Don't you understand you're all I've got?" she pleaded as she pushed the passenger door open.

He reluctantly climbed in, throwing his backpack on the floor as he closed the door. "Got any salsa CDs?" he asked, as she started the car.

"In the glove box."

He found some Cuban music amidst a pile of maps, Maxie's toys and loose coins and put it on, mouthing the words as she drove.

"I'm an idiot," she said.

"And I'm an arsehole, as you say in Australia."

They looked at each other and laughed.

"Why don't we go to your whale rock," he suggested. "We need to talk."

Shannon and Rafael had the rock to themselves. The joggers hadn't started the charge yet, and the cold wind kept many walkers away, except for an old lady and her pug. It was blowy but Shannon didn't mind. She needed the fresh air to sort out her feelings. They sat down facing the choppy sea. A cruise liner was moving north towards the heads, bringing its load of freezing tourists to dump at Circular Quay.

She decided to get right onto the topic that was bugging Rafael. "Why are you so against having a journalist write a story on the building site?" she asked.

"I just think it's dangerous," Rafael answered. "I don't trust the media. And I don't want anybody poking in my life, you know."

"But what have you got to hide?"

Rafael hesitated, then spoke slowly. "Nothing. I was just trying to protect her. "

"Who?"

"*Nada*, it's not important," he paused then turned to her and took her hands in his. "Look, I think it's time I explained to you about Lana."

She nodded. Her legs touched his.

"I worked with Lana, I told you before. We did have an affair and early on I did find her attractive. But her career always came first. And she didn't understand my country. She didn't understand how the revolution was a life and death situation for us. We couldn't let the *revolución* fail."

"I heard you in your sleep talk about a baby."

Sí, the baby. He would tell her about that. It was time.

Managua
February, 1986

We're in the doctor's waiting room – and waiting is the right word – for the nurse to bring the results of the test. Lana's tense, pushing her hair behind her ears every few minutes. The waiting room is full of happy couples; they want children, little Sandinos and Carlitos for the revolution.

A nurse comes over and hands me a piece of paper. Lana grabs it nervously. "Let me read it," but after running her eyes over it she groans and thrusts it at me. It's not her results, only the bill and I laugh. She hits me on the arm angrily: "You should have worn a condom, *mi amorsito*."

I can't use those things. They take all the pleasure away. *Desagradable*. What is wrong with making children for the revolution?

Then another nurse comes out of the doctor's room and smiles coming towards us.

"*Positivo*," she announces, her crooked white teeth showing.

I almost whoop with happiness but Lana groans again. "The Last Revolutionary," she announces as she picks up her bag and rushes out of the surgery.

Rafael looked at Shannon. "If Lana did what she did today in Nicaragua this dictator would put her in jail for life."

"What was that?"

"She got rid of my baby. Our baby."

"Go on." Shannon leant forward.

"There was just so much death and dying. I didn't want any more. I knew there was no future between us but I would have been willing to look after the baby. My mama would have helped. But Lana's career came first. It was illegal but she found somebody who would take *Gringo* dollars to do it."

Shannon bit her lip. "I understand Lana. Sometimes there's no choice."

"She had a choice."

"Rafael, now we are being honest," she paused. "I had an abortion."

Rafael nodded. "Oh?"

"I keep asking myself, is that why I lost Emma? Did it damage my body? I know Tom blames me."

"Was it his baby?"

"No, it happened a long time ago. Way before I met him."

"But he knows?"

"Yes I told him. I wish I hadn't. But you, please can we have no secrets between us?"

Rafael nodded. He pulled her up. "Why don't we go to my place?"

Managua
February, 1986

I'm outside the doctor's surgery waiting for Lana. I see the ugly, little man leave, counting notes as he shoves them into his wallet. But where is Lana? I push the door open and there doesn't seem to be anybody there. Then I hear somebody moving around in the next room. Lana is pulling on her clothes. She's thrown the hospital gown on the bed but is having difficulty getting dressed. I go to her and hold her tight. "What? He left you here on your own?"

"I woke up and he was taking the money out of my bag," Lana held her stomach.

"Are you in pain?"

"A little. Can you get a taxi to take us home. There's a phone here. Call the co-op."

We wait together until the taxi arrives, one of a very small fleet in my poor, earthquake-wrecked city. I want to talk about the operation but I know today is not the day.

Rafael unlocked the front door, the key turned easily in the lock since he'd sprayed WD40 on it. Nobody had seen them come inside the building or climb the stairs to his flat, which he was glad about. He still wanted to protect his privacy. "Da daa," he pushed the door open and waved his arm to welcome her in.

It was the first time Shannon had been here and she shivered as she walked inside. "Turn the heater on," she said as she looked around the room, taking in Mexican paintings, indoor plants, an old couch in front of the TV.

He pushed the button on the radiator. "Coffee? My turn to make you one."

"Do you have any tea?"

"I'll find something." He hoped he still had some teabags in the cupboard. The kitchen was spotless. Everything put away in perfect order. Coffee in a jar. Cans of beans on a shelf. But not much in the fridge. Only some butter and jam. "Sorry, I don't have milk. I'm on the Managua diet. No food. *No hay nada.*"

"It's OK, I can drink it black. Or just water." Her eyes moved to the hanging pot plant. "Your plant needs water too."

He filled a glass with water and poured it in the basket.

Shannon leant on the kitchen bench and watched him put a pot on the stove and prepare the tea. She smiled. "You don't cook much, Raf?"

"Nothing fancy. I'm an ordinary man." He handed her a cup. "You can drink it in my bedroom."

A red and yellow woven rug covered Rafael's bed, the neat blue sheets tucked in underneath matched the pillow cases. It was the only hint of colour in the bare room, even the walls were beige. That was apart from the pot plants on the windowsill and the view between the buildings out to the sea. On the bedside table was a pile of books almost as high as the bed. Most in Spanish.

Shannon picked one up and turned over its pages. Poetry. She didn't understand the words but she saw Nicaragua among them. "From home?" she said.

"I ordered them. I miss my Nica poets." He dragged the curtains together and turned down the sheets then undressed her.

But then she took over, unbuttoning his overalls, unlacing his boots and pushing him down onto the bed. She kissed every burn scar she could find on his body, working her way down his chest to where he really wanted to be touched. He moved her body around and opened her legs, going down on her till she climaxed.

"Nothing like makeup sex," she said.

"Shh, no more talking," he said as they lay back against his pillows.

Shannon cuddled up to him and they held each other until they both fell asleep.

Chapter Twenty-seven

Shannon couldn't believe that even without the new divorce lawyer hassling him Tom had relented and let her have Maxie for the weekend. He dropped him off at the café just at closing time on Friday as she was loading her car with her bags and boxes of food.

"Mummy," Maxie ran into her arms and they hugged like they'd never let go.

"I'll pick him up on Sunday night," Tom interrupted.

"I can take him to school on Monday morning," Shannon pleaded.

"No, Sunday night. Slowly, slowly Shannon. I didn't know you were going to the valley. Are you sure you can manage it?"

"Of course I can. He'll be alright, don't worry."

As she drove off, she turned to Maxie in the back, where he was hugging her teddy bear, thrown in with her clothes. "Always treat your girlfriend well, darling." And Rafael had been treating her very well, she thought

"Muum. I don't have a girlfriend," Maxie frowned.

"But doesn't Charlotte like you?"

"Oh mum, she's not my girlfriend. She's a friend."

Shannon laughed. "And I guess you're too young to go to a bar too?"

"Only the monkey bar, mum."

She laughed again. Witty, her boy. And smart. She remembered when he had come home from his first scripture class – before she'd removed him from it – and announced: "They tried to tell me Jesus was the son of God. But don't worry, mummy, I didn't believe them."

"Hey how'd you like to come and sit up the front? You're too old for that booster seat. You can bring Bear with you too." She smiled at the way he was holding it, remembering how he'd always loved cuddling up to it and not wanting another one of his own.

She pulled over to the side of the road in a No Stopping zone, and let him out. "Shh, just don't tell daddy, OK?"

"I think daddy has a girlfriend," Maxie said after she buckled him in.

"What?"

"Yeah I found some lipstick in the bathroom." He reached inside his jeans' pocket and handed it to her. "It's dark, like blood. You'd look pretty if you wore it."

Shannon took it from him. "It's not my colour, darling. You shouldn't have taken it." She imagined Tom's reaction if he knew his son had found the lipstick and kept it.

"Don't tell daddy. He'll get mad with me. He sure needs angry management, mummy."

Tom has a girlfriend, well what do you know? He's a sneaky bastard. Huh! Hope she can cope with Irina and know how to make Turkish coffee, or she won't last long.

Shannon threw the lipstick into the console between their seats. Maxie cracked her up. She knew what it was like to be on the receiving end of Tom's tantrums. He was so nice and polite to his clients but with his family he could lose his temper at the drop of a hat. About silly little things. If she hadn't bought bread that day. He couldn't survive a day without bread. If she let the Turkish coffee boil over and made a mess all over the stove. She'd had to learn to make that sort of coffee for when his mother visited, so she wouldn't look like an ignorant Irish housewife. Funny that now she ran a café. But Irina had never been there. Probably thought it wasn't hygienic enough. Oh well, she didn't want her breathing down her neck.

If dinner wasn't ready when Tom came home, he'd go into a huff and retreat to his little office. It got to the point where he never ate with her and Maxie. She'd eat standing up in the kitchen, while Maxie sat at the bench. No wonder she lost weight. He'd come out half an hour after she'd called him for dinner, grab his plate and take it back in front of his computer. She'd find it there the next morning, covered in leftovers. It was up to her to rinse and wash it.

"Do you put your plate in the dishwasher, Maxie?" she asked, squeezing his hand as she started the car again.

"Yeah, sometimes. But Baba does it when I stay at her house. She makes yummy cabbage rolls for me. And salad with fetta cheese. And baklava."

Oh that'd be right, Shannon thought, Tom's mother spoiling another male in the household.

"You should help her, darling. Show her you're a good housewife."

"Muum, housewife? You mean househusband."

"Yeah that's what I mean."

"It's Baba's birthday soon. She told me. You should come. We'll have banana cake and stuff."

"I'm not invited, sweetie. But maybe."

"Your cakes are the yummiest, mummy. I bet you're prettier than daddy's girlfriend. Oooh, I hope they're not sexing. Anyway, I don't like lipstick. Baba leaves marks like a clown on my face when she kisses me." Maxie stopped talking to his mum and chatted away to Bear, explaining where they were going and what animals they would see on the farm.

As she manoeuvred her way through the city's southern suburbs, Shannon tried to make the image of Tom and his girlfriend "sexing" disappear while the DVD player belted out Nick Cave. She felt sick, the thought of him being with another woman. But why? Surely she wasn't jealous? She used to say she didn't believe in monogamy, that women would be better off living in gatherer groups, taking any hunter men they wanted.

"Do you have a boyfriend, mummy?" Maxie's little voice disturbed her thoughts, as she turned down the music.

"Me? No." She couldn't call Rafael her boyfriend, that's for sure. She had hoped she could, but not quite yet.

"But I saw some clothes at your place. A scarf I think. It wasn't a girl's scarf."

She thought for a minute. "Oh, that must have been Rafael's."

"Rafael who?"

"Ramirez. Well, I do like him but I'm not sure he's my boyfriend. Too unpredictable."

"What does that mean?"

"You never know what's going to happen next. Don't ever get jealous with your girlfriend – when you do get one. Anyway, you're my only boyfriend, my darling."

"Muuum. I'm not your boyfriend," Maxie screwed up his face.

When she turned to look at him, she saw he had painted bright purple spots on his cheeks with the lipstick; she had to put her foot on the brake just in time to avoid slamming into the car in front of her.

"I'm a clown now, mummy," he said, turning to look out the window at the houses they were passing.

Shannon had bought Maxie his own pair of walking boots but he refused to put them on. He liked to go barefoot even in winter. Maybe he felt chained-in wearing shoes. She reluctantly gave in to him but put on her old boots. She'd trudged miles and miles with them, climbing the back blocks through the scrub, and up the creeks.

She grabbed her beaten up straw hat, her "farm hat" as she'd dubbed it, and her walking stick, a smooth piece of wood with a naturally knobbly handle that she'd picked up on a walk with Tom, in their happier times, way up the back of the property.

It was the bluest of blue autumn days, with only a hint of crispness in the air; the sun was shining over the escarpment, a single cloud reigning over everything below.

Shannon and Maxie crossed a swampy paddock past an ancient lemon tree, its fruit dominated by rind but still tangy. The birds had spread the seeds and you could find gnarly lemon trees in the strangest of places. They'd done the same with the damn lantana. It was a hybrid of town hedges, made tougher and stronger over the years and taking over everything in its way.

This is the country her parents had worked so hard to restore, spraying and hacking at the lantana for years on end. One day Shannon had gone for a walk up the back to where the lantana had taken hold again. She'd tried to get through but once inside the spiky growth of weed where fairy-wrens fed she'd worried she could never get out. She felt trapped, as the sky was shut out and darkness enveloped her. What if I'm stuck here forever, she'd thought but she'd managed to crawl backwards on her knees, covered in bloody scratches.

That part of the creek was full of rusting bits of machinery. They'd become part of the creek's slope, ironically holding it together, and slowing the erosion.

She remembered another glorious day – the first time she brought Tom to the valley. What a romantic weekend! It was like something out of one of those glossy travel magazines – picnics and fires and sex in front of the fire. He was so loving then, even made her tea in bed.

That's all she wanted from a man, she'd told Maxie later.

"I'll make you tea, mummy," he had said. "I won't burn myself."

Her sweet Maxie. She'd put a couple of carrots in her backpack so they could feed the old horse on the way up; he lolled over towards them as they came across the paddock. Maxie held his hand out flat with the carrot on top of it so the horse could gobble it. "Oooh yuk, my hand's all wet," he said as he wiped it on his pants.

Shannon stroked the horse's nose and snuggled up next to him. "He won't hurt you. Only people hurt you, darling boy."

Maxie spotted old Joe, who used to work for her dad and was now the caretaker of the neighbour's farm. Wearing his usual checked flannelette shirt, denim pants and clodhopper boots, he was working on his tractor behind the shed and the little boy ran over to hug him round his legs. "What are you doing, Joe?" he asked.

"I'm fixing the tractor. You got your licence yet?"

Maxie laughed. He knew he was joking. "Noooo but I found one in the rice bubbles' packet. Maybe I can use that."

"Oh well, that'll do," he hauled Maxie up onto the tractor seat. He reached forward to grab the steering wheel, making "brmm, brmm" noises.

"Probably a better driver than some of the P platers you get around here," Joe smiled. His laconic style left no room for fools. And that was what Shannon loved about him. You didn't have to put on an act in front of him or prove anything. He'd known her since she was a kid, and whenever they chatted they'd have a bitch about modern ways and the stupid government or local council or even some of the newcomers – Pitt Street farmers as they were known.

"You know why those people up the road haven't fixed their driveway into their property?"

"No."

"There's no grant for it."

Shannon laughed. "They probably are waiting until it's The Year of the Farmer or some such thing."

He raised one eyebrow and gave the cynical farmer look. "More like The Year of Living Dangerously."

"Joe, I've been wanting to ask you," Shannon changed the subject. "Do you remember Ainslie, who was a housekeeper who worked for mum and dad? A Koori."

Joe thought for a while. "Yeah I think so."

"Would she have come from the Bomaderry Children's Home?"

"Possibly. She didn't stay long."

"Any idea of her last name?"

"Wouldn't have a clue. Your parents had lots of housekeepers over the years. How's your sister?"

"She's good, kids are great. Five!"

Maxie was getting impatient, he wanted to keep exploring. They said good bye and held hands as they climbed higher, Maxie pointing out different birds – the willie wagtails and of course the kookaburra laughing at them.

"That means it's going to rain," Shannon said.

But she insisted on stopping at her favourite sun-baking spot, on top of a huge eucalypt which had fallen down in the strong winds the valley was known for, its roots dangling out the back in their nakedness. She pulled Maxie up onto the tree trunk and they lay down on its narrow, bark-covered length feeling the sun on their faces. A bit of rusty fence was lying against the other big gum tree. Willie wagtails flew from tree to tree and branch to branch. Their song reached out across the paddocks. She handed him an apple as she pointed out a wombat hole beneath the tree, with scats leading away from it.

"Look, they look like baked brown rolls from the bakery," Shannon said. "Remember that wombat we saw last night. Might be his home."

Caught in the car's high beam, it had slowly lumbered along the road, scared but not showing it, just moving at its own slow, sure pace. She dipped the lights so as not to blind the old fellow. He didn't turn around to check. Just wandered up a small hill to probably find his burrow. One of the few around here that hadn't succumbed to mange – a horrible, painful way to die.

Maxie munched the apple, then threw the core away. They climbed higher, Maxie running ahead, then stopping and attempting to do handstands in the long grass. "Be careful of snakes, make a lot of noise," she called after him.

"I'm not scared of snakes," he yelled back, running ahead. He seemed to hover over the ground.

"Maxie, come back." Shannon was worried a five-year-old would have no idea what to do if he came across a snake, and no boots didn't help.

But he kept running, not noticing a family of kangaroos up ahead and getting a fright when he disturbed them. They bounded off through the paddock and Maxie ran back to his mum. The huge male turned and stared at the pair of them, flicking his ears before he too hopped away. Shannon grabbed him by his arms.

"Don't be frightened. I'm here." She twirled him around in a circle until they were both giddy and fell on the ground.

"Do wombats hurt you, mummy?" he asked, picking himself up.

"Well they have sharp claws and can bite but they won't hurt you if you don't get too close."

"I'm not scared of them," Maxie was defiant. "I'm not scared of nothing."

Back at the house Shannon let Maxie watch *Dr Who* on TV while she poured herself a wine and sat on the verandah. She'd found her stash in its hiding place inside a bedroom cupboard – a small deal of dope – and she rolled herself a joint and drew it deep into her lungs. The birds were fluttering through the trees as the sky darkened. Always the sound of birds moving through the bush – the wrens, the robins and the cuckoos.

Soft pink light shone on the top of the trees and she could hear the cows mooing down below. She looked at her phone – no missed calls, no texts from Rafael or anybody else. Well, at least I know I can still do it, if nothing else, she thought.

Her eyes closed. She was tired, tired of all the fighting with Tom. And with Rafael, even though they'd made up. And sad. Anxious that it was too good to be true now with him. She could feel herself beginning to cry but didn't want to give way to it, instead bringing her ashtray and dope bag inside, leaving it on the table. She'd have to make some dinner soon.

She found Maxie standing in front of the wood stove, the door wide open. He was throwing sticks in the stove and lots of newspaper. There were spent matches everywhere and the newspaper was still alight, although the fire hadn't taken.

"Maxie, what are you doing?" She closed the stove door with a bang, and grabbed the matches from him. "You could have set the house on fire."

He was defiant. "It's OK, I can make a fire. Daddy showed me before."

She smacked him lightly on his bottom and he started crying. "I know how to make a fire. I told you."

Feeling bad, she hugged him and held him close, moving the cushions on the couch so they could snuggle up together as he pushed his snotty nose into her jumper. She wiped it with her sleeve and turned him around so that he could lean back on her tummy, their legs stretched out, intertwined. As he watched TV she fell fast asleep.

Shannon woke from the cold. The TV was on but she couldn't see Maxie. And the chops for dinner were still in the sink. The wood stove door was open again but the fire wasn't burning. She went to his bedroom to see if he'd put himself to sleep but he wasn't there. Bear was missing. The front door was also wide open. "Maxie, where are you?" She ran through the house looking for him, opening doors, pulling covers off beds. A cupboard door had been left open, the one where the torch was kept. It was gone. She went outside using the torch on her phone and called out to him but still there was no answer. The night was piercingly cold. The stars gave the only brightness.

Shannon had no idea what to do. Had he been taken by somebody when she was asleep or was he just exploring the bush? Even as a toddler he'd loved to go off into the paddocks in his bare feet but never during the night. She wished Rafael was here but what could he do? Instead she phoned Joe. "I'm really worried," she told him.

Soon she heard the sound of Joe's ute and saw the lights coming up the road. He pulled into her driveway and turned off the engine, emerging with a large torch.

"We'll find him, Shannon, don't worry." Always dependable even in the middle of the night.

"He might be looking for wombats, he likes wombats."

"Let's try that burrow up near the big gum tree."

Maxie was curled up like a wombat next to the hole, the torch still on in his dirty hand, Bear in the other. Face filthy. Fast asleep.

"Lucky a wombat didn't tread on him." Joe had to smile seeing him lying there.

Shannon fell on the ground next to the boy and hugged him with every bit of energy she had.

Maxie half opened his sleepy eyes and smiled. "I'm not scared of wombats, mummy. I'm Wombat Boy."

Joe didn't normally come inside. It was too much of an effort to take his boots off and usually he had plenty of other things to do but when Shannon asked if he'd like a cuppa to warm up, he agreed.

She carried Maxie into his bed, and scrubbed his face and hands with a face washer wrapped around some soap as he slept still clinging to Bear.

Joe had re-lit the fire and was piling it with bigger logs. She put the kettle on and spooned the tea into the pot.

"Just black for me," Joe said as the fire roared.

They sat at the kitchen table. Shannon was exhausted. She tried to push the ashtray away but Joe had already noticed the roach butt in it.

"Don't worry about it, Shannon. I already knew you liked a bit of the old marijooarna." He winked at her.

She laughed. "Well, please don't tell Tom. Poor Maxie, he must think I'm such a flake."

"No, he just loves you because you're his mum."

There was no need to talk until Shannon brought up the subject of Ainslie again. "Hey, you know we were talking about the Bomaderry Children's Home?"

"Yeah," he nodded.

"Well, they weren't orphans. Those kids were stolen from their parents. Like Ainslie."

"I know. Why are you so interested in her?"

"I've got a feeling she could have been the mum of a good friend of mine, Colin Barnett. Wouldn't that be a weird coincidence?" Joe put his cup down and stood up. He picked up the poker to move the logs around in the fire. "Tiny little one, if she's the one I'm thinking of. Your parents did get a few housekeepers from the home. Not sure about her though. She was older. Think she might have answered an ad. I met some of those Bomaderry girls at dances over the years."

"Dances? I didn't know you danced, Joe?"

"There's a lot of things you don't know about this old fella."

"So do you have any idea why she left or what happened to her?"

"No, Shannon. I don't know. Probably got a better job somewhere else. Anyway, better get home. Dot will be wondering if I'm the one who's fallen down a wombat hole." He gulped the last of his tea.

"Thanks so much for helping me find Maxie, Joe. I couldn't have done that on my own."

"No worries. He's a good kid."

"I know."

She opened the door for Joe, who pushed his beanie down on his head. He didn't need his torch to find his way back to his ute. He knew the old farm like the back of his hand.

Chapter Twenty-eight

Outside the Coroner's Court the usual gang of news crews and photographers waited. You always knew the commercial TV reporters by the amount of makeup they were wearing. One with stiff white hair, cut straight across at the ends and a face caked with foundation sat on the couch inside, checking her iPad and eating takeaway Chinese. Her jacket over a white dress couldn't have been a brighter pink.

They probably told her people will notice her more if she wears luminescent colours, Vesna thought, squeezing next to her on the couch.

"Oooh sorry, I didn't mean to take up so much room." She fluttered her eyelashes at Vesna, who grunted back.

Jeeze, the woman is wearing false eyelashes, Vesna noticed, wishing she'd at least put a bit of lipstick on. She looked in her makeup bag but couldn't see her favourite one. Oh well, who was here to impress anyway? Just the crusty old Coroner and the butch lawyers. Not a single spunk here.

"Are you covering the building site inquest?" she asked the TV reporter.

"Yeah, court room one. They were talking about safety standards this morning."

Vesna swore under her breath. She knew she should have got up earlier – on her day off – to get here. But at least she'd made it for the afternoon session.

False Eyelashes finished her noodles and stood up to throw the plastic container in the bin. She found her cameraman, pointing out some of the labourers from the Tamarama site making their way back into court. "Get a shot of them, OK."

Vesna went to the back of the court and found a seat. It was a small room and there was a media section but she didn't want to join the other reporters there, especially as she wasn't doing a news story.

The court rose when the Coroner walked in. Not so crusty, probably sixtyish with metal-framed glasses, a purple and blue striped tie, matching watch band and grey hair.He looked kindly, that was the word, Vesna thought.

A woman with short brown hair and a pin-striped suit who must have been Counsel assisting the Coroner called for Colin Barnett. He came inside and walked up to the witness stand, wearing a grey suit and a conservative navy tie.

"So this is Colin." Vesna had a feeling she'd seen him before. Shannon had never mentioned he was a Koori.

He looked uncomfortable and not very happy about being there, but he had that air of being used to authority and institutional situations. He made an affirmation, shaking his head when the Bible was offered. When he was cross-examined he didn't seem fazed by the questions.

Counsel Assisting asked if the deceased had held a legitimate occupational health and safety card – known colloquially as a white card – as well as a working-at-heights card, and Colin nodded. Then she asked what happened the day of Tony's death and Colin described the wasp attack and how Tony fell.

"So it wasn't a heart attack?" Counsel asked.

"Not that I'm aware of."

"One of the men – Rafael Ramirez – held his hand. Is this right?"

"Yes Raf did everything he could to ease it for him."

"But wouldn't it have been better to have somebody do mouth to mouth?"

"The first aiders in the team came to help. They wanted to do mouth to mouth, but Tony had hit the back of his head on the ground. Snapped his head right back. It was too late."

"Are you a member of the CFMEU, Mr Barnett?"

"I used to be, miss. For years. But since I've been a foreman I work for a salary. No overtime these days."

"So you were responsible that day?" A large woman in a purple pants suit, who Vesna guessed must be the lawyer working for the company, fired a question at him.

Colin looked at the woman lawyer; Vesna could see his hate towards her. "Yes, I was. It was an accident, pure and simple."

"You don't think safety procedures were breached?" Counsel asked.

"I really can't say, miss."

"Objection, there has been no question about safety procedures." Purple Pants Suit thought she was in an American TV show.

The Coroner just waved her away, while the journos scribbled in their note books.

Another lawyer, a thin man in a grey suit with scruffy shoulder-length hair, appeared to be working for the union. "Your honour, now that the subject has been brought up I'd like to ask the witness a question."

"Go ahead." The Coroner nodded.

"Mr Barnett, were there handrails on the scaffolding and had it been properly planked out?"

Colin stopped for a minute, his breathing got heavier. "There were handrails yes, and it had been planked out fully."

"Was there a reason why the safety netting hadn't been erected?"

"There was no reason, we were about to do it," Colin answered.

"And that's how the deceased fell?"

"It happened so fast. I just saw the wasps and Tony waving his arms around. And then, he hit the ground."

Sobbing was coming from the back of the court, where a large woman in jeans and a jumper was wiping tears from her eyes. "Tonyyyyyy," she mumbled.

On either side of her were teenage girls, their arms entwined in hers. Tony's widow and his kids, Vesna guessed.

"Who was in charge of the scaffolding?" the union lawyer asked.

"Well, the scaffolding company, they are a subcontractor. But as the foreman I manage the subcontractors."

"Mr Barnett, would you say the owners of the site were in a rush to get the building finished?"

"They're always in a rush, sir. It doesn't matter what site and what company it is."

"Objection." Purple Suit interrupted again.

"So would you say the CEO of the company should be held responsible?"

"It's not for me to say, but he is the top dog."

The Coroner coughed. "That'll be all for now, thank you, Mr Barnett. We'll have a break now for fifteen minutes."

As the court rose, Vesna watched Colin, without going up to him. All through the break waiting outside on the street he looked worried and fidgety. When he went to go back inside the camera crews followed him racing round to the front to get a shot for that night's news. He put his hand in front of his face and his head down as he walked in and took a seat.

Rafael Ramirez was called next. But he was a no show. Colin didn't even look around to see if he was there. She could see Colin knew he wouldn't turn up.

That evening Vesna gave Shannon a call to update her on the inquest and tell her about Colin's evidence. She felt a bit strange now knowing she was dating Shannon's ex but she wasn't going to say anything to her. She had been successful so far in pulling the wool over Tom's eyes as well.

"Poor Colin," Shannon said, opening the door of the fridge to see if there was anything for dinner while she spoke on the phone. "None of this is his fault. Or Rafael's. It's the bloody slack company. All for another ugly block of flats."

"Yes, I know, but that will come out eventually. You weren't around on the weekend?" She knew full well that Shannon had been allowed to have Maxie.

"No, I went to the country. With my little boy. It was so great but the funny little thing, he decided to go looking for wombats in the middle of the night. I found him curled up next to a wombat hole."

"What? Weren't you worried?"

"Oh yeah, but he's a smart kid. I knew he'd be alright."

Not for the first time Vesna wondered if she was dealing with somebody who was all there, or completely away with the fairies. She headed back up Parramatta Road, to the western suburbs of the city, miles from spoilt eastern suburbanites, their country estates and poor little rich children. She wasn't really looking forward to meeting this Maxie but Tom had invited her to his mother's birthday party that weekend, so she better brace herself for it.

Chapter Twenty-nine

Maybe it was the valley air or just having the previous weekend with Maxie but Shannon felt more energised this Saturday morning. She'd messaged Nick the night before asking him to fill in for her at the café as she was determined to face Tom and his mother and try to have a civilized discussion about her son.

She'd woken early, not this time because of the dreaded barking from the dog next door, but because the sounds of Indian Mynas had filled the room. Maybe she was dreaming but she woke feeling happy, rather than filled with the normal dread, even if the birds were an annoying introduced species.

Pulling on her slippers and dressing gown she padded into the kitchen and made herself a cup of tea. She turned her mobile on while she waited for the water to boil. Six missed calls from Rafael. And a text: Shannon, *mi amorcito, por favor, llámame.*

Writing to her in Spanish, that was a little weird but she gathered he wanted her to call him back. She needed the tea; she couldn't talk to anybody in the morning without a cuppa.

She also checked her emails and there was one from Deborah Secombe, the new divorce lawyer. She said she had looked at her case, and could not see why she shouldn't have equal custody of Maxie. She would be contacting Tom or his representative to discuss. Shannon almost whooped with happiness, even if a Saturday email from a lawyer would probably break her bank.

Back in bed, with the pillows propped up around her, she dialled his number. "Raf, it's Shannon. Is something urgent?"

"No. No, I just thought you were upset that I hadn't called during the week. Sorry I've been busy."

"That's OK. Me too."

She told him she was getting up the courage to go to Tom's

mother's house to wish her happy birthday, that it was time she grew up and tried to heal the rift – for Maxie's sake.

"*Buena suerte, cariño*. Call me when you come back. Maybe we can go out tonight, no?"

"OK, sure." Shannon's smiled widened.

"And Shannon, I suggest you take some flowers for Maxie's grandmother."

Irina lived at Rockdale – a suburb well known for its ethnic mix. Delis next to coffee shops on a strip facing the bay, fringed by brick blocks of flats. Where else could you find a shop dedicated to making and selling scrumptious *burek*, the cheese and spinach pastries she and Maxie loved. She'd have to buy some to take home later.

Shannon parked her car outside a yellow block, watching as some boys kicked a football around the cul de sac. Maxie would soon be old enough to do that, she hoped, if Tom ever bothered taking the time to play with him. She leant over the back seat to find the bunch of carnations she'd bought at the greengrocer, wrapped in matching pink crepe paper. Boring flowers but she knew Irina liked them.

Inside the front door the foyer was a bit grimy and a noticeboard had old notices pinned up, at least a year out of date. But she knew that Irina's flat would be spotless. She climbed a set of stairs to the first floor and with her hands trembling lifted the brass knocker.

An old lady with blue, permed hair and a neat brown pants suit opened the door."Shan-non. I wasn't expecting you." Irina looked behind her towards her lounge room which was full of the sound of people talking.

"I wouldn't forget your birthday, Irina," Shannon handed her the flowers.

Irina thanked her but smiled coldly, not fully opening the door to let her in.

"Can't I come in?"

"Oh of course but Shan-non ..."

Maxie came running, pulled the door open and jumped into his mother's arms. "Mummy, I knew you'd come," he kissed her on the cheek. "Daddy's girlfriend is here."

"Girlfriend? Oh I'd better go. Sorry for inviting myself. I just ..."

Irina shook her head. "Maxim, go back inside."

But the little boy ignored her. "No mummy, you can stay." Maxie took her by the hand and dragged her into the lounge room, Irina following, the flowers still in her hand.

The dining table in the next room, separated by a vinyl folding door, was covered with a white cloth, and four settings, with crystal wine glasses. Maxie's plastic baby cup, that Shannon knew he no longer needed, was perched at the end, in front of a stool.

"Hello Aleksandar," she smiled at Tom's father, who sat in a faded yellow wool rocking chair, sinking further and further down into its folds. Shannon was shocked to see how old he looked, and surprised that he didn't seem to recognise her. He didn't take his eyes off the television set, which was almost as big as the dining table. She would have gone over to kiss him except for her next sight.

In front of the pink floral brocaded lounge was a small table and on it was a tray with Turkish coffee cups, and a saucer of Turkish Delight. Sitting opposite were Tom and Vesna, whose face was rapidly turning the colour of the lounge.

"Shannon, hi," Vesna started to stand up but Tom pushed her down into the couch, as he almost knocked over the cups.

"Sit down," he hissed.

Vesna sunk back into the brocaded flowers.

"You know each other?" Tom asked. "What are you doing here, Shannon?"

"I wanted to say happy birthday to your mother, that's all," Shannon replied. "What about you, Vesna? What are you doing here?"

Tom stopped her answering but Maxie piped up. "She's daddy's girlfriend. She brought me lollies."

"Vesna's family is from Serbia," Irina pointed out. "I'll make you a Turkish coffee, Shannon or maybe you'd prefer a Nescafé?"

Shannon felt a whoosh of jealousy go through her. Vesna and Tom? It couldn't be. She'd been so open with her. Who was lying to whom? And lollies? What the hell? She looked at Tom. "No, no, don't do that. I'll leave. I wanted to talk to you and your mother about Maxie, but this is not the right time."

Tom stood up, and waved his finger at Shannon. "Don't think you can have him again. He could have died."

"What?"

"Lying next to a wombat hole," he was incandescent with rage. "How could you Shannon?"

"Vesna! I trusted you."

Vesna didn't answer, she just shook her head.

"You can't stop me seeing my son, Tom." Shannon turned to leave. "The lawyer told me. You'll be getting a letter."

Maxie started crying and grabbed at Shannon's legs.

"Maxie, let your mother go now, sweetie." Vesna tried to help but Tom gave her a withering look.

Shannon concentrated on her son, unpinning his clinging fingers. "Wombat Boy, you be strong now. I'll pick you up tomorrow from school, don't worry. You stay with Baba and Deda and daddy today – and Aunty Vesna."

Maxie climbed up onto his grandfather's lap and pushed his face into his grey vest. He sucked his thumb and held the old man tightly.

Shannon banged the front door behind her.

Shannon drove to a parking area next to the bay and turned off the engine. She stared out across the still water as the lights of the oil refineries sent lightning strikes across it. She was shaking and needed to think before going home or else there would be an accident. Her head felt like it was going to explode. Tom. And Vesna. How? Why? Oh, so what? What had she seen in him in the first place? Why did she ever marry him and have a child with him?

Maybe it was the sex. It had been great to start off with. So how was it with Vesna? The "sexing" that Maxie had talked about. She didn't want to think about it. She just hoped Vesna would chew him up and spit him out. He bloody well deserved it. She was surprised at her jealousy; it was like a flash of white heat running through her body. Did she still love him or was it just their normal family life she missed? And Vesna, of all people. She wasn't even good looking and really needed to go on a diet. But Serbian – of course, it fitted.

She wanted more, so much more but she couldn't put her finger on just what that 'more' was. Passion? Romance? Intensity? She'd had all three with Raf. Good sex too, but he was another one with a temper, although she felt Raf's love more keenly than Tom's. That is when Tom did love her. Raf's seemed more pure. He didn't expect anything of her, to be a good housekeeper or anything else. He'd just been mad at her going to the media. Well, maybe she should have listened to him. How could she trust Vesna now? It was all too close. How long had she been seeing Tom anyway?

Maybe she should have praised Tom more when they were

together. About what a good lover he was. Men need that. And certainly not to be lectured. Why had he acted so coldly towards her? Was it because his feelings had been hurt? She knew how much he had grieved for their baby too. But he'd hardly said anything. The perfect metrosexual. But deep down he was really just a Serb, who wanted a woman all to himself. And a Serb with a very controlling mother. Maxie's name was not Maxim, for heaven's sake. Poor old Aleksandar – no wonder he just stared at the TV these days. In a way, she was glad to be rid of the whole, bloody lot of them. Except for Maxie, of course.

As she drove home, she imagined what the evening would be like with Rafael; she hoped they wouldn't fight. Wait till he hears about Vesna! She owed him an apology.

Rafael picked Shannon up at eight and they walked down to Bondi together. He'd suggested a tapas bar where the Spanish food wasn't too bad, considering it was made in Australia. He wore his good black jeans and his leather jacket, his wavy hair out for a change and an unusual cologne that Shannon couldn't pick.

As they passed the headland, the beach swept out in an arc, once connected to the harbour by giant sand hills, now covered in mansions. Apartment blocks on the north side shone their lights down across the black water. It looked like Fairyland.

Shannon didn't want to ruin his good mood by mentioning Vesna but she was dying to tell him.

"But how on earth did she get together with Tom?" he sounded astonished.

"I still don't know. They're both Serbs, so maybe at some club or something. I got her name from Amany, the social worker. So maybe Tom gave her Amany's number. I've been trying to figure it out. The bloody bitch though, she must have told Tom about Maxie going missing at the valley."

"How did she know about that?"

"I'm the idiot who told her. I don't know, I thought I could trust her. I'm so sorry, Raf. I thought she'd write a great story and show how bad the construction company is. I just don't understand how I got it all so wrong."

Raf put his arm around her as they walked. "It's not your fault. It's mine."

"It's not, it really isn't. The inquest will show that. Did you go in the end?"

"No."

"But can't you get into trouble for that?"

"I don't know. I guess. Let's not talk about this anymore. We're meant to be having fun."

They pushed through the crowd at the bar and found a table at the restaurant. Shannon was surprised when Rafael ordered a bottle of white wine. He poured two big glasses and they clinked them together in a toast.

"*Salud,*" Rafael raised his glass. "Here's to both of us and our future."

"*Salud.*" Her voice could hardly be heard above the noise of the other patrons talking loudly and the music of the Gypsy Kings.

Shannon let Rafael order piles of food and she tasted everything. She hadn't been offered any food at Irina's and she was ravenous.

"It's good to see you eating." Rafael offered Shannon some garlic-covered prawns, spooning more rice on her plate.

"Well, I'm just glad we're both eating garlic tonight." She shovelled the prawn into her mouth.

"I really want to meet Maxie and take him to the zoo." He changed the subject.

"He'd love that, especially if there's wombats there." They laughed.

"Hopefully I'll have him more often now the lawyer says I should. But Tom was so angry, I just don't know."

"He has to let you have him."

"Yeah, I really hope so. You can come down to the valley with us too."

"I'd like that. The food here is good. We had nothing like this back home."

"You told me just beans and rice? But why?"

"It's a long story – the Americans put an economic embargo on us after the revolution."

"God, the bastards. Your country seemed to have had so many bad things happen to it. You spoke about the earthquake before?"

Rafael sat back in his chair, sipping his wine. "The one in 1972 in Managua, my home town?"

"Yes. You spoke of women being left to die in the factories while the owners only cared about their machinery. Unbelievable."

"I was only a kid then. It killed six thousand people, and

thousands more were injured, many more left with no home. They never rebuilt the centre of the city, just left it in ruins. Even today when people give their addresses, they say things like, two hundred metres from where the post office used to be, not the actual address. My country. It's a crazy place. Two streets below where the big fig tree used to be. You know what I mean?"

Shannon laughed. "Used to be! Huh! The café where the mummies go with the giant prams opposite where the general store used to be."

"That's it. Foreign governments, even the United States, and Mexico, well they gave us millions of dollars of aid money. But that bastard, Somoza, he kept most of it."

"Jesus! Didn't he have enough already? I hate greedy people, their mansions and their bloody BMWs and their birthday parties."

"The corruption was so bad in my country. The earthquake was the last straw and even the middle class and the rich eventually turned against Somoza. The whole country was shaken up when the editor, well the publisher really, of the opposition newspaper was assassinated."

"That's terrible."

"But in 1979 we won the *revolución*."

"And you were fighting in it too?"

"Yes, we all were. If we didn't have guns we threw rocks and sticks at the *guardia* in the streets, doing anything we could to stop that madman and his wife and their dynasty. You know her name was Hope? But we had no hope when they were there."

"Why did you leave, Raf?"

Rafael helped himself to some more rice and ate in silence. Shannon wondered if she would get an answer.

"I had no choice. I believed in the revolution. You know we have a saying: What is truth? This, or that? The only truth is: who knows?"

"I can relate to that. I'm glad you called me. It's so nice to go out to dinner with you and have a proper date."

He reached across the table and held her hand. "I think I'm falling in love with you, *mi periodista Gringa*."

"Who?" She pulled her hand away.

"I'm sorry," he looked embarrassed. "I didn't mean that."

"I know who you're talking about."

North of Ocotal
March, 1986

"Well, *Comandante* Manuel, what have we here?" Lana asks, once the greetings have been made.

"A hospital – I'm sure you can see that, *Señorita* Lopez. Our soldiers sometimes get sick."

"But this isn't the flu, is it *comandante*? They have war trauma, right?"

"War trauma?" A smear of a smile passes across *Com* Manuel's face. His long-sleeved khaki shirt is buttoned up, immaculate.

"Oh come on, not all your soldiers want to be fighting for the Fatherland." She gestures towards the woman soldier standing in the corner, whose tightly-pulled-back hair reveals a grim face.

"You and your government's secret deals with those muddle-headed ideologues." He laughs. "Your country always backs the wrong guys. Those counter-revolutionaries, only that crazy Reagan would support them. They are not the patriots. We are."

"I am an objective journalist. I'm not saying who I support. I just want to know what you are doing to these soldiers here."

"Objective!" he laughs again. "Then surely you can write the truth of how we care about our heroes. Come, I have somebody I want you both to meet." He calls out to the nun we just saw leaving. "Sister, can you bring Dr Krupitsky in, *por favor.*"

A few minutes later a tall, white-haired man in a matching coat, arrives. It's obvious he doesn't speak Spanish and *Com* Manuel interprets the Russian. "Dr Krupitsky has graciously come from the Saint Petersburg Regional Dispensary of Narcology to help us here at the military hospital. He is overseeing a group of twenty soldiers who are suffering from combat-induced Post Traumatic Stress Disorder, the current name for what you so quaintly call war trauma. He is overseeing our research team of three psychiatrists, two psychologists, several graduate psychology students, and other hospital staff. You'll be happy to know, my dear *Señorita* Lopez, that the funding has come from a wonderful North American organisation for the use of the drug, *3,4-methylenedioxy-methamphetamine*, also known as MDMA, to treat our soldiers."

"MDMA? Isn't that a party drug?"

"*Bueno*, maybe for spoilt teenagers in your country but this is in its most pure form. It is chemically similar to both stimulants and hallucinogens, producing feelings of increased energy, pleasure, emotional warmth, and distorted sensory and time perception. It alters mood and perception. We will be using it to help our warriors come to terms with their bad memories – what are known as traumatic flashbacks."

I can see Lana is hopelessly lost. She doesn't know whether to believe *Com* Manuel or not.

Dr Krupitsky nods at everything *Com* Manuel says as if he understands his words. Then he speaks to him in Russian. *Com* Manuel nods.

"We will be using a control group that will not receive MDMA," *Com* Manuel says. "The organisation supplying MDMA hopes that this study will generate data that will convince your Food and Drug Administration to allow this kind of psychotherapy in the United States."

Lana laughs cynically. "I don't think that will ever happen."

"Quite frankly, Ms Lopez, I don't care. We are much more foresighted here in Nicaragua and indeed in the Soviet Union than you will ever be in your so-called democratic country, run by the Mafia and despots."

"I don't think so, sir. You have no idea what the word, democracy, means. You are even too scared to hold elections."

I am feeling sick at this point. How could I ever have allowed her to come here? This story could so easily be twisted against us.

"I can assure you we are not in the slightest way scared to hold elections. No more talking now. We will visit the therapy room and see exactly what is going on."

Lana looks excited at this idea but her expression changes when *Com* Manuel says: "But *Capitán* Ramirez, you must stay outside. With your camera."

"But I need footage for my story," Lana interrupts.

"There will be no TV story, no filming until I say so. Just do as I say."

She gives me a look which says 'Get out there and film those patients'. "And since when have you been a *capitan*?"

I don't answer her question.

Rafael grabbed Shannon's hand again and held it tightly. What was he thinking? Talking about Lana? He was never in love with Lana. He could see a darkness cross Shannon's face. He didn't want to make her jealous. She had no reason to be. She was so much more to him than Lana.

"I'm so sorry, of course I meant you, Shannon."

"I damn well hope so. What is wrong with you, Rafael? You seemed miles away." She left her hand in his.

"Just memories I want to forget. Come on, let's walk to the beach." He paid the bill and led her down to the promenade where they leant over the rail towards the sand which had been raked like a Japanese garden. The wall behind them below the skateboard park was covered in graffiti, as if the people painted there were watching them, listening to their conversation. He kissed her on the cheek as tourists walking past pointed out to sea. They thought they could see a whale spouting.

Chapter Thirty

Vesna's fluffy pyjamas and ugg boots didn't really flatter her but she wasn't worried about that. Little cows and horses were perhaps not the right design for a woman in her early forties but the jarmies were comfortable and the ugg boots kept her feet warm as she tiptoed around her parents' kitchen at midnight, opening all the cupboards to see if she could find something to drink.

She had to keep wiping her runny nose, hoping it wasn't the beginnings of flu. She couldn't afford any time off work, having already taken all her leave. That lunch at Irina's hadn't left her mind. She'd been on her best behaviour all day, even wore a nice dress and stockings and spoke to her in her feeble Serbo-Croat. But it was exhausting, chopping up all those vegetables for the salad and trying to remember the words.

She really should have gone to Saturday School more often instead of escaping to the shopping centre with her friends to smoke and pick up boys. She just nodded and smiled most of the time, bored out of her wits when Tom and Irina yabbered on. Well, Tom did most of the talking. Irina sat there smiling at him; he hadn't wagged Saturday School, had he, Mr Goody-two-shoes? She'd picked up a lot in Kosovo sure but most was foul slang that she really couldn't use in that situation.

When Shannon turned up, she nearly died. Poor woman, all she wanted was her little boy. And Tom had been so angry. Wow, talk about a short fuse. She really hoped she'd never personally feel his anger, but she wasn't too sure. If he could lash out at his wife, or ex-wife, she'd probably be next. And why shouldn't Shannon see more of Maxie, even if she appeared to be a bit irresponsible? He was an OK kid, he was polite with her, although he seemed a little over-indulged by Irina. Shannon didn't need to be angry with her though;

she hadn't told Tom about Maxie going wombat-hunting. The ankle-biter had told him himself, boasting about being Wombat Boy.

Ah well, it was good while it lasted, she thought. And maybe it would last a little longer. Tom had put her on to some of his over-stayer clients, who were prepared to talk as long as they remained anonymous – and she'd interviewed contractors, unionists and other lawyers. She had enough material now for a really good exposé of how the underground, illegal migrant world worked. That would be her next big story.

Through money-launderers and criminal networks in their countries – often China – thousands of workers paid for four-five-seven and other visas to come here, making out they'd been sponsored. They'd get paid about ten per cent of their wages while the rest went to the middle-men, and it would take them years to pay back the around fifty thousand dollars they'd had to borrow with high interest. If they were caught and deported there was a good chance their debts would be taken out on their families – daughters raped and made prostitutes – or they'd get shot as soon as they got off the plane.

While here, they were able to obtain Medicare cards, drivers' licences and everything they needed – often via the "dark web". The government was aware of the whole sorry business but the "mob" never got charged. It only seemed to be interested in band-aid solutions like raids and deportation while others got rich, renting out "hot-bedder" apartments to whole families who used them on a rotation basis. These untouchables kept everybody quiet with huge political donations.

Vesna's slave trade feature was going to be a sizzler! Even Tom, who sometimes dreamt of a political career, had admitted that "politicians had no idea, no idea at all".

While her parents slept, Vesna poked around the kitchen. Surely there must be a bottle of plum brandy that Uncle Tesle made last summer. Her father couldn't have drunk all of it although it was his custom every morning to have a shot with his coffee. (Her mother always had the coffee going because "it keeps me up so I can do more housework".)

"I'll live to one hundred years after this," he would say the exact same thing every day. "It opens my digestion."

But, with her here, he might have hidden the *rakia*. Aha, here it is. Right at the back of the cupboard behind countless trays and coffee pots for making Turkish coffee she discovered it – about a glass's worth left in the bottom of an old soft drink bottle. Her father had said she could move back in – temporarily, on one condition – no drinking. The last time she'd got drunk at home was when her parents had had friends over for a barbecue and as the *cevapcici* grilled, sending tantalising garlic smells through the back yard, she'd berated the old couple about Serbian politics and how much she had despised the former president, Milosevic. They retorted that the Kosovars got everything they deserved.

"We hate Albanians," her father's friend said. "They have Kosovo now. It's not their country. It's part of Serbia. We should have killed all of them."

Vesna thought of the bastardry she had seen there. The KLA were animals but the Serbian Army were no angels either. Nobody deserved to be tortured by either side.

"Killing isn't going to help. People have to live somewhere. What's the point of all this hatred?" Vesna had not given up until her usually mild-mannered father had screamed at her. "Shut your mouth, Vesna. Enough. No more politics. This is my house."

She'd been on her best behaviour since because she had nowhere else to stay, at least until she saved some money for a bond and could find her own flat. She'd left the last place – a group house – because of arguments with her flatmates, and she wanted to live alone. So here she was back in Cabramatta, where the Yugos hated the Vietnamese and the Vietnamese hated the trendies who came for the "superb *pho*" and the police patrolled the streets looking for drug dealers, of any nationality.

At least she'd convinced her parents to get an internet account, so she took the glass of *rakia* gingerly up the stairs to her old bedroom to do some research. The room hadn't changed that much since she'd left it as a teenager. Still the same posters on the wall – Patti Smith, Cyndi Lauper, INXS and her heroes, Chrissy Amphlett and the Divinyls. Girls having fun with the boys in town.

She climbed under the covers on her bed, pulled the laptop up and logged into Facebook. God she hated Stalkbook, but it was a useful tool when she needed to find somebody. The dreary crap that people – she called them the 'faceless friends' – posted made her feel sick. She loved the analogy between Facebook and ancient Egypt – we're still putting cats on walls. Lost dogs, inbred cats, dead elephants, cryptic messages about people's boring lives, why would you bother? Distant, in-bred cousins trying to be deep and meaningful with posts from a Dalai Lama whose forte was not English grammar. Who thought of such drivel? Somebody somewhere in cyber space.

And the never-ending photos of food. Why if you're overweight would you stick up photos of the rich meals you'd consumed? She thought she might take a photo of her next Vegemite sandwich and put that up and see what people thought. Not that there was any Vegemite in this house. But the worst part was the hate posts, especially against outspoken Muslims. Vesna felt some sympathy for Amany when she read these.

Jenny George – pity that's such a common name, she thought. Shannon had said she was fiftyish, with red hair, in Sydney … da daaaa, a few Jenny Georges fitting that description popped up as she searched. Here was one. Gawd, how embarrassing – twenty friends only. At least she made it look like she had tons of faceless friends by friending people in third world countries. Yeah and guess what? Jenny George likes cats. And she's also a member of the Recognise Campaign. Oh my God – a politically correct Immigration officer. But she sounded like the one.

Toy farm animals were flung all over the floor as Maxie hunted high and low for his favourite truck in his bedroom at the Paddington house. It was a farm vehicle, a bit like the ute old Joe drove. He dragged his toy box over to his bed and pulled everything out of it. It was all Baba's fault. Why did she have to always clean up his toys? He knew where everything was before she started touching them. It was his room, not hers. "Daddy," he yelled. "Where's my farm truck?"

Tom appeared at the doorway. "I don't know, Max."

"But it was Baba who lost it. Tell her to stay out of my room."

Tom's face went red. "Stop this rudeness. Baba was only trying to help. Don't speak like that about her."

Maxie clenched his fists and screamed. "I want my truck. Where is it? She lost it."

Tom swept across the room and slapped Maxie on the bottom. "Stop that."

The little boy tried not to blubber like a baby. He climbed onto the bed and hugged one of his soft toys. "I want Bear."

"Stop crying, you have lots of other toys. I'm busy. I have a heap of work, and court in the morning. It's bed time. Go to bed."

"I want mummy. Why are you so mean to her all the time? Why couldn't she stay for Baba's birthday party? It's not fair."

Tom relented for a minute and sat down on the bed. He patted Maxie on his back. "You're too young. You don't understand. Come on, put your pyjamas on. We'll find your truck tomorrow."

"No! I want it now."

Tom pulled Maxie's pyjamas out from under the pillow and dragged his clothes off, and tucked him into bed. "Go to sleep now. And stop this nonsense." He turned to walk out of the room.

Maxie sat up and hissed at his father. "Anyway, you're not the only one with a new friend. Mummy has a boyfriend too – his name is Rafael. So there."

Tom slammed the door, went into the kitchen and poured himself a glass of red wine. "The sneaky little bitch. I knew it," he said out loud as he downed the glass in one go.

Chapter Thirty-one

Rafael was sitting at a corner table at the café with Colin, pretending to read the newspaper but really watching Shannon, who was at the cash register finding a customer's change. He recognised the woman whose daughter had caused so much chaos the first time he came here.

"Must have thick skin to come back here," he thought.

But he preferred to recall the weekend he'd had with Shannon. He'd come back to her flat after dinner on Saturday night and they'd made love as if they would never stop. He'd asked her to come to his place for dinner the following night, where he cooked her his mama's black bean soup. "*Sopa*, like my mother used to make," he announced, placing it before her at his kitchen bench and shaking out a cloth napkin to put on her lap. She'd loved it. Later they even danced the salsa together. He was happy; they were back on again.

Suddenly Tom came blasting into the café, all wind and bluster. The customer, who was waiting as Shannon tried to retrieve some coins she'd dropped on the floor, turned to him. "I haven't seen you at school lately, Tom."

"Been busy, Jane," he brushed her off.

Jane didn't seem worried. "Keep it," she said to Shannon about the coins. "A tip for your great coffee. I couldn't stay away." She took her cup to an outside bench.

"You just had to come over and spoil mum's birthday didn't you?" Tom ground his teeth as Shannon pulled herself up from the floor and went back to the cash register.

Rafael poked Colin, who was also watching. "Her bloody husband. Look," he said.

"I wanted to talk to you both about Maxie, I was trying to do the right thing." Shannon said.

"You're so irresponsible, I can't trust you with him anymore. That's the last time you're having him."

"But he's my son. You can't do this," Shannon pleaded.

"You've spoilt him. He's become very rude and naughty since he's been with you."

"He's never rude, he's adventurous, not naughty. He's Wombat Boy."

"Don't be ridiculous, Shannon. He's staying with me and mum. Just forget it."

"Why don't you just come out and say it. You think it's my fault I lost our baby."

"I didn't say that."

"You did. I tried to do everything right. I ate well. I exercised gently. I even gave up drinking and smoking for the pregnancy."

"Well, maybe you should have taken more care earlier than that. I know what you're like, always flirting with men."

"Oh stop it. Dr Taylor told me it's got nothing to do with what happened before I met you. Come on, Tom, Maxie needs me."

"How can I? You forgot to pick him up from school the other day. You're hopeless."

"I was just a little bit late. He was OK."

"He was scared, he thought nobody was coming for him."

"Oh bullshit. I'm so sick of you and your fucking perfect mother. And your trays of coffee cups and your *cevapcici*. Keep your glassware and thousand-year-old history and crazy legends about nymphs coming down from the sky. I wish the Turks had killed the lot of you."

"How dare you? You don't know anything about my culture. You don't know anything about me. You're a little slut. You flirted in front of my face, in front of my friends whenever you had a chance."

Hearing all this, Rafael threw his paper on the table and was about to pounce. Colin tried to pull him back down to his seat.

"My mother is just trying to help," Tom continued his tirade. "She's old. She shouldn't have to do all this. Don't you dare use your filthy language against her. OK, yes I do blame you. You're the one who slept around. God knows what that did to your body. It was my baby too, and you killed our baby. And you should be more careful who you fuck. Have you checked your boyfriend's visa lately? You can tell him he can't just ignore a subpoena from the Coroner's Court."

Shannon put her head down and Colin whistled under his breath. Rafael had heard enough; Tom must have done some research. He rushed at Tom; his right fist went straight into the side of Tom's head. He went down, immaculate suit and all. Tom's years of working out and early-morning cycling gave him the strength to pull himself up and swing back at Rafael. They pulled at each other's shirts; Rafael had Tom's tie twisted around his neck.

"Stop it! Stop it!" Shannon screamed at them.

The customers were pushing their chairs back, trying to get out of the way while the ones outside, including Jane, had jumped up to watch.

Colin lurched from his table, dropped his newspaper to the ground and threw his heavy frame at them, pulling them apart. Tom straightened his tie and suit and smoothed his hair with his hand.

"Don't you ever talk to her like that again," Rafael screamed at Tom. "She's not your possession to abuse."

"She's not yours either," Tom muttered as he turned, giving Shannon a last dig before he went outside. "Your wonderful lawyer is a coke addict. That's why he had to leave his practice. Walked out on his wife and kids too. Don't think that woman replacing him will be any better. You'll be hearing from my lawyer."

Colin put his arms around Shannon.

"I knew it, Colin."

As the whole café watched, Rafael chased Tom out onto the street, until he got into his car and drove away. He screamed a last: "*Hijo de puta!*" and sat down on the edge of the footpath staring into the rubbish blown there, as his breathing gradually slowed down.

North of Ocotal
March, 1986

While Lana's inside the therapy room with the *comandante* and the Russian doctor I'm running down the corridor trying to find patients I can film, people who will tell me why they're here. However you look at it, it's still a story the world needs to know – the effect of what the Contras have done to our best fighters. Have they gone mad from war and fighting? Our own *Los Locos*? I want to know the truth too. I was a soldier but I'm also a journalist, even if the title is cameraman.

I try a door handle expecting it to be locked but instead of a nurse barring me from entering I'm overwhelmed by the smell – antiseptic mixed with stale urine. It's the stare I can feel from across the room. A long, hard, unflinching look. No questions, no answers. *No pasaran.*

He's in bed, leaning on a pillow with a rolled-up towel under one arm, naked except for an orange washcloth placed discreetly across his private parts and a dirty white short-sleeved shirt draped across his shoulders. It looks as if he has one arm caught in one of its sleeves. I feel shamed for him but he doesn't appear at all concerned. He's handsome, a *guerillero herido* Romeo, with a beaded necklace around his neck. Perhaps nineteen or twenty years old.

But where his legs should be, from the knees down, are stumps wrapped in filthy bandages. *"Quién eres tú?"* he asks defiantly.

I answer I'm a cameraman making a film for television. But then I ask him if there's anything I can do for him. On both sides of his bed are small cupboards piled high with dirty cups, paper, tissues, candles, bottles of medicine – I guess pain killers. A small pink fan, a transistor radio.

"Nada," he shakes his head, his curly hair falling over his oval eyes.

"How did it happen, *hombre?*" I ask as I set up my camera and start filming.

"En la guerra."

"Sí, yo sé pero como? Yes, I know but how?" I ask again.

"En la frontera. The Contras. The land mine, it blew my legs off."

"My country – my poor, poor country," I think, but to him I say, *"Tranquilo, hombre."* And then I ask him: "Are they giving you drugs for your trauma?"

"No sé. I don't know. I was brought here by the *comandante.* They want to give me some special treatment."

"The drugs treatment?"

He shakes his head again.

"No sé. No sé. They'll make me new legs," the soldier says then groans from phantom pain from where his legs had been.

"Tranquilo, hombre." I repeat.

"Bastards. I'm going to push their heads under water, burn them with cigarettes, force them to cry for their *mamás.*"

"Tranquilo, tranquilo."

"And you? Are you a revolutionary? Or do you just carry that camera around?"

I pull up my shirt to show him my burns. There is no need for words.

"Ah *compañero*, I think you can help me."

"In what way, soldier? What do you need?"

"I need to get out of this place, I need to see my *compañera*."

"Wheelchair, we'll find a wheelchair," I say but I'm not sure why. Then I ask why they won't let him go.

"They say they have more work to do on me."

"And your new legs? When will they be ready?"

"They say they don't know. But they must do tests, more tests."

I feel guilty, I have survived. I still have my legs, my arms, my body. I lean over to shake his hand; I'm going to leave him to his sad daydreams but he grabs mine so tightly I can't let go. I try to pull away but he is the stronger of the two.

"Get me out of here," he says.

Colin walked over to Rafael; his knees clicked as he tried to squat down next to him. "Are you OK, mate?"

"Things too terrible to remember," Rafael kept his head down.

"I know he's an arsehole. I told you. Looks like you might get a black eye too."

"Cruel things. Cruel things. No legs. The hospital. Those scum, the Contras. In with the *cia*. Blowing people up."

"Are you talking about your country? We had wars here too, our warriors against the British, but that was a long time ago."

"It destroys you."

"Did they torture you?"

"I was a soldier." Rafael pulled up his sweater to show Colin his scars.

Colin touched them gently, speaking softly. "I was tortured too, my friend. They tied me to a tree and whipped me. Left me there for days. Put my tucker on a tin plate just out of reach."

Colin's words unleashed a torrent from Rafael. "I wake up sweating, remembering those terrible things I've seen. And then you ask the soldiers, what are you fighting for? And they say, the Fatherland. The Fatherland? What does that mean? Everybody's fighting for the Fatherland. It doesn't matter what side you are on. Up over there is the border. There's Contra camps tucked away in those mountains; they're training to fight for the Fatherland. I'm on our side doing the same thing. But what is the point? What does it mean?"

"Cruelty's not just a third-world notion, mate," Colin tried to counsel him. "Look what they did to us Blackfellas. But you can't hate forever. You have to move on."

"I don't want to move on. I've been here thirty years and this is where I want to stay."

"Well you better take some boxing lessons, mate. You wouldn't last one round here. Didn't they teach you to fist fight back home?"

Rafael took Colin's hand, pulling himself up slowly; his arms were sore and his eye and cheek throbbed. "They taught us how to keep our secrets, *compañero*."

"Come on, they'll be wondering where we are," Colin set off towards the building site.

Rafael slowly followed him, limping, hoping Tom hadn't blabbed about him to anybody official.

Shannon sent Nick home early. He had filled in for her so much and she really appreciated it. It was late afternoon and she was cleaning up in the kitchen when Rafael and Colin appeared back at the café.

"Just wanting to check how you are," Colin said. "Raf's sorry he took his training for the world heavyweight title out on your ex."

Rafael's eye was now deep purple.

Shannon laughed and put her hand on Rafael's face as he winced. "I'm OK and he'll survive. It was kinda nice to have my honour defended, even if it won't do much for business."

The men sat down at a table and Shannon closed the door.

"That is so terrible what Tom said, to blame you for your baby's death," Rafael began. "I have been blamed too, but it wasn't my fault."

"That's what I've been trying to tell you, Raf," Shannon said. "Tony's death wasn't your fault."

Colin nodded in agreement with Shannon.

"Not here. Back home," Rafael said.

"What happened? Is that why you left?" Colin asked.

He nodded. "I will tell you one day. I just want you to know I had no choice."

Both Shannon and Colin whistled. "You better be careful with Immigration hanging around," she said.

"I know. I know."

North of Ocotal
March, 1986

I wrench my hand from my limbless friend and leave. Then I enter another room, where there are four beds. In one an older man with a beard is screaming, tossing and turning, maybe imagining the *guardia* doing all sorts of evil things to him. In another, opposite him, a young, emaciated man with a week's growth on his chin is sitting up loosely holding onto something. What is it? Not his gun? Surely not.

He sees me and looks afraid.

"What are you doing here?" he asks.

"I was going to ask you that," I say, trying to be casual, rather unsuccessfully. This is madness. How can I film him without getting caught? "I'm doing a program about the war. Can I ask you some questions, *hombre*?"

"I'm fighting for the revolution. Free fatherland or death." He takes out what he has been hiding under his sheet and I jump back. But it's just a photo of his wife.

And then I look at the older man, the bearded one. I go over to him and touch his arm, hold his hand tight. He stops screaming and stares at me. There's a hint of recognition. I know this man. He was my cellmate when the *guardia* tortured us. I thought he was dead.

"Rafa?" He is coherent, if only for a minute. "The helicopters."

"No more helicopters," I say as I get my camera ready. "You're safe, old man. You're safe."

Shannon stood behind Rafael and massaged his neck but he pushed her hands away. "Please, I don't like massages."

Colin stood up. "OK you two lovebirds. I'll leave you to it."

"Come on, Raf, let's go upstairs," Shannon took him by the hand, closed the café door and led him up to her little flat overlooking the sea.

Chapter Thirty-two

The morning sun was shining through the window onto Jenny George's desk. She sat in front of her computer, right in the corner of her office, with her back to the window. On her desk was her name plate and title. She was the one who oversaw the raids. It was more important for her to see who was coming through the door than the view of the park below the office building.

She'd tried to make her office a bit more homely with framed photos of her two daughters, sitting next to her name plate. Jessica and Bianca. Not children anymore. All grown up, left home and out in the real world. They didn't need her now. Well, nobody did really. They'd call her every now and again and sometime she'd meet them for lunch. Or an occasional yoga class. She'd pay. They'd be getting married soon, both had boyfriends. She couldn't wait until the grandchildren came along. At least then somebody might appreciate her.

The phone rang, a colleague from Investigations asking about an over-stayer working on the Tamarama building site; she'd just got an anonymous tip-off from the "dob-in line", saying the department had missed somebody on their last raid there and he wasn't an Iranian or a Chinese.

"Yes, I've been to that site already," Jenny told her colleague. "The one where the accident happened. Everybody's papers were in order. I even checked the café across the road for escapees. So who's this POI? I'll do a computer check."

She hung up and logged on, speaking to herself. "Ramirez. R.A.M.I.R.E.Z. Rafael. It's a common name. At least it's not Jesus, Jesus Maria. I don't think they have the right to call themselves that. Still, nice change from Mohammed or Sultan. Why are they all named after religious figures? Maybe it's because they all think they're God. Next it'll be Buddha. God, why don't they all go home?

"So Rafael Ramirez, what's your story? Here he is: Ramirez, Rafael Martinez. Nicaraguan. Born June 10, 1963. Nailed it. Arrived May, 1986. My God, that's more than 30 years." She whistled under her breath. "Tourist visa. Looks like he's never been heard of since. Thank you Systems for People! That IT overhaul was worth the confusion it caused."

She turned to look out her window to see a cloudy winter's day with a hint of sun. She'd try and take a sandwich to the park at lunchtime and enjoy it before it rained again. Better give that charming Koori fellow a call. She bet he knew all about their mutual friend, Rafael Ramirez.

She got up and shut her office door, picking up the phone on her desk and copying the numbers from her mobile. "I'm wondering if you're feeling like a beer?" she asked when the phone was answered.

"Is that Ms George?" Colin sounded surprised.

"Yes it is. I thought, 'Well, I'm not doing anything tonight so why not?'"

"That's great. How about dinner? I know a beautiful little native tucker restaurant in Redfern. I think you'd like it, being a supporter of reconciliation and all."

Jenny laughed. This guy was going to be a pushover.

It was obvious to Vesna where the Immigration Department people hung out at lunch time. The park between their building and Central Railway suited their non-glamourous lifestyles. In one corner of the former swamp a group of homeless people had set up a tent city. They'd even managed to find clothes hoists abandoned by the apartment dwellers and had hung their clothes out to dry. The other side was full of Immigration staff and other office workers trying to ignore the homeless as they caught the muted sun while enjoying their wraps and takeaway coffees.

She already knew what Jenny looked like from Shannon's description and the Facebook photo, and laughed under her breath as she saw her eating her lunch at one of the benches. "Beautiful day," she smiled as she sat down next to her.

Jenny looked at her and went back to her sandwich.

"Not such a good one for catching illegals though?"

Jenny swung round. "Who are you?"

"Vesna Bojic. From aust.com.au."

"All media inquiries need to go through our Public Affairs Department. I really can't help you."

"Oh come on, Jenny, we don't want to have to worry about them. They just slow things down. And you're the one who knows it all. The whole story. Why were you at that building site at Tamarama the other day?"

"None of your business."

"Was it the Iranians?"

"Look if we get a tip-off we have to follow it up. Over-stayers can't expect to get away with ignoring the laws. Where did you get my name from?"

It was Vesna's turn to ignore the question. "I'm working on a story about the accident on the building site."

"This has nothing to do with that accident. That's WorkCover's area. Not ours."

"But somebody died."

"Not my problem," Jenny kept chewing her turkey and tomato, then picked at her teeth. "We just look after the over-stayers and the so-called refugees flooding into the country. I can't help you with your story."

"What if I was to give you some information in return?" Vesna was used to doing business Kosovo-style. A deal was a deal. And nothing was ever done without a deal. A quid pro quo. Dancing with the enemy. You didn't get into UN-secured areas without doing a deal. And you didn't get to report on the number of dead bodies piled up or emaciated prisoners in concentration camps without a deal either. She didn't see anything wrong with it. It was all about the end justifying the means. And she wanted to write "Ends" on her story as soon as she possibly could.

"What sort of information?" Jenny finished her sandwich and wiped her face with the napkin, then crumpled it up.

"About real illegals."

"Yes and …"

"Look, I understand you're still looking for the Iranians?"

"Everybody knows about that. You know where they are?"

"I can find out. I have good contacts. But I haven't yet witnessed an Immigration Department raid. I need that colour – and pics – for my articles. You let me know when you're about to do a raid and I'll give you some information."

Jenny stood up. "What was your phone number? I'll call you."
Vesna gave her number.
"And don't use my name, will you? Off the record, OK?"
"Sure," Vesna nodded. "Same here."

Chapter Thirty-three

The Green Goanna was owned by one of Colin's nephews – actually, the son of one of his cousins but in Koori terms, he was his uncle. In a sign of the times it was in Redfern's main street opposite new bars and coffee shops. The once-rundown suburb was going through a renaissance and the middle class who had been scared to go anywhere near it now drove their four-wheel drives there and even parked in side streets, although it was difficult to get their giant prams and babies out. They had gradually been buying up the two-up, two-down terraces, waiting with baited breath for the housing commission towers to be demolished and for everybody on the other side of the train station – don't mention the Aborigines – to be moved way out west.

It wasn't a place Colin frequented that much these days although he had lived in Redfern when he first came to Sydney in the 1980s. That was when The Block was a hive of activism, Radio Redfern blaring in every terrace house. The red, black and gold flag flew from a mast on top of the gym opposite the station. People were proud. But on Friday nights you were as likely to be picked up by a cop as you left the Clifton Hotel as to meet a friendly woman, who'd take you home for more than a cuppa. He wasn't interested in doing dope deals or getting blind drunk. He was there for the music his countrymen, Black Lace, played and the good sorts who lined up to dance with him. He was like a brolga on the dance floor. But getting married changed all that. He went straight and narrow – for a while.

Redfern was different now; the lefties might pay homage to Aboriginal "kulcher" but at the same time the real estate agents promised their clients a future Aboriginal-free suburb. Still he thought Jenny might like going out in Redfern. He found her attractive and he wanted to impress her. She was waiting for him outside the restaurant, sensible in her black pants suit, with matching high-heeled boots. Her silver loopy earrings featured scarlet parrots with a tinge of green and she wore an Aboriginal flag pendant on a chain around her neck.

Colin's nephew had gone to a bit of effort doing up the place. There were dot paintings on the walls and photos of local activists and the table cloths and napkins were made by women from a community in Central Australia.

"Let me get the seat for you, madam." Colin pulled out Jenny's chair so she could sit down.

"What a gentleman," Jenny smiled.

"Thank you, I try my best," he gestured for the waiter to come over. He ordered a bottle of house red wine and ginger ale for himself.

"You're an unusual man, Colin," she said.

"Why's that, my dear?" His scratchy suit was making him want to itch but he tried not to. The only time he normally wore a tie was for a funeral – or a coronial inquest.

"I thought Aboriginal people preferred to be in groups. You seem like a loner to me."

"I've had to, to survive." He started to sing:

'Cause we have survived, the white man's world …

She laughed. "Used to love No Fixed Address. Yes, we have that in common. I bet you were a bit of a heart throb in your time, lighting up the dance floor."

"A regular black John Travolta. I'll take you dancing sometime if you like."

She laughed again. "I'd like that. Have you got children?"

"Ah," Colin hesitated. "Yeah, maybe a few running around that nobody's told me about."

"Unusual you haven't been asked for maintenance."

"Well, we won't talk about that," and he certainly didn't want to talk about the daughter and grand-daughter he never saw. The bottle arrived and he poured her a glass of wine.

"What about you?" He sipped his soft drink.

"Two girls. Doing well. Jessica's studying physiotherapy. Hard for her, it's a lot of work. Bianca's into singing and dancing. She's always auditioning for shows. They're pretty independent these days."

"Their father not around?" He sounded hopeful.

"No. And I don't care. Glad to be rid of the bastard." She put the napkin on her lap.

"It must have been difficult for you bringing up kids on your own?"

"It was. But my career was important to me too."

"But what made you seek employment at that horrible department, hassling the poor, old illegals? They're even lower down the ladder than Blackfellas these days."

"Over-stayers, not illegals. Look, it's not my first choice of public service department. But it pays well. And they treat me OK. Super, holidays, all that. And plenty of overtime which really makes a difference. It's a tough job but somebody has to do it."

When Colin laughed, Jenny couldn't help smiling. "There's good sides to the job too."

"Oh like what?"

"We get to go to citizenship ceremonies and shake people's hands. We also go to humanitarian briefings. But we can't always say yes. We have to make tough decisions and when you get to know people the delivery of the news is hard for us too."

"Why can't you just say yes? We've got plenty of room." Colin was getting impatient although there was something he liked about this odd woman.

"Because the visa requirements often just don't allow it. It can be traumatic for us too. We have been trained though not to take the clients' reactions personally. And why should those people push in anyway? Did you know there's approximately fifty to sixty thousand unlawful foreigners in Australia, and meanwhile our strong policies have stopped the boat people coming here and drowning off Christmas Island. It's not fair, there's all these other people waiting who really do deserve to come here. Don't get sucked into the do-gooders going on about detention centres. There's a lot of con men out there; very few are real refugees."

"But what about the kids? Should they be in detention centres?"

"Would you prefer they were taken from their mothers?"

"Of course not. But there must be something else they can do."

"It's a tricky situation," Jenny poured herself another large glass of wine. "Look, the Minister had meetings in country towns suggesting they have the women and children living in government houses there. But the community rejected that. These protestors really don't have the full story. They'll be the first to complain when the Islamists bring in Sharia law. And don't talk to me about the media. They've all been spoon fed on leftist ideology at university; they're all biased."

"University? Most of them can't even spell. And it's taken Aboriginal issues off the front page."

"That's right," she showed her red-wine-stained teeth. "Trendies and greenies, they can only cope with protesting about one issue at a time. They don't seem to realise this country's suffering from a growing population of old people. Half the country will be on the pension in ten years' time. How are we going to pay for all that? And look at how many homeless there are. And what about the environment? The drought? There's plagues of kangaroos and emus bashing down fences and running into cars. You can't drive after four pm on outback roads. Trying to find a blade of grass, some tiny skerrick of water. Bushfires in October. Never heard of it before. That's only going to get worse with all these people overrunning the place."

Colin was beginning to wonder if a whole bottle of wine had been such a good idea.

"They all want to come to Sydney or Melbourne. They're not interested in staying in the country. Crammed into one-bedroom flats. Cooking over a single burner. No English. What are we going to do with them? And the family reunions? Mothers, brothers, uncles, aunts, step sisters of cousins who were married to their sisters. Any excuse. And the stories they make up? Couldn't lie straight in bed. Pathetic. It's so unfair to the genuine ones. Waiting in those camps for years and years. Dying in them, before they get the green light to come here.

"And what about the terrorists? You'd know about that wouldn't you? They say scores of Aboriginal – oh I'm sorry First Nations – prisoners are converting to Islam in Goulburn maximum security."

"Oh, did you read that in *The Daily Terrorist?*"

She laughed: "Well at least they pray before knifing each other."

"Spare me from the do-gooders, especially those terrible reconciliation people." Colin thought the only way to stop the diatribe was to throw in a joke.

Jenny hooted as she took yet another gulp of wine.

"And what's this First Nations business? What's wrong with calling us Blackfellas?"

"That's what we're now meant to be calling you Aboriginal folk."

"Cheers," Colin clinked her glass.

"I'm hungry." Jenny said. "The service here is pretty shocking. Sorry I know they're your rellies."

Colin's nephew had hauled in a few younger Kooris, with the promise of training and decent tips. They were having difficulty getting the orders right and the timing was way out. It'd been a good half hour since they'd ordered their meals when Colin noticed them being taken to the wrong table. "Hey, mate, I think that's what we ordered," he said, tapping the youngster on the arm.

The waiter swung around and nearly dropped the plates on the table. "Sorry, Uncle," he plonked them down in front of them.

Colin winked at Jenny who smiled back, and started tucking in.

"Wait, we can't eat yet," he interrupted her.

She stopped eating. "Oh do you have to say grace?"

"No, welcome to country."

"Oh right."

"Nah, just kidding," Colin grinned.

She laughed as she put her fork to her mouth and chewed her meat.

"What do you think of the fine food?" Colin asked, wiping the side of his mouth with the colourful napkin.

"It's different."

"Too much wattle seed sauce, if you ask me. Next time I'll take you to my local Chinese. They do a great sweet and sour pork."

Colin's nephew, a handsome man in his mid-thirties, brought a better bottle of Shiraz over to the table. "A little something to say sorry for the slow service," he patted Colin on the back. Jenny's eyes lit up.

"I won't be drinking that but I'm sure my lady friend will enjoy it," Colin smiled although he was worried about Jenny getting more intoxicated. "Thanks very much."

"Oh, still not drinking, Uncle? How have you been? We haven't seen you around for a while."

"Busy, working."

"You've always worked, Uncle. Too deadly."

"And so is your little establishment here. Have you applied for government assistance for the trainees?"

"We've put the application in but haven't heard anything yet.

Everything's been cut. I might have to hire Indian waiters soon. Enjoy your meal – and the wine." He winked at Jenny then moved on to the next table.

"He should have been round in the old days." Colin poured Jenny a glass from the new bottle, which she immediately switched to from the house red.

"Yes, before grants were invented. Did you grow up around here?" She seemed interested.

"No, madam. A little place called Kinchela."

"Not the boys' home? I went to a Sorry Day ceremony for the men from there. It was meant to be so cruel."

"Yes it was."

"Did you get into trouble?"

"Trouble, as they say, was my middle name. I seemed to always cop the floggings. For my own bloody good. Oh excuse me, Jenny, sorry for swearing."

"It doesn't bother me at all, Colin. I do work with men, you know. But you speak beautiful English."

"Yes, I'm an edumacated Aborigadidganee."

They both laughed.

"You have to learn the language of the coloniser if you are going to survive, my dear. In fact, I think I speak it better than most sons and daughters of colonialists, who actually don't speak English at all but some kind of slang strine. Dessert?"

She shook her head.

"Well let me pay the bill and then shall we take a walk?" He took Jenny by the arm, helping her with her coat and they left the restaurant. She was tipsy and leant on him as they walked, her high heels click-clacking on the footpath.

But just when he thought he might have half a chance with her, she dropped the clanger: "Now what about your mate, Wafael Wamiwez?" She had problems with the Rs. "What am I going to do about him?"

Colin's heart sank. He knew it would come up eventually but he was surprised that she knew his name. "I haven't got a mate called Rafael."

"I'm not stupid, Colin. I've done my homework. He's an over-stayer. He's broken the law."

"And you never have? Come on, Jenny. He's been here more

than thirty years. What does it matter if he didn't have the right piece of paper when he arrived? I bet none of your ancestors did either, unless it was a criminal charge."

"Mine were legal."

"Oh yeah on Aboriginal – oh I mean First Nations – land. You can't send him home. It's too dangerous." He pulled his arm away.

"He has to face the consequences of his actions." She slurred the words.

"And when have you ever done that?"

"Colin, I'm just doing my job."

"I've heard that one before." He hailed a taxi; the driver almost went straight past but when he saw Jenny he skidded to a stop. "Time for you to go home, Jennifer. You better give the driver your address."

"Colin, this has nothing to do with you." Jenny looked in her bag for her wallet, staring out miserably from the back seat. "But you know there are big fines for people who employ over-stayers. You and the company could get into a lot of trouble. I'm warning you because I like you."

Colin wasn't listening any more. He put his head down and walked as fast as he could back to the train station.

Chapter Thirty-four

Vesna was about to board a train from the ugly station near her office when her mobile rang. She didn't recognise the number but answered it anyway, hoping it wasn't some charity asking her for money.

"Vesna? Jenny from Immigration."

Vesna stayed on the platform. This was the call she'd been waiting for.

"We're doing an operation tomorrow, as early as possible. I'm just checking the access and egress. We don't want anybody doing the Harold Holt on us."

Vesna had to laugh, this was beginning to sound like something out of the 1950s. "Who do you suspect there?"

"A few Chinese with fake ABNs and forged visas. Possibly some Iranians and one other."

"Really?" Vesna was even more interested now. "Where is it and what time?"

"We're working on early, before they go for smoko. A site in Tamarama."

"Not the one where the accident happened?"

"Yes, but I don't want your fingerprints all over me, right? I'll call you around seven am and give you the details. Keep your mobile on. But I need information from you, remember."

"I have a lot, don't worry. Straight after the raid I'll give it you. Is there anybody specific you are looking for?"

"That's all the information I am prepared to give now."

Vesna jumped on the next train, deciding to get off at Central and take a bus to the site, to stake it out. She should tell Shannon what was going on, she thought. She was her original source after all. But this was turning into a totally different story, and she'd agreed to keep her mouth shut.

Her phone rang again. Work. She wondered why they'd be calling her, probably wanting to change her shift at the last minute. It was Liz, the deputy editor.

"Oh hi, I'm glad you called," Vesna answered it. "I'm onto a great story. An Immigration Department raid. I need a photographer in the morning."

"Since when have you been covering Immigration?" Liz sounded annoyed. "We have people in Canberra doing that."

"But I've got it on my own. It's a goodie, I'm telling you."

"Vesna, we've had a complaint about one of your stories, which by the way nobody knew you were doing. "

"What complaint? "

"One of the muftis at Lakemba Mosque thinking you were being disrespectful about Muslims."

"Oh, come off it. I gave them a good run. "

"Vesna!"

"But the closer I get the better the story."

Liz paused. "OK, if they're really going to arrest a few people then go. But I can't spare a photographer. You'll have to take the pics yourself. Get video too. And then come and see me about this complaint. They need an answer. By the way, you're on midday shift tomorrow. You'll be doing the raid story in your own time; we can't spare you from the desk."

That'd be right, Vesna thought, but she was pleased; she knew that Liz remembered her work in Kosovo and what a great foreign correspondent she'd been in the days when news services had overseas offices. At least somebody was prepared to trust her. The onto-a-scoop adrenalin was pumping. By the time she got to the café it was dark, and it was closed but she could see Shannon inside working on her computer.

Vesna tapped on the glass window and Shannon looked up with a start. She went to the door to open it. "What the fuck are you doing here?"

"Look, I didn't know Tom was your husband. I had no idea. I never told him about Maxie getting lost. I did get Amany's number from him but I didn't put two and two together."

"Great journalist you are."

Vesna shrugged, she had to agree. Sometimes she couldn't see the wood for the trees. But she wanted to set things right.

"You can have Tom," Shannon said. "I just want Maxie back. How is my baby?"

"He's OK, Shannon. He's a sweetie. He loves the presents I buy him."

"What do you buy him?" She looked apprehensive.

"Just action games, the sort of things little boys like playing with their dads. You know for Xbox."

"What? I don't want him playing war games."

"They're just games, Shannon."

"Vesna, it's not your place to bring my child gifts." She was burning up.

"Sorry, I was just trying to help. I felt sorry for the little thing. He seems so lost."

"Well, if your boyfriend let me have him more often he'd be fine. You have no idea what I've been through. Look, I think you should drop the whole safety story."

"Why? I thought you were keen on making the company own up to their mistakes."

"Maybe it's just not a story. Better to leave it."

"I've done a lot of work on it, Shannon. I went to the inquest. I'm waiting now for the Coroner's report. I'm not going to drop it."

"I think you've been using me," Shannon said.

"No I haven't." Vesna closed the door behind her, hoping Shannon would calm down but also pissed off with her. She still wasn't going to tell her about the raid. She couldn't see how it was going to affect Shannon anyway. It'd just be Iranians – and Albanians, she joked to herself.

As she left she spotted Colin across the road, waiting and watching. She went up the road to wait at a bus stop until he went into the café. When she was sure he couldn't see her she walked over to the building site to check out the exits. There was a small wall at the back that any fit labourer could climb over. Was it worth telling Jenny about that? No, she probably already knew.

Shannon was back on the computer when she saw Colin at the door.

"Who was that?" He was abrupt.

"Vesna, the journalist."

"Thought so. I saw her at the inquest. Be careful, Shannon, she could get Rafael into trouble."

"I tried to get her to drop the safety story. She seems to still want to do it, but nothing about immigration. She's a bitch; if she thinks she's going to be evil stepmother to my Maxie she's got another thing coming."

"What?"

"She's going out with Tom."

"Oh no. She probably knows everything."

"But I haven't said anything to her about Raf's status. Anyway, we really don't know what visa he has. I'm more worried about what happened in his country. I wish he would tell me the whole story."

"Why do you have to stick your nose into everything? Let people have their privacy. It isn't helping Raf and it isn't helping Tony's family. You white women, you think you're trying to help. But you're as bad as the Greenies, just making things worse."

"Don't talk to me like that, I can't deal with it."

"Oh you're always fragile. It's time, darling, to get a bit of backbone. Didn't Ainslie teach you that?"

"Colin, I loved her. I'm going to find out what happened to her."

"You mean the black maid?"

"No. I didn't know the situation; I was only a kid."

"At least you know where your parents are buried," he said as he walked out the door.

That was it. She didn't care what Colin said, she was going to call Rafael and find out what the hell had happened to him. If she was going to be involved she wanted to know the whole story. She called his mobile but there was no answer. She left a message: "Raf, call me please. I really need to talk to you. Please. I need you to finally answer my questions."

It was bad enough having Vesna trying to bring up her son. And now she'd lost Colin as well. She grabbed her handbag and locked the front door, then climbed the stairs to her flat and packed herself a small bag, including her new walking boots. Before leaving she called Nick to ask him to take over the café for a few days. "I've had it, Nick," she gulped.

He was surprisingly understanding. "Go, Shannon. You need a break with all this madness going on around you. I can look after things. Don't worry I won't burn the place down. And you know I have a thing about cougars!"

"Oh puke." But at least he made her laugh. Hiring Nick wasn't such a bad decision after all. "If Rafael comes in tomorrow morning could you let him know I've gone to the valley for a few days?" she asked.

"No worries, of course I'll do that," he answered.

Chapter Thirty-five

Winter was turning to spring, buds forming on the exotic trees in scrappy semi-tropical gardens. The mornings were not as cold; it was easier to get out of bed and pad across the lino floor to make a coffee.

The memories and dreams kept coming but Rafael tried to push them aside. He pulled on his green stubby shorts, belt and shirt. He still had good legs, he thought, as he admired himself in the mirror, remembering how *las chicas* would call him *guapa* as a joke. Brown skin, smooth with only the smallest amount of hair, as if he waxed his legs. He whistled at his reflection as the coffee pot bubbled.

He'd go and see Shannon after work; he'd got her message but he didn't feel like a heavy conversation. Later maybe after making love he'd tell her the whole story. She deserved to know. He thought about their last night together, the evening of the fight with Tom. She'd poured him a glass of wine – he enjoyed having an occasional one now. He had put on some salsa music on her CD player and taken her by the hand; they moved together to the beat, perfectly in rhythm. It was as if she was Nicaraguan, she knew the music and the steps so well. Later they'd wrapped themselves around each other in front of the TV. She even liked his favourite dance show. Life was looking up, at last.

And maybe Tom did know about his status but so what? Surely he wasn't that much of a bastard that he'd tell the department about him? He wasn't the one who broke up the marriage. He would never have done that. He had his morals. She was a gorgeous woman, she deserved better.

At the site, even the Mozzies had decided to return to work. There was only so much protesting you could do each day, especially when nobody took any notice of you and your placards. They stood in a circle, grasping hands. "For Tony," one of them called out and "For Tony," they echoed. And then the work began.

The company had been threatening to sack its sub-contractors and pull the plug unless shovels were picked up soon. Even the Chinese with their forged four five seven visas were getting twitchy. Rafael didn't have much choice either. He was always grateful to find a job where nobody asked any questions, and usually it was the Asians that got targeted first. The Latinos were normally ignored; nobody knew if they were Chilean, Mexican or any other damn race and they all came out years ago. *Viva la revolución.*

One of the Mozzies spoke as he passed him. "No hard feelings, bro. It was a bloody accident. Nothing more."

Rafael grabbed his hand and shook it hard.

Colin was nervous, hoping everything would go well this day. He was so fed up with this damned job. He could have found another one elsewhere. Tamarama could really do with another shoddy block of apartments, couldn't it? But he felt he owed it to Tony to get the job finished. The Iranians, on the other hand, had never come back. So he'd had to hire some Chinese and hope for the best.

He thought of Shannon. He didn't want to believe that his mum had worked for her parents. But she could be right. And that made him almost hate her. She'd never be the lovely, innocent girl he once knew. All gone. Too late. The Berlin Wall had gone up and it would take a revolution to break that down. Maybe he should have told her about dinner with Jenny. Even Rafael, he looked happy today. Should he warn him that Jenny was onto him? Surely she'd leave him alone, with sixty thousand other illegals to chase. With everything he'd gone through with the accident, it wasn't worth making him more nervous. Maybe at lunch time he could tell him the whole story.

And then the tranquillity of the day was shattered. White government cars seemed to come from every direction, skidding to a stop at the site entrance. Twenty men in badly-cut suits jumped out and ran towards the Chinese workers. Others raced to the back wall to secure it, while two stayed at the gate stopping people entering or leaving. Workers scattered – they'd already worked out the escape routes – but only a couple managed to hurdle the wall, with officials dragging the others down by their stubby shorts. They cornered whoever else they could, pulling them aside separately and checking their IDs. One was blissfully unaware of the raid as he worked on a jackhammer with his ear-muffs on until he got a tap on the shoulder that scared the living daylights out of him.

Jenny emerged from the front passenger seat of one of the cars. She wasn't going to waste her time with the Chinese, she headed straight for Colin, flashing her badge. "Hello, Colin. Thanks for a lovely dinner. Where's the Nicaraguan?"

Rafael, who was right next to Colin and didn't have the chance to get away, put down his saw and raised his arms in the air. "I'm not telling you anything, you *cia*."

Jenny and two of the burliest officials surrounded him. "Rafael Martinez Ramirez? Show me your ID please." She held her Blackberry, ready to key the information in.

North of Ocotal
March, 1986

I feel myself knocked to the ground as another patient, who I thought was asleep, runs at me. Luckily I've held onto the camera and it doesn't break as I go down.

I make such a noise I'm sure a soldier will come and get me, so I jump up and give the patient a huge sideswipe, getting out of that room as fast as I can, leaving him on the floor in the foetal position, weeping.

I run down to *Com* Manuel's office but the door is locked.

Where is Lana? What is going on in there?

One of the officials put his hand on Rafael's carpenter's belt.

Colin grabbed Jenny by the arm. "Don't."

She swung round and faced him, shaking his arm off. "He's an illegal over-stayer."

"But he's been here for years, without hurting anybody." Colin turned to Rafael. "Come on, Raf just show her your white card and your working-at-heights licence."

"We need his passport, even driving licence," Jenny was adamant.

Rafael ignored their requests. His brown eyes seemed to change colour – turning misty, almost opaque. They stared into the distance, his face stern. He was no longer on a building site in Tamarama but back home, captured by the *guardia*. "My name is *Capitán* Rafael Martinez Ramirez of the Sandinista Army. I am The Last Revolutionary. You can torture me but I will never give you nothing."

Colin and Jenny looked at each other, while another official fastened his hands with plastic ties.

"Can't you see he's not well?" Colin pleaded. "Where are you taking him?"

"He'll be detained at Villawood," Jenny said. "Possibly repatriated to his home country. If you really think he deserves to stay you need to find a lawyer. They can help him lodge a request for ministerial intervention."

Colin used the F word for the first time in years. "You fucking bitch."

The officials led Rafael to the waiting van. One pulled open the sliding door and pushed Rafael in, making sure his seat belt was done up. He climbed into the barricaded front seat to keep watch. Rafael was staring way into his past, muttering to himself as he crawled into a ball on the vinyl seat.

Managua
May, 1978

Yes, it is my turn for giving up secrets, but I have none to give. So the *guardia* just keep torturing me. First, it's the water treatment again and then out comes the cigarettes. Half smoked, locally-made ones in the American-owned factory that uses child slave labour. One of the guards has taken his time, smoking it half way down then laughing as he moves towards me huddled on the floor of the torture cell. The burning on my stomach is hard to describe, it's almost a euphoric pain that goes deep into my soul. I must be screaming but I can't hear anything coming out, except their sarcastic laughter. One ciggie after the other, deep into my flesh, leaving rude, red marks I'll never be able to erase.

"You scum, tell us when the next attack is planned."

I am a lowly foot soldier. I have no idea about attacks. I just fight in the streets, which is where they picked me up. I have no idea either why I'm still alive. "*No sé. No sé.*" I just don't know.

Colin followed the officials. He could hear Raf in the van screaming something about helicopters, but then he saw Vesna on the kerb scribbling notes and taking photos of the parade of shame. He might have known the bitch would be here. It was a long time since he'd run. He did his exercises but he only walked around the headland. He arrived at the café puffing so hard Nick brought him a glass of water and sat him down. "What's wrong, mate? Immigration again?"

"Shannon. Where's Shannon?"

"She's in the country. I'm looking after things."

"It's Raf. They're taking him to Villawood. I need to talk to her."

"She's not in a good way, Col. But I'll try and call her." He picked up the café phone and called Shannon's number, but the call rang out. He shrugged his shoulders as he put the phone back.

And then Colin remembered he still had Tom's number. Where did he put it after he'd called him that time to tell him Shannon had been taken to hospital? He pulled his phone out of his pocket and checked his contacts. Yes. Let's hope he didn't mention the last time they met – when he broke up the fight.

Tom wasn't at all happy to be disturbed at work and he had no idea whose number was on his screen, but he took the call. He almost laughed when he realised that Colin was asking him to help Rafael.

"He can't be deported. It'll kill him, if the detention centre doesn't," Colin begged.

Tom saw a flashback of the day Shannon lost the baby, remembering it was Colin who had called the ambulance. He'd never thanked him for that or for everything he'd done for his wife. Why hadn't he? Too caught up in his own grief? For a brief moment he felt guilty about that.

Colin's shoulders collapsed as he described what happened. "There was a girl reporter there, taking photos."

"What did she look like?"

"I don't know, a bit scraggy. Plump with shoulder-length dark hair. I've seen her before, she was at the inquest when I gave evidence. I think her name's Vesna."

"Vesna!"

"Yeah, she's the one who's been hassling Rafael for weeks and talking to Shannon all the time."

Tom was furious. Vesna. What the fuck was she up to? Talking to bloody Shannon? "I can't do anything for Rafael, Colin."

"You're kidding aren't you? You're an Immigration lawyer."

Tom didn't have to be reminded of that. But he didn't want anything to do with Shannon's loopy boyfriend or with her, for that matter. And the thought of Vesna in cahoots with his ex-wife turned his blood cold. "I'll ask one of my colleagues. He's a bleeding heart." He hung up leaving Colin waiting on the other end of the line.

"Fuck!" Colin screamed.

Two F words in one day.

Chapter Thirty-six

Shannon woke up in her bedroom at the farm house at the valley feeling a little better and took a cup of tea back to bed. She was determined to forget about everybody and everything by doing a walk up a trail once used by the cedar cutters one hundred years ago. It was a beautiful clear but cold day. She pulled her new boots on, lacing them up as firmly as she could. Her old ones had finally given up the ghost.

A family of roos was lying in the paddock below the house but bounded off when they heard her coming. A tiger snake was not so fast. It was curled up in the sun on a dirt patch next to an old bit of iron and didn't move an inch even though she was sure it could feel her presence. Didn't even move his head. She got a fright when she saw him but then she was mesmerised by the vivid yellow patterns on his skin.

I like snakes, she thought. What's wrong with them? Even spiders don't bother me. It's people who worry me. They scare the life out of me. Shannon thought of her meetings with the cocaine-addict divorce lawyer, his red eyes popping out of his head like neon dollar signs. She could hear the sound of the cash register as she walked in the door. Good riddance to him and his cocaine habit.

But then she thought of all the good, old women, some in their eighties, who lived around here. Up bush tracks hidden away in their shacks or even brick houses. No modern weekenders for them. They survived. They weren't worried about snakes or spiders. Not so long ago she'd visited one of these women, so strong even as she leant on her walking stick. They'd had tea in front of the fire and listened to the sound of light rain on the roof. She'd given Shannon a bag of kindling as she left. "I've plenty," she said, pressing it into Shannon's arms as her old blue cattle dog, Ally, nudged her leg.

"Will you stay here for ever?"

"It's my country," she said. "Me and Ally here, we're caretakers."

Shannon called these women the valley dolls – a bunch of tough, clever, practical women who knew all about the trees and the plants and the native animals. Some had partners but most were alone. Nobody really cares when you get divorced or your husband leaves you for another woman. You become invisible to the wider world.

She made her slippery way across the creek, weaving its own way out of the escarpment, fringed by native pines, cedars and lilly pillies. In between barbed wire fences, lantana and stinging nettles, the water moved over slimy rocks and into deep pools, where she and Maxie had cooled down and played that past summer. She missed him and wished he was here.

Apart from the call of birds and the sound of water it was as if peace had never been shattered by humans. But then Shannon's body shook with the blast of a chain saw, over the other side of the creek. Or was it a lyrebird mimicking old Joe cutting wood? Those cheeky lyrebirds! She'd woken that morning to tap-tapping on the glass bedroom door that led to the verandah. A lyrebird was dancing with his reflection, believing so strongly he had a beautiful mate that performed as well as he did.

She waved to Joe as she noticed some dark clouds gathering in the distance, hanging over the top of the escarpment. "Rain coming?" she asked.

"Could be," his gnarled hands gently holding the saw, his dark blue beanie pulled down over his forehead.

"Do you think the creek will come up?"

"That waterfall needs to go somewhere."

"I guess we need rain."

"Yes, but not this much; the paddocks are drenched. How's that little fellow of yours? No more wombat hunting or running away from home?"

She smiled, trying to pretend all was well, and shook her head. "He's with Tom."

Joe nodded.

"I heard there's a track that's meant to lead through the rainforest to Red Roof Farm."

"Yeah that's an old fire trail," Joe said, knowing every track in the valley. "There's a few waterfalls along the way."

"Pity about the lantana."

"If it's not lantana, it's cabbage weed." Clear one weed and another one pops up. It's a never-ending job and one Joe, after working more than fifty years in the valley, had pretty well given up on.

They turned their backs on each other as, climbing the hill, she felt the unknown track calling to her. It could have been an ancient Aboriginal path before the cedar-cutters used it. She made her way to the site of a slab hut, where now there were only bits of timber lying around and some sandstone stumps. The hut's roof had fallen in and the walls collapsed, so that it all had deteriorated into a home for animals and insects, not people anymore. Who had lived here after the Aboriginal people had been driven out? Did the cedar-cutters build huts? She'd heard they camped in the hollows of enormous trees. She wondered about all the families that must have passed through here. You could hear the cries of children building tree houses and playing by the creek. Who was keeping watch of their memories now?

As she pushed her way through the lantana it opened out and she could see it was a decent sort of track. It wound its way down to another small creek where a stump was the only remnant of a once great cedar. She touched the bark softly, whispering her commiserations. The track then became part of the creek and she could see up ahead a staircase of rock platforms that descended into a pool. The rain from the night before had led to a series of trickles flowing into the pool. She imagined Joe's spectacular waterfall after a flood.

Pulling herself up over the rocks, and being careful not to slip on the moss, she managed to reach the pool. A dragonfly hovered over the water; the sun reflected its silky wings before hiding behind new, grey clouds. She looked up to see a boulder but it seemed odd. Is that a rock, she wondered. It was bluey grey with white lines on it. As she peered closer it appeared to be wrapped in some old material. Was that lines on the rock or rib bones? Was it a dead body? It was really hard to tell. She climbed around to get closer and crouching down, leaning over, she was just able to prod it with her stick. She reeled back when the stick sunk into the mass. That was no rock! The smell of death erupted into the air. God, she thought, what kind of animal is that? It could have been a mangy wombat washed down the creek or even a newly-born calf still wrapped in its amniotic sac. Or was it a baby?

"Rest in peace," she spoke out loud to the corpse, leaving the stick stuck inside it.

The police, she thought without wanting to. She took out her phone and snapped a photo of it, deciding she would email it to people who might actually know. People who grew up in the country and knew what a long-dead wombat really looked like. People like Colin. He was a country boy. But no, Colin, her only real friend, hated her now. She was surprised to see there were five missed calls from him – as well as one from the café – but she was still upset with him and didn't want to answer him. Why was he calling so much? To abuse her even more. She didn't feel like a lecture. She waved the phone in the air to get some reception. And a text message pinged: "Raf's been picked up by Immigration. Come home." Picked up? No. Immigration finally found him? Did Vesna dob him in? My fault. It's all my fault. Oh fuck, I caused all this. She tried to call but she'd lost reception again.

That dead wombat looked like a baby and the thought of some poor child that never had a life hit her like a volcano erupting. They'd dressed her darling baby in what looked like a pink doll's dress and crocheted cap, cardigan and booties, took her tiny body off to a funeral home and cremated her. Her little Emma. Somebody came and delivered the ashes to her. In a nice, little white box.

She turned and slid, as tears streamed down her face, like the water over the rocks' cool surfaces. The now-dark sky and the red mud were almost touching. Get out of here. Now. She gasped as she ran, pushing her way back through the lantana, scratching her hands and face and brushing past stinging nettles, her legs raw. The rain was coming down in sheets. Shannon wasn't sure which way to go. She took refuge inside the lantana to wait for the rain to ease. It was warm inside, like a womb, and she crouched low to stop herself being scratched by its thorny branches. Must wait, must wait. For rain to stop. No. No. Mummy, come on, come home.

She emerged and ran back down the track, past Joe's abandoned work site, jumping over the cattle grid and turning into the garden. The kitchen door was open and she heaved herself inside. Make a fire, warm yourself. But your stick is gone. No wood, no kindling. She edged her way down the dark corridor and fell on her bed, letting the tears flow.

She woke several hours later from a bad dream. She had puffy eyes from sobbing in her sleep. She'd been in a cave, a deep, dark cave that echoed with the sound of bats and gushing water coming from the hanging swamps on the plateau above. Wombats were crouching around one of their dead. She could see some light from outside the cave and stumbled towards the entrance. But how did she get here from the hospital? She had come in an ambulance. They'd carried her through on a stretcher and she heard a voice say: "Oh no, it's the baby." But it wasn't the baby, it was the dead wombat, its smell overpowering her.

Another loud crash of thunder. Clouds covered the stars. Her faithful friends, her guardians. She was still in the dream, huddling inside the cave. It was dank and smelt of dirt. How many millions of years had it been like this? Or was it once all under the sea? No, the land went out further, much further. Soon the water would be coming back, claiming the land, icebergs melting, oceans swelling. There'd be no valley, no farm, only these caves. She could hide here for years. Some kid in the next century exploring them would find her remains. Just her bones, a banana chair and a pair of rotten, old boots – but no wedding ring. They even found boots in the wreck of the Titanic. They last forever.

The water was pouring in the entrance of the cave. The waterfall was sweeping her cave away. She was being swept down the escarpment, bumping over rocks and sliding through rapids, the corpse in the water with her. Gotta get out, gotta get home. Gotta save Raf. Gotta save baby.

She swept past the man who lived behind the waterfall. She knew about him, he ate whatever he could find, even insects. An old misfit. Maybe the great grandson of one of those tough cedar-cutters and his woman. Those bearded men wielding those giant saws and sending hundreds-of-years-old cedars crashing to the ground. Their strong women holding the other end of the saw. But she couldn't reach her destination, she just kept getting further and further away.

Something flapped past her in the dark. Was it a baby flying fox, who had flown in her bedroom door, frightened, its little wings tearing through her mosquito net? Hiding under the bed now. "We're trapped together," she said. And the lyrebirds weren't dancing now, they were fighting at the window, trying to get in to attack her.

She was back in the operating theatre. Blood on the sheets. Neat, hospital corners. Scuffed, green lino, marked by so many feet, so many patients, nurses, doctors, labourers with work-place accidents, men who'd fallen off scaffolding, children with raging earaches. The voices of Dr Taylor and the nurses floated up to her. "She's losing a lot of blood. She needs a transfusion."

"Remember we've still got Maxie." Tom's words echoed like a lyrebird's song.

Her nightie was covered with blood. She asked the nurse over and over, "Please can you change the sheets".

"Soon, soon," but she never came back.

Her breasts were full of milk, engorged, sore. Why didn't they give me those tablets to stop my milk?

Lightning tore through the sky and lit up the room, like a white-walled gallery. She and Tom are at an exhibition opening together. It's one of women artists from the desert and she's hoeing into the champagne. A group of the artists stand shyly in the corner in front of their brightly-coloured canvasses, dressed in equally bright cotton shifts, well-worn cardigans and pullovers and running shoes. One of them has a baby, a chubby, cuddly thing. Shannon goes straight for it, holding her hands out. The shy young mother hands the baby over. She kisses and coos with the baby, who smiles at all the attention he's receiving. But then she shrieks. It's not a baby, it's a wombat. The baby keeps crying even when he's back in his mother's arms.

"Now look what you've done," Tom hands Shannon a fresh flute of champagne, and apologises to the mother. The mother turns to the other women and says something in language. Tom takes Shannon by the hand and draws her away from the desert women.

Shannon got out of bed and stumbled, still half asleep, into the kitchen. Her watch said twelve but she felt like it was much later. The door was open and the rain had caused a flood, washing in over the timber floor. It was so loud it almost drowned out the sound of branches hitting the roof. "I'll never get across the creek in the morning," she said out loud. "Gotta get to Raf. Now. Gotta see what's happening with the creek."

Shannon found her keys on the kitchen table, and ran through the rain to the car. Her hair was dripping. She started the car and drove down the hill past shivering cows and the grey horse, trying to shelter under a tree. The creek was no longer pretty and clear and bubbling but a wild, brown sea, risen from the heathland on top of the escarpment and coming down the mountain taking fences and trees and debris along with it.

Once when she'd been pregnant with Maxie she'd driven from town and had to leave the car on the other side because the creek was too high. She'd managed to wade across and walk up to the farmhouse. She was brave then. Poor brave Maxie. Where is his little sister? "Baby, baby," he'd said when he came into the hospital room, rushing to the bassinette. He thought the baby was just sleeping. Poor, poor baby. She would get across now, she knew she could.

Emma's spirit was related to here, her place of conception, not her place of death, that horrible hospital ward. Her spirit had returned here. That's what Colin had told her about his people. Their dreaming related to their conception place. He had wanted to ask Lily, "Where was I conceived?" But he never got the chance did he? But Emma was conceived here, here in the valley. She was sure of it. Shannon was from the valley, this was her place of conception too.

"Kumanjayi, kumanjayi. We have to go now. We have to get to Raf. I have to save him," she called out to the dead, as she nosed the vehicle onto the concrete causeway. The rain banged loudly on the roof. The water was swelling and rising around the car. She pushed her foot down on the accelerator. "Hold tight, Maxie, my beautiful boy. Just a little bit further." She turned to the back seat to talk to her absent son. And then the car stalled. She turned the keys in the ignition but it revved for only a second. She slipped her foot off the pedal and tried to open her door but the water came rushing in, swirling around her feet. She slammed the door shut. She tried the ignition again; there was just enough power to open the windows. But then it went dead. Dead. "Come on Maxie. Climb over, I'll help you."

Unbuckling her safety belt, she climbed over to the passenger side and squeezed her way out through the window, belly-flopping into the creek. The water was up to her chest and she could feel herself going under as she moved in the direction of the current. "Gotta keep going, swim, swim. We'll get to the other side, Maxie."

Just then a wave crashed into the car, pushing it off the causeway like a slippery ice cube, sending it floating downstream, until it came to a crashing stop against a huge boulder, the whole side bent in.

Five metres felt like five hundred. But she kept forcing herself against the dark tide. "Keep going. Maxie. Raf. Baby, kumanjayi." She muttered. "Green lino. Ugly grey walls. Doctors. Nurses. What are they saying?" The water was rushing, moving. And then another rush swept her closer to the bank downstream. Something swept past her.

A dead bird? The wombat? She smashed onto a rock and tried to cling on. "Lights above me. The hospital. Operating room. Shining down. On me. On baby. Perfect baby. Baby's not moving. No sound. No crying. What's that sound? Where's it coming from? Is that me? Tom? Are you crying? 'Shan-non, put your slippers on. Shan-non, you shouldn't have run around so much. It's your fault'. Irina's crying. 'Poor, poor Tom.' No, Irina, I did everything right. It's not my fault. Tom is looking out the window. He's quiet. He must be crying. Hold onto the rock, Maxie, Maxie hold on. No, it is all my fault. I have to save the baby. Emma, I'm coming for you. Raf, I'm coming. Maxie, we have to save my boyfriend. No, I'm slipping off. Lights. Operating lights. I'm going to die in a hospital bed. Blood on the sheets, blood on the sheets. I'm coming to you, baby Emma. Floating, floating. I'm coming, kumanjayi."

And then a black wave hurled Shannon back down into the water and she stopped remembering anything.

Chapter Thirty-seven

Giant waves crashed the headlands and tore at the walls of surf clubs. Swimming pools fell right off the end of cliffs into infinity, as the deluge continued. It was as if Mother Nature had said, "OK I'm going to prove all those climate change deniers wrong. I'm going to wreak havoc on the world".

Mother Nature's panic at how humans had wrecked the earth, God's wrath against sinners, or just an unlikely event – it didn't really matter. The super storm passed and the clean-up began.

At the detention centre, Rafael was locked in, away from nature. He belted the door with all the force he could find. He had to get out; the walls were closing in on him. They'd stuck him in here in the Iron Curtain high security area after he wouldn't come down from the roof. As visitors reached for their umbrellas and the rain started, he'd escaped the visitors' area and climbed up, threatening to stay there forever unless they let him out. He called out constantly, demanding they send him back to his mama's house. His feet were pulled up to his chin as he tried to stop himself sliding down the tin. He didn't want to budge, even as he felt the rain penetrating his skin.

"*Mamá*," he yelled.

He could see a helicopter above him and shaded his eyes, worried it was going to land, drag him up and take him away. Throw him into the volcano.

A cameraman leant out of the copter filming him. Rafael covered his face with his T-shirt and bent down low over his knees. "Leave me alone, bastards," he muttered.

The helicopter hovered then climbed back into the sky doing a turn, ready to come down again. In the short time between its manoeuvres the guards acted. Rafael felt a strong pain to his legs. Realising he'd been tasered, he yelled out as one of the guards pounced on him, grabbing his pants. Another dragged him down a ladder and onto the ground, face down in the dirt. The first pulled his arms back; the second was about to hit him when the helicopter swooped down closer to film. Quickly, they wrenched him up and dragged him away, and back to his cell.

He hammered the door again but with nobody answering his calls, he went back to his hard bunk and curled into the thin foam mattress. It smelt of stale urine.

He mumbled: "The soldiers. Stop!

"Come on, pay him the money. We'll get some drugs. We'll stop the pain. You'll have another baby. Don't cry.

"Don't go, Tony. Mate. Don't leave us. Don't die. Don't die."

A slot in his door was pulled back and two deep, blue eyes peered through. "You OK mate?"

The door opened and the guard brought in a tray of food. Bland, mashed potatoes, two sausages smothered in tomato sauce, still frozen peas. He set it on the floor next to the bunk. "Raf, got you some lunch."

"*Patria libre o muerte.* For the fatherland. I will fight for the fatherland."

"Yeah, sure Raf. Now come on, have something to eat."

"The food must feed the children. I care only about the children."

The guard picked up the plastic fork to hand to him but Rafael pushed it away; peas went flying all over the floor. "Where am I?"

"It's a special place for people we need to watch. It's OK, you're safe," the guard touched him lightly on his arm.

"No! Don't touch me. I will do it. Whatever you want. What do you want to know? Please, please don't hurt me. I will tell you everything."

"It's OK, Raf, I'm not going to hurt you."

"Do you want my body?" Rafael stood up, moving closer to the guard. "Anything. I can please you." He wedged his way closer, trying to unbuckle the guard's belt. "I'll make you feel like Heaven."

The guard pushed him. "Get away from me, you little poofter. Jesus!"

Rafael dropped to the floor again, muttering to himself: "Cigarettes into my flesh. Wound on wound. Crucified. Stop, I'll give you my secrets. All the secrets. Just stop.

"*Sopa. Mamá. Necesito sopa.*

"We're all human. We're all flawed. We're not Jesus Christ. Sandino. Carlos Fonseca. We're all depraved, no morals, no feelings even.

"Is that what I fought for?

"Helicopter – coming to get me. Take me. Throw me into the volcano's murkiness. I'm dead already.

"Lana, why did you get rid of the baby? My baby. *Comandante* stop! You can't do that to a woman who just had a baby inside her. Pig! Stop!"

The guard shook his head. "I can't help you, Rafael," he said. "Just eat your food." He banged the door shut, bolting the lock, leaving Rafael sunk on the floor in a pool of squashed peas and mushy potato.

Chapter Thirty-eight

It was Tom's turn to be late to pick up Maxie this day. He'd booked him into after-care but even those extra couple of hours weren't enough. He was swamped with work. The woman with the Balinese gigolo wouldn't stop calling him and he'd had to waste time having an appointment with his own divorce lawyer to sort out a financial agreement with Shannon. He almost hit a huge four-wheel drive reversing out of the school grounds as he pulled up in front of the gate.

God, hope that wasn't Jane, he thought as he shoved his car into reverse and parked, blocking the turning circle. He clicked the remote over his shoulder as he ran through the gate.

Maxie was holding the care-worker's hand and sucking his thumb.

"I thought you forgot me, daddy."

Tom took his hand and thanked the worker. "I wouldn't do that, my boy. Come on, let's go to the park for a little while."

At Centennial Park, about fifteen minutes' drive away, Tom took their two bikes off the rack at the back of his car. He helped Maxie with his helmet after slipping his suit off and his Lycra on, and they rode slowly together on the bike track past swamps, football fields and lakes filled with waterlilies and ducks. They only had twenty minutes until the park closed but he needed that time to let all the stress of the day dissipate.

He'd reluctantly asked his colleague to take up Rafael's case but he wasn't sure if he was having much luck. Too bad, it wasn't his problem. Trust Shannon to get involved with an over-stayer. She was a do-gooder as well, but an ignorant one which could be very dangerous. And she wasn't even in town to help him. Maybe she didn't even know that Rafael had been picked up. He'd had a message from old Joe at the valley but he hadn't had time to call him back. He would when he got home. And why was she speaking to that idiot Vesna? How did he ever get involved with her? It was all too much. "Spare me from do-gooders," he spoke out loud.

Maxie, riding just in front of him, turned round. "What did you say, daddy? I'm being good."

"Not you, my boy, nothing. Come on, we better turn back."

"But I want to keep riding."

"No, the park rangers will be after us. They'll be locking the gates soon."

"I don't want to go home. I want to stay here." Maxie tried to speed up, his little legs working as hard as they could.

Tom rode in front of him and stopped his bike, grabbing the handle bars so he nearly fell over. Maxie jumped off and sat in the middle of the track crying. "I don't want to go home. I don't want to go to school. I just want to ride my bike forever."

Tom got off his bike. "Well, you can't. Come on, don't be silly."

"I want Aunty Vesna."

Tom almost laughed but Maxie's next line stopped him.

"I miss mummy. Anyway, Rafael isn't really her boyfriend. I'm her boyfriend. I just told you that to make you jealous because you smacked me."

"You're too young for all this stuff, Maxie."

"Don't call me Maxie. I'm Wombat Boy. And I'm not going home."

Tom was tired and worn out and he didn't want to be stuck in the park overnight. "Yes, you are. Get back on your bike." He grabbed Maxie's arm but he started crying.

"You're hurting me. You're always angry. You need angry management."

"You need to do what you're told."

Maxie refused to move, sitting cross-legged and staring at the ground. Still crying, he mumbled: "I want a baby brother or sister. I'm sick of it just being me. Why can't you and mummy have another baby?"

Tom was startled by his words. He let his precious bike crash to the ground, and knelt down, then sat cross-legged next to Maxie. He cradled him in his arms and rocked him. "I want a baby too. I want everything to be alright again. I want mummy to come home."

When the park ranger drove up he found a middle aged man and a kid sitting on the ground next to their higgledy-piggledy bikes crying together.

Living at home with her parents was driving Vesna mad. Every morning her father and his bloody Turkish coffee and *rakia*, and her mother sighing about how hard she had to clean, but it was her duty. And the TV always turned up so loud it hurt your ears – stuck on commercial channels.

Her father still bossed her into picking up her dirty clothes from the floor and helping her mother with the cooking. It was as if she'd never grown up – they treated her like she was fourteen. She was a former foreign correspondent, for God's sake. They hadn't even figured out she was working as a hack sub-editor for a news service.

And now her car had had it and she didn't have the money to buy a new one. She was even more stuck. For a moment there, she had seen a light at the end of the tunnel. She thought Tom might just invite her to live with him. She could get used to his damask bed coverings and state-of-the-art coffee machine. It was a world she could be very comfortable in.

She'd even been kidding herself that Maxie liked her and her weird sense of humour. He did laugh at her jokes and, no matter what Shannon said, he liked her presents – she'd found them at Cash Converters and Vinnies when she was looking for a work jacket. She'd never wanted kids and had no desire to be a step-mother but if that was part of the deal she'd cope, and bugger Shannon.

But Tom's temper was another matter. And she soon got to feel it. After Rafael got picked up she'd filed her story and pics as quickly as she could and the story went to number one on the site – for at least a good fifteen minutes.

Liz was pleased enough to tell her: "Just send a crawly email to the Mufti about your story, say sorry and leave it at that." And even Steve, the editor-in-chief said, "Well done, Vesna" that afternoon when she saw him sleazing over another young reporter in the kitchen.

Jenny, of course, was after her for information about illegals and she'd tried to fob her off with some details about how they obtained tax file numbers and Medicare cards. Jenny was not impressed. She already knew all that. She wanted names and news on where the Iranians were. A deal was a deal, Vesna.

"What about those people you interviewed?" Jenny had asked. "Where are they now?"

"Oh those. I don't know. I'll check and get back to you."

As she popped a Prince CD into the player in her bedroom, Vesna saw Tom's name come up on her phone. Her gut instinct was to not answer it. She knew he'd be furious. Well, she couldn't tell him everything could she? Otherwise it wouldn't be a scoop, the word would get out and there'd be ten TV crews waiting at the site. She didn't know Rafael was going to be one of the victims. The third time he rang she answered it.

"Vesna, what the fuck were you doing?"

"I needed a raid for my feature and it was too good a story not to file."

"But they picked up Rafael."

"I didn't know they were going to nab him. I thought they were going for the Chinese."

"And you call yourself a gun journo? You're an idiot."

"Hey, don't talk to me like that. I have to trust my sources."

"What? You didn't give Immigration his name? I find that hard to believe."

"Tom, I didn't even know he was illegal. You never told me. I could have used him for my feature."

"He wasn't my client. They might deport him."

"Can't you do something?"

"My office is working on it, Vesna."

"Can't you take over the case?"

"Maybe, I'll try and sort something out. If you really want to help you can write a story about what a waste of money and time it is to lock up and then deport a peaceful, hard-working man from Latin America who's been here nearly thirty years."

"I thought you'd be glad to be rid of him."

"Come to my place in an hour. I can't leave, I've got Maxie. We'll work on it together." Tom said. "You have to fix this."

Vesna felt a shift in her guilt. Maybe they could turn all this around. They'd get Raf out and she'd have the best story yet. She knew though that her affair with Tom was over. Oh well, he was so eastern suburbs. Didn't he realise that on public transport it would take a lot more than an hour to get from her place to Paddington?

Chapter Thirty-nine

As dusk was falling the Green Cat-bird called its strange 'meow'. A woman sat huddled at Joe's kitchen table, a tartan blanket around her shoulders, staring into the distance. Joe's wife, Dorothy, brought over a cup of tea with three teaspoons of sugar and put it on the table. Shannon said nothing. There was no acknowledgement. Dorothy looked at Joe and he shrugged.

Shannon picked up the cup and sipped it but she didn't detect the tea's sweetness. It tasted bitter. The room was spinning around. How did she get here? Who saved her? "Is this what it feels like to die in somebody else's kitchen?" she blurted out. She took no notice when Joe picked up the telephone on the hall wall and dialled a Sydney number. Neither did she recognise or care about the voice on the other end. "Message ... secretary ... sleeping all day ... creek ... nearly drowned ... clinging to a tree." Shannon heard the words wash over like the water that had almost swept her away. Her nose dripped as she pushed a tissue to it and she sneezed continuously.

Joe stretched the phone's long cord around the corner from the hall to check on Shannon, hanging it back up on its hook. "Can't believe it took Tom so long to return my call," he told Dorothy.

"You shouldn't have had to chase him. What did he say?"

"He's coming in the morning. Has to re-arrange his appointments or something. Tells me they're not together any more. Separated."

"She's lucky you got there in time, Joe."

"Hmm," he whispered to her. "City people!" He turned to Shannon. "Hey, Shannon, remember when you were Maxie's age, always a bit cheeky but interested in everything? You loved it when I took you for rides on the back of the tractor laughing and calling out for me to go, 'Faster, Joe, faster'. You'd ask the names of plants, name all the calves, giggle when your dog chased the poor cows. Jumping into creeks, running barefoot."

Shannon heard the words but didn't take in the meaning. Her face was blank.

"Poor thing," Dorothy took the now-cold cup from Shannon and led her to the couch. She'd made up a bed, moving all the washing and ironing onto the already piled-up ironing board. "Try and sleep, dear."

Still shivering, Shannon leant her head back on a cushion, but kept her eyes open, staring with no recognition at the inane music show on the TV screen while Dorothy returned to the kitchen.

"You dry." Dorothy held out a tea towel which Joe took with his large farmer's hands, covered in scratches and cuts. She flicked her long, grey plaits out of the way and dipped her equally weather-beaten and sun-spotted hands into the soapy water.

"She was such a happy kid, Dot," Joe whispered again. "Why do things go so wrong?"

"Marrying the wrong man maybe, Joe, I don't know."

He laughed. "Are you glad you married the right one then?"

"Who?" She smiled as she wiped down the sink and filled the kettle with water. "Can you put a bit more wood on the fire, love? It's freezing. Another cuppa?"

He nodded. Shannon hadn't eaten much of the lamb roast, so she put some back in the oven for her. "Can make fritters out of it for brekky," she said, sighing.

Joe threw a log inside the wood stove then turned to Dorothy. "Hey, how about some dessert? I'll open a tin of peaches." He found a can in the cupboard and used the wall can opener.

Dorothy's eyebrows lifted. "What a gentleman!"

"Shannon, feel like some?" He poured the peaches into a bowl, adding ice cream from the freezer and a little bit of cream he'd got from the local dairy. He put it on a tray for her.

"Not hungry." She looked at it but didn't touch it.

"Shhh. Just eat. Try not to think about it all. Tom's coming to get you. I think you need to see a doctor."

"Tom? Yeah like Christmas. No doctors." She picked up the spoon and slurped her peaches. She felt some energy return as a memory came back to her of Ainslie. "Ainslie made peach crumble. With custard."

"Who dear?" Dorothy asked.

"Ainslie. Told me ghost stories."

"I don't know her."

"She's talking about the coloured housekeeper they used to have." Joe licked the last of the ice cream from his spoon.

"Who would have thought Ainslie would have a son called Colin." Shannon stared into her peaches, taking a last mouthful before putting the bowl back onto the tray.

"Don't know about that." Joe got up from the table, taking his and Shannon's bowls to the sink.

"Ainslie had a mother. What tribe was she?"

"Oh, they lost that long ago." Dorothy spoke to Shannon as she handed her bowl to Joe.

"Did they, Dot?" Joe said.

"I'm not a racist, you know that. I've taught Aboriginal kids, jeeze, and you know all the ones that used to come over here after school with the boys. They were alright."

"And the ones at the dairy, bloody good workers."

"Yeah, but the kids are on the back foot when their parents are alchies. That's what I'm talking about. Some of those so-called Stolen Generations were better off away from their drunken parents. You've gotta agree with me on that, Joe."

"I don't know. I didn't know their parents. But I do remember Ainslie a bit. Could have answered an ad, I'm not sure. Shannon's mum often had maids. She was never one for housework. A bit above all that. Preferred playing Bridge with her girlfriends or tennis or horse riding out in the paddocks."

"Horses. We had horses." Shannon spoke up again. Shadowy figures in the stables, a slight brown woman feeding hay to the horses, memories coming back. In black and white. No colour.

"How old was this Ainslie?" Dorothy asked.

"Hard to tell – forties maybe," Joe answered. "She'd been around a bit. Didn't talk much. But she told me she'd been at Bomaderry, the home for Aboriginal kids. I did know some of those Bomaderry girls. They'd go to dances, you know."

"Oh right," Dot looked knowing.

Shannon blurted. "They'd put her in the morgue at night, scared the hell out of her." She pulled the blanket up higher but was still shaking. "So sad. Johnny died. Burst appendix."

Dorothy shivered. "What's she yabbering on in Double Dutch

about?"

"She must still be in shock," Joe said.

Shannon's teeth were chattering. She didn't think she'd ever be warm again. "Her sister died. At the home. Only a baby. Head caught in the cot rungs. Taken from her mum. And then same again. Her kids taken."

Joe looked like he was the one who'd seen a ghost, turning his back to the women as he washed the bowls.

Dorothy walked over to the TV and picked up the remote control, turning the volume up as she took a seat on the battered armchair. "Now how would you know that, Shannon?"

"She told me." Shannon remembered Ainslie sitting on the end of her bed, telling her those sad stories. She was right back there. The faded sheets, the pink eiderdown. Her teddy bear.

"She mustn't have been a good mother," Dorothy put a cushion behind her head to make herself more comfortable. "Some Blackfellas neglected their kids, would get on the grog and just leave them. Somebody had to look after the little buggers."

Joe hung up the tea towel. "Sh sh. No more talking. You need to rest, Shannon, and I need to go and work on that tractor engine."

As he opened the back door, their Collie lumbered into the lounge room and made straight for the couch. Shannon leant down and pulled her up next to her. She was about to drop pups and just needed a cuddle. Shannon hugged the affectionate old bitch. Joe looked at Dot. Dogs weren't normally allowed inside the house but this time they both nodded.

Tom's gleaming black BMW never did look quite at home in the valley. He had also never taken to the local custom of raising one or two fingers off the steering wheel just for a second to acknowledge the other driver coming towards him. Driving around a hundred Ks along a road most people did seventy on didn't help him rise to Mr Popularity with the local community neither. He sped past a station wagon, which swerved onto the damp grass to avoid him. Further down the road, he arrived at the one-lane bridge and made the local bushfire brigade captain stop his four-wheel drive coming towards him so that he could pass. "Great, I won't be invited to join the bushfire brigade now," Tom laughed to himself, recognising him from barbecues Shannon had forced him to go to. He pulled in through the wire gate at Joe's, and wondered where the old man's battered truck was.

The garden was wet and squelchy and he worried the grass would wreck his new shoes. Why the fuck did he have to come all this way for Shannon? What was wrong with her? Stacking on the bullshit as usual. Poor little Shannon. Maxie had begged to come but he didn't want him to miss school; better to keep him out of it. Not good for him to always see his mother like this. He knocked on the half-open door, the smell of lamb fritters and bubble and squeak wafting from the kitchen. God, this place hasn't changed in years, he thought. Like something out of a 1960s magazine, only a lot more untidy.

Shannon was sitting on the couch, a tray of breakfast food in front of her, but she didn't seem to have touched it. She was staring at the TV, showing some kind of breakfast show, the presenter's hair held together like glue. She put the tray on the floor when she saw Tom and pulled the blanket up, leaning back into the cushions. "I don't want to go back with you," she said before he'd even had a chance to say hullo.

Dorothy swung round from the stove, where she was piling eggs onto a plate. "Oh Tom, you're here."

"Thought I better make an early start," he pecked her on the cheek. "Have a lot of appointments today. Gotta get back. How are you anyway, Dorothy? And Joe?"

"I'm fine. He's out mending fences. Cuppa?"

"No thanks, I bought a coffee on the way. But thank you, and thanks for looking after Shannon."

"She's not in a good way, Tom," Dorothy whispered to him.

"I can see. How did you find her?"

"It was just luck, Joe went down to check on a cow about to drop a calf. He'd been worrying all night about her, the rain was that heavy. Got the shock of his life when he saw Shannon clinging to a log wedged between two rocks in the creek."

"I can stay here can't I, Dorothy?" Shannon pleaded. "Just a day or two then I can go home."

"No, really Shannon I think you need to see a doctor," Dorothy answered. "It's lucky you didn't get the flu after getting so wet too." She turned to Tom. "Really, Tom, it's lucky she's alive."

"Where's her car?" Tom gripped the back of a kitchen chair; he was seething. Why did Joe and Dorothy have to become involved in their problems? Would his embarrassment never end at having the whole world seeing his private life? Shannon was a nut case. Driving into a flooded creek! What next? He'd get her to a GP and have her put away. He couldn't help her. Nobody could.

"It's OK," Dorothy said. "Joe and some of the others managed to winch it out of the creek. Will take a while to dry out though and will definitely need panel beating."

"Christ, it has to be a write-off. The insurance company will be thrilled. I'll organise a tow-truck, don't worry," Tom looked at his watch. "Have you got some clothes to put on, Shannon?"

Dorothy had lent Shannon some pyjamas. She gave Tom her freshly-washed and dried jeans, jumper and underwear, which had been neatly folded on a chair.

Shannon got up from the couch slowly, but with a burst of unexpected energy knocked the clothes out of Tom's hands. "Stop treating me a like a child, I can dress myself."

"Well, you're acting like a child, you loopy bitch," he yelled back at her.

"How about a shower, dear," Dorothy interceded, giving Tom a stern look. "I'll get you a towel."

"Yeah, but not a long one." Tom was still angry. "Maxie's waiting for you."

The sound of his name forced Shannon to move just a little bit faster.

Shannon stared into her reflection in the bathroom cabinet's mildewed and cracked mirror. But there was no recognition. She opened the cabinet door, seeing shelves crammed with old toothpaste, a shaving cup and brush, ancient bottles of medicine, squeezed tubes of ointment and some bottles of pills. The Green Cat-bird shrieked again outside the bathroom window, its cry like that of an abandoned infant.

"Baby, baby. Where's my baby?" She spoke out loud as she closed the cabinet door.

"Blood on the sheets. So much blood.

"The baby can't breathe. Her lungs just aren't strong enough.

"Tom, Tom, where are you?"

At the sound of his name, Tom called out to ask if she was OK. But when there was no answer, he tried the door which was locked. "Open the door, what are you doing?"

Dorothy tried it too. "Don't yell at her. Let me talk to her. Shannon, darling, let me in."

Tom looked like he had a bomb strapped to him which was about to go off. "Stop stuffing around, Shannon. I'll have you committed. You're completely mad. You're losing any chance of getting Maxie back."

Dorothy swung round and grabbed Tom by the arm. "Calm down, that's not helping."

They heard the shower water and then Shannon's voice, singing something about graveyards and flowers.

They looked at each other, moving back to the kitchen. After about ten minutes Shannon emerged with a towel wrapped around her.

"Ah Shannon, you're wet. Come in front of the fire." Dorothy nudged Shannon. "I'll give you some privacy," she said, going out to the vegie garden.

Tom put another log in the wood stove, noticing a pile of cruise ship travel brochures in the newspaper and kindling basket. Poor Dorothy, so much for her plans for a cruise holiday. He dried Shannon in front of the fire, softly patting the cuts and bruises all over her body. "You'll need some ointment for these. We'll get it in town," he said. He dressed her and grabbed the beanie Joe had left for her. He squashed it down on her head, finding a coat to put over her. "Let's go, Shannon. It's time to go home," and he led her out the door to his car.

Chapter Forty

Colin knew he had to visit Rafael. He hated the thought of it, of going anywhere that had razor wire surrounding it and guards. Too many bad memories of being inside for that. He'd never turned back. But Rafael needed him. He was his mate. He had to go.

It took a bus, two trains, another bus and a great deal of humiliation to get to the detention centre. And now he felt anxious as he surveyed the waiting area, a scruffy garden with more dirt than flowers, benches filled with inmates and visitors. He thought about what Raf had told him about torture. He'd heard of lots of soldiers who suffered from PTSD – mates a bit older who were Vets. He had brothers who had come back all quiet and leaden from Vietnam. And he'd heard about the experience of others who had immigrated here from repressive regimes. Raf only ever hinted at his past, except for the day of the fight with Tom. Colin hardly knew anything except that he had fought in a war and been tortured, it seemed.

In some ways, he thought of himself, too, as a soldier, even if an unrecognised one, in a frontier war. They tortured us, too, he thought. We were kidnapped. And we were just little kids. Why? Why did they tell us so many lies? They told us we were orphans; that our mothers had died. Or if they were still alive, that they didn't love us. Why?

Rafael appeared, brought to Colin by a guard. He was wearing overalls and looking thinner than usual. His hair, normally in a neat ponytail, was un-brushed and tangled. He didn't seem to recognise Colin, but took a seat at the table without a word.

"Can I get you a cuppa, mate?" Colin asked but Raf didn't answer. He got up and made two teas at a bench filled with plastic mugs, tea bags and sugar. "Here you go. Black as usual." He placed the mugs on the bench. "How are you going? The job's going fine without you." He made an attempt at a feeble joke.

No answer.

"We're working on getting you out. Funny part is Tom's now helping too. He called me last night. It shouldn't take too much longer. Just hang in there."

No answer. Colin could feel himself babbling on, just to fill in the space between them. He didn't want the guard to come and take Rafael back. "I saw my brother die. His appendix burst. It was too late. They said they were protecting us but what sort of protection was that? Do you know what they did? The punishments they used to think up?

"They were sick at bloody Kinchela. If you ran away they always got you, they always brought you back, severely flogged you with a six-foot cane. I was black and blue from one end to the other. They tied me to the old fig tree – the one where the ancestors had died. There's bones buried under that rocky, hard, hard ground. I can feel them, my ancestors, hear their groaning, their whispering in the trees. Feel their icy shadows. Gunned down by police troops, or even hung from those branches. They say it was women and children too. The sister girls talk of how they were punished – locking them in the old morgue. It used to be a hospital. They'd leave them all night freezing in their nighties, alone in the dark. They were scared out of their wits. They did that to my mum. They punished me too, they tied me to that tree. The ghost tree. The death tree of my ancestors.

"So the first chance I got I left that hellhole. Well, they kicked me out when I was old enough to get a job. Very unceremoniously, I can tell you now. They say you become the victim or the victimiser. I was a victim. But then I became violent. I made the choice to change to a victimiser. Killed a man. My daughter's man. He was hitting her, just a little bit too much for my liking."

Colin began to cry, it was so long since he'd felt tears on his cheeks that the salty taste was a surprise to him. He found a hanky in his pants' pocket and dried his eyes. "Yeah, Raf we've been through torture too. I was trained to be a white man. And when I wasn't accepted as a white man I went crazy. Almost drank myself to death. A violent drunk too. So I became the abuser. Violent, cruel. Murderous. Yeah – I'm a murderer. I did my time. They say you can do it easy or hard. Well, I did it hard just like most of the other stolen Blackfellas in that jail. My only family. I'll tell you something though, mate, jail was paradise compared to that bloody home. Now all I want is peace and quiet – just peace, restful peace and no more trouble."

Colin looked up to see some sort of recognition in Rafael's eyes, and felt relieved, but not at the words that he spoke next. "You had dinner with her? Why?"

Colin took his hand. He felt sick to his stomach. "I was trying to help, mate. Just trying to help."

Rafael didn't move his hand away but looked at the sky. "You gave me up to the *guadia*."

"No, Raf, no." Colin was shocked. He would never have ratted on his friend.

"No more helicopters," Rafael stared at the clouds. "You're safe old man, safe."

"I'm sorry, Raf. I'm so sorry." Colin stroked Rafael's lined palms, sitting with him for what seemed like hours, letting him mumble his memories, just like he had done for him. Two men, in trauma together.

Chapter Forty-one

Tom took Shannon home to his house, and let her lie in front of the TV for a couple of days. He thought she would be safe on her own as he had to go to work, and seeing Maxie would be the best medicine for her.

But even he couldn't break through her melancholy – despite bringing her presents of flowers from the garden and reading to her from the tiny books he'd made at school and even attempting to make her tea with warm water. Shannon took a sip and turned back to the television. Maxie didn't know what was wrong with her. He cuddled up on the couch with her and gave her Bear to hold. "Don't be sad, mummy. I'll look after you."

Tom was still angry but also worried about her. The threat to have her committed was a real one; she obviously needed some kind of counselling or psychological help. He had no idea where to turn. His mother didn't want to know and his father was incapable of sympathy even if he normally would have had it in bucket loads. Aleksandar had always liked Shannon – for some unfathomable reason. They shared a sense of humour, especially of the absurd, he supposed.

Amany was the only person he could think of. He wondered how her husband and brother were going. He hadn't been able to help her, and he felt bad about this. But what could he really do? Still, it was her job to keep an eye on her clients. He took his phone outside to call her so Shannon wouldn't hear. Amany picked up after a couple of rings. "Shannon's sick. She almost drowned herself." Tom got to the point immediately. "I'm pretty busy and I've lost a couple of days of work. Anyway I don't think she'd go with me. Do you think you could take her to her doctor, you know Dr Taylor in the clinic next to the hospital? I'll pay you."

"That won't be necessary," Amany said. She agreed to meet Tom and Shannon in the hospital foyer once he made an appointment and she would take over from there. She also agreed she would talk to her about Rafael after Tom explained what had happened to him.

"She knows he was detained but she doesn't seem to want to contact him or her friend, Colin. She's really out of it, Amany." Tom said. "She's lost so much weight. Her ribs are showing. She was such a beautiful woman when I first met her. Lovely soft skin, strong and fit ..." his voice petered out.

Dr Taylor's waiting room was jolly and comfortable. Children's toys were littered on the floor where a toddler had been playing and the receptionist made chatty conversation with all the patients. A nice change from the overworked staff at other parts of the hospital.

Amany took a women's magazine from the low table and flicked through it. The way she dressed you could see she liked fashion. She preferred the elegance of long tops over pants herself, which suited her tall, slim frame.

Shannon just stared into her lap; she didn't want to be here with Amany. She felt like she had lost her life to Tom, all over again. She was too scared to even think about Rafael.

Dr Taylor, an Amazonian, picked up her file and called Shannon's name. In heeled court shoes she towered even over Amany, who stood up too, and began to explain that Shannon should perhaps get a referral for a psychologist. The doctor nodded at her, but didn't say anything. She closed her surgery door, leaving Amany in the waiting room.

Shannon sat at the desk, clinging to her handbag, not wanting to look at Dr Taylor. She didn't want to be sent to a mental asylum. She muttered under her breath, but the doctor didn't catch it.

"Oh Shannon, you've lost weight. Here let's weigh you." She pulled her scales out from beneath her examination bed. "Fifty kilos," she was concerned, indicating she climb up onto the bed. "Don't you want to eat the delicious food you serve in your café?"

"Not really," Shannon sat down on the bed. "Tom wants me put in a mental hospital."

"Well, that's not going to happen." The doctor took her blood pressure, which was a little low and then felt her pulse. "Have you done a pregnancy test? Lie down."

"Pregnancy? Oh ha ha."

Dr Taylor felt her tummy. "I'm not joking. I felt two heartbeats. When was your last period?"

"Period? I don't remember. I just thought, after the baby, you know …"

"Right. Here take this and do a wee in it." She handed Shannon a small plastic container, helping her down off the bed. "You know where the bathroom is."

Shannon was still a bit shaky and with trepidation inched her way into the bathroom, making sure Amany didn't see her. On the toilet, she made a mess trying to piss into the jar, and used some toilet paper to clean it up. She screwed on the lid and washed her hands, trying not to look at herself in the mirror. But she couldn't help a glance, and saw a pale, thin woman with greasy hair and a few spots developing on her chin.

Back in the surgery, Dr Taylor took the jar and dipped the tester into it. "Congratulations." She smiled and walked round her desk to give Shannon a hug.

"But Tom will be furious." Shannon couldn't believe the news.

"Why?"

"It's not his. It just can't be."

Dr Taylor sighed. "Whoever the father is, you're going to have the baby you want."

"But when?"

"You're around four weeks I'd say, so in eight months. I'll write you a referral for a brilliant gynaecologist and obstetrician. She can closely monitor the pregnancy. You might need a cervical stitch. I'm pretty sure you've got an incompetent cervix."

"Incompetent? Yeah, that'd be right."

The doctor smiled wanly. "Don't worry it's all going to work out this time. Be happy, Shannon."

"So I'm not going to be committed?"

Dr Taylor smiled again. "Not on my watch, my dear. But I can give you a referral to a psychologist like Amany suggested, if that's what you want. Sometimes it does help to talk to somebody."

Shannon nodded. "I guess so."

"And, Shannon, stop smoking OK?"

"Well?" Amany smiled at Shannon as she came back into the waiting room, holding some bits of paper.

"I'm not going to the loony bin," Shannon's tone was flat. "But there's something else."

"Tell me."

"Four weeks pregnant."

"Oh praise be." Amany hugged her, then took her by the hand and led her down to the hospital coffee shop. She offered to buy her a biscuit with her coffee but Shannon shook her head. She still didn't feel up to talking much so Amany took over. "Think of your family, Shannon."

"But it's not Tom's baby. It's Raf's."

She nodded. "I thought so. Look, he's in Villawood."

"I know. But they'll let him out."

"I'm not sure. They could deport him back to Nicaragua."

"No!" Shannon screamed. "They can't do that."

"Tom is doing everything he can to get him out."

"Tom? Why? How do you know?"

"He told me your friend, Colin, begged him to and he knows the system. He'll figure something out. I have my problems too, Shannon, and he has tried to help me. He's a good man, deep down."

Tom helping Raf? Shannon stared at her coffee. She couldn't comprehend what was happening. "But Tom's with Vesna now anyway. It was all her fault."

"Vesna?" Amany was surprised. "But Tom's a married man. What is she doing with him? She has no right to break up a family."

Shannon didn't reply.

When they finished their coffees, Amany took Shannon by the hand again. "I want to take you somewhere now. It might help you."

"Where?" Shannon was worried she meant the mosque or a prayer room, but followed Amany up in the lift anyway. They got out and walked down the corridor to a red, yellow and blue swinging double door, with a bell on the side. Amany rang it and a nurse opened it a few minutes later.

"Hello, Amany," she whispered, letting them in. The social worker often brought women up here who were experiencing difficult pregnancies and needed to learn what it was like to have a premature baby.

The room was full of humidicribs, with tiny babies and tubes connecting them to heart monitors. Mothers and a father were sitting next to a couple of them. At one a nurse wearing an apron was feeding a larger baby with a bottle. Suddenly a loud, beeping alarm went off and Shannon jumped back. "Why are you bringing me here?" she asked. "I want to go."

"I have a story to tell you," Amany was firm as she led her across to one of the cribs. "See how tiny these babies are. Well, most of them will survive. Modern medicine and parents' love is amazing.

"I get very sick when I get pregnant, Shannon. Placenta praevia. I spent months in hospital. I lost three babies. The first one only lived for a few weeks in a neo-natal unit, but not as bright and cheerful as this one."

Shannon clung on to the side of the crib, wishing she could touch the translucent pink skin of the baby lying flat on his back wearing the tiniest nappy she'd ever seen. The Perspex stopped her but she could almost feel his will to live as his diaphragm lifted with each breath and he held his arms outstretched above his head. "Go on."

"My faith. I finally had my beautiful daughter. It's God sending something back to us. My belief in God is very strong. I felt I could overcome this."

"What about your husband?"

"Well, I guess he tried to help. It's hard for men too."

"I'm scared, Amany. I can't lose another baby."

Amany squeezed Shannon's hand. "Be strong, do what the doctor and nurses tell you, and have faith. You will have this baby."

After a few moments Shannon spoke again. "When I'm feeling up to it, I would like to visit your home and meet your daughter. And hear your problems, for a change." It had been a long time since she'd felt hope. She was going to have a baby. She had to let Rafael know. He would be so happy. Surely they couldn't deport a man who was about to be a father?

Chapter Forty-two

Colin saw Shannon from a distance, sitting in her old spot at the whale rock. The deep blue sea drifted out beyond her, filling up his whole vision, going on forever. Past the last Ice Age. Past all of human history. Covering up long-gone peoples and their stories but its dark depths always there, below, teeming with life. He felt as if he'd sunk to his own deepest depths, and that life was slipping away from him.

She was staring out to sea, quietly sitting cross-legged on the grey rock, tufts of green mossy grass either side of her. Her pink jumper contrasted with her pale face. He'd never seen it so pale, so grey around the eyes. She looked like a fading sunset, drained of feeling.

He didn't want to disturb her, or speak to her. He hadn't spoken to her for days, not since before Raf had been picked up. She just disappeared. Didn't answer his calls. She was meant to be in love with him, wasn't she? Typical Whitefellas – cold, no feelings. How could she have abandoned him to that hell hole? He was still shocked that somebody who had seemed so caring, cared nothing at all. He thought of that song from *Hair* which asked how people could have no feelings and ignore their friends.

Well, what did you expect? Her parents were quite happy to employ his mum and other Aboriginal girls, work them hard and pay them almost nothing. They were the ones who owned the land. As if she'd be different.

He hurried past so she wouldn't see him. Over in the east the ocean was changing colour, from deep blue to deep grey almost black. To Colin it was as if the sky and the sea were reflected in the shadow that crossed Shannon's face.

As a lone light shone down through the clouds as if from heaven, Shannon could feel somebody watching her. She turned towards the path and glimpsed Colin scurrying up the hill and back onto the road towards Bondi. The coastal path had been badly damaged in the storm so he couldn't go that way. She knew his flat was somewhere close. Hadn't he seen her? Why hadn't he stopped? She wanted to tell him about the baby.

She stood up shakily and took a step, about to call out but he was gone. She put one foot in front of the other – like a walking meditation – breathe in, breathe out. One. Breathe in, breathe out. Two.

Colin turned onto the unswept path to his apartment block. The grass hadn't been cut and leaves were everywhere. Jacaranda flowers had blown in from the neighbour's tree and were turning mushy inside the foyer. The smell of gas was as strong as ever. He'd been wanting to get that gas leak fixed for a long time. He'd tried the body corporate and the owner of the flat, but had been ignored. He'd even called a plumber himself who quoted him ten thousand dollars and who knew if he could fix it? The smell was coming from beneath the tiles, somewhere in the basement. He'd been down several times to have a look and deduced it was coming from the hot water service.

But now he realised there was a solution to the problem. He'd just light a match near it and blow the whole block up. And all the memories would be gone – including that of a girl he once helped when she lost her baby.

He opened his letterbox and took out a pile of bills including a very thick one from MasterCard in among pamphlets advertising last-minute sales and politicians smiling broadly at him. A gold-embossed white envelope stood out. It was from the Coroner's Court.

He made himself a cup of tea, slowly filling the pot with boiling water, and sat at the kitchen bench just staring at the envelope. He thought of the illegals that worked on building sites all over Sydney. He'd tried to be careful. He always checked their white cards, made sure they were legit. Made sure they had CBUS super cover. They couldn't get on a site without it. At least Tony's family should get some money even if they also had to pay a fine because he'd been such an idiot. But the forgers were so good these days. And anyway, wasn't that the government's responsibility? They knew who was running the show. The whole industry was illegal really, making billions out of these poor bastards. Raf had worked the system –

bloody hell, thirty years underground. They must have trained him well back in Nicaragua.

But he wasn't the one who dobbed him in, even if that was what Raf must have thought after he heard Jenny talk about the dinner. What was he thinking having anything to do with her? She used him, like all Whitefellas use Blackfellas. OK yes, he was jealous of Raf's relationship with that stupid Shannon but he would never had stooped so low to give her information. Rafael was his mate. And now he was stuck behind barbed wire, going madder and madder.

Colin put his mug on the pile of library papers about Barangaroo and colonial history. No time for that now. He felt sick as he ripped open the official letter. It was a subpoena calling for his attendance as a witness – again.

"That's that," he thought, sipping his tea as slowly as he had made it. "They have to blame somebody. Well I'm not copping a five thousand dollar fine, or a criminal charge."

In the hallway cupboard was a vacuum cleaner. He took it out and carefully sucked up all the dust and dirt in each of the rooms. He filled a bucket with water and Domestos and mopped the floors in the kitchen and bathroom. He wiped down the sinks and benches with Ajax. Everything was gleaming.

He really only had one suit. For funerals these days, rarely for weddings. Or for going out to dinner with immigration officers. He cringed. It was kept in a suit holder in his bedroom cupboard. The white shirt he normally wore with it didn't look so flash. Better give it an iron and find a tie.

"You brush up well, my dear," he told his reflection in the mirror. "Not bad for an old Koori." He put the ironing board and iron away. Everything was tidy. The card from Lowanna on the mantelpiece next to the photo of his mum looked down sadly at him. "Sorry, love. I tried, I really tried." Why bother writing a note? He left his keys and wallet next to Lowanna's card. Nothing to leave her, only a few dollars and lots of debts.

Yes, he remembered the words of the song about surviving the white man's world.

He remembered too as a kid before he was taken to the home how he and his brothers would get a few bob for the carcass of a feral cat. They'd trap them in cages and then attach an old bit of hose to the exhaust pipe of a car. In thirty seconds the cat was asleep, in one minute dead. It wasn't going to take that long. He made sure all the doors and windows were closed, blinds drawn and the racks from the oven taken out. Can't be bothered cleaning these, he thought as he put them in the sink. "Investigate this death, Mr Coroner," he said out loud.

The kitchen seemed to take on a pink glow as he turned the gas on, knelt down and stuck his head in as far as he could reach. He thought of his mum's watermelon-pink dress that she made herself. The matching pillbox hat like the one Jackie Kennedy wore the day JFK was shot. His mum was always a cool dresser. Never mind Jackie wore hers blood-stained for many hours after the tragedy. He'd only seen his mum in that dress in those photos the neighbour sent him. On the edge of drifting away he heard a scream. Was that his mum calling him to hurry up and come?

"Colin!"

He felt somebody drag him out and an almighty slap to his face. And then he heard the ambulance sirens.

Chapter Forty-three

It was Vesna's turn to do the morning shift. She hated getting up in the dark and catching the train with a whole bunch of exhausted office-workers. She was a night person; those late shifts suited her better. And she could raid the fridge without anybody noticing.

This morning, her eyes were bleary and the air in the office was icy. There seemed to be more management people than journos hanging around, whispering and looking serious. Skinny Human Resources girls in black mini-skirts and stilettos were weaving in and out of the editor-in-chief's office, like seagulls picking at a packet of cold fish and chips. Something was wrong. When she logged in, she saw the email. She had a meeting with the sleazebag in the boardroom and HR on the fifth floor at ten am. At the desk next to her, Gary's face was white; he must have the same email.

"What does yours say, Gary?" she asked, but he just shook his head. He wasn't going to talk about it.

At nine am he disappeared from his spot.

"Where's Gary?" Liz looked up from her computer a few minutes later.

"I think he must be at his meeting," Vesna answered.

Liz nodded. She obviously knew more about what was going on than Vesna. "Just take over his queue can you, Vesna? Just for now. He's locked a story. I can't get into it."

Gary's job was to check the stories before sending them to the subbing baskets and Vesna had authority to do the same job when she was needed. She shifted some of the backlog of stories out to the other subs.

He was back in fifteen minutes. It was as if the computer had frozen. He sat in front of his screen staring at it, not saying a word.

"Liz asked me to take over while you were away, Gary," Vesna tried to coax him out of his coma, as her stomach churned.

"Well, there's no point me subbing this story," he said. "I don't work here anymore."

Vesna didn't know what to say. Not Gary? He was part of the furniture here. He packed up his bag with his papers, threw a few pens in and pushed his chair back. Before Liz had looked up again from the computer, Gary had walked out the door, leaving his lists behind him.

There were twenty-five redundancies handed out that day. Around six months' pay. You had to leave immediately. No checking of emails, no photocopying of records. No good-byes. Just out.

Different people had different reactions. Some were angry, furious that after thirty years of working for the same organisation they were treated so badly. Some were incredulous that the organisation could sack such a talented person. Surely it couldn't operate without them? People who thought they'd be retiring with a company dinner or even just a cake and a speech were unceremoniously kicked out the door. Some cried. Some raged. But Vesna was not among the twenty-five, she was relieved to hear at her meeting. Neither was Sarah although she was moved from being Features Editor to the Digital desk and the sub-editor Vesna called Pollyanna was made Chief Sub, even though she'd only been in the building a few months.

"This means there will be new jobs, but it also means there will be fewer jobs," the human resources skeleton told her at her meeting while Steve grinned. She would be taking over "extra duties" – Gary's job plus her own. For no extra pay. No time for writing features or do-gooder stories, Steve laughed – ones she had thought she had so successfully sneaked out. Leave that to Canberra and the new "national correspondent" who was going to be hired from outside. Hiring people when they just sacked twenty-five? It was hard to believe.

"Your job title is curator," Skeleton Legs said.

Vesna thought that was what they usually called people who put art exhibitions together, not news people.

She was told that the company was "continuing to evolve in this rapidly-changing media environment".

"Along the way we sometimes make some difficult decisions and even though most would see these as necessary, we want to ensure that the philosophy that makes us unique is preserved," Skeleton Legs continued. "Culture is important to all of us and you can help."

She was invited to join the Operations and Engagement Group (OEG), which would report to management on the needs of staff culture. Vesna tried not to laugh. The company's idea of culture was a sausage sizzle, tomato sauce and a beer on the sixth floor balcony before sending staff home to watch the footy.

But as she walked out of the boardroom, still shaking and astonished she hadn't been handed a redundancy package, all she could think about was how with all this chaos it was the perfect time to send her over-stayers' feature out on the wire. Gary was no longer there to block it, and with everything else going on, Liz probably didn't care too much.

She had almost finished her latest news story on Rafael. Tom had told her that provisions existed under the Migration Act where under exceptional circumstances an over-stayer could be granted permanent residency. He was arguing in his application to the Minister for Rafael's status to be normalised because for one, he had not been a leech on the state, had no criminal record, paid his tax, and had set down his roots here. He believed he had a really good case of convincing the minister that Rafael should stay. All Vesna needed now for her story was a comment from Immigration. After her shift finished she moved over to the Features' desk and called Jenny.

"I've washed my hands of him," Jenny answered. "That's not my business anymore. Try the minister's office. And Vesna, I'm still waiting for names."

"Yeah. Yeah." Vesna was sick of this woman but annoyed she had to make another call.

"Yeah, that's right. I'd be careful if I was you." Jenny's tone turned decidedly nasty.

Jenny sat back in her ergonomic office chair. Well no, she hadn't quite finished with Rafael. Or with Vesna, whose anti-department stories weren't helping her reputation. And like the UN and international diplomats she also believed a deal was a deal. She wasn't going to get into any trouble because of that Serbian bitch, or that stupid Blackfella. He wasn't going to swear at her and get away with it.

Naïve, that's what they were. There was more to this Rafael Ramirez case than met the eye. His fancy lawyer – God knows how he could afford him? – could push for ministerial intervention and the media could make a big show of it but she doubted he was quite the angel he made himself out to be.

How could he have hid here since 1986? What sort of outside help was he getting? Was he a terrorist? Who else wanted to know about him? Yep and what else had he done that had flown under the radar? It was time to contact some of her colleagues at the Federal Police and the Health Department. Maybe even ASIO or Interpol. She started tapping her keyboard as she logged back into the system. "OK, *Señor* Ramirez, you could be your average, common-or-garden over-stayer or ... you could be wanted in a whole bunch of jurisdictions. Senior Executive Service here I come." Jenny lifted the phone and dialled a number in Canberra.

Chapter Forty-four

Even being a lawyer with a client inside didn't mean you could skip security at Villawood. First, a guard must open a gate between two fences covered in razor wire. Then the guard unlocks the padlock to the outer gate, lets you in, then locks it again. Then he unlocks the padlock to the inner gate and lets you out. And that's where you take your place in a line. A long line. People push in front of you, the whole time.

"There's more queue jumpers here than the ones coming in boats." Shannon made an attempt at a Colin joke to Tom, who at least smiled. "Why does this place have to be so barbaric?"

"Well it's not meant to be the Hilton. They're trying to turn people off overstaying," Tom said. He had let Shannon come with him on this visit because she'd begged him. She wanted to tell Rafael about the baby. She seemed a bit better since spending time with Amany and getting the good news but he felt as if he was being torn in half. Would he end up being the one bringing up the baby if Rafael didn't recover from this ordeal? Was she sure it was his anyway? Who else had she slept with?

They made their way to the waiting room away from the strong wind which was blowing up. A spring storm. There was dust everywhere. Inside, a woman guard told them to put their bags and belongings in a locker and keep the key.

"I just brought some fruit," Shannon said.

"Fruit's OK," said the guard, who must have modelled her look on the TV serial, *Wentworth*.

"Then do I have to wait in the line all over again?"

"'Fraid so, love."

Tom waited on the other side while Shannon put her bag in the locker and lined up again before going through the metal detector.

"They're getting lots of fruit today," a male guard said.

"Oh, right," Shannon nodded.

"Who do you want to see?"

"Rafael Ramirez."

The guard spoke into the microphone. "Rafael Ramirez, come to the visiting area. Rafael Ramirez come to the visiting area."

Tom led her to a group of plastic chairs under a tree, where they waited.

"Well I hope Vesna's story helps," Shannon said, referring to the one she had written with Tom's help. It had got a very good run and others had taken up the cause.

"Yeah, about time she did something right."

"Better than giving Maxie Xbox games."

Tom smiled.

"Surely the Minister will let him stay," Shannon waved some flies away. Summer was on the way.

"You'd hope so." Tom wasn't so sure. Immigration was so political these days, anything could happen. But he was damn well trying his hardest and his request for ministerial intervention was on the man's desk.

The guard brought Rafael over, even more dishevelled than when Colin had visited. He'd been out of the Iron Curtain maximum security area for more than a week but he was still meant to be on suicide-watch. Shannon jumped up to hug him but he pushed her away. "What are you doing here?" he asked, sitting down.

"I came to see you, of course," Shannon said.

"Why?"

"Because I'm worried about you. We're trying to get you out of here."

"Just leave me. I deserve it. I asked for it. They are cleansing me. They are making me whole."

Shannon reached her hand out but Rafael ignored her. "Tom's a lawyer, remember? He's working on your case. He needs to ask you some questions."

"No, no lawyers. I deserve what I am getting. I did wrong." He stood up. "Guards. Take me back."

Tom touched Rafael on the arm, who jumped back, startled. "Hey, wait. You don't want to be deported do you? We're appealing to the Minister on humanitarian grounds. You've been here so long,

I'm sure they'll let you stay. Shannon has some news for you." He looked at her. "Shannon."

She sighed as if she was ridding herself of all the troubles of the past winter, and all the longing and sadness. "Raf, I'm going to have your baby."

"Baby? Lana." He was still standing.

"I'm not Lana. I'm me, Shannon, and I love you, Rafael. Try and keep calm. You have to have hope."

"You had a termination. You killed my baby. Get out! Get out!" Rafael jumped up and down waving his arms in the air.

Tom and Shannon looked at each other. Neither knew what to do.

"Aye, Rosita, we are only doing this for your benefit." Rafael was acting out a scene from his past, speaking in rapid Spanish: "The revolution believes you are being exploited. We want to eliminate prostitution. It's a social evil that exploits women and hurts their dignity. I know you have to eat, *amor*. Even if there is no food to buy. And when there is food you have to stand in line half the day for it. Aye, *compañera*, the government says that apart from the war the big problem is *machismo*. *Sí, machismo* in Latin America is the first thing we have to tackle. We consider it a retrograde ideological position unacceptable by true revolutionaries."

"I don't know what he's saying." Tom looked bewildered.

"Raf, don't you recognise me," Shannon begged. "Here, I brought you some fruit." She took an apple out of her bag, but Rafael knocked it out of her hand.

"You're poisoning me. You're Eve. Take your apples and go."

"Don't worry, Rafael," Tom said. "We're going to get you out of here."

"Guards," Rafael waved for the guard to come over. "Take me to *Com* Manuel."

Tom recognised the guard as a former inmate he'd met on other occasions here.

The big Tongan took Rafael gently by the arm. "No good, mate," he said to Tom. "It's too late."

"What do you mean?" Shannon asked.

"He's flying out tonight. The removals team's already scheduled to begin the removal at four pm."

Tom's face went red. "But I've put in an appeal, they can't do that."

"Oh yes they can. The Nicaraguans are keen to have him back, apparently. They'll be meeting up with him in LA. Of course the department will be sending him a bill for his stay at the Hotel Villawood."

Shannon bent over and shook but Rafael didn't turn around as he was led away.

Tom was boiling with rage as he steered his Beema out of the detention centre car park and onto the main road, past vacant lots and piles of rubbish. How could his request for ministerial intervention have been ignored? He had good contacts and an almost one hundred per cent success rate. Why did the Nicaraguans want Rafael back? He didn't need that surprise. Shannon and even Colin weren't telling the whole story about Raf.

Shannon had said nothing since they left the centre, appearing to be in shock but Tom couldn't contain his anger. "I had no idea Raf was wanted by his government. What the hell did he do?"

"It was war, Tom," Shannon answered.

"What do you mean war?"

"The revolution and then they fought the Contras. He told me."

"The revolution?"

"Yeah, but Tom he told me he was only protecting Lana."

"Who the fuck is Lana?" Tom swore as a car he almost clipped in his blind spot honked him as he moved into the left lane.

"The American TV journalist he worked with. An old girlfriend. Something terrible happened. That's all he told me."

"What? No wonder he was illegal."

"It was so long ago. I thought you said you could get him out."

"How can I if I don't have all the facts?" He was at a set of lights, waiting to turn left. The arrow was green but the car in front of him wasn't budging. This time Tom honked his horn but it still didn't move.

"It's not left turn only, Tom. Calm down," Shannon counselled.

Tom yelled out his window at the driver, waving his arms. "Move your fucking car, you moron."

"Tom, stop, stop," Shannon tried to pull his hand off the horn.

"Fuck off, Shannon," Tom bashed the accelerator as the car finally moved. He looked at her; she was searching through her bag for a tissue, gulping. He pulled over to the side of the road as soon as he could stop and turned to her. "Why, Shannon? Why? Why the hell didn't you use contraceptives? What possessed you to get pregnant to a criminal?"

Shannon kept crying. "Everything I do is wrong. Maybe I should just end it all."

Tom didn't want to hear this. "Shannon, you're a mother. You have a little boy. You stop it."

He sat in silence and tried to breathe, to calm down, to stop being so angry all the time. He felt so ripped off. First he lost his baby daughter, and then other people wouldn't allow him the feelings he so desperately needed to let out. The emptiness hurt physically – it was like a piece of his own flesh had been cut out of him. He hated seeing Shannon suffer so much, but he'd also died inside. It was really only his mother who understood. He could feel that although she never said anything to him. He had to be a man, for the outside world, at least. But deep down he felt he was going mad. "You never loved me enough, Shannon. I wish you had loved me the way you love Rafael."

"But I did, Tom. Is that why you left?" Shannon looked shocked at his words. "I was just so sad."

"It wasn't just you. She was my baby too. I felt so hopeless. One day in the tea room one of the women lawyers told me, 'It was probably for the best anyway'. What did she know? Emma was perfect in every way. There was nothing wrong with her."

"She was beautiful. It was my body that messed it up."

"But it wasn't your fault, don't you see?"

"I know that now but you said terrible things to me. Even that abortion – Dr Taylor told me it wouldn't have made any difference, it was before twelve weeks."

"I never should have blamed you, Shannon. That abortion stuff is bullshit, I know. But I didn't know what to do. Maybe I didn't look after you well enough. When I saw you smoking and drinking and not coping ... and I was jealous too. I'm sorry, I'm so sorry."

"It's a big, bloody mess."

Tom took Shannon's hand in his and kissed it as he cried. "Where is your wedding ring?" he finally asked.

"I took it off long ago, Tom. Remember, we're getting a divorce." After a while she pulled her hand away to look for another tissue and he started the car.

Chapter Forty-five

Vesna was feeling cheery for a change. Even though she was single again and still living at home, she was saving a bit and would have the money any time soon to move out. She'd even bought a new car, a smooth, white Kia – with a loan from the bank.

She was driving to the beach on her afternoon off. The weather had turned and she wanted to make the most of it. Unnaturally high temperatures for spring but hey, global warming had to come in handy sometime. No local swimming pools full of dive-bombing pimply adolescents for her; she wanted to feel the sea on her skin, even if she would go numb as soon as she jumped in. Normally she wouldn't want to be seen dead in a bathing costume, but today she didn't care.

At least she'd tried to make up for her mistakes, she thought. Her critical stories on Rafael's detention had gone out and the reaction on Social Media had been huge. There'd been a Change.org petition to keep him here and QCs offering their services Pro Bono. Her feature on illegal immigrants had also been picked up widely, and even her photos were being used. They couldn't keep her on the subs desk much longer now, subbing woeful copy and hoping she wouldn't drop dead in a shopping centre like poor, old Grahame. Maybe she'd even get a gig in Canberra – that couldn't be too bad. She quite liked men in suits, these days. If not the Press Gallery, perhaps they'd give her the Jakarta job or another foreign posting.

Her phone rang and she saw on the screen it was the general work number. She put it on speaker as she answered it. It was Steve, the editor in chief. She nearly swerved the car she was so surprised. Aha, the Jakarta job offer.

"Ah, Vesna, I want you to drop that illegal immigrant story," Steve began.

"Have you had pressure from Immigration?" Vesna guessed Jenny had made a complaint. Her good mood disappeared out the window.

"I'm not going to answer that. I'm the boss here, Vesna, not you."

"Well, I can't drop the story. It's in the national interest now."

"I don't care, Vesna. You've become too pro boatpeople."

"Rafael Ramirez is not a boatperson." She was furious.

"Somebody else can write about this from now on. Somebody more objective. You're too emotionally involved. Anyway, you're obviously behind with the news. He's being deported. Tonight. It's become very political. Something about being listed as a wanted person by Interpol."

"What the fuck?" Vesna couldn't pull over; she was right in the middle of traffic.

"One more word, Vesna, and you're out," he spoke steadily. "And there won't be any redundancy package for you."

"That's OK, I quit." She threw the phone down on the passenger seat but kept driving. Nothing was going to stop her going to the beach that day, but she needed to make another phone call. She changed lanes and stopped the car in a No Parking zone, grabbed the phone and punched the numbers in.

Tom picked up after a few rings. That was a nice surprise. "Tom, Rafael's being deported. He's a wanted person."

"I already know that, Vesna. I was at the detention centre this morning. There's nothing more I can do."

"But do you know what he's wanted for?"

"They won't tell me. Something to do with his ex-girlfriend, an American TV reporter called Lana. Anyway that's what Shannon thinks."

"Lana who?" A memory was coming back to her.

"I wouldn't have a clue. And don't try and write any more stories. You'll just make it worse."

"Tom, I did everything I could to help. I won't be editing the next edition of How to Win Friends and Influence People, that's for sure."

"Just shut up, Vesna. Never call me or contact me again."

For once Vesna didn't know what to say. She knew she'd pissed Tom off but she didn't know he hated her that much. Bloody upstart

Serb, thought he was better than everybody, just because he went to Saturday School. Oh, stuff him and his Oedipus complex. "Give my love to Maxie," she said, but he'd already ended the call.

She tried to think of work, of stories, of being professional, of finding this Lana. Lana, Lana? She thought for a while. She'd met a Lana in Kosovo years ago. She'd been in Latin America in the eighties working for CNN. Oh my God, yes, they got really drunk together one night at some horrible hotel bar in Pristina, she remembered. She was American-Latina, maybe Chicana. She could easily have reported from Nicaragua back then. It was the biggest story in Latin America at that time. Lana Lopez. Yes, that was her name.

Vesna Googled Lana Lopez on her phone. Here she is. Still alive. And a pic. Looks like she's had a fair bit of work done on her face. Former CNN anchor. Had her own current affairs program. That'd be right. Always found her to be a know-it-all and a bit paranoid too. And conservative. She kept reading. Won a TV award for her story on the secret use of illegal drugs to treat traumatised soldiers in Nicaragua in 1986. Gave President Reagan even more reason for funding his beloved Contras, probably. He used to say they were drug-runners. Jeeze, bloody Americans and their stupid War on Drugs.

Vesna started the car again and drove towards Tamarama, her mind ticking over the whole way. I have to track Lana down. She has to be on Facebook. She stopped a block past Shannon's café, hoping she wouldn't spot her. She'd heard about the whale rock from Maxie but had never been there. Today she needed that solace before she went for a swim. She was still upset by Tom's words. And that bloody Jenny dobbing her in. What a bitch. Thank God I never did give her any info. But then her phone rang again. Her parents' home number.

"Vesna, you must come home now. Your *tata*. His heart. Ambulance came. We're at hospital. Why you not here? We need you."

"I'm coming, mama." Just five minutes at the whale rock, please. Only five minutes.

She stumbled out of the car and walked past the playground in the park where one lone child was playing. No steep, iron slippery dip. Just some plastic roundabout thing that didn't quite make sense. His overweight mother stood over him to make sure he didn't fall off or actually have some fun. He escaped over to the outside gym where a young man in shorts and a singlet was pulling himself up on a chin-up bar. The toddler jumped up and down trying to reach the bar.

As Vesna looked at him a déjà vu hit her. Then she remembered what she saw that day in the Kosovo village, something she'd tried to forget ever since.

She arrives at the square with the soldiers from the Serbian Army. All is quiet except the caw of crows as they circle above a rusting piece of fencing. Hanging from it: the bodies of a young man and a young woman. Probably teenagers. Both naked. Not a stitch of clothing. Blood down their bodies. Her breasts have been cut off. They have done the same to his private parts. Around their necks are placards in Albanian: "Traitors." Even the war-weary soldiers are stunned. Her guard soldier who has shadowed her the whole time explains: "He's Albanian, she's Serb." Lovers in real life, destined to the after-life together, where Vesna hopes nobody gives a damn about religion nor race.

Vesna tried to erase the memory but it wouldn't go away. She climbed down the grassy bank to the cliff walk. She soon found the whale rock; it was the one ignored by the tourists. Maxie had given her good directions. She stood next to the engraving but she felt herself panicking – her heart raced and her throat went dry. Clouds blocked the sun as the waves crashed below. I'm an idiot. I buggered up everything. Gotta get away. Gotta go. Can't take any more. Over it. Had it. Everybody hates me. I'm done for. *Tata*, are you OK? Don't leave me. She walked to the edge of the rock and gazed down at the sea moving in and out. It would be easy to jump, to just get the hell out of here.

But then her phone rang. She let it ring a few times but then she couldn't help herself. She had to answer it, especially as her mate, Sarah's name popped up. "Vesna, did you really resign? I heard Steve telling Liz."

"Yep. Enough is enough."

"Well, you'll never believe it but Peter Robinson, who used to work here, just called me. He's starting a new paper in Melbourne, bankrolled by a shopping centre billionaire. They're looking for ace feature writers and I mentioned you. He knows your work. He's going to call you."

"Peter, Grahame's mate? Wow. Thanks, Sarah." Vesna put her phone back in her bag and looked down at the black waves smashing against the rocks. It was too windy for a swim anyway. Her father needed her, she had to get to the hospital and tell him the good news. She wouldn't be drinking his *rakia* anymore. She was off to Melbourne.

Chapter Forty-six

The air hostess took Rafael's ticket and tore it, giving him back the stub. "Fifty-two A," she looked down at the purple swirly carpet, not wanting to meet his eyes.

The Immigration officer and the guard escorting him had waited until all the other passengers had gone on board. Now there'd be no room left for any hand luggage in the overhead compartments, not that Rafael had any. He'd been thrashing around so much at the detention centre they'd put the plastic cuffs on him again and he hadn't spoken in the van the whole way to the airport.

After being contacted by the Australian authorities, the Nicaraguan government had dispatched a new passport for Rafael (he burnt his years before after he arrived in Sydney) and the Australian government had bought him a ticket to Managua via Los Angeles. A one-way ticket home.

"I'm OK," he told the guards, slurring his words. "You can go. I'm no danger to nobody."

"We can't let you go until somebody from the airline meets you, mate." The Tongan guard, who had tried to help Rafael at the centre, made an attempt at kindness, knowing it would be fourteen hours of eternity for the poor bastard.

An officious representative from the airline arrived and he and Rafael disappeared down the jet way and onto the plane. The other passengers stared as Rafael climbed into the window seat and the airline rep made sure he had his seatbelt buckled. "Have a safe flight," he said as he walked back down the aisle. Rafael didn't answer him. No thank you from him. He ignored the passenger in the middle seat, who had tried to say hullo before putting on his headphones and watching a movie on his in-flight entertainment. Rafael wasn't capable of watching films. His knuckles gripped the seat-rest to his right; his neighbour had no chance of using it on this flight. He stared out the foggy window at the other planes on the wet tarmac. Home. Nicaragua. Would he be met by guards there too? Taken to yet another jail cell? Did they know about *Com* Manuel? What would his family think? What would be his fate?

Once the plane was in the air, the passenger in front of him suddenly reclined her seat almost into his lap. She was so close he could touch her long, blonde hair pulled up into a ponytail. Lana. He'd written to her but she'd never replied. The last time he saw her was at the hospital entrance at Tegucigalpa in Honduras. As they'd driven along the treacherous roads through the night, she'd filled him in on what had happened to her in *Com* Manuel's office while he was out filming.

He had pulled up at Emergency and, as she took her bags and the all-important video cartridge out of Carlos's Datsun, she'd told him: "I'll be OK, Rafael. Just go, go."

North of Ocotal
March, 1986

Lana followed *Com* Manuel and Dr Krupitsky into the therapy room. Lying in a bed was a woman, her black hair plastered over the pillow, her white hospital gown stuck to her body with sweat. A lone fan hummed from the ceiling, moving the languid air around in circles and flapping the dirty, grey lace curtains against the closed window.

The patient's eyes were glazed, she stared towards the window as if she could see something beyond its painted panes. The war? The fighting? Torture by the Contras? Her toes stuck out from under the sheet, raggedy, dirty, un-cut. Now that woman needs a pedicure, Lana's mind was racing.

The patient was wearing headphones that were attached to a cassette recorder in her lap. Dr Krupitsky explained she was listening to calming music. Next to her on a hard, plastic chair sat a man in civilian clothes. A suit seemed out of place here. *Com* Manuel introduced him as a Nicaraguan therapist, who was there to assist the patient through her MDMA experience. As they spoke, the therapist leant over the woman fixing eyeshades to her eyes. She didn't object, but leant back, putting her head on the pillow, as the therapist held her hand.

"MDMA has a unique ability to reduce fear and increase interpersonal trust," the doctor said. "This makes it well suited as an adjunct to psychotherapy for PTSD, opening a window of tolerance in patients. They are then able to experience and express fear, anger and grief with less likelihood of feeling overwhelmed."

Lana looked like she didn't believe this. "Oh come on, *Com* Manuel, is all this rubbish really going to do anything for the poor woman?"

"*Por favor, Señorita* Lana, you should have patience like the therapist. He will wait for the participant to take her time. She has already been given the MDMA. It is non-directive. We believe the participants themselves will decide how the session should unfold. The therapist doesn't force the participant to face their trauma. He can bring it up if it doesn't arise spontaneously but so far we have not had to do that."

"Yes I can imagine they all want to talk about their torture." She couldn't help being sarcastic.

"Come, I think you've seen enough for now," *Com* Manuel led Lana out the door, leaving the doctor with the therapist and patient.

Outside, *Com* Manuel looked around for Rafael. "Where is *Capitan* Ramirez?"

"You mean Rafael? He must have gone to the bathroom."

Com Manuel laughed. "I'm not stupid. So I guess he is trying to sneak around and do some filming without us?"

Lana didn't answer, hoping that Rafael at least would get some decent footage before being caught.

"You see, Lana, the *capitán* is one of our warriors too. He was tortured in the revolution by the *guardia*, but he still came back and fought for us against the Contras."

"He never told me but I guessed it. Maybe he needs some of your assistance for trauma as well," Lana suggested.

"Perhaps. But you would have to leave him here for his treatment."

"No, he comes with me."

He laughed again. "Don't worry your pretty little head. Follow me now, I will order refreshments and I will send somebody for young Rafael."

She followed *Com* Manuel down the long hallway, her sandalled feet creaking on the floor until they reached his office.

"So this was a convent?" Lana nodded towards a large, wooden crucifix on the wall. "And this is the Mother Superior's desk?"

"*Sí*, it once was but we were in need of the building for our work. The nuns understand; they believe that Jesus was a true revolutionary. Can I offer you a coffee?"

She nodded: "*Bueno*, OK."

"*Sí*, looking for conspiracies in the jungle would be thirsty work." *Com* Manuel waved to the woman soldier to bring a tray of coffee.

Lana glanced towards *Com* Manuel and could see he was staring at her breasts. Just like the young soldiers. Men, they were no different, no matter what age and part of the world they came from. They still saw women as pawns on a chess board. Well, she needed his help to pin down this story. She smiled at him.

"Is there something in particular you want from me, *Señorita* Lana?" He looked amused. "I have nothing to hide."

"Well, then, you'll do an interview on camera about your work here?" She took out her lipstick and applied it with the help of her compact mirror.

"Certainly, but first I need a favour from you."

The woman soldier pushed the door open with her tray, setting it on the desk. She gave Lana a warning look, her eyes moving sideways towards *Com* Manuel but Lana ignored the gesture and the soldier left.

"I need you to make a video to show you Americans that we look after our people, that we don't let them rot, or jeer at them like you did to yours coming back from Vietnam. We respect our soldiers."

"*Comandante* Manuel, I'm not one of your visiting Russian poets or third world documentary makers. I can't make a propaganda program."

"I can explain everything. But first, your coffee?"

Lana pulled her heavy, teak chair closer to the desk, putting a lump of sugar in the thick liquid, the grains sticking to her red lips as she drank from the small, white cup.

Com Manuel lit up a cigarette and walked to the door. He pulled the knob, clicking it shut. He turned the key in the lock, then put it in his trouser pockets. Turning to Lana again he smiled as he smoked: "How is your coffee?"

"Why are you locking the door?"

"I'm sure you know why, Lana. Isn't it what you always wanted?"

"No, *Comandante*. Not at all. I only want a story, the real story of what's going on here. What are you and the military doing here?"

A storm was gathering outside and the clouds weighed down from a sky as thick as the coffee she was drinking. The room had gone pitch black and the temperature had dropped one or two degrees but the air was still suffocating.

Lana looked at *Com* Manuel's desk and the papers, which appeared to be lists of patients, then out the window to the dense garden, full of tropical plants, hibiscus trees and orchids wet by a sudden shower. It smelt like a florist's shop; the scent floating through the window was intoxicating. But now it mixed with the smell of *Com* Manuel's cigarette smoke.

"You ask too many questions, my dear. Far too many. That is not your right. We are helping our soldiers, not leaving them to suffer. You speak out too much criticising our noble military who have fought for our freedom."

"I am only doing my job. I need to report the truth."

"Truth!" *Com* Manuel's face was going red. "You know nothing about truth. You are a loud mouth. You think you know everything. Did you spend days and weeks with a hood over your head? Were you ever tortured? I've forgiven enough. Your hypocrisy sickens me. How dare you belittle what we are doing here?"

Lana's heart began to beat faster. For once, she was not sure of what was happening around her. She realised she was scared. Not nervous. Scared. What was happening here? Was she now the prisoner, not the one in charge? How could he do this to her? She was an American, a journalist. Neutral. Not on anybody's side. This was outrageous. She went to do up the top button of her blouse but *Com* Manuel took her arm and pushed it away.

"Leave it, I want to see what you have." He opened another button, to reveal her large, creamy breasts.

"Stop it."

"Oh now you say you don't want it. But there's always a quid pro quo, my charming American *periodista*. And it's time you were punished."

"You're mad, you can't do this." She tried to push him away but his grip grew tighter, squeezing her like the Chinese burn games she used to play with her brother as a child.

"You *Gringos*, with your philistine sexual philosophy, your barbaric prohibition of sexual pleasure. If you don't like my deal, *bueno*, we can try something else." He pulled her up from the chair and kissed her hard on the mouth with his full lips. One hand ripped the rest of the buttons, then he turned her around, pushing her hard against the desk, her head knocking over the coffee cups and scattering the sugar, as he wrenched down her jeans.

"Stop, stop. Jesus, stop," Lana tried to get away, but he pushed her head down again leaving her only a view of the crucifix on the wall.

I see through another door into a room with a single woman patient. Her arm is attached to a drip but I can't see exactly how. I wait, frozen, for the nurse to leave, hiding in the darkest part of the corridor I can find. After the nurse gently closes the door, I sneak into the room. The smell of disinfectant is overpowering. I reel back. Has the patient been sick? Was that what the nurse was doing here?

Close to the bed I can see a bucket full of yellow vomit. As if reading my thoughts, the woman stares at me but says nothing.

"*Hola, chica. ¿Cómo estás?*" I feel the question is slightly hysterical in the context but what else can I say?

"*Agua,*" she answers. Only one word. Water.

Next to the bed on a small table is an empty glass. I pick it up, looking around the room for water, my camera in my other hand. "I'll come back," I say, not understanding my weird behaviour. Why would I go for water when all I want to do is ask the woman why she is here? It doesn't make sense. Nothing here makes sense.

I open the door into the corridor, looking left and right. Is there a bathroom here? I find a small bathroom with a grimy sink and fill the glass. But as I turn to head back to the woman, a firm hand grips my arm. It's the nun we'd seen earlier.

"What are you doing?"

"Water. I was thirsty."

The nun lunges for the glass knocking it out of my hand. It bounces across the floor and smashes into pieces. "You have no right to be here, follow me."

The nun leaves me in the waiting room before *Com* Manuel's office. I try his door but it's locked. I can hear Lana screaming. I rattle the knob but I can't open it. It's one of those old fashioned doors with a big keyhole. I crouch down and put my eye to it.

It's blurry but then I can see what's going on. *Com* Manuel has Lana from the back and is going at it like a rabid dog. And I know for sure he's not wearing *anticonceptivos*. It's unbelievable but he seems to be smoking at the same time.

I pull the cartridge out of my camera and stick it down my shirt. I have to keep the evidence. It's the only thing that will tell the truth about this place.

I run down the corridor and out the front door and the side of the building. I'm trudging on wet grass as the rain pelts down on my head and body. I find the room which I believe to be *Com* Manuel's and yes, the window is open.

With all my strength, I heave myself through it, jumping onto the polished, wooden floor. The smell of sex is rising from his desk and Lana, her lipstick's streaked across her mouth – like a clown. She's not beautiful, not any more.

Manuel has his back to her and is pulling up his pants with one hand and the other holds his cigarette, when he turns to see me lunging towards him. I've grabbed the first thing I see on his desk – a long, gold paper knife and I'm coming straight towards him with it.

"Raf," Lana yells out. "No!"

But it's too late, I've stabbed Manuel in the belly, perhaps the only real wound the bastard's ever felt. The great revolutionary hero, the tortured one, the *comandante*. Is any of this true? I doubt it all now as I see him fall to the floor.

"Quick, Lana." I kick him over. The room stinks of blood and I retch. But then, just for good measure, I take his cigarette from the floor and put it out deep into his chest, so that it looks as if it's a tattoo on his body.

I help Lana out the window and to freedom.

The rain has already turned the dirt road to mud – we're sloshing through puddles and running through slippery, red clay. As fast as we can go. Coffee bushes picked clean not so long ago by *campesinos* fringe the track and I veer through them to make it harder for the soldiers to get to us. I pull Lana along – she's bedraggled, her blonde hair stuck to her face by the rain. Her jeans are falling down and she tries to grab them with one hand to do them up. "Wait, Raf, I can't do this."

Her bag is slung across her chest, her blouse unbuttoned to her waist and her black bra showing.

"Yes, you can, come on." I keep pulling. Her long, slim fingers are enveloped in mine. The red and green parrots are screeching in the trees, warning the soldiers of our whereabouts. Sandinista parrots, I should have known! It's about a kilometre from the hospital to our car. The bushes are thick and my boots are sinking into the mud. I tread into ground so wet I almost lose my boot, but drag my leg out just in time. Wet mud has a particular smell – of animals – lizards, iguanas, maybe even jaguars – that have passed through it during the night. But all I can think of are the sounds that bastard made when the knife went in. Like a pig's piercing squeals as it's killed for a *barbacoa*. Those leaders I fought under, I dedicated my whole life to. *Patria libre o muerte*. Perhaps it's *muerte* for *Com* Manuel. I really don't give a fuck.

I almost cry when I see our trusty little Datsun. Still there, thank the Lord. The double iron gate is closed but not locked and I wedge it open, dragging Lana through. I can hear a jeep screaming down the track, we've got to get out. I clank the gate shut.

Inside the car Lana is heaving with exhaustion, puffing and crying at the same time. I can still smell *Comandante* Manuel on her. It sickens me. The odour seems to fill the whole car. I find a rag in the side pocket of my door and hand it to her; she takes it feebly. I put the key in the ignition and thank God again when the car starts with no trouble. I may end up a Catholic at this rate.

"Where can we go?" Lana asks. "They'll find us."

"Honduras. We're close to the border – we'll make it."

"You can go on to Mexico," she nods. "I know people at the Australian Embassy who can help you."

I head the car north up the winding mountain road, driving as fast as that Datsun can go.

Chapter Forty-seven

Colin was sitting up in bed wearing a blue hospital gown. He pulled at it to try and make it more comfortable but there was nothing he could do; it kept riding up his bum. He was waiting for the nurse to arrive so he could get out of this moronic place as soon as possible. OK, he'd done something very stupid, and now reality was setting in. He felt awful.

The bills would still be there when he got home, the letter from the Coroner's Court, the memories, the fears, the resentment, the sadness. He had a criminal record, would that affect the Coroner's decision? Why hadn't Shannon just let him die? Bloody do-gooders! He'd survived this far, he'd done what he could. He had no desire to hang around.

An efficient-looking nurse in a pale pink uniform arrived in the ward, the three other beds were taken up by two men and a woman snuffling and shifting and snoring and complaining. The nurse told Colin he could leave that day, as soon as the doctor had seen him and signed him off.

"Great, thanks, nurse," he said, still ever polite. The first thing he would do was go and see Rafael, the poor bastard. The nurse brushed past two people at the door. A teenage girl peering around it, followed by Shannon. She had golden brown skin and dark hair down to her waist, wearing jeans and a pullover and well-worn gym shoes. A pair of small gold sleepers, no makeup. "Grandpa," she whispered. It was if the sun had just come out and lit up the whole room. There were miles of ocean in front of them, not medical charts and bed pans.

"Lowanna? Is that you?" Colin pulled the sheets up to cover his hospital gown. He felt as if he was sliding down the bed and would get caught up in the worn sheets and thin blanket.

She danced across the room. "Here let me help you." She fluffed up the pillow and pulled Colin up so he could sit up straighter.

"How did you find her?" he asked Shannon.

She smiled. "It didn't take that much detective work. Her card and envelope with her address, remember, on your mantelpiece?"

"And your mum let you come?"

"She had no choice," Lowanna said. "I haven't seen you in so long, Grandpa. And Shannon told me you'd want to see me." She held Colin's hand as she sat on the edge of the bed. "Don't ever do this again, Grandpa, OK?"

He nodded, trying to hold back the tears. As Shannon stood up to leave, he mouthed: "Thank you."

Chapter Forty-eight

Rafael's outside room was still much the same as when he left it more than thirty years before, but instead of cigarette butts strewn across the floor there were kids' toys. Luis, Rafael's nephew, now lived there with his wife and daughter and son. It was too expensive to own or rent their own house so they shared what had been Rafael's mother's home. The bathroom and kitchen were now inside – the old outhouse had been pulled down – but the concrete courtyard and the mango tree were still there. The kids climbed it each day to gather mangoes and eat them till their tummies hurt.

Rafael slept inside the house in his mama's room. She had died two years before, with no knowledge of what had happened to her favourite child. He had never dared contact her from Australia, worried the knowledge of where he was would endanger her. He lay on her bed shirtless as the late afternoon sun drenched the room and thought of her. The smells wafting from the kitchen of black bean soup cooking on the stove made him feel that she was still here. How she must have missed him. How could he have been so cruel? He thought of all the wasted years and the loneliness of being a fugitive. Had it been a huge mistake? Should he have turned himself in years ago? What was the point of all that fear?

He was gradually beginning to feel sane again since receiving psychiatric counselling. Being home with his own people, speaking his own language, had helped restore his balance. He enjoyed joking with his limbless *compañeros* when he walked past them sitting in their wheelchairs on their verandahs. They'd ask for cigarettes like the old days. And he would reply, just like the old days, "*Lo siento, no hay.*" The love of Luis and his family was restoring him to health.

He'd spent his first weeks back in another cell in Managua's prison but he'd been freed when Lana travelled to Nicaragua after that ratbag journalist, Vesna, tracked her down. She gave evidence that *Com* Manuel's killing was an act of heroism; it had saved her from what could have been more abuse or even death. The President pardoned Rafael; he had no wish to keep a revolutionary hero on a pedestal when it was proved he was a rapist. And anyway, Nicaragua needed that trade agreement with the United States, and Lana Lopez was an influential journalist.

Rafael remembered their last meeting at a bar in the rebuilt city centre. Cuban hip-hop played on the sound system, different from the salsa they used to dance to. The clientele were spoilt, rich kids but Lana seemed to like the place. No Rosita and Maria here, they worked from home these days. The revolution never did eliminate prostitution – or machismo. It was deeply rooted, but not just in Latin America.

"Did you ever have children, Lana?" he asked.

"No, never. It would have been difficult to share custody, wouldn't it, *cariño?*"

Rafael winced. More sad memories. And still so cynical.

"Anyway, I was married to my career." She'd aged a lot, as people do. There were streaks of grey in her blonde, coiffured hair. No more pony tails, they would've showed off her lined neck. She still wore bright red lipstick that she'd apply in front of a small mirror in her left hand, her lips pursed. It matched her fancy Italian leather stilettos and handbag, and floral, wraparound dress. "And you? What happened in Australia?"

"No children. But there's one on the way."

Lana whistled. "And the mother, what's she like?"

"Beautiful. A country girl but she owns a café in Sydney. A good dancer too. *Mi bonita* Shannon."

"Will you see her again?"

"*Sí.* I hope so. She says she'll come here one day. Lana, I'm so grateful for what you have done."

She nodded. "I had to."

He was nervous about asking her. "Have you had any therapy, you know for what happened that day?"

"Me? We didn't believe in therapy back then. Work was my therapy." She sipped her chardonnay. They had good Chilean wine in Nicaragua these days. Rafael was on water, back to being a teetotaller. She commented how he no longer smoked; he said he hadn't since 1986.

"I needed to come home, Lana."

"Thank you, Australian Immigration." She shrugged.

"*Bueno*, I really needed treatment. It's amazing I was still alive. I needed to forgive my enemies."

"You're a better person than me. I'll never forgive that arsehole."

"Not him," he shuddered. "But the Sandinistas meant well. They were trying to help our soldiers, those poor mad bastards – like me."

"They had a strange way of showing it."

"Maybe but they were experimenting with new techniques. Those were radical days. You know what we saw. It was brother against brother, sister against sister. Neighbour against neighbour. Now it's happening again. Will we ever really heal?"

"At least you're not fighting against the Contras anymore."

"No, but we might have to start another revolution."

They'd kissed goodbye as Lana climbed into her rental car. Carlos, who they had rented their trusty Datsun from, now had a big business. "*Adios*, my New Man," she laughed. She waved as she closed the window and sunk into the air conditioning.

Rafael wondered how Lana could have put on such a pretty face and professional coolness. He guessed she'd had years to practise covering up her past or coming to terms with what had happened to her. He still had flashbacks of the knife going in, the squealing like a pig. In his sessions with the psychiatrist he was gradually allowing himself to open up about everything that had happened to him – in the revolution and later at the hospital in the mountains. Still he wondered if his scars – like his country's – would ever really heal. Not the cigarette burns all over his body but the memories of the volcano, the torture and then that stinking afternoon at the hospital. Like his *compañeros*, he'd taken a few shaky steps on the path to recovery. But there were those who were suspicious of him – why did he disappear during the worst years of the war? Why was he on the other side of the world meeting women, enjoying life when they stood in food queues and lost their brothers? Why did so many of his friends die?

Nicaragua was a traumatised country – but now it was back to being a capitalist one once more. What did the revolution achieve? Luis and his wife worked as therapists at the hospital, struggling on their limited funding to look after former soldiers and *campesinos* suffering from PTSD. At least they'd managed to get an education due to the revolution; his wife also came from a poor Sandinista family. Despite their work, Luis had told him that the psychic recovery of his country had never been pursued in any significant way. Past traumas meant many people had psychological problems they were confronting today – alcoholism, violence, child sex abuse and rape.

Rafael hoped too he could work again, perhaps with Luis and his wife at the hospital to help others suffering trauma or even those who were maimed from land mines and the war.

He'd taken a bus home from the centre after meeting with Lana. As bad as ever, with the music blaring, the driver rude and the people crammed together so that you could feel their sweat – but not the hands of the pickpockets. He would never complain again about Sydney buses.

The trip took even longer than usual with road blocks along the way as students mounted protests about pension cuts, soldiers on every corner.

"Time to oust another dictator," Rafael had thought.

He got up from the bed, sat at his desk and turned his computer on. It buzzed. A Skype call. From Shannon. One of her regular ones.

"*¿Hola, cómo estás?*" she said.

"*Muy bien.* I'm glad you're speaking Spanish."

"I'll need it for when I come to visit."

He laughed. "I can be your interpreter. But wait till it's safe, please. It's dangerous now. How are you feeling anyway? What did the doctor say?"

"All good. The stitch is holding. I have something to show you." She held up an ultrasound photo. "She seems happy too."

"She?"

"Yes. We're having a daughter, Raf."

His face opened into a wide smile. "Ah, a beautiful *compañera.* You were born to be a mother, *amor.*"

"*Gracias.* And guess what? I've learnt to cook casseroles. I might even turn out to be a good wife too."

"You still make me laugh."

"Gotta go. Customers coming. *Hasta luego,* see you later, darling. Miss you."

"Miss you too."

There was a tap on the door and he turned round. His great niece and nephew were staring at him holding mango pips in their hands, their faces dripping with goo. "Come here," he gestured as they shyly waved to Shannon's face on the screen. He turned the computer off, then went to the bed, pulling them up to sit with him. There was no mama there to scold about orange stains on the sheets.

The pair looked at him solemnly as the little boy touched the scars on his chest. "Does it hurt, *Tío* Rafa?" he asked as he sucked his pip, tracing the other hand over the scars.

"Not anymore," Rafael answered.

After they had licked every last drop of juice from the pips they handed them to him and climbed back down, going outside to climb the tree again.

"No, not anymore," Rafael repeated.

Chapter Forty-Nine

As usual the whale rock was empty. As usual the runners and the walkers jogged and walked right past, without noticing a thing. It was surprising if they even saw a whale breaching out to sea they were so intent on their exercise and fitness routines. Sleek, glossy gym pants, all the right shoes from the most expensive exercise shoe shops. Everything was just right. Neat ponytails poking out of caps. Designer sunglasses. Phone apps. Heart monitors. Calorie counters. Babies looking shell-shocked ensconced in special prams pushed by yummy-mummy Olympians.

Shannon was tempted to trip the runners over, but instead smiled sweetly as, despite her big belly, she climbed over the fence and onto the rock. She nodded at the whale and her baby as she sat down on the mossy grass. The rock jutted out to sea, broken at the edges like an iceberg floating in the ocean. Freezing cold bits of solid ice breaking up into the sea.

Shannon wondered what the last Ice Age must have been like. How did people survive it? Huge drops in temperature caused by the ice build-up, at the same time as falls in sea level. Then later rising sea levels as the ice melted, waves of water gushing in and filling up areas that were once land. Like the creek when it flooded at the valley but one hundred thousand times bigger and grander. Salt and sea and blue depths covering up thousands of years of rock engravings, petroglyphs and etchings and paintings of ancient animals – giant kangaroos and wombats and dinosaur-type beings.

In the distance she saw that landscape – people walking on the same territory as giant animals – throwing spears at these lumbering creatures and lassoing them for dinner, gnawing on the huge bones as they sat around the campfire discussing the day's events. The café of the great outdoors.

She smiled. She knew her idea of ancient Aboriginal Australia wasn't quite the same as Colin's. But then maybe they were her ancestors too – well, all of mankind's. The last Ice Age happened around twenty thousand years ago. That was long before the Irish were trying to stay warm by burning peat in their fires. What were these peoples' secrets? What could they tell her about life, her problems, her future? Did they have the same worries back then, which went far beyond what huge animal they'd have for dinner? Did they care about love and children and divorce lawyers?

She removed her boots and socks and felt the sensation of warm rock on her feet. She imagined the rhythm of the whale songline, the chants that told the story. She thought of what Colin had told her about Barangaroo, and her incredible generosity – to try and bring the colonialists and her people together by the birth of her child. She looked far out to sea as she moved – beyond the last Ice Age – and then down to her favourite whale engraving. She sensed the whale could feel her questions and her loss and fears but it couldn't answer her. But perhaps it could give her messages or hints that might fill up the emptiness since Rafael left. It might be saying, "I have a baby inside me and it will be born one day". It might be showing that the sea path up north to give birth and back south to the frozen icebergs of Antarctica would never change, would happen every year without fail and that life would go on, whatever happened to her or anybody else.

She felt comfort from this. It's what drew her to this spot. It's what made it her rock, her whale rock, and nobody else's. Apart from Colin. He understood and he had been coming for a lot longer than she had. Even Vesna had come here for help, she'd told her later. She'd had a call from her that week, checking to see how Maxie was. The Melbourne job was going well, she was scooping her competitors every week. Her father was recovering from his heart attack and she'd even given up smoking. Miracles could happen.

Shannon felt the sun on the back of her neck. Summer was on the way. Something made her look up and, out past the choppy sea and the small boats, she saw a tower of water shoot up into the sky. "It's a whale," she called out excitedly. "Oh and a calf. Thank you, whale rock," she spoke to the engraving.

"It's a sign, Shannon."

She swung round to see Colin lifting his weighty body over the rail, and puffing, come to stand next to her beside the rock. She hadn't seen him for weeks. He sat down next to her, patted her tummy and held her hand. They looked out to sea together, not speaking for ten minutes until the whales were out of sight. "Are you feeling stronger, Colin?" Shannon finally asked.

He nodded. "I think I can handle the Coroner's Court. Tom has offered to represent me."

"Really?" Shannon smiled. "Well, what do you know! And Lowanna? How is she?"

"She's a sweetheart. Been coming round to my place and borrowing my history books. She's involved in an oral history project with our mob. About post-contact times. She'll know more than me soon. And did I tell you? I've enrolled in History at the uni. Hope I can manage to live on a student allowance."

"Wow, you should be teaching the teachers, but that's great."

"How is Maxie?"

"He's learning to become a barista," she laughed. "Good, ol' Nick is teaching him."

Colin laughed. "Just so long as he doesn't get a tattoo."

"Better not, but Nick's got a full beard now."

He laughed again. Then he paused. "How's Raf?"

"He's fine, he's good."

"I miss the mystery man."

"You're not the only one." She missed him so much her whole body hurt. Shannon hesitated. She was nervous about bringing up the subject of Ainslie but Joe had called her from the valley. The story about the baby dying in the cot at the home had fuelled his memory and he'd finally recalled what happened.

"I knew that story, Shannon," Joe had said on the phone. "Ainslie told me. At one of those dances. That was her baby, not her little sister. She first came to work at the farm when she was in her early twenties, she was married then and had a little boy. Her husband was in the army still."

"Yes, Colin's dad was in the army and he had an older brother, Johnny. So she worked at our farm before I was born?"

"Yeah she worked for your grandparents when your dad was also in his early twenties. I wasn't around then but later she came back when you were a little girl. Must have been at least twenty-five years later. And that's when she told me her story. I had a dance with her, just cause I knew her, she was much older of course. And we went out on the verandah to get some air. I don't know why but it all came out. All her kids had been taken away. First the baby and the boy. And the baby had died. In the cot at the home. Then her other daughters and son taken. Maybe one was your friend, Colin." He went very quiet.

"What else, Joe? Why did she come back to our farm after all those years?"

"I remember one night in the stables," he said. "I saw something. Just as I was finishing work. A man and a woman. She left soon after."

"A man?" Her memories became clearer. "Not dad? I thought I saw something too but I was only a kid."

"She was sitting on his knee. I don't know for sure what was going on."

"Joe, I think we both know."

"Too late, Shannon. We can't ask them now. But I have a feeling your dad called her Lily. I'm sorry but you wanted to know." He hung up.

She had to tell Colin about this, although it terrified her. More whales were arriving, coming closer in, past the ships and small boats. "Colin, did your mum ever tell you anything about a baby dying at the Bomaderry home, got her head caught in the rungs of a cot?"

Colin's eyes widened. "Yes, I did hear that story. I wasn't sure it was Bomaderry. I thought it was mum's little sister in one of the homes."

"Do you mind if I have a look at that photo of your mum and dad and Johnny?"

He took it out of his wallet – he'd used sticky tape to hold it together – and handed it to her.

Shannon stared at it for a while then said, "Colin, it's Ainslie for sure. She must be Lily, she must be."

He took the photo back, saying nothing.

Shannon got all her courage up. "Old Joe at the farm thinks the baby who died was actually Ainslie's baby, your older sister I guess. And it was at Bomaderry."

Colin whistled. "Well there you go."

"There's more. Old Joe thinks that she worked at our farm when she was young and then came back a good twenty-five years later. She'd had more kids by then, all taken away. You, and Johnny, the baby, your sisters. Colin, what happened to your dad?"

"From what I've heard he drank himself to death. After we were taken. Of grief, I suppose. Fought in the war and couldn't even get his kids back. I have a feeling mum moved back up the coast later to be nearer to me but we just never found each other."

"I would like to help, really." She lowered her eyes.

He looked straight at her. "What else, Shannon? What's bothering you?"

"Well," she was very nervous. "Joe thinks he saw something once. Ainslie and my dad, she was sitting on his knee. Maybe but he won't say for sure."

Colin held his breath. He gestured for her to go on.

"Maybe that's why she left so suddenly. Never said goodbye to me. Maybe that baby was your sister? And mine? Maybe they did love each other. Why else would she come back?"

Again, he went quiet then he spoke slowly. "She was Aboriginal, wasn't she? He couldn't leave your mum for a black woman."

They were both silent until Shannon spoke again. "I wish I could do something to make up for all this. I want to help you, Colin."

"No need, you've done enough," Colin said. "Lowanna's going to help me. One day, she and I will go home together. My mum was used and abused by white people everywhere, I know that much."

"I was thinking about Barangaroo and how courageous she was," Shannon said. She needed her as a role model, somebody to look up to, to move on. "Our histories are intertwined, whatever people think."

"She wanted the land to heal too," Colin said. "We still do. We're going to be OK, Shannon. We're going to be brave like Barangaroo. Like my mum – and me – you're going to survive. You'll have a beautiful baby and you'll see Rafael again one day. And Lowanna and I will find my mum's story. It will all work out somehow."

Shannon hugged him. "I really hope so, mate. It's about bloody time things went better, isn't it? For all of us."

He swept her fringe out of her eyes. "Yes my dear, it's about fucking time."

She laughed. "Swearing, Colin?"

And they both looked out to sea.

I have given suck, and know
How tender 'tis to love the babe that milks me.

LADY MACBETH, *William Shakespeare, Macbeth*

Acknowledgements

To my editors: Jan Cornall, Alison Lyssa and David Rapsey, I can't thank you enough.

Thanks also to Zoja Bojic and Alejandro Pérez for their encouragement and belief in me and April Fonti, Natalie Turner, Glenda Hambly and Zeinab El hares, who read parts of the book or the whole manuscript in different stages and offered invaluable advice.

To those who have helped with my research: David Lloyd, Mujib Abid, Mohammed Sabsabi, Sonia Sabsabi, Peter Rochfort, Rima Allouche, Simon Corden, Victor Flores Garcia, Sandi Logan, Martyn Wyer, Arnold (Pudding) Smith, Ray Minniecon and the survivors of the Kinchela Boys Home, Maryann Young, Simon Dodshon, Abbie Fields, Danica Maroya, Dr Aamer Sultan, the Muslim Women's Association and staff at STARTTS.

To my Western Sydney University Masters supervisor, Christopher Andrews, lecturers and fellow students.

And to those who gave support along the way: Helen Attwater, Mare Carter, Lucy de Bruce, Brian Brennan, Mira Joksovic, Annemarie Nelson, Michael Visontay, Jan Mayman, Tom Blacket, Nengah Arsana, Andrew Puris and Rebecca Wilson.

To Silvio Leal, who inspired the original story, and the late Tanny Polster, who always knew exactly what I was trying to say.

To my publisher, Jennifer Mosher and all at IndieMosh. And to Bart Willoughby for permission to use a line from his song, *We Have Survived*.

And to my children, Amelia and Marco Stojanovik, for their patience, humour and practical assistance.

The information on Barangaroo was gleaned from the accounts of the First Fleet diarists and the writings of Ann McGrath.

About the Author

Diana Plater was born in Boston, Massachusetts, USA but grew up in Sydney, Australia. Her journalism has appeared widely in newspapers, magazines and online. She has covered Indigenous and race issues since the beginning of her career and was based in Nicaragua in the mid-1980s during the Sandinista/Contra war. She has written several non-fiction books, including *Taking Control: How to aim for a successful pregnancy after miscarriage, stillbirth or neo-natal loss,* and the Cootamundra Girls Home chapter in *Many Voices, Reflections on experiences of Indigenous child separation* published by the National Library as well as a play, *Havana, Harlem. Raging Partners,* written with Ollie Smith, was short-listed for a 2001 NSW Premier's Literary Award. *Whale Rock* is her first novel.

CPSIA information can be obtained
at www.ICGtesting.com
Printed in the USA
BVHW030951210319
543224BV00026B/15/P